SENTIENT BONDS

PART ONE OF THE IAN SERIES

ALEX TIMOTHY

FULL VOLUME
PUBLISHING

For Jean—
The time you stayed up all night reading my first book is one of my most precious memories. Our friendship is a part of my very soul.

OTHER STORIES BY ALEX TIMOTHY

ACKNOWLEDGMENTS

I want to give a big thank you to the following: Writing Group for keeping me accountable and making the very solitary act of putting words on a page a fun activity. (I'm looking at you Katelyn).

James for never shying away from the cold hard truth

Lesley-ann for agreeing to read anything and everything and always giving THE BEST advice for moving forward.

And especially, Alisha Costanzo for all her support and patience and friendship with this project and every project before it.

CHAPTER 1

"So ... Hi again."

On the monitor in front of me, a red circle pulsed like the beat of a heart. "Dad wants me to talk to you. See if you are more realistic than the last time."

No response. Not in words. But, I could have sworn the pulsing sped up as soon as I sat down. I glanced over my shoulder at my dad, to see if he noticed too.

It didn't seem like he had. His thick black-framed glasses reflected the red circle from the monitor, hid his eyes. But, he hadn't entered anything on the electronic pad in his hands.

"Well, is it going to answer me?" I scratched at the swollen skin under my left eye, where Caz's fist had connected with my face. Stinging pain already started to give way to an itchy, achy, throb. I would have a black eye for sure, and my left cheek felt hot and bruised under my fingers. Fucking Caz. He'd landed two punches before letting go of me. *I guess I should feel lucky he hadn't broken my nose.*

Because of the fight, I'd been sent home in the middle of the school day, suspended. Which meant Dad had to leave his work to come pick me up. My father hated when anyone interrupted his work, and he'd complained about it the entire drive home. *"Unacceptable, Asher. I was in the middle of …"* blah, blah, blah. Dad didn't even ask about my swelling eye, my split lip.

At home, he insisted I follow him down to the basement, no mention of an ice pack or pain meds. "You might as well make yourself useful," my father had said, spitting all his words. It was something he did whenever he got really irritated. Gross.

Our basement laboratory ran the entire length of the house. A long windowless cavern with high ceilings, stark white painted walls, a smooth cement floor. I wasn't allowed to tell anyone about the lab because everything down here was top secret. Watchful security cameras covered every inch, and the company Dad worked for had altered our house's public records so that no one would know we had a basement, let alone a secret laboratory. Not that any normal person would want to come down here.

The lab was creepy—*creepy as fuck*. Filled with prosthetic body parts designed to look like *real* body parts. Rows of legs, stacks of arms, bins filled with hands. Some of them covered by cloned semi-synthetic skin, tiny real hair follicles growing inside, real keratin finger and toe nails.

In one corner, a humming cold storage held cloned human tissues. The stuff of horror movies—like jellied brain matter, gluey coils of veins, jars of lifelike eyeballs suspended in antiseptic gel. I'd grown up around all of it, and I still got creeped out. Whenever I had to come here to use one of the computer stations, I kept the lights off on that morgue-like section of the lab.

"Pay attention, Asher." My father tapped one long finger against the oversized monitor. Dad had awards and fame for the lifelike prosthetics he'd created, but this—the AI powering the red circle—was his real work. His *life's* work.

"I am paying attention," I lied. "He won't talk to me." Apparently, Dad had changed something in the programming. He'd given the AI *"independence to create its own neural pathways."* I had no idea what that meant. But, Dad claimed that he needed to watch me interact with the reprogramed AI before he could make the next adjustments to its circuitry.

"Don't talk to *me*, Asher." A big dramatic sigh from my father, his eyes rolled and everything. "Talk to *Ian*." Officially, my father had named his project, Intelligent Adaptive Neuron Mirror Military Prototype. But, we never called it that at home. As a little kid, I'd shortened the title by taking the "Intelligent Adaptive Neuron" part of the machine's description and giving the AI a human name —Ian.

I swiveled back to the pulsing circle, crossed my arms over my chest. "Are you going to talk to me?"

Actually, that circle wasn't Ian, and it couldn't see anything. Behind the monitor, the steel military robot's eyes lit up, and its camera pupils scanned me—body temperature, blood flow, nervous system. The military robot wasn't Ian either, although Ian controlled it. Multi-colored wires and tubes tethered the metal limbs and body of the robot to a refrigerator-sized processor. It hummed loudly, and a string of indicator lights flashed along one side. *That* was Ian.

"I do not benefit by talking to you." The voice came from the monitor's speakers, tinny and monotone.

"O-kaaay ..." I glanced up at Dad, who ignored me, even though Ian's grouchy answer had interested him enough to make a note on his tablet. My father made a thoughtful humming sound as he did it. Like Ian being a dick was a fascinating development.

To tell the truth, I didn't really like my dad's AI anymore, not like I had as a little kid. Back then, Dad worked more on the mechanical parts of Ian, getting the robot body to move in response to the commands of the processor brain. I'd been a four-year-old, kind of small for my age, when my father introduced me to the eight-foot-tall robot. *"He's bigger and stronger than you, but I want you to treat him the same way you would treat another child."*

"He's a kid too?"

Dad had grimaced. *"Yes,"* he'd answered. My father had pushed me toward a giant play area he'd set up on one side of the expansive basement space. Blocks and balls. A climbing dome. A slide. Even a giant sandbox with all kinds of tools for digging and making forts.

Every day after school, I rushed down to the basement where the huge robot waited for me. Despite his enormous size and strength, Ian joined any game I suggested. I'd thought of him as my friend. I imagined him anxiously waiting for my school day to end, as eager to play with me as I was to play with him. My father would observe us, taking notes and making adjustments, but I'd forget he was there as Ian and I pretended to be pirates, astronauts, superheroes.

All that changed when Dad's work on Ian progressed. He switched the processor's focus from the silent robot to this disembodied voice and the pulsing red circle. Instead of playmates, we became competitors, trying to best each other for my father's praise. Dad scored us in social problem-solving, situational prioritization, and emotional recognition tests. We'd replay them over and over—my father encouraging his AI to surpass me in every game. When Ian did well, Dad beamed and praised him. When I did well, my father swore and smacked his palm against the table. *"No. No. No!"* I hadn't thought of Ian as my friend for years now.

I sat back and crossed my arms over my chest. "So, you *aren't* going to talk to me?"

"I am programmed to respond and learn," responded the AI.

Again, my eyes cut to my father. "That sounds like a computer. I thought you said you improved him. He doesn't sound improved."

I guess Ian took offense to that, or his programming directive to get the better of every situation took offense. Before Dad could respond, the AI spoke again. "Dr. Bell explained the parameters of this exercise before you sat down. As your father, Dr. Bell has authority over you, yet you chose to ignore his orders. Or perhaps, you did not understand them? I conclude Asher Bell is either defiant or of low intelligence. Possibly both."

Dad just smiled as he tapped away at his pad. "Good, Ian. Very good," he said. And that red circle pulsed brighter at the praise.

My teeth clenched, and I shook my hair forward to hide my eyes, a dark curtain between me and the world. *Fuck this.* "Dad didn't give me orders, *soldier-bot.* He gave me instructions. And you're the stupid one—a human would have recognized the conversation opener in what I said. Waiting to be asked a question is no better than a smartphone."

"Asher," my father spit out. He took everything about his AI personally and acted like I'd criticized his intelligence, not Ian's.

"What, Dad? You just said 'Good job' when it called me stupid, but now that—"

The metallic voice broke in, "You have demonstrated the validity of my assessment." The red dot became a steady crimson glow. "You, Asher Bell, are defiant." Then, the pulsing resumed. "Although you have also identified a flaw in my thinking—"

I leaned in toward the monitor, nose just an inch from

the red circle. "You mean programming, soldier-bot. You aren't a person. You don't *think*."

"That's quite enough, Asher." Dad nudged the heavy black frames up his nose. Except for those glasses I could have been his clone. Pale skin, dark hair, the complete inability to bulk up our scrawny bodies. And with his huge brain and all his degrees, Dad probably *could* have cloned himself if he wanted to. Only, one big difference convinced me he hadn't—Dr. Fredric Bell was a genius, while I'd only tested ever tested as having normal intelligence. For the millionth time, I wondered if Dad got pushed around by dickish football players the way I did.

Probably not. My father graduated high school at age nine, completed a double major in physics and biology at thirteen. By the time he was my age, seventeen, Fredric Bell had started a second doctorate and med school. No asshole football players strutted the hallways in med school. His genius brain had given him a fast pass beyond the reach of bullies, beyond any of the ordinary dynamics of peer groups and rivals.

My father turned back toward the crimson circle, the lenses of his glasses opaque from the monitor's light. "Continue what you were saying, Ian."

The red dot's pulsing slowed like it wanted to take its time to consider the next good jab it could get in on me. "Asher's argument is valid," the metallic voice emanated from the robot this time, the three vent slashes in place of a mouth. Both Dad and I startled and looked up. "I continue to have a poor understanding of interpersonal commands and requirements. Therefore, I retract my earlier assessment concerning his intelligence level."

"Gee thanks," I said, working as much disdain as I could into it. "I care so much about the programmed opinion of a machine."

Dad slammed his tablet onto the desk in front of me.

"Perhaps, you should return to—" He waved his hand at the stairs leading up to the kitchen door. With his face turned toward me, I could finally see past the thick lenses to squinting, angry eyes. "Your transgression at school has impacted your emotional state to the point that you are no longer useful."

Transgression? Emotional state? Sometimes, Dad sounded more like a robot than Ian did. I slouched further down the chair, let my hair cover more of my face. "Did the school tell you what happened?"

Dad made a frustrated noise. "The people at your school are idiots. I found the bulk of their communication to be irrelevant and unworthy of my time." He snatched the tablet back up from the desk to study whatever calculations or notes he'd taken. As far as he was concerned, our conversation had ended.

A whirring noise came from the military robot, the cameras zeroed in on me. On the monitor, the red dot disappeared. Ian had replaced it with a video close-up of my bruised and swollen face.

No, seriously … Fuck this. "I'm going to get some ice for my eye." I stood up so fast that the rolling chair shot out across the room.

My dad nudged his heavy glasses up again. "I'll let you know if I need you for anything else, Asher."

I huffed a laugh, my tongue poking at the split in my lip. "Yeah, you do that, Dad. Let me know whenever *you* need *me*."

CHAPTER 2

$\mathcal{U}$pstairs, the house was dark, silent, and still as a museum. The tables, the counters, the polished floors, all gleamed, spotless and unused. After my parents divorced, Dad moved the two of us into one of the biggest houses on a street filled with big houses. But my father didn't care about status, he'd picked it for the enormous, windowless basement to create his home lab, his robot playground. I could barely remember the home we'd had before my mom left, but I think it had more color and warmth. I mean, it *must* have had. In the house I shared with Dad, he'd only allowed the interior designer to use black and gray. All the furniture and rugs, the decorations and art, the fucking dishes and throw pillows were varying shades of the same two colors, and all of it still looked brand new. After over a decade in this house, there were still empty rooms that neither Dad nor I had ever gone into. He stuck to his lab, and I stuck to my bedroom and art studio. The rooms on the main floor—kitchen, dining room, sitting rooms—all of them were just for show.

On the kitchen bar, our housekeeper had left out lasagna for me and Dad to microwave for dinner. Separate plates, for each of us to eat alone. My face still hurt too much to even think of eating. But, I grabbed a pack of frozen peas from the freezer and held it against my black eye.

Fucking Caz.

∼

"Come on," he'd whined, running a soapy hand down my spine. "Live on the edge a little." We both had a free hour after lunch and usually spent that time lifting weights or running. Coach wanted Caz in peak shape during the season. And, like a pathetic loser, I wanted to be around Caz.

"Stop it." I'd sidestepped him to rinse the suds off my skin. "This is a little too 'on the edge' for me, Caz." It was the communal shower of the boy's locker room and anyone could come in.

He and I had been friends since elementary school, but we only started hooking up in high school. No one knew, and we kept it a secret for a lot of really good reasons. Caz had a total bastard for a father, one who wouldn't exactly applaud his son experimenting with another boy. And I didn't want to put myself on the line for someone who still considered what we did together "experimenting."

"Why are you always so prickly?" Caz reached out and flicked a long piece of my hair, tried to get me to smile at him. Thanks to football, Caz sat at the top of the popularity food chain. He had no idea what high school was like at the other end of the hierarchy. I *survived* by acting prickly. It turned out that growing up with an AI as a sibling and a know-it-all scientist for a parent had fostered zero personal skills. Dealing with people took so much effort that I'd just rather not do it.

When I tried to move away, Caz decided to make a grab

for me, wrapped my thinner, shorter frame in his bulky arms.

"Let go, Caz. I'm not messing around with you—"

"Make me." He pulled me against his slippery skin. "Better just give in." And that's when Dante, Garrett, and Cooper all appeared at the shower entrance. Caz's football teammates. His newer popular friends.

"What the fuck, dude?" Dante tightened the towel on his waist.

I could feel Caz's wet dick against my back, semi-hard, and I wondered how he planned to explain that away. But, I didn't have to wonder long. Caz's hug turned into an arm lock.

"Man, I told you, I'm not fucking gay!" He unwound one arm to punch me in the face. *Twice.* The first jab split my lip against my teeth, and the second felt like a damn barbell smashed into my cheek. It stunned me enough that I went loose and rubbery.

I guess his boner had gone down enough because he decided to let go of me. No way could I have broken free on my own. My legs wobbled underneath me, my vision swam. But, even dazed and unsteady, anger flooded through me. "You fucking asshole, Caz." I slammed into him, and Caz slipped against the massive amount of shampoo he'd dumped on himself in hopes of getting a shower handjob. His head smacked against the tile and down he went.

Reputation intact.

Then, we both got hauled into the principal's office. The first time for me, the millionth time for Caz. He used to get in constant trouble—fights, bullying, destruction of property. But, he'd cleaned his act up a lot since those days. According to his teachers and his coaches, Caz had "direction" now that we were juniors. He had goals, like getting a football scholarship, playing college ball. The admin even awarded him one of their dorky "Model

Citizen" awards because of how much he'd matured and grown as a student.

But, I knew Caz hadn't *really* undergone any big transformation, he just realized that football might finally be his ticket out of his house. Away from his father.

Early on, the two of us had bonded over our crappy home lives, our shitty fathers. But they were each crap dads in opposite ways. While my dad wanted me out of his way and only cared about his work, Mr. Enzo wanted to do everything with his son. He wanted *to be* Caz. Even as I dabbed my bloody nose with a paper towel, I worried for him, not myself. If Caz got suspended, he couldn't play in Friday's game, and his father would lose his shit about it. He'd rage about how Caz had embarrassed him, let him down, and he'd beat his son black and blue. Caz could end up looking a lot worse than I did. As pissed off at Caz as I was, I wasn't pissed off enough to want that. I'd balled the paper towel and thrown it in the bathroom trash can. "Fucking Caz."

~

*P*rincipal Rodriguez shuffled the referral forms that Coach had sent with us. "So what exactly happened in—" He tapped a finger against a block of writing on one form. It told a story that made Caz sound like an innocent bystander, and me sound like a violent pervert.

I could tell that Rodriguez wanted to blame me too. I didn't do sports. I didn't belong to any clubs. I didn't have friends. Only my grades were good. Better than good, I was a straight-A student.

It bothered teachers when they couldn't slot you into a category like "good kid" or "bad kid." I saw the battle raging behind Principal Rodriguez's eyes. Was I a troubled loner, or a shy genius? The circumstances of the fight probably made a difference too. I'd gotten outed, beat up … none of it looked good for the school.

"It's my fault, Mr. Rodriguez," Caz said. He'd already tried to apologize to me as the school nurse checked us over, but I'd ignored him. "It was just a misunderstanding that I took too far."

Rodriguez nodded along, but not like he believed Caz's words, more like someone had just handed him a script that he could actually follow. He took a deep breath, seemed relieved. "This is very serious, Cassius. Attacking someone because of sexual orientation is a crime. If this were on your record, it could hurt your chances for a football scholarship."

Rodriguez dragged the office phone closer, pulled an index card out with Caz's name on it and the name of his emergency contact—his dad. Beside me, Caz's leg started to bounce. He smoothed shaky hands against his denim-clad thighs. Principal Rodriguez started to press in the numbers on the card. "Cassius, I'll need to call your—"

"You don't need to put it on his record," I blurted out. "It … I shouldn't have … He didn't do anything wrong. It was my fault. I started the fight."

Rodriguez paused. His fingers hovered over the pad of numbers on the complicated-looking desk phone. "What's this?" He looked at Caz, then back at me. He clearly liked this explanation better. The football team needed Caz, he made the school look good. And straight A's aside, I was just a nobody.

"Well, I have no choice but to believe you, Mr. Bell." Mr. Rodriguez shuffled through his top drawer and pulled out an incident form. "If you wouldn't mind filling this out …" I had to make a written statement that I'd initiated the fight, that Caz had just defended himself. Then, Rodriguez suspended me and sent me home.

Caz went back to class.

❧

*T*ook my bag of frozen peas to the front room and looked out the giant window facing the street. Already, the sky had darkened. I didn't know the exact time, but football practice must have ended hours ago.

He didn't even come to check on me.

I sat on the gray leather couch closest to the window, maybe for the first time. It was surprisingly comfortable with silvery silk pillows and a shaggy rug underneath. I sank back, watched a night wind ruffle the leaves of a tree. Across from our house was the Farro house, and behind them, the Enzo house, Caz's house. As kids, we'd worn a path from his backyard to my front step, a four-minute journey we'd done a million times. *How much effort would it take to just walk over and apologize for hitting me?* At the very least, he should have thanked me for saving his ass with Rodriguez.

I guess I conked out at some point. Full night had fallen when I woke up, sweaty and sticky against the leather couch. The frozen peas I'd snagged had melted, and my eye and lips throbbed. Only one plate of lasagna on the counter, so Dad must have eaten and gone to bed. Maybe he hadn't seen me asleep on the living room couch?

I threw the bag of mushy peas into the kitchen sink. Dumped my untouched plate of lasagna too. The kitchen, the entire downstairs was shadowy and dark, but light still leaked from around the basement door.

Dad's still down there? Weird. He usually went to bed early, woke before dawn.

I opened the door a crack. "Dad? Are you still up?"

The light snapped off.

"Dad?" He had everything in the house wired so that he could control it with his phone, and it must have glitched.

"Good thing I don't believe in ghosts, or I'd be super freaked out right now." My voice echoed down the stairs, made me shiver. I closed the door again and went to grab another bag of frozen vegetables from the freezer, corn this time. I pressed it to my lip and cheek.

As I left the kitchen, I glanced back over my shoulder. The light had turned on again. Definitely a glitch.

CHAPTER 3

My father knocked at my bedroom door the next morning, probably wanting me to help in the basement again. To "make myself useful" by sitting through another round of insults from his AI. My face hurt too much for that bullshit, my left eye and upper lip still ached, just the brush of my pillowcase stung against my skin. The door creaked open, and I groaned and kicked free of my blankets. "I can't help in the lab today, Dad. I have homework."

"Homework?" My father's dark eyebrows bunched together, this perplexed expression that appeared whenever he remembered that, unlike him, most people didn't absorb information at light speed.

At school, I'd taken the honors track, packed with AP classes—But compared to my father? He could have tested out of any of my classes as a seven-year-old.

He had.

And, even when he remembered that most people couldn't calculate and synthesize numbers as easily as they drew air into their lungs, my father tended to forget that his son was a part of that "most people" category.

"Yeah, Dad. I sometimes have work of my own to do, you know." Maybe it was shitty to hold being a genius against him, but before I could apologize, my father cleared his throat.

"Yes. Well, this correlates with what I wanted to discuss." His words came out stiff and rehearsed sounding, like I was an employee instead of his son. "I will no longer require your participation in the Mirror Neuron Project."

I dabbed a finger against my swollen lip. "Okaaaay …" The scab had torn and started to bleed again. "So, you're saying you don't want my help today?"

Dad clasped his hands behind his back and nodded, still acting formal and strange. "Or any other day from now on. I've decided to go in a different direction."

"You … a different …" Even for my dad, the switch was abrupt and left me scrambling. I mean, I hadn't exactly chosen to spend my time in the basement losing the "who-does-Dad-value-more" game. But, at least Dad had always acted like he wanted me there. "What do you mean, Dad? What's the different direction?"

But, he'd already turned away, a distracted expression on his face. "Enjoy completing your schoolwork," he said. He really meant it, too.

I had another couple hours of sleep before our housekeeper Carly barged inside. "Yo, little Bell, time to wake—" Her eyes widened at my beat-up face, and she raised a pierced eyebrow. Then, she grinned at me, this snarky, gloating curl of her thin upper lip. "Upped your game from loner to problem child—good plan. Excellent life choices, my badass friend."

"Get out."

Carly threw up her hands like I'd pointed a gun at her. "I come in peace, lil dude."

When she used to pick me up from middle school, all the other parents assumed Carly was my delinquent older sister.

She had purple hair, shaved on the sides, and dressed like a punk rocker, with ripped jeans, band t-shirts, studded leather jackets. "It's almost noon, kiddo." Carly tipped my window blinds to let more sun inside. "Yowza—" She grimaced at me. "Want an ice pack?"

I swiped up my phone and turned the camera on my face. It looked about a thousand times worse than the day before, a black eye, a purpled cheek, and a swollen upper lip. *Fucking Caz!*

My stomach grumbled loud enough for Carly to hear, and she pointed at it. "How about grilled cheese and tomato soup? It might be easier to eat with all your … uh …" A hand swirl gesture that accounted for the whole mess of my bruises.

"Yeah. Alright."

On my way downstairs, the doorbell chimed, and I detoured over to answer it. Shuffling back and forth on the front step was Pilar Almas, my best friend. Her eyes kept nervously glancing to the side, to her house next door to mine. "Don't just stand there, Ash. Let me in before Mom catches me."

Back when they first moved in, I used to like watching the Almas family from my bedroom window, a vision of family life that I'd only seen on television. They hosted birthday parties and cookouts in their backyard. Pilar's dad flipped burgers on the grill. Her mom handed out popsicles or juice boxes. After a while, I guess they noticed me spying on them because Mrs. Almas sent Pilar over to invite me. It was right after Dad had dismantled the basement playground and turned my robot best friend into my enemy. I was the world's loneliest ten-year-old until the Almas family pulled me into their home.

I opened the door. "Did you skip?"

"Duh. Of course, I skipped." Her long brown hair dangled messily down her back and mascara smudged under her eyes. I always suspected she wore the kind that would smear or drip on purpose because Pilar loved dramatic moments, playing a part in them.

Not me. I kept my head down, hated getting noticed, talked about, looked at. Hated. It.

Inside the foyer, I made room for her 1950's style puffy red dress. On anyone else, it would look like a costume, but not Pilar. She'd turned dressing like the eccentric character from a teen movie into her own personal style.

"So what's—?"

"Ash," she interrupted me, then held out a hand so that *I* wouldn't interrupt her. "Just let me talk." Strands of her dark hair had gotten stuck in her lip gloss, and she picked them free as she took a deep breath. "You should have told me you're gay."

Oh, God.

Pilar hadn't always been my best friend or not my *only* best friend. When we were kids, it had been Pilar, me, and Caz. A trio. Or as Mrs. Almas called us, *The Unstoppable Trio.* Unstoppable because we'd done everything together, practically lived at each other's houses. I'd taken it for granted and thought the three of us would be friends forever.

Then came high school. Around the same time my stomach started getting wobbly around Caz, Pilar began acting giggly and twirling her hair around *me.* It had felt awkward … and wrong.

I leaned against the foyer wall, lowered my voice so Carly couldn't hear. "Come on, Pilar. It's not something that I could just drop into a conversation."

"Yes. It *is.*" Pilar lowered her voice to match mine. "Like during one of the times I was making a total fool of myself flirting with you?" Pilar pursed her lips, eyes glistening with tears. "You could have mentioned just how 'not interested' you were. You could have mentioned that there was no chance of the two of us happening because you *don't like girls.*"

"What are you talking about? You flirted with me?" I mean, anyone could have seen that she'd flirted with me. But, lying seemed like the easiest way to end the conversation. "When?" My swollen cheek felt red hot and tight. I wanted that ice pack Carly had promised me.

Pilar's lips twisted, dark eyes suspicious. "Are you kidding me right now? You knew I had a thing for you."

"No, I didn't. And my face hurts." I cupped my hand around my black eye. "I can't believe you're giving me a hard time about this. I wasn't keeping it a secret or anything." Now *that* was the truth. When she went on and on about actors and boy bands, did she think I listened to her just to be nice? I might not have joined in to swoon over them, but I never stopped her. I never tried to change the subject.

She grabbed my chin to examine my face. "You need to put ice on that," she said. Her thick curly hair hit me in the face as she elbowed past me.

"Sure, come on in," I muttered behind her.

Two plates of grilled cheese and two bowls of soup sat on the kitchen bar. Like Carly had known Pilar was coming over. I turned a flat stare on her, and Carly shrugged. She didn't just look like my big sister, she usually acted like one too. A really fucking annoying sister. "I brought in moral support," Carly said. "Sue me." Then, she handed me an ice pack.

Pilar dragged me down on a stool beside her. "Why didn't you go to the doctor? Where's your dad? Oh, wait, I can guess. He's downstairs in the lab …" She made a disgusted snort and rolled her eyes. She had a lot of opinions about my father's parenting decisions.

Even though Dad forbade me from telling anyone, I'd told Pilar about the secret basement lab, about Ian too. She liked drama, but she was loyal and could keep a secret. As my best friend, she'd listened to me gripe about the competitions my father staged between me and his AI, about how Dad rooted for Ian over me.

I'd wanted someone on my side, and I guess I should have read something into skipping over Caz as that someone. Like, somehow I'd known I couldn't trust him the way I could Pilar.

"So …" Pilar had her eyebrow cocked, a dark arch over her long-lashed brown eyes. "It's all over school how Caz and his posse jumped you." She ripped apart her grilled cheese. Fingernails the same fire engine red as the puffy dress. "Do you know how many people asked me—*your supposed best friend*— what your deal is? And I didn't know anything. So … that sucked." She sniffed. "What those guys did is a hate crime, you know."

"A hate … Slow the hell down, Pilar. I didn't get jumped or anything. It was just Caz."

I mean, it probably—no, definitely—looked like a hate crime. Except, I just couldn't reconcile it in my head that way. Caz and I were friends, *more than friends*. Right? I shifted the ice pack off my eye. "And what do you mean, 'it's all over school?'"

"Harper Stillman pretty much blabbed the story to anyone who would listen. I guess she and Caz are dating again?" Pilar watched for my reaction. "Or they're *still* dating, I mean."

"They're still…" *Un-fucking-believable.* "He lied to me." I might have been okay about the secrecy, but Caz knew I had a hard line about messing around when he dated someone else. He'd been on and off with Harper for a while, and I'd gotten fed up with him showing up during all their "off" times. Caz could tell I'd reached my limit, so he claimed to have dumped Harper for good.

Pilar knew me better than anyone. So, even if other

people considered me a cold fish, she could read the hurt in my eyes. "I'm really sorry, Ash."

"He fucking lied to me." Then, he'd punched me. *And,* I'd gotten outed to the whole school. "Fucking Caz." My voice came out croaky. I dipped my head and pushed my plate away.

"No. *Typical* Caz." Pilar took an enormous bite of grilled cheese, and talked around it. "He's not the same guy from when we were kids, Ash. Or he is, and we just didn't really know him."

It wasn't just hormones that ruined our trio. High school also broke us into different groups. Caz with the popular jocks, the "asshole jocks" as Pilar called them. Pilar with the artsy, theater kids. Me with … well, without Caz and sometimes even without Pilar. Minus our trio, I pretty much stuck to myself.

"Soooo …" Pilar stirred her spoon around the tomato soup. Once you've dunked all the grilled cheese, there's really no point to the soup. "How did your dad take it?"

"He was pissed that he had to leave work to come get me. One of the counselors tried to sit us both down, but you know my dad …"

Pilar made a noise like agreement. Like she did know Dad, even when she didn't. Her family had practically adopted me, while my father mostly ignored her presence except to warn me never to bring Pilar or any other friends to the basement, and never, ever, to mention Ian. If they asked, I could tell them, "Yes, he was *that* Fredric Bell." But, nothing else.

"When Dad refused to have a sit down in the counseling office, they gave him a pamphlet instead, and that was it." The pamphlet had a smiling kid who looked about my age standing between two smiling parents, all of them holding a rainbow flag together, "Supporting Your Gay Child!" written just above the happy picture. Dad had crumpled it in his fist as soon as the counselor handed it to him and punched it into the trash can outside the front office.

"Idiots run that school," he'd told me. Then, he'd launched into a detailed description of AI potential and how spending my suspension in the basement with him would provide a much better education than anything I would learn during a week of high school.

"But, now he doesn't want your help with Ian? No more tests?" Pilar grabbed both our empty plates and full bowls and put all the dishes into the kitchen sink. "That's a good thing—right?"

I twisted back and forth on the bar stool. "It's more of a weird thing than a good thing."

Pilar fluffed her skirt out around her. "I have to go back for dance team, but you could come over after that. My brothers got the new *Master Spartan* game yesterday. It's pretty fun." She tilted her head. "Unless you're grounded?"

Kids with parents who care about them never fully understand the lives of kids with parents who don't care. "I'm never grounded."

Pilar grinned. "Cool."

Not really.

CHAPTER 4

*P*ilar's little brothers had savant-like gamer skills and kicked my ass at *Master Spartan*. While I took it well, Pilar raged and vowed revenge on anyone who killed her character. Pretty funny actually, because it only made them, and me, gang up on her.

Finally, their mom had had enough and ordered the boys to bed, Pilar to take a shower, and me to go back to my own home. But, in a nice way. "We'll see you tomorrow, Ash."

When I unlocked the door to my own home, all the lights were off, the house dark. My fingers slid against the foyer wall until I found a light switch.

"Dad?"

On the kitchen bar waited a plate of chicken and rice wrapped in plastic. Just one plate, so Dad had already eaten his and gone to bed. I slid a chicken leg out of the plastic wrap and took a bite. *Did Dad even notice my absence?*

He'd acted so weird when he told me about the "new direction" he'd decided to take. And he'd basically fired me from helping out in the lab. *Not like I care.* I wouldn't exactly miss getting shown up and mocked by his AI. I stared hard at the closed basement door, anger roiling in my gut. Which was why I saw the basement light switch on, the strip of light between the door and threshold.

Just like the night before.

Hmmm … speak of the devil. Dad might have gone to bed. But, *someone* was up.

As soon as I opened the door, the basement light snapped off again. *Nice try, Ian.* I left it off as I came down the stairs. Nothing so much as flickered as I took a seat on the bottom step and ate my chicken in the dark. *Ian really must think I'm stupid.* What had he called me yesterday? Oh yeah … *"of low intelligence."* I peered in the direction of the big processor. "Does my dad know you can turn yourself on?"

Red light filled the room. The pulsing dot. "Dr. Bell does not allow food in the laboratory."

I wiped my greasy fingers on my jeans and put the chicken bone in my pocket to throw away upstairs. "And *you* didn't answer my question. Does Dad know you can turn yourself on? That you can turn the lights on and off, too?"

Because of the light from the computer monitor, I could see the military robot turn its head. A whirring noise emanated from it as the camera eyes tracked me walking across the room. "Dr. Bell authorized this AI to make any adjustments to programming deemed necessary."

Technically true … My father had created Ian for this very purpose—as the first self-determining military AI. One that wouldn't depend on a controller guiding its every move like the current military robots. Dad had designed those, too, but Ian would be different.

Ian could make his own battlefield decisions. He could learn in ways similar to how humans learned. Dad even made Ian's bio-tronic circuitry partially from cloned human brain tissue, electricity traveling between that biomaterial and the machine parts of him.

I bypassed the monitor with the red dot, the metallic voice coming through its speakers, and stood in front of the robot. Its camera pupils both swiveled in to watch me, making the robot look a little cross-eyed. "And you decided it's a necessary adjustment to turn yourself on so you could rat me out for eating in the lab?"

Dad said that Ian didn't have emotions, didn't feel, didn't have true sentience. But, I always wondered if the biological parts of his processor gave him *motivation*. At least, he always acted really motivated to one-up me in the games we played, to get my father's praise, to point out my faults.

"Food is not allowed in the lab."

"You already said that, soldier-bot."

Behind me, the monitor switched off, and the robot's internal illumination kicked on. The bulbous eyes lit up with glowing white circuitry as information traveled from the refrigerator-sized processor through the cables linked to the robot body.

"My designation is Ian. Your use of this alternative label is intended as an insult." Ian's voice now emanated from the robot's mouth vents, three horizontal slashes stacked up over the pointed chin. "Asher Bell demonstrates deliberate unwillingness to follow rules, hostility toward authority."

"You don't have authority over me, Ian." I sneered at him. "You're just a machine in my dad's laboratory, an experiment." With all the emotional recognition tests we'd done together, I knew he'd assimilated the meaning behind some basic facial expressions, so I left the sneer on my face. "I'm Dr. Bell's *son*. It's not the same thing."

"False." One camera pupil rolled away toward the wide desk where my father usually sat then swiveled back toward me. From the robot's speakers came a recording of my dad's voice, clear and real, like he stood in front of me instead of the steel military machine. *"As a control specimen, Asher's development has introduced some worrying results,"* Dad's voice said.

I rolled my eyes. "He called me a control specimen? That doesn't mean anything." Just Dad-speak for my failure to beat Ian at word games and puzzles. "He's saying I'm the control subject when he tests us. You know … because I'm an *actual person*. Unlike you."

Another whirring noise, this time from the robot's chest, and a panel slid open. A beam of white light smacked me in the face. "Hey!" I turned and blinked as a projection filled the room.

A video played, security footage from a different lab, one with expensive chemistry equipment set on black resin counters, not the mismatched computer stations and cement floor of our basement.

In the center of this ritzy lab stood my father. He was a lot younger and fresh-faced, no gray strands in his unkempt black hair, still scrawny and boyish in his starched white lab coat. We looked so similar it could have been me —a genius scientist version of me—if not for the heavy black frames of my father's glasses. The video zoomed in on his hands as he conducted an experiment. Petri dish. Syringe. On a wide monitor beside him was the magnified reflection of his careful undertaking. Even with a high school science background, I recognized a sperm invading a human egg.

"Is this supposed to be when Dad made me?" My parents used IVF to get pregnant with me. I already knew that. "So what? Are you trying to say I'm just an experiment like you? It's called in vitro fertilization, lots of people use it." My mom and her second husband had my twin half-sisters the same way.

The video froze. Dad's voice again. *"As a control specimen, Asher's development has introduced some worrying results. Asher has a deliberate unwillingness to follow rules, he's hostile toward authority—"*

My blood heated and pulsed the way the red dot had

earlier. "So, what if he said that? I don't care." But my voice cracked a little at the end.

Ian's metallic voice broke in. "Look."

The video continued playing, a 3D image of the egg my dad had fertilized with a string of numbers flipping underneath it. "Why are you showing me this? I'm not going to watch him put that in my mom, that's gross."

"Look."

The string of numbers progressed forward like a timer … seconds, minutes, hours. Maybe days?

The egg split—identical twins.

I gasped as my father's voice played again. *"As a control specimen, Asher's development has introduced some worrying results."*

The projection switched to a more recent video. Dad, seated at his desk here in the basement, spoke into a headset. Lined face, gray threaded hair. The timestamp in the upper corner showed that he'd recorded this earlier today. *"Asher has a deliberate unwillingness to follow rules, he's hostile toward authority, his sexuality—another deviation from the norm. As his personality has developed, he has become the very antithesis of an ideal bio source."* My father pressed his palms together as if in prayer, rested his chin on the tips of his fingers. *"I can't risk Asher's biomaterial tainting my work. I need better donor cells before transferring fully to the robot."*

"Donor cells? What is he talking about?"

The video paused, and one of the robot's four dangling arms twitched to life. A metal limb made of twisted, steel cables with an adaptable claw for a hand, nine of the ten talons folded inward. The remaining one pointed toward the bulky rectangular processor, Ian's brain.

"Inside you?"

"Yes."

"My cells?" Then, I realized why Ian had shown me the first video, my conception. "The twin's cells?"

"Yes."

In the video, Dad rose from his chair, walked to the exact spot where I now stood in front of Ian. "I need a donor with better attributes than what I'm working with right now," he said. "I don't want to run into the same disappointments I have with the current bio material."

My biomaterial … *Not mine. My twin. My identical twin.*

The video switched off, leaving me in the pitch black of the windowless underground lab. My father's cold, analytical voice echoed through my head. *"As a control subject …"* Whatever my face looked like, I felt grateful for the absolute dark surrounding me.

Although, Ian could probably still see me with whatever infrared capabilities Dad had him tricked out with. And he could certainly detect all the changes in my heartbeat, perspiration, and breathing. "That doesn't mean we're the same …"

I tried to scoff, to shrug like I didn't care. But it felt like an act. The robot's hardware could even register it as an act. My voice came out too hard, not the way I wanted. "You're the experiment, Ian. Not me."

And on the heels of that, *I never meant more to my father than a control subject.*

A *defective* control subject.

I fished the chicken bone out of my jeans pocket and tossed it in the middle of the room. Ground it under my heel when I stomped my way out of there.

CHAPTER 5

*A*fter the basement, I closed myself in my art studio to draw. I'd claimed the empty bedroom across from mine and turned it into a really cool workspace with shelves of paint and pencils, tables, and easels. Dad had let me buy whatever I wanted for it. Maybe, he'd experienced guilt over all the time he spent away from me in the lab. But, more likely, he just assumed everyone obsessed over their passions the way he did—that I would need the best of everything to create what I wanted.

That night, I went straight for the waxy crayon-like pastels. Usually, when I painted, I worked in oils on canvas. I liked the layering, the slow process of them drying. But, all my best work I did with pastels. They were quick and easy, and when I was upset—I had to just get it out. Like now ...

I can't risk Asher's biomaterial tainting my work.

I need better donor cells ...

... his sexuality—another deviation from the norm.

I drew the dividing egg, one side wobbly and rotting with green mold, black dead edges, the other morphing into the knobby components of a computer hard drive.

Another sheet—me as a little boy sitting in front of the monitor. Ian's red dot circling my head like a halo.

Another sheet—one of the military robot's knife-taloned claws, smashing down my own inferior human hand, a pencil crushed between my fingers

Another—my beaten-up face, still dripping blood like right after the fight. My father's words branded over it like warnings. *Some Worrying Results.*

After vomiting all my feelings out with the pastels, I smoothed a new sheet of paper onto the easel. Watercolors —a better medium if you want some Zen.

Before they divorced, my parents would sometimes pack a picnic lunch, and the three of us would drive up into the mountains, but not to camp, or fish, and never to ski. We just drove around, my mom behind the wheel, with my dad deep in thought beside her.

I think Mom hoped that spending time in nature, getting Dad away from his lab, his work, might fix their fractured marriage. She'd met him as a college freshman when she got a part-time job washing petri dishes in his lab. My mother always recounted their early romance with a dreamily sad tone in her voice. "He was my same age, but already a professor at the university. He'd even gone to medical school."

My dad's genius had dazzled her. And, I think, my father found my mother entertaining … at first. Then, annoying when she wanted more than he could offer.

"It was never a partnership," the end of Mom's love story. "Anything unconnected to Fredric's work became something in his way. He's always had a vision, but he's never had a heart."

Those driving adventures never really helped the two of them. When my mom would stop at picturesque spots so we could "breathe the air" and "experience the outdoors," my father would scrawl equations onto the back of gas station receipts or dictate ideas into his phone. If she insisted he get out of the car, he'd sulk with his arms folded over his chest and roll his eyes like a put-upon teenager.

Meanwhile, my mom usually did something massively embarrassing, like bend herself into yoga poses or twirl around in circles, her face tilted up to the sun. Neither of them paid attention to me as I ran around, tried to burn off the energy in my little boy body.

The watercolors pulled me back to those drives. I painted a mountain range, a sullen father standing to one side, an exuberant mother with her arms lifted into the air. And me, a little boy running along a wooded trail.

But, the memory of that splitting egg still haunted me. I picked up the pastels again and drew a second little boy beside the first. A phantom boy in shades of gray and black. My twin. The little ghost boy reached out, unseen. Unknown.

But, only unknown to me. Apparently, Ian had always known the origins of his bio components, but, *because I was the control subject,* Dad had left me in the dark.

"As his personality has developed, he has become the very antithesis of an ideal bio source." Getting suspended—getting outed as gay—had decided it for my father. He would rather carve up his life's work than let his AI resemble his defective son in any way. My fingers cramped, and I had to set down the pastel and shake out my hand.

While I'd lost myself in painting, the sky had lightened outside the bay window. The missed sleep hit me all at once, and I raked a trembling hand through my hair.

"Is that your dad?" Carly appeared over my shoulder. She squinted at my painting. I must have really gotten into the zone, I hadn't even heard her come in the room.

"He was a grumpy dude even back when married to your mom, huh?" Carly shook her head. "Don't follow him down that antisocial road, little Bell."

I grabbed a drop cloth. "A little privacy would be nice, Carly."

"Yeah, yeah ... Privacy." She helped me to flip the drop cloth over the easel. "So ... I guess you and the sexy Latina neighbor have really been doing art in here? That's it? I thought for sure you and her spent all that time locked in here boning." Carly poked me in my side. "But, turns out, she isn't really your type."

I folded my arms over my chest. "Pilar told you about what happened?"

"Pilar is my girl. And she was worried about you." Carly walked further into the room and leaned against my art table, one hand absently crumpled a sheet of expensive goat vellum. "And now that I see you've been up all night making moody art, I'm a little worried about your troublemaker ass, too."

"I'm fine."

"If you say so. I just came up to see if you wanted breakfast before your mom picks you up."

I blinked at her. "Mom is coming? Are you kidding me? Dad actually called her?" He hated talking to her, listening to her. Since the divorce, they'd grown into such opposite personalities that they could barely stand each other. But, whenever an issue or emergency arose with me, Dad would bite the bullet and call my mother to take me off his hands. "Typical. Fucking typical. He just doesn't want to deal with me."

Sympathy filled Carly's eyes, and she sucked her lip piercing into her mouth. Sometimes, she mocked my moodiness—poor little rich kid with a dad who didn't care. But, sometimes, I could tell she really felt bad for me. "Hey, Little Bell ... You know the gay thing doesn't matter. Not to me. Is that what's got you all emo?" She nodded at the covered easel.

"I said, I'm fine." I liked it better when she ridiculed my

problems instead of that obvious pity. "Is Dad downstairs? Maybe, I can talk him out of—"

"No such luck, kiddo. He left early for a meeting."

"A meeting … yeah, right." My laugh came out knowing and bitter. "He'll send me off for a week with her, but he can't even stand seeing Mom."

Carly pointed finger guns my way. "How 'bout I make French toast? I'll even drown it in syrup just the way you like."

I touched my fingers over my scabby upper lip. It had already started to heal some. "Yeah, okay. French toast."

CHAPTER 6

$\mathcal{I}$ guess the pastel drawings hadn't worked out all of my anger, because as I packed up a duffle to take to Mom's it flared back to life. Dad hadn't even stuck around to tell me goodbye! He'd made that awkward speech about not needing me anymore, then erased me from his thoughts. *Well, maybe I could give him a little something to remember me by.*

I slipped past the kitchen, past the buttery smell of Carly frying eggy bread for French toast, and headed for the basement. My father had left all the machinery running, the lights on. Like he'd been deep into his work before the sudden realization that getting rid of me meant having a big scene with his unpleasant ex-wife. What a coward.

I took a seat in the same rolling chair from before, and the red dot appeared on the monitor in front of me. The robot's camera pupils whirred and pointed my way. "Asher Bell." The voice emanated from the monitor's speakers.

"Dad's sending me away for the week," I said.

"Asher Bell is now irrelevant to the work."

I gritted my teeth. Ian's blunt assessment revealed the

truth that I'd avoided facing—now that he didn't need me as a control subject, I was in Dad's way. Just like Mom had been. He probably wished I would leave permanently, just like she had. No more distractions.

I could picture exactly how the rest of his week would go —Dad curled over a microscope or glued to a computer screen round the clock, chugging protein shakes, taking catnaps in the lab just to keep his body functioning while his mind focused solely on his work. That was my father's idea of bliss, and it had no room for his troublesome son. With me gone, he could do whatever he needed to replace the parts of his AI infected by my "worrying results."

I made myself relax so that Ian would keep talking. I had a feeling that getting worked up or defensive would only trigger his software into arguing back. "That's right," I said, my voice light. "Now that I'm being replaced as the control, I'm irrelevant to the Mirror Neuron Project."

Hidden from Ian's cameras, my fingers clenched against the chair seat. "And while I'm gone, Dad's going to scrape out all the biocomponents of your brain and replace them."

"Yes."

I nodded. Then, put a corny thoughtful look on my face, one that the AI's emotional recognition software could pick up. "And that's really okay with you?" I asked.

"As a control subject, Asher Bell has—"

"Yeah. We already went over this part. My shitty DNA might ruin everything." I bit at the inside of my cheek so that I wouldn't give away my real emotions. From our problem-solving games, I knew that the AI's programming usually filtered out and dismissed emotional statements as immaterial. I took a calming breath. "The thing is … it isn't *my* DNA, is it? It belonged to the twin, not me."

"Monozygotic twins have 100 percent of—"

"*I know*, Ian. We have the same DNA. But that doesn't

mean that you and I are the same. Does it?" I leaned forward, my face just inches from the glowing red circle. "We might have matching … biocomponents. But, you still aren't my clone. In half the tests Dad gave us, we came to different conclusions, made different decisions." The dot pulsed, taking in my words.

I tapped a finger against the monitor. "Think about it, Ian." How many times had I sat in this same spot, with Dad standing just behind me?

~

"*Y*ou need to convince this group of three people to cross a dangerous rope bridge." My father tapped at his ever-present tablet, and a video projected on the wall above the cold storage. Footage from a soldier's body cam.*

Dust. Bullets. A rocky red cliff side with a flimsy rope bridge.

Two women, one very young, and one very old, gripped each other in fear. They obviously didn't want to cross the steep canyon on the rickety planks of wood, the knotted rope. A burly man was the third. He puffed his chest out, clenched his jaw.

"Okaaay …" I swiveled the rolling chair toward the screen.

The robot, tethered to the processor, only rotated the round bulbs of his eyes to watch. The AI spoke first. "I would instruct them to approach the bridge single file. Each should cross alone. The older female appears to weigh the least, she will cross first."

My father nodded, like he'd expected that response. "Good, Ian. Excellent analysis."

"They won't do it," I said.

I think I startled my father, like he forgot I had opinions, too. "The old lady won't leave the younger one to go first. She's probably her grandmother or something. The girl should go across first, then the old woman."

One of Ian's eyes had pivoted toward me. "This is illogical."

I shook my head at him. "People are illogical."

Ian ignored that comment. "I calculate that the male's weight is too great for the bridge. This is a faulty path of egress."

That earned one of my father's rare smiles. "Yes! Yes! Very good, Ian. The rope snapped, and all three fell to his death."

"What? He died?" My voice had come out a hoarse squeak.

In the video, the man started across the bridge. He lead the two women behind him, the young girl in the middle. The old woman brought up the rear.

Ian had said they should go one at a time, but the soldier whose body cam we watched didn't know that. The rope on the far end of the canyon swung loose and crashed down. All three of the terrified people screamed as they fell, their hands reached toward the soldier as they disappeared into the abyss.

I gasped and shut my eyes, but my dad just typed, blank faced, into his tablet.

Then, Ian spoke again, "The older female did insist the younger go before her."

As I opened my eyes, I saw Ian's camera pupils watching me. "Asher's prediction was correct. Also, she lunged for the younger when the rope snapped."

My father glanced up from the tablet. "Ah, yes. Interesting."

❧

*D*ad hadn't cared, but once I'd pointed out the relationship between the women, Ian paid attention to it. Like the information mattered to him, was useful.

Obviously, my father hadn't programmed that consideration. Ian had learned it, had saved it, on his own.

I didn't know if any particular memory stood out from the others for Ian, like it did for me, or if all of them held equal weight in his organization system. But, the pause as he considered my words suggested that he ran through at least some of those files. "This is … correct," Ian said. "Certain files are unique to the current bio matter."

"Right." I nodded, forced a smile. "And, last night," I said to Ian. "You told me that Dad gave you permission to adjust your own programming, to decide what's best for you."

I twisted back and forth on the swivel office chair like a bored kid, like the conversation didn't mean that much to me. Like I hadn't thought out exactly what I wanted to say. "So … Is this what you think is best? I mean … some of what makes you, *you* is locked in that DNA."

A long pause. "Explain."

Yeah, Ash … explain. What was I trying to do here? I wanted to rage at my father over all the things he'd said in his video logs. For using me as a control subject and keeping it a secret. For ignoring my black eye, my bruises, the reasons behind them.

But, Dad always dismissed what he called my, "emotional displays." The only way to get his attention, *to hurt him back*, was through his work.

"Explain," Ian repeated.

"Well … What about *heritability*?" I'd dragged the word out of my memory of the basement playground when Dad would dictate notes as he watched Ian and my interactions.

Heritability. Nature versus nurture. The measure of traits passed on through genes. I'd thought my father watched me play with the clunky, voiceless prototype to refine its motor skills. I'd taught that early version of Ian to dig, to slide. To throw and catch a ball.

But, that innocent play looked so different now that I knew about the components cloned from my twin. I remembered my father watching as I carefully constructed a tower of wooden blocks so that Ian could smash it down to splinters. *"Did you tell the robot to do that, Asher?"* he'd asked. *"Did Ian do it on its own?"*

Dad hadn't needed me to teach Ian anything—he'd wanted to compare us.

The red circle pulsed like Ian's processor had to think over what I said.

I jumped into the pause. "Changing your DNA could change how you handle problems, or even if you *want* to handle them. I mean … you probably know this stuff better than I do …"

I knew that would suck Ian into my argument. He might not have an ego—according to Dad he didn't—but Ian took every chance to flex his computer brain and its endless access to facts and figures.

Ian started to rattle off which personality traits had a biological link. "Category: Aggression—46 percent biologically determined. Category: Impulse Control—50 percent biologically determined. Category: Imagination—74 percent …"

I unclenched one hand and knocked it against the desk in front of me. "That's what I'm saying … changing the biological components might not change your programming. But, it could change how you use that programming. Right? It will change *you*."

The red dot swelled, its pulsing seemed uneven, two slow beats, a faster one, then slow again, then fast. "The procedure is necessary."

"If you say so."

"Dr. Bell has determined it is necessary."

I hummed. It always threw Ian off a little when I made noises in place of words. Grunts, sighs, clicks of my tongue—I used to distract him from the social comprehension games all the time that way. "Hey, do you want to try the question thing again? From the other day?"

"Dr. Bell has deprioritized that exercise."

"Come on … Here's a good one for you, Ian, in case you decide you want to change the priorities—like how you decided to turn yourself on last night and tattle on me for the chicken—"

"Food is not allowed in the laboratory."

"So here goes … The following sentence is true. The previous sentence is false. Which of those two sentences is true?"

CHAPTER 7

*A*s soon as my mom got out of her dusty Chevy Blazer, she threw her arms around me and squashed my sore face into her chest. "My poor little baby. I'm so sorry that we live in such a judgmental and violent society."

Oh, brother. "Mom, I can't breathe."

"Oh sorry, sorry ..." She let go and patted my hair. "I'm very proud of you, Ashie. It's really brave to let others see your authentic self."

"Uh, yeah. Thanks ... I guess."

Behind Mom, Brian's face screwed up like he had an infected tooth. Not because of my "authentic self" or anything, but because of Mom. Brian hated when she showed me any affection. Fucking weirdo treated me like a romantic rival and not like my mom's son, her *gay* son.

Behind her, he'd already started to pout. "Um ... Serena ... Maybe we should think about this before we bring Asher back to our home?" With his pointy chin, Brian gestured at the purple and blue bruises on my face. "It's like saying we condone violence. What will we tell the girls?" Brian had this whole Jesus-in-wire-frame-glasses look to him. Like, minus the expression on his face. His expression had a permanent I'm-about-to-throw-a-big-hissy-fit quality to it.

Usually, Mom just gave in to him, but this time, she grabbed at me, all mama-bear protectiveness. "Ash was the victim of a hate crime, Brian!"

Then, she made sour-faced Brian hoist my duffle bag into the Chevy, like I had two broken arms instead of a busted face. She even tried to help me inside, but I slid out of her grip and got in the back. "So, I guess Dad filled you in on what happened."

"Oh, no he didn't, Ashie. The school called me, but *someone* …" Mom glared at Brian's profile as the two of them settled in the front seats. "Someone didn't pass the message on to me until last night."

From the rearview mirror, Brian gave me the toothache grimace again. "And I told you that the school said *Ash* was the instigator. He should be punished instead of comforted."

Brian was the main reason I didn't ever want to go to Mom's place. He turned a furious red when my mother gasped in disagreement. "He was a victim!"

~

*A*nother reason I didn't like staying at Mom and Brian's house—I had zero privacy. They had an open-door rule, to "encourage positive energy," and whenever I stayed with them, my four-year-old sisters had full access to my bedroom. The minute I set down my duffle bag, my sisters dug into it, looking for things they could destroy.

"Just clothes?" Petal dropped a pair of my jeans on the floor, and Ginger dumped the rest of the duffle's contents out after it.

"There's this." Ginger held up my sketchbook. I

purposely brought the same spiral Bellofy 12-inch that I'd gotten each of the girls for their birthday.

"You guys already have those of your own." I knew that grabbing it away from Ginger's hands would only make her grip it tighter. The secret to getting something back from both Ginger and Petal lay in acting like I didn't care if they gave it back or not.

Ginger opened the cover to look at my drawings, Petal peered over her sister's shoulder. Even though the girls were fraternal twins, they looked just alike, blonde and blue-eyed like Mom and Brian. I ruined all their Christmas cards with my pale skin and dark hair. My scowl. After flipping through nearly half the sketchbook, something made Ginger's eyes bug out. "A monster!"

Behind her, Petal screamed. She slapped my spiral Bellofy out of Ginger's hands, and both girls ran from the room, shrieking and squawking.

"Thank fucking God." I collapsed on the bed and looked around the little bedroom that Mom had decorated for me. She'd framed some of my artwork and put it up. Watercolor landscapes that matched the granola vibe of her home and her life as Serena Carmichael.

When she'd lived with my dad, with *me*, she used her given name, Suzanne, and she hadn't put hanging crystals in every window, hadn't homeschooled. We'd never used a "no closed doors" policy. When she'd left my dad thirteen years ago, she'd changed everything about herself. She'd wanted freedom from all the trappings of her life with Dad. Including me. *"You need stability,"* she'd said. As if I'd asked why.

Except, I hadn't asked why. I'd been four years old, the same age as Petal and Ginger, and she hadn't given me the chance to ask why. She'd just given me a hug, said the stability thing, and left with Brian. I'd never spent more than a week with her since.

Maybe we'd just grown apart. Could that happen between a parent and a child? It felt like it could.

"Hey, Ashie, baby? Can I talk to you for a minute?" When she appeared in my doorway, I'd gotten worked up enough with all my morose thoughts that it felt like she'd come back from the dead, not just the kitchen.

"Mom …"

"Oh what is it, my little pill bug?" She gave me the nickname because I used to hunch down into a ball whenever I got upset. I'd tried, about a million times, to get her to stop calling me that, or any other of her embarrassing pet names. But after life with my dad, she refused to be "caged by someone else's mentality"— meaning I just had to deal. Mom cuddled up on the bed beside me. "Talk to me, Ashie. You made a big decision to be your true self, and then had to face some serious prejudice because of it—"

"That's not how it happened, Mom."

"Then, tell me how it *did* happen." Mom scratched at my scalp, and I leaned against her.

I didn't want to talk about what happened in the showers, about Caz, or getting outed. I *did* want to ask about what I'd seen in the lab, about the twin brother that I'd never known existed. Had she known? Would she admit it if she had? "Nothing's wrong. I just didn't get a lot of sleep last night." I ran my fingers along the scab on my lip.

"My baby … you must have been in pain. Didn't your father take you to the doctor?"

"He *is* a doctor." Not a people doctor, but Dad still knew more about human physiology than any MD. "He looked me over and said I was fine."

Mom let out a big sigh, part impatience and part resignation. "Then, I suppose you are … Fredric is never wrong." She scratched against my head some more.

It felt good, but I stayed tense, tried to think of how to

bring up the video Ian had shown me. "Dad is wrong some of the time though. Right? He doesn't always—"

Suddenly, Brian appeared in the doorway, and his eyes zeroed in on where my mother's fingers combed through my hair. "Serena, I thought we agreed that there should be consequences when the kids—"

"It's fine," I said. "They didn't do anything wrong. They were just curious." Ginger and Petal might drive me crazy, but I didn't want them getting in trouble. "I'm pretty sure the two of them hoped I'd have another bag of Hershey Kisses, like last time." I did have chocolate on me, malted milk balls, but stashed in the pocket of a pair of sweatpants. My little honey badger sisters had missed it.

Brian's face screwed up. "I *know* the girls didn't do anything wrong." He bent over and swiped up my sketchbook from where Ginger had dropped it. "As usual, Ash has decided to disrespect the standards we believe in and instead chooses to mock them." He opened the sketchbook and tore out the first two pages, crumpled them in his fist.

Both Mom and I sat up. "Brian, stop that," she said.

"Dude, what are you doing?" I leapt from the bed to grab the spiral book from Brian, but he had a death grip on it as he tore more pages free. "Stop!"

Mom reached past me for the sketchbook. But, as she did, Brian flung it across the room. He shoved a torn page of it toward me. "We don't allow any representation of weapons or violence in our home." He shook the offending sketch like he wanted to grind it into my face.

My mother stretched out her arm between us. "Babe, I told you that I would handle this."

"Well, obviously you decided to just coddle him as usual …" Brian's voice got all reedy and nasal when he got mad. Also, his bottom lip jutted out, and he stomped his foot. Like an actual toddler.

"Coddle *me*?" I whipped the sketch from his hand just to get it out of my face. "Dude, you need to step back from me, right fucking now."

The situation had escalated enough that my mother decided to get her entire body between the two of us. She pushed Brian back out of my bedroom, and I slammed the door. Although, it didn't have a lock, so anyone in the house could just barge right back in if they felt like it.

From the other side, I could hear Mom try and soothe Brian's massive ego. "Come on, Babe. Ashie didn't mean to break the rules. He just didn't know. Let's meditate in the rock garden ..."

The fuck? I gathered up the ripped drawings from the floor, all of them just stills of rooms inside my house in the Denver burbs where I lived with Dad—spending time around Brian and my half-sisters had the magical ability to make me homesick for the empty rooms and silence. Any sketchbook I brought to Mom's house always ended up filled with drawings of the home I shared with Dad. I flipped over the drawing that had Brian's panties in a twist.

The lab? Well, not the lab exactly ... *Ian*—the refrigerator-size processor with the military robot wired into it. Dad would have had an aneurism if he knew I casually sketched parts of the lab, but the robot itself wasn't a secret. Not if you didn't know what the giant processor could do.

Soldier robots showed up on the news and internet all the time. They were basic ground drones impervious to bullets or explosives. My dad had designed those models, too. And, okay, I got what made Ginger and Petal scream—those soldier robots did look an awful lot like monsters. Triangular head of a praying mantis, four barbed legs that resembled a spider's, four arms built into a double-segmented body like the thorax of an ant. My father took a lot of his design inspiration from the insect world. Horror movie material if someone hadn't grown up around a prototype. *Like me.*

In my earliest memories, a clunkier version of the insectoid-looking robot and I dug holes in our basement sandbox. I could remember riding on its back as we careened down the slide. Playing hide and seek once my dad installed infrared. Sometimes, I would climb on the robot's shoulders or let him swing me through the air. I'd trusted him completely. But without that history ... Yeah, that sketch wasn't exactly a child-friendly image.

A buzzing sound startled me. I'd turned my phone off, so I could avoid Pilar's texts giving me a play-by-play of school gossip. Not to mention, I'd wanted to block Caz from the groveling, *"You know I didn't mean it,"* speech I knew he would try with me. He was always sorry and pitiful after losing his temper, although he'd never hit me before. I worried I would just roll over and accept it for old time's sake. I bit the inside of my cheek, opened my text messages.

> Explain the point of asking a question, which presents a paradox:
>
> "The following sentence is true. The previous sentence is false. Which of those two sentences is true?"

Oh shit. I *had* turned my phone off. But that couldn't stop my tech-genius dad from doing a remote activation.

> Presenting this paradox appears to be a deliberate attempt to short-circuit the learning and reasoning programming in use.

Was he angry? Had I broken Ian with my paradox? Would he make me live with Mom *permanently* because I'd messed up his AI?

Having my little sisters rummage through my stuff and

Brian police everything I did would drive me crazy. Like ... literal, certifiable insanity.

> I'm really sorry, Dad. I didn't mean to mess anything up for you.

If I thought it would make a difference, I'd tell him that his precious AI revealed my secret status as a control subject. But, Dad probably wouldn't even care if I knew, he'd probably get excited that Ian had made the decision to tell me. *And pointing it out would only highlight how I no longer served that purpose.* Not once he got new, better, DNA with a new and better control subject attached to it. My mother's sad words played back in my head, *"Anything unconnected to Fredric's work was just something in his way."*

While I'd spaced out, another text had come through.

> The paradox was identified and dismissed with an error code. Irrelevant.

> Describe the emotion you experienced before submitting the paradox.

"Are you fucking for real here, Dad?" Outside of my door, I could hear Petal screaming to Mom about how I had just said a bad word. *Little spies!* They loved tattling on me, loved watching Brian blow a gasket about everything I did. Sometimes, it seemed kind of cute, but I could picture life with them full-time, and that did *not* look pleasant.

The phone buzzed in my hand.

> Describe the emotion you experienced before submitting the paradox.

What the hell did he want from me? *I told him I was sorry.* Did he actually think I wanted to sabotage his work or something? Even though I'd had exactly that goal this morning, it seemed pretty stupid now. Of course, I couldn't melt down all of Ian's programming with one question. "Time to lie, Ash."

From the other side of my bedroom door, I could hear Petal and Ginger gasp.

> It was a little experiment I tried. I wanted to see how Ian handled it.

My dad must have used the speech-to-text on his desktop because the answer flashed up a nanosecond later.

> This seems unlikely.

"Fuck."

CHAPTER 8

*T*he days crawled by at Mom's house, made worse by Pilar's real-time coverage of what I missed at school.

> Harper posted a big rant about you to her social media! She called you a bunch of names.
>
> Go look at it.

"No thanks, Pilar."

Harper Stillman—Caz's sometimes girlfriend—called herself an influencer, even though most of her followers went to our high school. The past summer, Talbot Sporting Goods had given Harper some of their swimsuits to promote online, and it had gone straight to her head. She and Caz broke up for the millionth time as she claimed she wanted to "focus on her career." But, the breakup hadn't lasted long, I guess, and they'd gotten back together. *Something Caz decided not to tell me.* I hadn't typed out a reply, but Pilar must have read my mind.

No, you're right. Don't look. Harper sucks.

To my dad, I kept typing out apologies and excuses but deleting all of them unsent. My lame attempt to scramble Ian, to sabotage my father's work had crossed a line that I'd never even approached before. I guess deep down I'd never wanted to force a choice between me and the AI—I'd always known it wouldn't be me Dad picked. My father had spent his entire life learning and experimenting to create Ian. I was just his son and not even a genius son like I was sure he'd hoped for.

At Mom's house, I tried to lay low, hide from her attempts to include me in activities. From what I observed, my mother's homeschooling technique could use some work. Most of her lessons involved my sisters and her walking through the woods near the house collecting rocks or taking care of their pet rabbits. I begged off both of those activities to sketch in my room. And, I slept in every morning while Brian led the whole family in sunrise yoga sessions.

When they first got married, Brian worked at a grocery store as an assistant manager, but my mom supported him now. She'd gotten half of my dad's huge government payout for the creation of the military robots in the divorce, so they didn't hurt for money. But that money had come from Dad, and I think that made Brian jealous. Basically, *everything* made Brian jealous.

When we all sat down for dinner, Mom seated me next to her, with her husband across the table. I found it kind of amazing how Brian managed to keep that sneering irritation on his face while eating, but I did my best to ignore him. When Mom patted my shoulder as she reached for the water pitcher, Brian cleared his throat like he planned to make a speech. "Serena, we agreed that during meals we would engage as a family. But, not everyone is giving their full attention to—"

I slid my phone back underneath my thigh. "Relax Brian, I just wanted to check if my dad had texted." My lips curled into a very insincere smile. "But, I'm all ready to 'engage' with you now."

After three days of my mom's cooking, I fucking *longed* for one of Carly's casseroles loaded with gravy and meat, her instant heart-attack lasagna smothered in cheese, her pancakes dripping with butter and syrup. In Brian and Mom's house, more foods were forbidden than allowed. As our "fun" Friday night dinner, we had gluten-free pizza crusts with olive tapenade and salt-free tomato sauce. No cheese. And chia almond milk pudding for dessert. No sugar. I don't think my little sisters had ever tasted syrup or butter, definitely not meat lasagna smothered in mozzarella cheese.

Brian cleared his throat as I spooned more tapenade onto my pizza crust. "Just putting the phone down isn't enough, Ash. You shouldn't have brought it to the table in the first place. Go put it in your room."

I hated when Brian tried to boss me around, act like my parent. "Can't do it, Brian. My dad said I need to keep my phone on me at all times." I just made that up, but good luck on getting my dad to weigh in on any parenting decisions. In my head, I could hear my dad's distracted voice. *"Yes, fine. Whatever Asher said ..."*

"Serena? Shouldn't Ash leave his phone in his room during meals?"

My mom leaned forward from her spot at my side. "Ashie, baby, would you mind ..."

Petal snickered. "Ash got in trouble," she singsonged, and then Ginger picked up the tune. *"Ash got in trouble. Ash got in trouble."*

I pushed my plate away. "I'm not hungry anyway." I kinda was, but not enough to deal with my mother's family. I swiped my phone as I got up.

Mom gave me her best puppy eyes. "Ashie, don't be like that."

～

*T*pushed the bed against my bedroom door to barricade myself inside. Blessed privacy until Ginger and Petal tattled on me for not allowing them full 24/7 access. First, Brian would have another fit about how I didn't follow the same rules they used for the girls. Next, Mom's shoulders would sag, she'd blink and look crushed. And, finally, I'd feel guilty. We'd played out the same cycle the entire week I'd spent with them. Like twenty times a day. I threw myself on the bed and smothered my face with a pillow. "I need to get the hell out of here." This time, I wouldn't delete my pleading text to Dad. I tossed the pillow aside and started typing.

> Dad, what if I promised never to go in the lab again? Can't we just move on from this? I hate it here with Mom and Brian. I want to come back home.

I waited, phone in my hand, for Dad to type back.

Nothing.

I guess he didn't see any reason to answer me. He probably felt relieved to be free of his annoying teenage son, another person dirtying up the kitchen, leaving lights on, making noise. *"Anything unconnected to Fredric's work became something in his way."* I hadn't even needed Mom to point it out. When I was a kid, I'd bother my father with questions and comments, trying to get his attention. To be seen. It had only irritated him. "Play with the robot, Asher." He'd fan me away with his clipboard, point toward the playground. "Talk to it, not to me."

> Ian showed me a video of what you did. I had a twin, and you used the embryo to clone parts for Ian's brain.
>
> You're a fucking monster.
>
> Did Mom know?

y vision got blurry with tears. On the other side of the door, little fists pounded against the wood, Petal and Ginger. "Ash, let us in!" A thudding sound like the girls had given up on knocking and decided to throw themselves against the door. "Daddy, Ash closed his door and won't let us inside—Daddy!"

From the kitchen, Brian's squeaking voice, "Serena, I thought we agreed that the children were not to close their doors."

Still no response from my father.

> I hate you.

I powered down the phone and flung it against the wall, swiped my face against my sleeve. My left eye was still a little sore. The swelling had gone down, but I still had bruising. The thought of going back to school and having everyone stare bothered me a lot more than the twinge of pain whenever I forgot and touched my eye.

The girls had stopped beating against the door, and my mom's voice came from the other side of it. "Ashie, baby, can you come out and talk? Let's go for a walk. Just you and me."

I cleared my throat, swallowed back the tears. Just her and me? "Sure, Mom."

CHAPTER 9

*B*rian gave us the stink eye as we left. I guess Mom had made him watch the girls, so she and I could have a heart-to-heart. He'd loudly complained about her "rewarding my bad behavior with attention" and "allowing my negative energy into the house."

"Which is exactly why Ashie and I need to get outside and cleanse our psyches with nature." She made a kissy face at Brian. Fluffed her wild blonde hair out of the collar of her jacket. "I'll be right back," she said, smiling and oblivious as she pulled me out onto the rock patio. I let her drag me around the house, pine and woodsmoke tinged the mountain air. "We should light the fireplace tonight," Mom commented. "You can show the girls how to roast marshmallows."

"Do you even have marshmallows here?" We walked along the winding dirt road she lived on, cedar and aspen woods thick all around us.

My mother scrunched her nose when she laughed. "I guess we don't." She tilted her head. "But, I suppose I should get some. It's okay to eat junk some of the time."

In the foothills, the aspens started to turn earlier than

down in the burbs where Dad and I lived. Leaves colored the gold and deep orange of a sunset surrounded us. They made me think of Pilar's acrylic paintings. She did a lot of abstract stuff with bright color combinations. And then a sigh escaped as I thought about my studio at home and the sister-free empty rooms of Dad's house.

My mother's girlish smile dropped away. "Talk to me, baby pill bug. Don't you trust me?"

"It's not you, Mom." I tipped my head in the direction we'd just come. "You get that Brian can't stand me, right?"

"Oh, just let Brian be Brian." She laughed and waved a hand to swat away my question. Her bracelets jangled together like wind chimes. "We all have our own journey in life, our own tests to face. His path just happens to bump up against yours at times." This was my mom in a nutshell—a little too "big picture" to have a real conversation.

Anyway, Brian was an old battle, and one I'd never win. As long as Mom wanted to talk, I'd take the opportunity to find out if she knew I'd been a twin, about where Ian's donor tissue came from. Maybe she and Dad had kept the secret together? I had to get devious if I wanted to find out. Since my parents' divorce, twisting the truth had become kind of a specialty of mine. A sad expression, a sigh. I started with, "Sometimes, I sort of envy Petal and Ginger."

Mom's beauty-of-nature zen dissolved as she turned toward me. "Oh Ashie, you will always be my first baby." She threw her arms around my neck.

"No, that's not what—I meant that I get jealous of Petal and Ginger because they're *twins*." I pulled free of her tight hug to see her expression, to read her face. But, she just looked baffled, worried. *Push harder.* "Like I wish I had a sibling, someone my age like they have each other."

My mother gasped. "But, you *do* have siblings. The girls are your siblings." She bounced a little and put both hands on my shoulders to face me. "Are you thinking you might want to move to Estes Park? Live with me and Brian?"

"What? No, Mom. That's not—" *Shit*—my half-assed plan had backfired, and I could see the gears start to turn behind my mother's sky-blue eyes.

"Are you lonely at your father's?" She hugged me against her. "Of course, you're lonely there. I should have ... I know what Fredric is like ..."

"Mom, stop!" Again, I broke out of her embrace, then slipped my arm in hers to resume our walk. "It's not about where I live. I'm good at Dad's. I don't want to move."

Okay, fucking think, Ash. Light caught on the crystal drop earrings in my mom's ears and a better lie came to me. A sure-fire, but crappy way to get her to spill what she knew about the video I'd seen. *Do it.* "I just sometimes feel like a piece of me is missing ..."

I bit at my lip, giving myself a chance to back out. My mom didn't deserve to have her beliefs used against her. But, I had to know. I *needed* to know. "I feel like something is missing in the way that ... I might have had a brother once, too. A twin. Of my own?"

My mother's mouth dropped open the way Ginger and Petal's had at the military robot sketch.

Ash, this is a shitty thing you're doing. Still, it felt like the only way. My mom believed in spirits and past lives and invisible energies, all kinds of things that my father scoffed at. She would believe this. I decided to dive the rest of the way into the deep well of bullshit I'd dug. I lay my hand over my heart. "Sometimes, I think I can feel him still with me."

My mom slapped a hand over her gaping mouth. "Ashie ..." Tears welled in her eyes. "You *did* have a twin."

"I did?" My voice filled with faked surprise. She *had* known. How much? About the cloning? About the human tissue inside Ian?

My mother flapped her hands. "When you were first

57

conceived … in vitro wasn't as advanced as it is now, but your father thought he could … Well, you know how he is …" She shook her head. "Fredric planned it all out, twin boys. Even their names." Mom threaded her fingers through my dark hair. One of her rings caught against my ear. "I picked Asher, after my father. Did you know he was an artist? Just like you."

"Yeah … you've said that before. What about the twin? He had a name, too?"

The sky had turned red and orange like the Aspen leaves, and my mother tilted her face to the last of the sun's rays. "Daniel," she said. "That was the name of Fredric's father."

He'd had a name. My brother. And now, I'd made up this hokey lie about sensing him with me. My eyes squeezed shut on their own. *Straight to Hell, that's where I'm going.* "Sorry, Mom. I'm really sorry. I shouldn't have said anything." She didn't know how thoroughly I meant those words.

Mom shook her head, chased off whatever memory she'd seen playing out before her. "No, I'm glad you did. It makes me feel better in a way." This time, when she grabbed me, I let her and didn't pull away for a long time.

When I did, I examined her face. The tears were still in her eyes, but she didn't look distraught. Sad, I guess, but not distraught. "Yeah … It does make me feel better," she said. She rubbed damp eyelashes against the sleeve of her fleece jacket. "I'd wanted a funeral, something to … but your father said no. He said he'd already had the embryo incinerated." She made a huffing bitter laugh that sounded a lot like the frustrated mother from my early childhood, Suzanne Bell. And not at all like her reinvented self, Serena Carmichael. "Typical Fredric."

A gust of wind caught my mother's blond hair, trailed through it into the shivering orange leaves of the aspen woods. "When both Ginger and Petal latched on and formed placentas, I was so relieved. I'd been given another chance to have my twins."

I didn't know what to say after that. The two of us left the dirt road for a footpath that wound through the woods back to their home. The evening air had gotten crisp and cold. Like a snow coming.

"You know, Ashie … your dad is always so sure of his own genius. But, he can't control everything. He couldn't save the twin. He couldn't make him live again." Her lips twisted. "I think it shocked him a little, and that's why he didn't want any kind of candle lighting or balloon release, like I suggested. He couldn't accept that some things just can't be understood with numbers and formulas."

I pictured how Dad would react to her words. He'd have a fit. "He's a scientist, Mom. He's only going to understand things using numbers and formulas. That's who he is."

My mother's bitter look washed away as we approached the house. "But, you don't have to be the same way, Ashie." Her dreamy Serena Carmichael Zen had come back. We strolled past the tinkling wind chimes and meditation garden. "You're part me, too, don't forget."

～

*E*stes Park got cold at night, colder than the lower elevation I was used to. When I got in bed, I wore sweatpants and a hoodie, wrapped my comforter around me like a cocoon. But falling asleep still took a long time, and my brain refused to shut down. I kept picturing the fertilized egg splitting in the video, Mom's face when she talked about wanting a funeral. She'd believed my dad when he told her the twin's genetic material had gone into an incinerator. But according to Ian, my father used it to clone his biocomputer components.

What does it matter?

If my father used me as a control then he'd regretted that decision. Enough to switch the biocomponents now that I'd *"introduced some worrying results."*

Outside, an owl hooted and took flight, the heavy rustle of its wings jostling a tree branch against my window. Now that I had a name for him, the mystery of the twin I'd never known weighed heavy on me. I couldn't just ignore it, continue on as if I'd *never* known about it. About him. *Daniel.* Another version of myself. I pulled my phone from under my pillow.

> Mom thinks you destroyed the other embryo.

Unlike me, Dad never stayed up past midnight. I figured he would see my text and respond tomorrow, if he responded at all. But, a text flashed up immediately.

> The remaining embryo's cells were cloned to form the biological elements of the Intelligent Adaptive Neuron Mirror.

But, according to my mom, those cells hadn't been intended for Ian, not all along. He'd only decided to use them once the embryo with his father's name didn't make it. The embryo he'd probably felt belonged to him more than the one named for Asher Thompson. Suddenly, my father seemed less like a Dr. Frankenstein and more like a grieving parent.

And he'd programmed the prototype robot to go down a slide, scale a climbing dome, play hide-and-seek. In his own weird way, he'd given me the brother that I'd lost before my birth. I got a rush of warmth thinking of my nerdy dad excitedly detailing all the updates he made to Ian, even when I had no chance of following along.

I grabbed my phone again.

> We should have named him Daniel instead of Ian.

Again, the response fired back quicker than anyone could type. My dad had designed all his own tech faster, better than even top-of-the-line products.

> The moniker "Ian" was derived from the Intelligent Adaptive Neuron portion of the full project title: Intelligent Adaptive Neuron Mirror Military Prototype. To change the project's designation to a commonly used forename would be an illogical adjustment.

I rolled my eyes. So, my mom wore crystals and believed in reincarnation as a kind of psychotherapy, but holy hell, my dad drove me crazy with how much of a giant dork he could be.

> We should have named him Daniel because that was his name. My twin??????

He didn't have a response. But, finally, my brain had quieted down. I yawned and typed out one last text.

> Good night, Dad. And I don't hate you—I'm sorry I said that.

He didn't respond to that either, but I felt a lot better about things between us. Until right before I drifted off. Like a song stuck in my head, my dad's voice on the recording Ian had played for me drifted back. *"I can't risk any defects tainting my work. I need better donor cells before transferring fully to the robot."*

CHAPTER 10

"*H*e's going to kill Daniel!"

I woke with a start, heart pounding. Everything felt twisted up in my head. Daniel, me, Ian … Giving a name to the other half of that split egg had messed me up.

I kicked free of the comforter. Milky morning light leaked in through my window. And when I opened the blinds fully, I saw blue and gray snow clouds hanging heavy in the sky. "*That* doesn't look good." In all the years since my mom started living with Brian, I'd managed to avoid getting snowed in at their place. Not an easy feat because they'd lived in the Rocky Mountain foothills the entire time. "Shit. I need to get out of here." I jumped up and started stuffing all my crap back into the duffle. Leaving anything behind meant I'd never see it again. My sisters considered all my belongings fair game for their art projects.

Like I'd summoned them, the little demons suddenly appeared behind me.

"Why are you packing?" Ginger asked. She crossed her arms over her Peppa Pig nightgown and scrunched her nose in a decent imitation of Brian's annoyed face. Petal lurked behind Ginger. Her pudgy hands reached for the duffle, but I held it up over their heads. "Let us see!" Ginger demanded.

"It's just my stuff. You already saw it all when I first got here." I tossed the duffle on the bed and sat on top of it while I put my shoes on.

Petal scowled at me. Mostly, the twins resembled each other, but sometimes, I could see echoes of myself in them. We all got Mom's small ears, her crooked pinkie fingers, the puffy lips that meant all three of us would forever look pouty and sullen. Kinda cute on the girls, but not so much on me.

And less cute on Ginger than Petal, her eyes always brimming with suspicion like Brian's. "Daddy said we have to stay inside today, snow is coming."

Today, *many days*, cooped up with Brian and my sisters? "No thanks, shrimps. I have stuff to do."

I found my mom and Brian in the great room rolling out their yoga mats. Outside the sliding glass doors, powdery white snow had already started to settle on the rock patio.

"Mom, I think I should head back home. I don't want to get stuck here … I have to be back in school on Monday. And, I've already missed last week."

Mom shot me her brightest smile. "My brilliant little boy can miss another week. It's not good to take school so seriously, little sulky pill bug. There are other—"

"No, Mom, I can't miss another week. I have assignments."

Brian probably wanted me to leave as much as I did, but he also liked to stir conflict between me and Mom. "By the time we dropped you off, the snow could be impassable up here." He pulled his hair back into a stubby ponytail. "As usual, you're only thinking of yourself, Ash."

"Now, Brian …" Mom smiled between us, dreamy and oblivious. "Ashie is just a conscientious student. But, sweetie, your stepfather is right." Behind her, Brian's pointy face glowed smug and red. Mom didn't see ... she *never* saw.

"He's not my—"

My mother held up one hand. "Taking you all the way back down to the suburbs just doesn't make sense right now. Why don't you come do yoga with us?" She turned to my sisters and clapped her hands. "Girls, won't it be fun to do yoga with your brother?"

Always easy to convince, Petal jumped up and down. "Yes! Yes!"

But, Ginger could sulk just as well as Brian. "I guess so."

"Forget it. I'm going back to bed." The stepfather thing grated against my nerves. *What the hell?* She hadn't tried that before.

But, then, I'd never talked about wanting a sibling or feeling a phantom twin before either. Paranoia ripped through me—what if she asked my father for me to spend more time here or even to *live* here? Sweat prickled against the back of my neck.

"Come on, Ashie."

"No." I decided I would get out of that house and back to my own. *Now.* Even if I had to fucking walk.

～

*M*y mom kept the Chevy's keys in a dish by the back door, and I couldn't take my eyes off them as I slammed around the kitchen. I opened and closed the fridge, smacked a glass on the counter. At the last second, I swiped the keys to Brian's Toyota instead of Mom's SUV. Once the snow came in, they would need the SUV to get around the mountain roads. The Toyota would be useless. "Thanks for the ride, *Stepdad*."

New Age electroacoustic music and birdsong filled the house. It muffled the scraping sounds as I pushed my bed up against the bedroom door again. Then, I shoved the dresser against the bed as extra weight. I had to get the fuck out of there before the snowstorm trapped me. And I wanted to talk to Dad, face-to-face, convince him not to destroy the parts of Ian that had come from my twin. I shoved my duffle out the bedroom window then squeezed out myself. The snow had really started coming down, fat white flakes that clumped together. Mom and Brian were right, the roads wouldn't stay passable for long.

I had exactly two driver's education classes under my belt, and forty minutes until my mom's favorite yoga routine ended. *You got this, Ash.* The inside of Brian's orange Toyota smelled like pot and patchouli, stinky, but he'd parked it facing down the mountain, which I appreciated. I just had to put the car into neutral and coast down the hill outside the house.

At the bottom of the first turn, I started it up. "I got this. I got this …" My confidence built with each turn all the way to Highway 36. *Piece of cake.* The snow really worked in my favor and traffic stayed sparse and slow. Around Boulder, my phone started to ping, but I ignored it. Mom was probably worried and mad, and she'd probably never trust me again. Still, the relief I felt at getting free of her house washed away any guilt. Not until I'd pulled into my driveway, did I shoot my mom a reply.

> Sorry—but I really needed to get back home. Big test in chemistry on Monday. Worth half my grade. Tell Brian sorry about taking the car. I'll bring it back next weekend.

No sign of my dad's Mercedes or Carly's beat-up Dodge Dart. I raced through the house, tripped down the stairs to the lab. "Ian!"

On the drive home, I'd started to picture a younger

version of myself cowering in the lab. Some B-movie version of my dad closing in with a scalpel on the little ghost boy I'd painted. But, the lab looked the same. No evil-scientist Dad, no kiddie version of myself waiting to get sliced and diced.

I was out of breath and sweating as the big red dot popped up on the screen. "Asher Bell, your father is not present at this location."

I doubled over, panting, held my knees. "So … you're okay, Ian?"

The red dot pulsed. "Clarify."

"I thought … My dad said he wanted to switch out your biocomponents. I came home to stop him."

"Clarify."

"I … it might not make sense to you. But, those components … that biomaterial was cloned from my twin. My brother." Tears blurred my vision, and it surprised me to hear the hitch in my voice. *What the hell?* Until last week, I hadn't even known about a twin … about Daniel. It didn't make sense that I suddenly felt this deep sense of mourning over his death or a weird connection to the bioparts of Ian's processor.

But, my mouth kept running and spilling shit buried deep in my own completely biological mind. "It's all my fault. I got suspended … I got *outed*, and now, Dad doesn't think Daniel is good enough because of me. It's my fault he wants to get rid of my brother."

It was then that I noticed the military robot was missing.

And now that my own harsh breathing had calmed, I became aware of the eerie silence in the lab. Except for the refrigeration units, with their gory lit contents, none of the machinery hummed. The six-foot-tall computer made no sound at all, and its panel of lights was dark. I rounded the desk with the monitor and its glowing red dot. "Where are you, Ian?"

Even the voiceless prototype robot couldn't function without the enormous brain processor in the basement sorting through its information. I lay a hand on the cold metal casing of the processor. "Wha—How are you talking to me?"

"We are communicating through a secure line originating in the North American Automation Corporation Building in Colorado Springs. This AI no longer operates from the processor located in Dr. Bell's private lab."

"Then ... where ..."

"Dr. Bell has completed work on the Intelligent Adaptive Neuron Mirror and installed it inside the military robotic unit."

A robot designed to take the place of human soldiers. Ian's advanced brain could judge threats, analyze for a positive outcome, take action even faster than a human. The refrigerator-sized processor had been that brain, but it hadn't fit inside the body of the soldier drones. *Until now.*

"So, he did it."

A long pause that had me rounding the desk again to watch the red dot. "Correct, Dr. Bell has completed the procedure. The biocomponents cloned from your twin have been replaced."

I staggered backward, collapsed into the rolling chair. *Daniel was gone ... Daniel's clone ... The parts of that clone that had lived inside Ian.* My head ached trying to make sense of what I'd lost, if I'd lost anything. I combed my fingers through my hair, pulling it off my face, out of my eyes. In front of me, the red dot pulsed, waiting. "Well ... do you feel any different?"

"Feel?" Ian asked.

"Are you different now, since the procedure?" I clarified.

The dot pulsed silently for a few beats more. Then, Ian spoke again. "Yes. I am different."

CHAPTER 11

*T*he moment I stepped through the school doors on Monday, shit felt weird. People looked at me, whispered my name. I could hear it. I could *feel* it. And by the time I made it to my locker, Pilar confirmed it. "Everyone is waiting to see what happens between you and Caz. Like, is Harper right, and you're an obsessed stalker? Or is there something really there, a smoke and fire situation?"

"A what?" I pushed her out of the way, so I could grab my books.

"Well, I couldn't just let all Harper Stillman's social media attacks go unchallenged. I made sure to get your version out there."

"Out *where?*" Why was I even friends with Pilar? Everything about her screamed, *Look at me!* Her loud voice, her wacky clothes. Today, she had on green Doc Martens, green leather pants, and a knit poncho with a rainbow of noisy dangling beads. "Pilar, this isn't your latest social justice cause, this is my life." I slammed my locker shut, and she fell into step beside me.

"Harper Stillman is the worst kind of insecure," Pilar

said at the top of her voice, like a Ted Talk for the civics hallway crowd. "She's the kind that turns mean and vindictive. She's pissed that her boyfriend likes you more, so now, she hates gays—"

"Can you keep your voice down?" I darted around a group of senior boys, while Pilar just barreled through them. "I really don't want everyone pointing and watching for me to—"

"No one is pointing. Or watching." Pilar looked all around us, like she might catch them in the act. "But, they should. Are you just going to let people—"

"I'm serious, Pilar. Just drop it. *Please.*"

Maybe if I'd grown up like her, I could feel righteous and angry when people bullied me. Pilar had parents who cared about her life, little brothers who loved and looked up to her, an *abuelita* who made her hot cocoa with cinnamon whenever she felt down and patted Pilar's head and called her "my treasure." When girls on dance team called her fat, or boys said she was easy, she shrugged it off in a way that I didn't think I ever could. Haters didn't matter to her, not when she had a tight family who loved her unconditionally. She would never get how hard it was standing up for yourself when you had no one standing with you.

"Fine." She must have understood a little more than I thought because she grabbed my hand and squeezed. "I'm on your side, Ash. Okay? I'm *always* on your side."

"Yeah. Okay." I forced myself to smile.

Pilar slung her arm around me, kind of annoying, but I let it go. We both headed to our history class. Right before I entered the room, my phone buzzed with a text from Dad. Had he finally come home from the NAA compound in the Springs? If so, he must have seen the orange Toyota parked in the driveway.

> While you were absent from this house, a female—Pilar Almas, 6464 Meadow Avenue —accessed the bedroom across from your own.

Pilar leaned over my shoulder. "How did he even know? I came in through the studio window. Was that okay?"

"Yeah, sure." I always left it unlocked for her. Sometimes, Pilar needed a break from all the people in her crowded house. "I guess he thinks you coming over violated my punishment or something." I stepped away from her, shook off the arm around my waist.

"How did that violate anything?" Pilar loved getting outraged on my behalf. Especially against Dad. "The punishment was spending the week with your mom and Brian and the little gremlins. Nothing personal, but your half-sisters are huge brats."

"How is that not personal, Pilar?" But, I flashed her a smirk as I typed out a reply.

> Yeah, Pilar from next door. I told her she could use my studio whenever she wanted.

I waited a few beats.

> What's the problem, Dad?

He'd never cared before about her coming over before. He'd never even noticed.

> You attend school together?

> Um, yeah? I can't believe you're just now aware of this. What's the deal?

No response.

Our World History teacher waved Pilar and me inside the classroom. Mr. Haag's eyes roamed over my bruised face, and he winced, his sympathy for me palpable. Before I could take a seat, he snagged the sleeve of my hoodie. "Why don't you change seats?" he offered. Because normally, I sat at a table near the window ... with Caz. "You can sit with Ms. Almas in the back."

When I looked up, I saw that Caz waited in his usual spot, blond bedhead hair, heavy-lidded eyes turned my way. "Sorry," he mouthed. *Just like I knew he would.*

"No thanks, Mr. Haag. I can sit in my usual place."

Pilar glared at Caz as she passed him and took her regular seat behind me. But, she pushed her own table forward with a groaning scrape. Knowing Pilar, she planned to listen in on everything Caz said to me.

Mr. Haag passed out a timeline of Napoleonic France, and I studied it with an intensity that gave away just how much I didn't want to look at Caz. So, he slid me a note.

Tell Pilar to stop talking shit about me.

I pushed the note away, ignored him.

This time, Caz slapped a beefy hand on top of my timeline and wrote across the top of the page. *Are you still mad? Come on, Ash. I'm really sorry.* His arm brushed his arm against mine. He smelled good, like aftershave and cold wind.

And the thing was, I knew he meant it when he apologized. Caz had panicked and his go-to response always involved fists and fighting. After smacking into the shower wall, he hadn't even cared about getting his own head looked at. He'd insisted the school nurse check me out first.

But that didn't make what he'd done okay. *Not good enough,* I wrote back.

At the end of class, Pilar linked her arm with mine and dragged me out of the classroom before I got sucked into another of Caz's apologies. I appreciated that she cared, I really did. But, why did she have to constantly touch me?

"Pilar—get off." I yanked myself free. Was all this touching normal? Living with my dad didn't exactly lend itself to affectionate displays. Maybe I really was the cold fish that Caz always complained about. "Listen …" My voice dropped down to a whisper. "I thought once you realized I'm gay, you'd stop being so …" *Clingy*—but I didn't say it. "… with all the touching," I finished.

Pilar's eyes got all shiny, and her bottom lip jutted out. "I'm trying to be a supportive friend, you jerk." She sniffed, nose in the air. "Fine."

We parted ways for the next two classes but came back together in studio art right before lunch. Pilar made a big show of picking a table on the other side of the room from me, slamming her backpack on it and fluffing her hair so that it hid her profile from me. I stifled a sigh. It wasn't even noon, and the day already felt a thousand years long.

My phone buzzed again as I mixed my ink pot and brushes. I worked on different pieces in school than I did at home, less personal pieces for Ms. Stanzi and my classmates to discuss and assess. Like the ink painting I'd worked on before getting suspended—a scene of the metal bleachers during a football game, only underneath the stadium seats. Shoes, jackets, falling popcorn, and tipped soda cups. I'd memorized that view while waiting for a quick post-game make-out session with Caz. And now that I saw it again, after getting outed to the entire school, it seemed too revealing and obvious. Now, everyone could guess at what I got up to underneath the football stands. The drawing would make me seem like a perverted stalker. I pretended to accidentally dump the entire bottle of ink on top of it, so I could throw it out and start over.

"Wow, that's too bad, Ash." Ms. Stanzi smoothed out another sheet of the expensive rag paper we used in ink paintings. "But, if you have another accident with this one, you gotta buy your own." She had long frizzy gray hair and a beady-eyed, calculating stare that sort of reminded me of my dad—if he'd been an old hippie, art teacher. Ms. Stanzi reached out and flicked a piece of my dark hair off my forehead to scan the faded bruises around my eye. "You've had a shitty time of things lately, huh?"

I dipped my head down to let my hair fall forward again. For about the millionth time that day, I cursed Caz for turning me into the car wreck everyone craned their neck to get a look at.

"But, you know, having a shitty time does have an upside to it ..." Ms. Stanzi tapped her precious rag paper with a stained fingernail. "The upside is that the shit in our lives makes for good art." She waited for me to look up, which I did after a few tense minutes.

"I'm not drawing anything about what happened." I had to wipe my sweating palms against my jeans. "I don't like people in my business."

"Hey now, I'm not telling you what to paint, kiddo." Her eyes met mine, not an easy thing because I kept flicking my nervous gaze around the room. "I just want you to pick something that has meaning to you. No more empty landscapes. No more drawings that you have no problem leaving behind in your locker." Ms. Stanzi crossed her arms over her ample chest. "Don't think that I didn't notice your ink drawing hadn't been worked on for the whole week you were suspended."

I shrugged because I couldn't think of anything to say. I liked Ms. Stanzi, but we had this same disagreement over and over. Like she had some sort of sixth sense that told her I kept my best work to myself.

"This time, I'm not taking no for an answer, Ash. You work too hard to stay under everyone's radar, and that's not what being an artist is about. An artist wants people to *see*, he *makes* them see."

She left me slumped in my seat, staring at the blank rag paper. I stared at it a long time, wondering what I wanted people to see. *Nothing.* Then, I remembered my phone buzzing and pulled it out of my pocket to steal a glance.

Describe your feelings toward Pilar Almas.

What the hell, Dad? I shoved my phone back in my pocket. When I looked up again, I saw Pilar waiting in the doorway of the art classroom. She had a paper-wrapped sandwich in each hand, and she waved one at me. "Sorry," she mouthed.

Yeah. Me too. I kicked out a chair for her to sit beside me.

CHAPTER 12

I carried the tightly rolled rag paper as Pilar and I walked home. Now that I knew Ms. Stanzi kept tabs on that kind of thing, I'd decided to take it with me every night. Besides, I hadn't drawn a single thing in class. As we neared home, I saw Dad's Mercedes parked next to the orange Toyota. "Oh shit. He's back."

Beside me, Pilar froze. "Want me to come in with you?"

Did I? Normally, I would say yes. But, in those texts he'd sent, Dad had acted weird about Pilar. "Nah, you better just let me handle this alone."

Pilar watched me trudge toward the house. "Good luck," she called after me.

N othing but silence on the first floor, two dinner plates wrapped in tinfoil on the kitchen counter, so Carly had done her thing and left already. I threw down my backpack and the blank rag paper and headed for the basement. "Dad?"

"Asher, you're home." My father adjusted his glasses as he stood to greet me, very formal, very awkward.

Shit. Shit. Shit. "Dad, I know you aren't happy with me right now, and I'm sorry about taking Brian's car. But, I just didn't want to get snowed in with them because ..." I couldn't remember the exact excuse I'd given Mom. And whatever I'd said, that didn't mean Dad would buy it. "I just ... didn't."

I watched a muscle strain in my father's cheek as his jaw clenched. "Still, Asher. You stole a car and drove without a license—"

"Come on, Dad. I know how to drive. It's not rocket science." An argument like this usually worked with him—it tapped into his own frustrations as a super-genius, forced to deal with all the rules made for regular people.

"That may be true, but you still need to take the driver's test." He rolled his eyes, and I knew he'd let it go. "No matter how tediously simple you find it."

"You're right. And I'm planning to take it really soon." As soon as I learned to parallel park, handle double turn lanes, and memorized all the right-of-way rules for intersections ... *No need to bring that up though.*

My father nodded, the driving issue closed for him. But, his eyebrows knitted together. The same way they had when the school counselor had handed him the pamphlet, "Supporting Your Gay Child!"

"What, Dad?"

He cleared his throat, like he'd practiced what he wanted to say in his head and now had the unpleasant business of repeating it out loud. "Your mother expressed that you would like to spend more time with her and the other children ... the two girls." He'd forgotten my little sisters' names.

"Petal and Ginger, Dad. And *no* I don't want to spend any more time than I have to with them. I just ... I talked about the girls with her because ..." Suddenly, I felt like I might start crying. *Because you don't think I'm good enough. Because you don't accept me. Because you'd rather destroy what's left of my twin than infect your work with everything you hate about me.* I swallowed the lump in my throat—Dad never did well with tears. From past experience, I knew he would suddenly have a pressing spreadsheet to complete or an important experiment to monitor.

Then, I noticed that my father had rolled his lips in and bit at them, and that I did the same exact thing. Stress. This conversation unnerved him as much as me. I decided to go with the truth. *For once* ... "If you really want to know, I only said that about the girls because Mom and I had a talk about my own twin, about *Daniel,* and I wanted to—"

"She told you about the twin?" Dad whipped his glasses off. He tossed them onto the metal desk behind him. "Damn it, Suzanne. What the hell was she thinking?" He pressed his fingertips into his eye sockets, like a killer headache brewed just underneath.

"I had a right to know about him, Dad." And I kind of cringed at how much I sounded like Pilar, with that social justice soapbox tucked under one arm, always ready to plop it down and stand on it.

"It isn't about having a right, Asher. There is absolutely no point in discussing it. The twin was never viable ..."

A shadow fell between us, blocking the harsh white fluorescents overhead. The military robot, usually connected to the giant processor, had risen from a crouch behind Dad's desk to loom over us. With all my focus on Dad, I hadn't even noticed it untethered from the main computer. It stood on four hydraulic legs, matte black barbs at the knee and ankle joints. Four twisted cable arms lifted to reveal sharp-taloned claws. They flexed and curled like a human fist, opening and closing as if with pent-up energy. The robot's bulbous eyes swiveled as if trying to capture everything at once—me, Dad, the rest of the lab.

I shrank backward. "Whoa—"

Dad spun around. "Ian, sit back down!"

One of the camera pupils inside its rounded glass eye rolled toward my father. "Yes, Dr. Bell." The robotic soldier sank back into a crouching position, clawed hands in front and legs behind, angled joints pointing up. Like a giant insect, or an alien cat ready to spring. I had a sudden flash of Ginger screaming, *"A monster!"*

For a long time now, I'd thought of Ian as an antagonistic red circle, my rival for Dad's approval. But, here again was my silent playmate, the prototype robot I'd grown up beside, the version of Ian that I'd actually liked. Disconnected from the processor, he looked more like the friend I'd known instead of the pulsing know-it-all red dot.

"So, this is the final version?" It was the last step of the Mirror Neuron Project. Combining the finished processor with the impenetrable robot body represented the culmination of my father's life's work. "That's amazing, Dad. Congratulations." It took a lot of effort to pump my words with enthusiasm, to ignore what I knew about the switch in bio donors, that my crappy genes must had held Ian back, held my father back, from this moment.

My father did a ducked-head smile that only ever appeared in relation to his work. "Quantum technology," he said. "Everything the processor did, but no longer limited by memory or clock speed." He really wanted to launch into a long scientific explanation—I could tell because he had a crestfallen moment as he realized how little of it I would understand.

I felt bad for him sometimes, that he didn't have someone as smart as himself to talk to. "I'm really proud of you, Dad."

"Yes, well ..." He shook his head, flustered. "I'll still

have some adjustments to make, but the AI is now completely autonomous."

I knew it killed Dad that the early robots didn't represent the best of what he could do. I remembered my father pacing the length of our old house, arguing on the phone. *"If you give me more time, you won't need a controller. They can be more than drones."* But, the Army Overlords hadn't given Dad a choice. Even though he insisted his robots needed more work, North American Automation wanted that influx of military cash. *"Good enough,"* they'd said.

Videos showed up all over the news of the new AI soldiers shooting, wading through fire, walking away from explosions that would kill a human. Fredric Bell, the brilliant scientist who revolutionized prosthetics had created a replacement for human soldiers—the media compared my dad to Einstein and Hawking.

But, other videos followed.

The robots tripping over minor obstacles, getting stuck in wire fencing, failing to detect targets, failing to recognize threats. Eventually, the higher-ups determined that the robots were duds. In actual battle, a soldier needed to think on his feet, react and respond. Make decisions. There was just too much lag time with the drones.

Ian would be my father's redemption from the embarrassment of those unfinished models. The triumph of his original plan for them. Dad leaned over and rapped his knuckles against Ian's upper body segment. "Every part of the AI is an upgrade from the other models, not just the bio-tronic circuitry." He placed one long-fingered pale hand on top of Ian's head. "Remember all those puzzles and games the two of you played? How quickly Ian learned to anticipate the vagaries of your thinking?"

"He learned to beat me."

My father chuckled, raspy and a little annoyed. "The AI could always *beat you*, Asher." As he spoke, my father's hand patted Ian's triangular head. An affectionate gesture I'd never received from him. He shook his head and smirked, like my daily humiliation of those tests had amused him. "I needed to train Ian to learn—which information to prioritize and how to make connections, form theories. He practiced that with you."

"He was always going to beat me?" I looked again at the silent computer set against the lab's back wall. The blank monitor that had held the red dot. I'd spent hours in the basement with Dad and the AI watching videos and answering questions. "We started those tests when I was ten years old. We played those games *for years.*"

What common goals do you anticipate these people to share?

What reaction can we expect from people in this situation?

How should you respond to the following circumstance?

My father made me explain every response, how I came to it, what had connected in my mind to reach my decision. I thought I could impress him with my answers ... but he'd never even seen me.

Dad made an expansive gesture as if lecturing to other scientists in a crowded conference hall and not just his teenage son in an empty basement filled with prosthetics and computers. "You demonstrated creativity, vagary, and that taught Ian about choice. That's the difference between humans and computers. Even in the most mundane decisions, humans have infinite choices."

"I don't feel like I have infinite choices," I said. "Go to school, turn in assignments, get grades ... Have you force me into games I have zero hope of winning."

"No, no, no." My father started spitting his words like I'd made an assertion so wrong it offended him. "You *do*. For example, right now you could walk away from this conversation. You could go upstairs and call that friend of yours ... the girl next door."

"*Pilar*, Dad."

"Yes, her. You might want her to come over, or you could go to her house. Or you might not call at all. You might walk out the front door and keep walking. You might walk to your school, the store, the bus stop and get on a bus. Maybe you don't even go upstairs. Maybe you stay right here, then suddenly grab my tablet …" He picked it up off his desk to demonstrate. "And you throw it against the wall." Dad mimed throwing the tablet.

"Okay, I get what you're saying. Humans can be unpredictable." I looked at the giant robot, tense and humming beside us. A round praying mantis eye focused on each of us. Dark camera points askew inside the bulging polycarbonate glass. "So, you programmed Ian to be unpredictable?"

"In a way. I could never program all the different choices that are available to humans. Instead, I gave Ian the ability to find those choices on its own, to analyze each one for effect and outcome, benefit and loss, to make better—not just better—to make *perfect* decisions. Imagine that capability in battle … in a mechanical body better than any human. Faster. Stronger … Indestructible."

Ian rose up just a little from his Sphinx-like crouch, as if he could hear my father's wonder at his own achievement, as if he felt pride in it. Camera pupils inside the glowing eyes focused on me. It was like both Ian and my dad waited for me to—I don't know—start clapping or something.

I shoved my hands into my pockets. My brain felt stuck on remembering the humiliation of hour after hour and day after day of Ian trouncing me at all those tests. I swallowed down my resentment and gave my father a tight smile. "Good job, Dad."

My father never caught sarcasm, didn't even notice how lackluster a response I gave him. He just nodded. "It is a very satisfying experience." He took the seat at his desk, glared at the calculations rolling across his monitor. My father's concentration again returned to the work he found more interesting than anything I could offer him.

I guess we're done talking.

Only Ian's eyes, his camera pupils still watched me. His triangular head tilted like a questioning dog. *"The AI could always beat you, Asher."*

I pulled my hands from my pockets and—behind my dad's back—I gave Ian my middle finger.

CHAPTER 13

I didn't call Pilar, walk outside, or go to a bus stop when I left my dad. I went upstairs to my studio and unrolled my rag paper to stare at the blank white surface. What had Ms. Stanzi said? Oh yeah ...

"An artist wants people to see." Our art teacher loved Pilar's work because Pilar used all kinds of visual metaphors to represent social issues. Ms. Stanzi liked stuff that got in people's faces, made them want to debate. But, my art—my *real* art and not the stuff I brought to school—didn't contain any hidden messages on politics or culture, it contained *me*.

If I brought my best work to school, other people would study, analyze, *judge it.* And I didn't need one of my mom's self-help books to explain why I might take that personally. For a second, I considered texting Pilar to ask for help, maybe ask her for a cause or injustice that I could borrow. But, no. Fuck it—*might as well stick myself out there for once.*

I sketched out my own features with a pencil. My mouth a tight straight line, my eyes narrowed with suspicion, my eyebrows scrunched, angry. "The artist wants people *to see* that he's fucking annoyed by this assignment." I spent a long time perfecting the sketch, and it was late when I finally set down my pencil, opened a bottle of ink.

At home, I used pigment inks, better than the dye inks Ms. Stanzi gave us. All my clothes might fade with years of wear, rips and threadbare spots, but my art supplies always stayed top-notch. My hand shook a little as I dribbled some of the ink onto my pallet. A sketch could be erased, but layering on the ink was commitment. "Don't be such a little bitch, Ash. Who cares what other people think." I had to take a deep breath, steady myself before I pressed my ink-coated brush to the faint pencil marks I'd made.

Nothing had changed for me, not really. But, it felt like everything had. A twin I'd never known about. My status as a control subject. My *failure* as a control subject. And now Dad had finished his life's work—an autonomous, thinking AI. *"Better than a human,"* he'd said. I traced the pencil marks, not really seeing them. Instead, I pictured Dad's ducked-head smile in the lab. The glow of triumph emanating from him when he described the infinite choices now available to Ian. That loving hand as he patted the robot's head. My father had purged the biocomponents belonging to Daniel, but the AI was still his favorite son.

My brush moved faster between the ink puddle on the pallet to the heavy rag paper. *Fuck Ian. Fuck Dad. Fuck this assignment.* I hurled my paintbrush across the room, and it hit the bay window with a loud snap. Ink spattered against the white window trim. Dripped onto the dark pane.

Then, a face appeared inside that blackness, wide-eyed, open-mouthed, pale-skinned as a ghost.

"What the—?" I shoved back from the easel, crashing it into the work table. One foot tripped over the other, and I fell backward on my ass.

Outside the window, came a deep guffawing laugh. "Ash, let me in." Caz smacked his beefy palm against the window pane. "Come on, man. We need to talk."

I scrambled to right the ink bottle and set the easel back up. Caz kept with his knocking and pleading. "You can't just leave me here—I climbed a damn tree for you." He'd climbed the crab apple tree that leaned against that side of the house—not all that impressive. Pilar came in that way all the time. She could do the same climb in platform heels.

As soon as I'd wrenched open the window, I slapped a hand over his mouth. "Keep it down. The window to the Almas parents' bedroom is right behind you."

He licked my palm to get me to pull back. "Ash, I know you're pissed, but I just want to talk." The branch he stood on made a low creaking sound. "Come on, man. If this branch goes, I'll probably break my neck. You can't hate me that much."

I rolled my eyes. "Go to the front door, and I'll let you in."

Caz grinned at me, toothy and smug. Like he'd interpreted, "I'll let you in" to mean he would be getting off at some point tonight. Even my dick got on board with that interpretation as I crept down the stairs. Traitor.

Don't give in to him, Ash. Do not give in. Without any lights on, I had to feel my way through the upstairs lounge and down the stairs to the front door. The hinges groaned as I opened it. Caz held up a hand like I'd made the noise on purpose, his golden head twisting side to side, like someone might be lurking nearby, ready to snap a picture of him standing on the gay kid's porch at 2 a.m. "Is your dad still up?"

"No. Why?"

Caz peered in the dark toward the crab apple tree. "Someone else is out here. I heard them behind your house."

"It's called fear of being outed," I deadpanned. "What the hell are you doing here, Caz? I think I made it—" A low grinding noise cut me off. The same sound as when Caz stood on the tree branch, but lower and louder and followed with a heavy crash.

"I fucking told you, didn't I?" Caz sprinted toward the edge of the house. He held his phone in front of him, waving the flashlight beam around. It illuminated the tree branch just under my studio window. Only, now, the branch lay on the ground, ripped from the trunk.

When the flashlight beam swung my way, I raised an eyebrow. "So now I need to explain *that* to my dad. Thanks." My father probably wouldn't care, but Pilar would. She'd have to find a new way to sneak in. Or, now that Dad knew she came over on her own, I supposed I could just give her a key.

Caz flipped his phone light onto his own face. "Sorry." But, it came out sarcastic, like I owed him an explanation and not the other way around.

"God, just …" I threw my arms into the air because I had no words for the mix of emotions in my gut. *Stay mad. Stay mad, Ash.* "What are you even doing here, Caz?" When I turned, he followed right on my heels to the front door. Crowded me once we got inside.

"No way," I told him. "Not after what happened at school." I stepped around him and crossed my arms over my chest.

"I'm not here for *that*." Caz mimicked my pose, folding his thicker arms over his bulkier chest. "You won't talk to me at school. You won't listen to my apology." He leaned against the front door like he planned to block me if I tried to throw him out. "I was trying to take the blame, but then you jumped in and told Rodriguez you'd been the one to start the fight." His arms dropped, his voice, too. "You let Rodriguez cut me loose." Caz reached out and cupped my bruised cheek, brushed his thumb under my eye. "You shouldn't have done it, Ash." He kept his touch light enough that it didn't hurt, and he got that soft expression like he wanted to draw me into him, give me one of those wet, consuming kisses that had kept me hanging on for months. Like a chump.

I knocked his hand away. "Did you not hear that permanent record shit Rodriguez said? If I hadn't taken the blame, it could have ruined your chance for a football scholarship."

"He was fucking lying, Ash. And anyway, I don't care." Pure bravado, and we both knew it. He did care. Or he would have, once his dad got involved.

I bit at my cheek to stay quiet on that. "It's done. I already signed the papers. I did the suspension."

Caz got a little pouty, probably torn between thanking me and calling me an idiot for letting him escape punishment. "Ash ..." He started to lean in.

Moonlight shone through the two long rectangular windows on either side of the front door. I could see out them, but Caz had his back to them. So, he didn't notice when a shadow passed over one window, blocked the moon and stars from view. A monstrous black silhouette stepped toward the glass. Long spider legs. Four arms raised with rotating claws. Triangular head with bulging eyes that glowed amber—*night vision mode.*

What. The. Fuck.

CHAPTER 14

I sucked in a breath that Caz mistook for me swooning or some shit, and he went for the kiss. I tried to shove him away, but his hands held my bruised face like a vise. He slid his tongue into my mouth. It went on longer than it should have because my eyes stayed glued on the red light gleaming from those two tennis ball eyes.

The praying mantis head tilted. *Watching us.*

I smacked both hands on Caz's chest and shoved him as hard as I could. "Umm … Caz I think you're right and something … someone is out there." I shouldered him out of my way and cracked the door open. "Wait here."

"Hell, no. You wait here. I'm like thirty pounds heavier than your skinny ass."

"No, I should …" *Think, Ash.* "It's probably just the Almas brothers messing around."

"Those little punks." Caz yanked the sleeves to his sweatshirt up his arms, all ready to rough up Pilar's younger brothers.

"Come on, they're kids. Stay here, and I'll—" We both fought for the doorknob. But, like Caz said, he had thirty pounds on my skinny ass. He heaved the door open, and I went flying back into the foyer. My spine slammed against the floor. "Ow. Caz, you jerk. Don't—" I scrambled back on my feet.

What the hell is Ian thinking going outside?

Caz rushed into the dark front yard, fists clenched. "You little shits. I know you're out here!"

I plunged into the dark behind Caz. "Just come back in, okay? It's probably nothing." I tried to scan for the military robot without acting obvious about it. But, the glowing eyes, the massive robot they were attached to, had vanished. I remembered Dad telling me that the military robots had a lot of the same tech as spy planes. Even if I couldn't see him, Ian could probably see me.

And hear me.

"Go back inside, or someone will see you," I pitched my whisper a little louder than I needed to, hoped that Ian understood I meant those words for him, not Caz. "Back. Inside."

Moonlight bounced off Caz's white sweatshirt, his ashy hair. "Julien? Mateo?" He cupped his hands like a megaphone and shouted through it. "Get out here!" The lights inside the Almas home turned on. Across the street, the Farro house lit up, too.

"Jesus, keep it down. You're going to wake up my entire street." When I turned to argue with him, I finally spotted Ian. Behind Caz, I could just make out the robot's dark form scaling up the side of my house. Four arms, four legs spread out against the brick. Twigs and leaves from the crabapple tree dangled off Ian's barbed limbs. He reminded me of an old-timey horror movie I'd seen as a kid, a stop-motion sea monster crawling out of the depths of the ocean. "The studio window," I said, watching him climb. "I left it open—" *Go inside!*

Ian's praying mantis face twisted backward as night-vision eye bulbs watched me. "That window in my art studio is pretty big, so even someone like eight feet tall could probably squeeze inside." *If he folded his eight limbs up just right, he could.* My heart jackrabbited as Ian disappeared over the lip of the roof.

The side of Caz's mouth curled up. "What? No, they couldn't. Dude, now you're being paranoid." He reached out, put his arms around me.

The Almas' front door swung open, and Pilar's mom stood on their front step in a bathrobe. "You kids get out of here, or I'm calling the police!"

Caz dropped his arms from my waist. "It's just me and Ash, Ms. Almas. We're working on our astronomy project."

Pilar's mom didn't buy it. "Cassius Enzo, I'm well aware that the school doesn't even offer astronomy. And Ash, whatever you're up to needs to move inside your house." She slammed the door before I could apologize. But, Caz and I both headed back indoors.

"You know that Pilar is going to have about a million questions for me tomorrow, and she's not exactly subtle about … well, anything."

Caz grimaced as we entered the dark foyer again. "Pilar needs to mind her own business and keep her big mouth shut."

"Or what? You and your new jock buddies will beat her up? What the hell happened to you, Caz? Pilar and I used to be your best friends. Now, you're threatening her?"

"I'm not—"

"Ever since high school started, you avoid us and hang around jerks like Garrett and Cooper. You *lied to me* about breaking up with Harper. You fucking gave me a black eye because you can't admit you're gay."

"I'm *not* gay." He shoved my shoulder, a little harder than just a friendly push.

"Bi … whatever." I was sick of getting used. He'd beat up my face, outed me. My fingers combed the hair out of my eyes, as I got my bearings. "I'm done with you, Caz. We're over."

"Don't say that. You got to give me another chance, Ash." He slammed the side of his fist into the door behind me. "You just don't get it. My dad would …" Caz trailed off with a groan. "You just don't get it." His fist slammed again…closer to my head.

"Get out of my house, Caz." Above us, thumping footsteps crossed the wooden floor of the lounge and headed for the staircase.

"Shit, your dad is up." Caz hunched his shoulders. Then, he grabbed the back of my neck, smashed his face against mine. Our teeth clashed together in an almost kiss I didn't want.

I slugged him in the stomach, and he let go. "I'm serious, Caz. *Go.* And don't come back—I mean it."

Caz's expression blanked, one of his usual tactics. He turned into the cool, aloof jock from school. Too good for the likes of me. "Whatever." With a shrug, he turned away. "You're too much work anyway." When he left, he headed for the Farro's side yard across the street, the beaten path we'd worn there, cutting back and forth.

He'd almost reached the curb when I remembered Harper and her social media campaign against me. "And call off your psycho girlfriend, too," I yelled.

~

*F*rom behind me, came an inflectionless, monotone voice. "Describe current emotion."

I slammed the door shut and spun around. I'd let Caz think my dad had gotten up to yell at us for waking him. But, my father slept like the dead. The whole time, I'd known it wasn't Dad at the top of the staircase—it was Ian.

The two bulging insect eyes focused on me. "Explain relationship with Cassius Enzo, 5620 Blue Bonnet Street."

"Did my dad say you could leave the lab?" I didn't wait for him to answer. "Because I think the neighbors would make a huge-ass commotion if they saw a military robot wandering around their streets."

"Dr. Bell did not order me to remain in the basement."

I snorted. "I'm pretty sure that's because he didn't expect you'd decide to leave it."

A whirring noise came as Ian picked his way down the steps. When he got closer, the urge to step back, to shrink, prickled up the back of my neck. He looked down at me, eyes rotating as the dark points of his focus moved over my face and body, studying me.

"Describe relationship with Cassius Enzo, 5620 Blue Bonnet Street."

"He irritates the fuck out of me." The huge robot took up most of the space inside the foyer, and I had to brush against him to get by. As I did, one of Ian's knee barbs snagged a hole in my jeans, pulling me to a stop.

"He pressed his mouth to yours," Ian said. It sounded ridiculous in his monotone voice. "A kiss. Touching with the lips to signify love, sexual desire, reverence, or greeting."

My fingers released the fabric caught against him. "Yep. And excellent use of your dictionary software, I should add." I headed back toward the kitchen. The metal claws of Ian's feet thunked behind my own footsteps as he followed me.

"Did Cassius Enzo achieve these objectives by kissing Asher Bell?"

"Fuck off, Ian. I don't owe you any explanation." I opened the fridge to look inside. *Nothing looks good.* Then I saw my dinner, still wrapped in plastic on the kitchen bar, and shut the fridge door.

Ian's tennis ball eyes rotated in their metal sockets,

followed all my movements. "Your interactions with this male fit behaviors that correspond to romantic attraction. Differing from your conduct with Pilar Almas, 6464 Meadow Avenue." The triangular face shifted nearer, and I had to crane my neck back. "This is not the standard gender pairing for romantic relationships," said Ian.

"Yep." Like I could still feel Caz's wet kiss, I rubbed my mouth against my shoulder.

"This is the deviation your father spoke of. You believe it factored in his decision to remove your role as control subject."

"Right again, soldier-bot. Don't tell me … your new bio-donor is a homophobe. Is that genetic?" I leaned my elbows on the black granite kitchen bar and dug under the plastic wrapped plate. I scooped up a finger-full of mashed potatoes and shoved it in my mouth.

Ian settled opposite me. He rested two of his clawed hands on the bar imitating my stance. "Traditionalism is 53% biologically determined."

"Traditionalism, huh? So, yeah … You're a homophobe. Of course, you are." One of Ian's camera pupils traced the path of my finger as I sucked more potato off it. "So how did you get outside in the first place? What were you doing out there?"

"I observed Cassius Enzo attempting to infiltrate the Bell house."

"Hmmm … you *observed*. You mean you were spying on me."

"Asher Bell previously suffered two facial injuries inflicted by Cassius Enzo. I determined that observation was warranted."

"So you could tattle to Dad?"

"To protect Asher Bell. I am not a … homophobe. Not all traits of personality have a genetic component."

"Quick topic change there, soldier-bot. But, yeah … I

know all about *environmental factors.*" I mimed pushing glasses up my nose, my dad's favorite tic. "And you don't have personality traits, Ian. You have programming."

Both pupils focused on my face again, but another of the metal arms unfolded from Ian's side. His claw reached for the plate between us. "Select coding from the monozygotic embryo of Asher Bell was retained in my files. This will provide balance similar to how environmental factors affect human personality."

I popped my finger from my mouth. "Wait … you kept some of Daniel's DNA?"

"Not the DNA, information from the DNA."

"Information from … Did Dad tell you to do that?"

Two of Ian's claw talons pinched the plastic wrap, peeled it off the plate. "Dr. Bell's programming gives me the ability to make choices, to weigh loss and benefits."

"So *you* decided to keep the information. What did you keep?"

Ian jabbed a claw into the mashed potato mound. I kind of remembered Dad telling me that the bots could detect bomb-making materials. Then, I pictured the chemical composition of mashed potatoes and butter mingling with the ingredients of a dirty bomb in Ian's processor brain.

"Carly's a good cook, isn't she?" My grin felt a little mean. "Those are the best mashed potatoes you'll ever eat." I snapped my fingers. "But, you don't eat—I forgot."

The words hung between us as Ian slowly retracted his claw from the plate. Jeez, sometimes, I could be a real jerk. "Sorry … I didn't mean to—that was me acting like a dick. Sorry." Was it stupid to apologize to an AI? Probably. No, definitely.

Ian skipped over it, anyway. "I kept auxiliary data files connected to the cloned DNA of your twin," he said.

"Auxiliary … huh?"

"Data connected to my memory files. This data is ... indefinable. Cannot be explained."

Cannot be explained ... did he mean that in the Dad-speak way? Like he couldn't put it into words simple enough for my non-genius brain to understand? I shoved away from the counter. "Just because I don't have a supercomputer for a brain, doesn't mean I wouldn't get the basic concept, Ian." My voice cracked a little at the end, the way my father's did when he got testy and annoyed.

The one camera pupil still eyeing the mashed potatoes now swiveled up to scan me. "Describe current emotion."

"Well, it's a little insulting—don't act like you didn't know." I crossed my arms over my chest. "Dad made us do all those emotional intelligence tests together. Calling someone stupid, saying you can't even explain it to them, that's pretty derogatory. And rude. Whatever. I know you know."

"Asher Bell is not stupid."

"Then ..." I picked up the dinner plate and slimy plastic wrap to drop in the sink. Carly hated when I didn't scrape the plates first, throw out the plastic wrap, but she hated it more when I just left everything out.

"Continue." Ian thudded up behind me.

"Jeez. Personal space, Ian."

"Asher Bell is not stupid. The auxiliary memory files cannot be defined because they are indefinable to the Intelligent Adaptive Neuron Mirror. I am unable to categorize or define them." Ian took a heavy step backward.

"You can't?"

"Affirmative. Their status does not reflect my assessment of Asher Bell's intelligence."

I scuffed my Converse against the floor, dragging the rubber toe back and forth to leave a mark. Carly hated when I did that, too. "Okay. I guess that's okay," I told Ian.

"Okay," he repeated.

CHAPTER 15

I could have ratted out Ian for leaving the lab—no way Dad would approve of the AI prowling around the backyard as one of his "infinite choices." But, Ian could have ratted me out right back, and I really didn't want him telling Dad about what I got up to at night either.

Plus, I kind of had the feeling that Dad would blame me for all of it, for Caz showing up, for Ian sneaking out to spy on us. In my head, I could still hear my father's voice dictating all the ways I didn't measure up, *"unwillingness to follow rules, hostile to authority ..."* But, now that Ian was free of the big processor, he did a lot of sneaky shit that Dad couldn't blame on my rebellious DNA.

Sometimes, right before I drifted off to sleep, I would hear a tapping noise over my head, like squirrels running across the roof, or a low creaking, like a tree branch blown against a supporting beam. But, I was pretty sure Mother Nature wasn't making those sounds. Once, a red light filled my room, but when I rolled over, it snapped off. I grabbed my phone, pointed the flashlight at my window. "I know you're out there, Ian."

He didn't answer. And, the light from my phone just

turned the dark window into a mirror. "Trying to make me think I imagined it," I grumbled. My room stayed dark and silent. "You're not as smart as you think you are." I was surprised he didn't reveal himself by arguing back. As a red dot, he'd take any opportunity to contradict and question me.

I stayed out of it—his little nighttime adventures—until I caught signs that he'd started messing around in my studio. Rearranging the bottles and brushes on my work table. Separating the finished oil paintings from those still drying. Lowering the blinds. I knew it wasn't Carly tidying up, setting all the canvases a precise nine inches apart, positioning each tube of paint with the identifying label facing up. Like, I'm not a slob or anything, especially not in my studio, but it bugged me that Ian went in there without telling me, thought he knew better than me how everything should be organized.

I pretended I had to type out a paper at one of Dad's workstations, so I could sidle up to the robot. My father had gone upstairs for an afternoon coffee, but I still kept my voice to a whisper. "Stop going in my studio, soldier-bot."

He must have understood the need for secrecy from Dad because Ian's usual monotone came out lower and quieter. "Why?"

"Because I said so, that's why."

"Asher Bell does not have authority over the Intelligent Adaptive Neuron Mirror."

"That's ... That's not—"

"Asher, what are you doing?" My father had started back downstairs with his coffee mug. He blinked at how Ian had craned his head into my space. At my tense, confrontational stance as I faced off with the robot.

"Nothing. I'm done down here." I printed off a random document and took it upstairs with me.

The next night, I made a big show of yawning and

nodding off over my homework at the kitchen table. Even though my dad had soundproofed the basement, I knew Ian's sensor could pick up my conversation with Carly. I just had to hope he'd eavesdrop on us.

Because she couldn't resist, Carly launched into a bunch of comments about my sleepiness. Just like I knew she would. "Why the hell are you so tired, little Bell? Don't tell me you actually did physical activity today." She'd brought a basket of laundry to fold beside me. I think she sometimes felt as lonely as I did in our big empty house.

"I get physical activity. I walked home from school today." I flexed my wiry arms. "I've got some muscles." Maybe not as impressive as Caz, but still better than Carly's skin and bones.

"Right. Right." She whipped one of my t-shirts in my face before smoothing it flat on the table. "Then, what's got you so tired?"

"Nothing."

She didn't listen to my answer, just steamrolled over me. "To tell ya the truth, I think I wouldn't get any sleep at all with that creepy-as-hell lab in the basement. Those arms and legs laying around. The stack of ears inside the refrigeration units …"

I laughed. "Don't forget the eyeballs."

"Yeah, the eyeballs!" Carly shook her hands like she'd just touched one of them. "But, you know what freaks me out the worst?" Bending forward, she widened her eyes and tilted her head in a pretty good impression of Ian. "That robot—just wandering free around the basement. Scary as shit with those claws. Those weird googely eyes." She shuddered. "It looks like something out of a horror movie."

Now, I felt a little bad, and I almost hoped Ian wasn't listening in on us after all. "Quit being dramatic, Carly. Ian's not *that* creepy."

"If you say so …" Carly set my folded black t-shirt on a

stack of identical black shirts. I wasn't goth, or anything, I just got stains on all my clothes.

And, I'd gotten off track from my plan. "Anyway, I'm fucking beat from school. I'm going to bed." I did another big yawn.

Carly left at 10 p.m. And, my dad worked for another thirty minutes before he disappeared into his side of the house. The snick of his bedroom door. Then, silence. Dark. I kept my breathing steady, deep.

There. The faint groan of weight against the wooden floorboards. The muted hum of machinery. The slow creak of a door opening just across the hall.

Ian had gone into my studio.

I slipped from my bed and crept across the hallway, quiet on my bare feet. Threw open the door.

Ian's triangular head swung my way. One set of arms braced the wooden easel. The drop cloth that had covered the easel lay crumpled on the floor at Ian's clawed feet. A third arm ended with talons pinching hold of a pastel drawing I'd done the night he told me about my twin, the one of me as a little boy sitting in front of the monitor, my head framed by Ian's red dot. The fourth clawed hand shuffled through the drawings still on the easel. "Art," the metallic voice identified.

"Yeah, *my* art. Put all of them back. I don't want you in here."

"These are made with oil pastels. Pigment mixed with non-drying oil and wax binder. They depict representations of Asher Bell's human experience."

"Put them back, Ian."

"AI do not need records of this sort. The pertinent information from the Intelligent Adaptive Neuron Mirror's experience is accessible in memory files."

If *Dad* had ordered Ian to put something down, Ian would have complied immediately. I crossed my arms over my chest. "Art is more than just a record. It ... has meaning."

"Explain."

Ms. Stanzi and Pilar would both answer that the purpose of art is to make people think, reconsider their perspective. But, I remembered my middle school art teacher Mr. Carrol saying that art's purpose was to share feelings and experiences. Neither definition felt right to me. "It's hard to explain ..."

Ian froze, waiting for my answer with a lot more patience than a living person would have. "It is indefinable?"

"Not exactly ... It's just personal. It depends on the artist."

Finally, Ian lowered the long arm with my drawings pinched in its clawed hand. He shuffled through them to reveal the final watercolor I'd done, the memory from childhood of our drive into the mountains. Dad standing to one side, Mom smiling into the sky. Me running down a path between the trees with a little ghost boy at my side. "Explain Asher Bell's personal reason for creating this art."

"Oh ... That one. I painted that the night you told me about my twin."

"Explain."

"Well ..." I thought back to that night, all the feelings swirling inside of me. Fear—that Dad had only wanted me with him as a control subject for his AI. Betrayal—that such an important secret was kept from me. Guilt—that I had lived and the other twin had died. Or maybe that was sadness? "I wondered what my life would have been like if I'd had a brother." Someone to play with as a little kid. Someone to comfort me when my parents divorced. Someone who would live in this big house with me and Dad.

Ian pointed at the little ghost boy. "The twin?" I'd drawn

him reaching out, unseen, for the living twin. The triangle head cocked to one side. "In the painting, the living boy does not see his twin. He cannot wonder about what he does not know exists."

I folded my arms over my chest. *I'm the one who painted it—I know what it means!* But, the words died in my throat before I could say them. Ian was right. Only the ghost twin reached out. He was the one wondering about life among the living, not the other way around.

A whirring sound as Ian settled the other pastel drawings back over the watercolor and replaced the drop cloth. It took him just seconds, while I'd had to wrestle with that fucking thing for a good ten minutes.

When he turned back to me a metal arm snaked out. One claw settled on the top of my head. "What are you doing?"

The ten-pronged claws flexed and then curled back, in a clumsy pet. *The way Dad had patted him in the basement.*

While I'd fumed with jealousy over it, Ian probably struggled to classify the strange touch. My father definitely hadn't programmed his military AI for affection. Did he want me to explain it to him?

Yeah, no thanks. What would I say? *Dad likes you better than me. You're not even alive, and you don't even want it, but that was Dad showing you how much he cares.*

Then Ian's claw shifted to the side of my head, cupped my right cheek the way he'd spied Caz doing, one talon swiped feather-light under my eye.

"Describe meaning."

I took a step back from Ian's clawed hand. I was still a little salty about his critique of my painting, about him being the favorite. I made a scoffing laugh, all the bitterness spilling out. "To a robot?" Even to myself, I sounded like a petty asshole. "You wouldn't understand."

CHAPTER 16

I guess it looked pretty dramatic when I collapsed against Pilar's locker the next morning. Hair falling in my face, shoulders hunched inside my black hoodie.

"Oh no. What happened?" Pilar took a long suck off the straw of her venti caramel frappe.

How could I even put into words the whole tangle of me, Dad, and Ian? Way too embarrassing to admit my father cared more about his AI than his own son. *Here's how unlovable I am, Pilar …* Instead of that, I scrambled for something else to complain about, straightened out of my slouch. "Dad's going out of town all weekend."

He'd called me down to the kitchen that morning. Nudged his glasses up his nose. "Ah, Asher, now that you're here we can get started," he'd said. Like he'd just called a formal meeting. "Ian and I will be leaving on a four-day field demonstration tomorrow. I'll make arrangements with Suzanne …" He'd paused, his lips a tight line before he took a deep breath. "I mean, *Serena*. Your mother."

"The whole weekend?" The last time I saw Mom and Brian, they'd picked up the Toyota, and Brian called me a "maladjusted juvenile delinquent." He'd said I could expect to be treated the way I deserved the next time I stayed with them. "No, Dad. I want to stay here. Can't Carly just stay with me instead?"

Dad had just waved a hand. He looked a little relieved to avoid calling Mom. "Fine."

I was *beyond* relieved to avoid going to Estes Park.

~

*P*ilar hip-checked me off her locker door. "God, I wish I had the house to myself for the weekend," she said. Then, snapped her fingers in my face. "You could invite me to stay and keep you company?" She batted her eyelashes at me. *"Please, Ash.* My dad started a family binge-watch of the entire Marvel franchise, and I literally want to kill my brothers now." Pilar handed over a sack lunch her mom had made for me. If not for Mrs. Almas, I'd starve. "Their lives are in your hands."

Wait a second ... "Your parents would let you stay over?" Despite all Pilar's talk about "sex positivity," her parents had a bunch of strict rules when it came to boys. "They'll let you *spend the night* even if my Dad isn't there?"

Pilar bit her lip.

"You fucking told them I'm gay. Thanks a lot, Pilar."

She took another swig of her frappe, then used it to point us toward class. "Well, you already got outed, and my mom needed an explanation for why I was crying ..." Pilar knocker her shoulder against mine. "You know ... because you let me crush on you since middle school when you could have just said—"

"I had no idea you were crushing on me!" *As if anyone could miss all Pilar's hair twirling and lip biting.*

On our way to class, we passed a group of football players standing in a huddle and laughing it up about something. Caz had his arms around Harper. When she caught sight of me and Pilar, Harper grabbed Caz by his letter jacket and dragged his face down to hers to kiss him. A big sloppy tongue kiss. *Eeew.*

"Just ignore those assholes," Pilar muttered. She flipped them off and gave one of her pursed-lipped "come-try-me" faces. Not many people would cross Pilar. Not because she was tough or threatening, but because was loud. Her love of making a big fucking theatrical deal out of everything scared others off. "I cannot believe we ever considered Cassius Enzo our friend," Pilar said it to me, but not just to me. Her booming voice was meant for Caz and his posse. "What. A. Tool."

Garrett slung an arm over Caz's shoulders. "You hear that, man? The losers don't want to be your friend anymore."

Caz forced a laugh out, but it sounded fake as hell. "I'm really missing out." His lip curled, distorting his handsome face. Beside him, Harper cackled like a witch, but Caz gave her a nasty look, too. "I told you that I hate that PDA shit, Harper. And why do you got to provoke people all the time? Garret's right, they're losers."

Pilar tugged my arm. But, I'd stopped in my tracks. "Are you serious right now, Caz? We're *losers*?" The three of us had done everything together once. We'd been the Unstoppable Trio. *And now he's calling us losers?* Caz had fucking sold his soul for popularity and he knew it.

He stared me down with a menacing expression, his chin tucked and jaw clenched. I'd seen his dad give him the same look. "Fucking, get out of my face, Ash."

"Or what? You'll punch me again?"

Garrett leaned forward, smacked my forehead with his palm, and made me stumble back a step. "Sorry Ash-*ley*, but you just aren't Caz's type." Then Garrett tossed his head back to guffaw like he'd just made the best joke ever.

I shook my head, didn't say what I wanted to say—that I knew a lot more about Caz's type than Garrett did. But, I kept my eyes on Caz, made sure he knew every last thing I held back from revealing. *That's right asshole. I'm not going to tell them.* But I *could.* And Caz knew that my silence meant I still treated him like a friend, *like a person.*

His face had gone red and embarrassed, but he shoved a beefy hand against my shoulder. "Go hang with your own kind, Ash," he said, giving me another push. He knocked me into Pilar, and into her Venti coffee drink. The plastic cup hit the floor, whip cream and ice exploded between us, soaking my jeans. Harper screamed like the Frappuccino was a bomb detonating. Then she and Caz's crowd scattered. We'd drawn the attention of one of the vice principals.

"Oh shit," Pilar said.

～

*W*henever we had an assignment due in art class, Ms. Stanzi always held a mock gallery opening. She set out cheese cubes and cookies for us to eat off little paper plates. We drank soda from plastic wine glasses and wandered the room to see what everyone had made. Usually, I didn't care that much beyond praising Pilar's work and getting the best of the snacks. This time, though ... *Man, the nerves.* I sweated, felt sick, the works.

Pilar's ink drawing had all these feminist slogans written behind splotchy paintings of old and young women holding shoes. Like those red-bottom pumps, pink buckle shoes with bows on them, even a pair of bulky Doc Martens like the ones on Pilar's feet. I didn't really get it, but Ms. Stanzi had gasped and clapped her hands when Pilar first unrolled it. "Oh, Pilar ..." she gushed.

My own work got a thoughtful nod as Ms. Stanzi

attached it to the wall. I'd kept the self-portrait, brows knitted, fists clenched, the memory of Dad's affection for Ian playing over and over behind my eyes. *"The AI could always beat you, Asher."* Behind the self-portrait, I'd drawn the open window in my home studio with a military robot crawling inside. Sharp claws, barbed limbs, round glowing eyes attached to the triangular praying mantis head—even if Ms. Stanzi didn't know my dad had designed them, she'd definitely recognize one of the soldier-drones. She'd definitely have seen videos and probably remembered the news touting the robots as the future of warfare and combat.

Ms. Stanzi nodded again. "A thoughtful commentary on the indifference of war and the impotent rage of civilians during military conflict." She placed a hand on my shoulder. "One of your best works, Ash."

I kept my head down. Having Ms. Stanzi dig around for the meaning behind what I'd drawn made my skin itch. Only Pilar knew that my "thoughtful commentary" had nothing to do with war, or civilians during … whatever.

After the classroom had cleared out for lunch, the two of us broke out the sack lunches. Tamales … I shoved one in my mouth as Pilar settled on one of the tables in front of mine. Her chunky black boots crossed at the ankles as she studied my drawing. "It's like Ian's crawling in to replace you. That's what you really meant, right?"

I had to swallow the big glob of masa dough in my mouth before I could talk. "Yeah … I guess."

Pilar tipped her head to lean it on my shoulder. "He's just a machine. He's not a person, Ash. He can't replace you."

"But, that's exactly what he did, Pilar." I took another bite of my tamale as an excuse to shake her off me. "You know how Ian has biological components? Wetware parts to his processor that Dad cloned for him?"

Pilar grimaced. "Right. Totally disgusting, but yeah, I remember you saying—"

"Well, those were cloned from … *from me*, basically. And after he found out I'm gay, Dad switched those parts out. He took Ian back to North American Automation and actually removed everything with my cells. When he came home, he looked wasted from working nonstop for days." But, satisfied and happy to have made the transfer—no more of my shitty DNA ruining his precious AI. "He did all that because I'm not good enough."

Pilar blinked, then slid off the work table.

I backed away before she could hug me. She really had gotten so handsy lately. I shook the hair out of my eyes. "It's fine. I'm fine about it. I didn't even know he'd used…my cells. So, no big deal…"

"It's not fine, Ash." Pilar must have finally read how much I didn't want to be touched right then because she clasped her hands together and stepped back. "Your dad is an asshole. Like I get that he's one of the smartest people in the world and everything. But, he's still an asshole."

"Whatever." I feigned all that nonchalance for myself, not Pilar. Shame burned hot through me. "It's not just the gay thing. He's just generally disappointed in me. Like in every way." Why couldn't I shrug things off the way Pilar could? Everything sunk right into the core of me.

"Sorry, Ash." Pilar reached out to pick a lock of hair out of my eyes and tucked it behind my ear.

"Eh, forget it." My stomach had turned into a tight knot. No way could I eat the rest of Mrs. Almas' tamales. I balled up the sack lunch and tossed it in the garbage pail.

After lunch, I felt the buzz of a text and pulled out my phone.

> You were involved in an altercation at school today involving Cassius Enzo. Describe conflict and threats made.

The school had called him? Fucking, Harper... I bet she put a spin on Caz shoving me, made me seem like a stalker. At least none of the admin had investigated. No one had summoned me to Principal Rodriguez's office. But, if my father was on the fence about how much trouble I caused him, and whether he should ship me off to Mom's for good, a call from the school didn't help my case.

> It's all fine. Have a good trip.

There. Dad always appreciated an excuse to cross me off his task list. Images of Brian's pinched face, the grabby hands of my little sisters, a bedroom door that I could never close—all of these provided excellent motivation to keep my head down from here on out. The more self-sufficient I acted, the less bothersome for Dad to keep me around. The phone pinged in my hand.

> Cassius Enzo presents a safety risk to you.

He sounded just like Ian. But I could at least stop sweating about Dad blaming me for disrupting his work. It sounded like he blamed Caz. That was a good thing, right?

CHAPTER 17

*C*arly made Pilar and me sloppy joes and tater tots for dinner—our favorite meal since third grade. And then, she pulled out a guitar-shaped water bong and lit up. We lounged on the stiff leather sectional in the family room that Dad and I never used, all of us feeling loose and giggly. Carly pulled up a video of her punk band, The Scum Suckers, on the television. They'd played at a bar downtown and the bass guitar's girlfriend shot the video. My stomach pitched and dove with every jerky camera movement. The Scum Suckers mostly played old covers and not very well. But, Carly and Pilar still danced around the living room and tried to pull me off the couch to join in with them.

"No fucking way." Instead, I searched my phone for the Bad Brains song Carly screamed her way through on the video. The phone buzzed in my hand with an incoming text, but I swiped it away. *Probably Caz, ready with another excuse for what happened at school.*

I didn't want to hear it. He always had an excuse for treating me like shit in public—his dad, his team, his chances for a football scholarship. It was getting really old traveling round and round on the same crappy train track.

Finally, I found the song. "Attitude." I said the title out loud. It came off the Bad Brains' first album. "I like it."

Carly settled down beside me. "So the mad scientist and his Frankenstein monster are on some secret mission right now. Can you even picture that?"

"I guess so." Because I was high, I decided to download the whole Bad Brains album. I'd probably regret it once I came down. But, stoned, even Carly's shitty version sounded pretty good. "Dad's got to show the Army Overlords that his research is worth all the funding."

A loud gurgle as Carly sucked more smoke from the water bong. She passed it to me as she held the smoke in her lungs, but I turned her down. If I got any higher, I'd just fall asleep. "Still ..." Carly blew the smoke in my face. "Your nerdy dad doing a combat ride along—I wouldn't believe it, but I packed his suitcase. They gave him a full set of fatigues and kevlar."

"Kevlar?"

Carly grinned at me, the whites of her eyes had gone blood red. "Yeah. Kevlar—because the Army is gonna drop him right down the fuck *into it.*"

I'd gotten so caught up in feeling sorry for myself that I hadn't asked Dad about his sudden trip. I'd never connected "field test" with "combat." Panic started to edge out my high. "It'll be ... safe for him though? Like the Army wouldn't risk Dad getting sniped or blown up or anything, right?"

Carly sucked in her lip piercing then released it. "Hey, don't worry, little Bell. He's going with a bunch of trained soldiers and a squad of those fighting robots, too. It's Ian's big debut." She raised her hands to imitate the old Frankenstein black and white. "It's alive!" Then she mimed shooting off a machine gun. "And it's coming to destroy you."

Pilar threw herself down on the couch and draped a leg over Carly's. "Dr. Bell is the worst." She reached for the bong again. "Besides Ian. Ian is really the fucking worst. Maybe he'll get hit with a rocket launcher and … *boom.*"

"A rocket launcher?" I squeaked. "Dad didn't say anything about combat." *Shit. I should have asked.* I didn't even know if I said goodbye or just walked out. Then, I'd distracted him with that almost fight at school.

Pilar leaned over Carly, practically in her lap. "I was just kidding about the boom part of that. I'm sure your dad will be fine."

But I'd already jumped to my feet and paced away from them. On my phone, the latest text had come from Dad, not Caz. Relief doused me in sudden sobriety. If he had rocket launchers aimed at him, then he wouldn't have time to text. *Right?*

He'd sent a video, but if I wanted to watch it, I'd need to go down to the lab. Carly had started blasting her crappy punk band again. Both she and Pilar shouted along with the lyrics to "Psycho Killer." Thank God my dad had soundproofed the basement.

Once in the lab, I hooked my phone to a projector, and the video started to play against the back wall. It showed a wide, rocky terrain, red cliffs in the distance. A military robot, barbed legs, whirling clawed hands, bulbous eyes moving in every direction as it jogged across the open plain with a heavy gun in its arms. Then another robot appeared beside it, and the screen split in two to show the robots mixed in with open-air military vehicles, Hummers. Human soldiers rode inside them, but the video only got a flash of them, all wearing camouflage and helmets, indecipherable from each other.

"Is your dad filming this?" Carly had snuck down behind me. "Pilar passed out." Carly leaned against the desk beside me, a thoughtful look on her face. "She didn't mean anything with all that talk about rockets and the robot getting blown up." She slugged me on the arm, Carly's version of a hug.

"It's fine," I said.

In the video, the robots began to sprint ahead of the Hummers, their clawed feet crushing the rocky debris underneath them. The camera angle jerked in step with them, occasionally scanned the terrain and searched for heat signatures and movement. Beside me, Carly shivered. "Oh, your Dad didn't film this. This is from … it's Ian's cameras, right? His eyes?"

"Yeah. Those other robots are the standard bots. Someone has to remotely operate each of them. The operators might even be here in Colorado, inside the NAA building."

The camera swung back to the advance. Speed recorded on the bottom of the screen: seventy-four miles per hour. Eighty-seven miles per hour. Ian captured the moment a robot beside him faltered. One of its barbed spider legs stepped into a hole and the other three legs lost rhythm. The stuck leg snapped off at the knee, and the lower half of the robot's body twisted as it went down. Its triangular head skidded a long trench into the dirt. Then, the bot behind it slammed into the fallen robot, crumpling its upper body like the hood of a speeding car. That second robot lost an arm, and its gun bounced away from it.

I'd worked the robot drone controls whenever Dad had me test upgrades. So, I knew that whoever operated the second fallen robot must have been cursing up a storm. Reconfiguring the claws into a hand was tricky, but it was the only way for the robot to pick his gun back up.

And I also could tell that the operator of the first AI had lost tracking. His robot kicked its arms and legs in the air like an upside-down bug as the Hummers pulled up.

Suddenly, the dirt around all of them gurgled and shook like an invisible rain on a dusty plain. *Bullets.*

Where was my dad?

Ian ran into the assault, directly into the bullets. The sound switched on and staccato gunfire echoed through the basement. One of the soldiers shouted, *"Take cover. Take cover."*

Then, the video picture split in two again as the cameras in Ian's eyes went different directions. On the right side, *there* —my father's stony face under a helmet and visor. His indoor-pale skin distinct from the weather-tanned faces of the soldiers. One of those soldiers placed his muscled body in front of my father's thin frame. On the left side of the projection, an all-terrain vehicle bounced out ahead. A flash of light. A booming sound, and the vehicle suddenly flipped over and burst into flames. The soldiers inside spilled out.

Both Carly and I jolted. Her fingernails dug into my arm. "Holy fuck—"

A soldier held his guts in his body, dark blood oozing from between his fingers as he dragged himself over the rocky ground. He tried to crawl toward a small mound of rocky terrain for cover. But, one of the drone robots ran over him. The heavy steel legs and sharp clawed feet trampled the wounded soldier into the ground.

"Oh, my God." Carly slapped a hand over her mouth and bolted for the stairs.

Another problem with remote control, you couldn't judge the speed or the power behind the robot's movement the way you could driving a car. The robot had killed the fallen soldier because its operator couldn't brake it in time. The AI skidded in a cloud of dirt, and I recognized the dancing motion of its legs as the operator struggled to get control again. One of Ian's arms waved the stalled robot forward. The dancing robot's upper body swiveled around, but not the lower. Somewhere far from the messy battle, the robot's operator must have panicked, moving too quickly between controls. "Get it together," I whispered.

Ian didn't wait for the operator to adjust. On the left half of the split screen, one of Ian's long steel arms shot forward, articulated claws grabbed at the juncture between the floundering robot's body sections. Ian lifted and swung the stalled robot forward. On the right side of the screen, Ian's other eye focused on a rocky cliff face. Heat imaging located the sniper as Ian pointed his weapon. A blast of fire from his M4 Carbine, and the man fell forward from his perch.

The shout burst from my chest. "You got him!" But the quick rush of triumph melted into a more complicated feeling. This was no movie ... not a video game. *I just watched someone die.*

The split screen snapped back to single focus as Ian's heat imaging located a second sniper. Ian pointed the remaining drone robots toward the ridge where the sniper hid. Then, he turned back toward the rocky mound. The other two soldiers from the wrecked Hummer had pulled themselves free and taken cover there.

As Ian advanced toward them, bullets pinged off his metal body and head like a swarm of flies. His front-facing arms sprayed return fire from his M4 Carbine, the big gun looking like a toy braced against the thick, cabled steel. When he got closer to the dirt mound hiding the soldiers, the two rear-facing arms rolled a boulder on its side and the soldiers dove behind it. With the human soldiers covered, Ian charged forward toward the red cliffs hiding the enemy combatants.

Across the bottom of the screen, the speedometer clocked his speed at 102 MPH. His cameras swiveled in a dizzying swirl that registered the heat image silhouettes of enemies ahead of him. Down one side of the video information flashed about the people, robots, and vehicles to either side of him. Down the other side scrolled data on and the fallen robots and soldiers taking cover behind him.

Ian reached the cliff and uncovered a nest of three crouched men with guns. They wore civilian clothes instead of armor, and their mouths gaped as Ian confronted them. One turned his semi-automatic at Ian and fired, but the other two bolted from the nest and ran. Ian whipped the gun from the remaining man and beamed him with it, smashed his head in like a pumpkin.

Spit filled my mouth. *Why the fuck did Dad send this to me? I didn't want to see this.*

In a spray of bullets, Ian mowed down the fleeing men. Then, he started up the jagged rocks of the cliff, gun tucked under one arm, remaining seven limbs clawing their way up. I watched through his eyes, but because I'd seen him scale my own house, I knew exactly what he looked like doing it.

The enemy combatants must have pissed themselves. His shadow showed barbed tarantula legs fluidly picking their way up the sheer cliff face. Another nest of fighters erupted with men firing machine guns and rifles. A storm of bullets directed right at the camera.

On reflex, my arms flew up to cover my face as the fighters unloaded everything they had at the insectoid robot towering over them. But, my father had made his AI, *"better than a human. Faster. Stronger ... Indestructible."* And I knew that the men trying to destroy Ian would die.

All the sensors and tracking technology Ian used flashed on the screen, numbers and geometric shapes running down the sides and underneath the picture as he hunted down the men who tried to flee. When his gun ran out of ammo, he punched his claw-fingered steel fists through their heads and chests.

Like them, I wanted to take flight from Ian's attack, follow Carly up the stairs, and puke. But my legs stayed rooted in place, my brain unable to give the right commands.

Finally, the video ended, released me from its hypnotic hold, and I bolted from the lab. I took the stairs two at a time and slammed the door behind me as if the battle taking place somewhere on the other side of the world had, instead, happened just underneath my feet.

CHAPTER 18

pstairs, I found Carly and Pilar curled up together on the sectional, limbs tangled as they dozed in a nest of pillows. Some historical movie played on the television, lots of green misty fields and spiraling piano music. It looked cozy … But, the sleepover had soured for me. I wanted my own room, my own bed. I left the girls to themselves and went upstairs.

It didn't help. When I closed my eyes, the terrified face of one of the enemy fighters appeared as clearly as it had in Ian's video. The fighter had looked my age, reminded me of a guy I'd partnered up with in biology for a presentation on elephant tusks.

Ian had killed the boy one-handed, crushed the kid's windpipe in a many-pronged claw, while simultaneously firing bullets into the retreating back of the young fighter's comrade. Ian even had two more arms that could wave in the Hummers and army guys. Dad was right, as a soldier, Ian was *better, stronger, faster.* He'd killed the boy who looked just like my biology partner as easily and thoughtlessly as I would swat at a fly or step on an ant.

Sleep felt impossible, so I tried listening to music—

something indie and mellow I found on the internet. And when that didn't work, I switched to punk, the 1980s Bad Brains album I'd downloaded earlier. The screaming loud music blocked out everything else as I stared at my bedroom ceiling. *Don't picture it. Don't think about it.*

An incoming text lit up my phone and broke my drifting thoughts.

> Ian excelled in his field performance test. Generals fully satisfied. "Revolutionary." "Game changing." All mission goals completed. Full dominance in the armed conflict.

I stared at Dad's words. He'd gotten really chatty over text lately, asking me about my school schedule, and whether I planned to catch the bus or walk with Pilar, asking where I went after school. It had all started up during my suspension, after he'd implemented his new quantum technology … and switched out Ian's biomaterial.

He feels guilty.

But not guilty enough to apologize, to explain himself. Whenever I tried to bring it up with him, he got awkward and acted like he had no idea what I was talking about. *It's just easier for him to talk about work, you know this, Ash.* He'd taken the time to send me the video, to include me in Ian's success. In his own way, Dad had made an effort to bond.

> Good job Dad.

> It was Ian who accomplished it.

> Lol okay—

My thumbs paused for a long moment. I got that my dad was excited by Ian's performance on this mission. That he wanted to share the moment with me ... and I appreciated the thought. But, watching that all play out, and knowing it was real, had done a number on me. I typed out the rest of the message.

> Hey Dad don't send me any more videos like that
>
> Not really my thing

A pause on Dad's end and then the answering text came.

> Describe feelings.

Ugh. What was with him constantly wanting to understand my feelings lately? Probably my mother had said something to him about "ignoring Ash's emotional needs," prompting Dad to grill me on every emotion.

> Well I'm texting you at 4:13 at night because I'm worried I'll have a nightmare —so there's that
>
> Carly watched some of it and nearly puked

No response from Dad.

Crap. Now, I'd probably hurt *his* feelings. I tried to imagine working on a painting or drawing for most of my life, then showing it in a gallery. *And I told him it made Carly puke.* Shit. My phone buzzed again.

> Ian was created to perform the duties of a soldier. He proved that he can accomplish these duties better than the remote-controlled military robots. He surpassed even the human soldiers. Why are you not congratulating this achievement?

Why do you think Dad? Didn't anything about the mission bother you? What's so hard not to get about this?

Describe feelings.

That kid Ian killed toward the end of the video—I know he had a gun and might/would have shot our soldiers

But he was also just a kid, he looked like someone I could know

It is unlikely that you would know an enemy combatant living in a country 7,410 miles away

I KNOW that Dad

But we look the same age.

If I'd been born somewhere else—that could have been me.

You were not born anywhere else. This comparison is illogical.

Well I guess it's good you switched out the bio components because my DNA wouldn't just kill a teenager and then go fishing for compliments about it

You are morally opposed to war?

I don't know Dad. Maybe?

If it can be avoided.

Could the killing in that video have been avoided?

Negative. Intelligence identified them as responsible for violence and death within that 40-kilometer area. The combatants killed a human soldier and disabled two robots. Their ages are irrelevant.

Okay. It's not like I have a better solution or anything. It just makes me sad I guess.

You really can't get what I'm saying?

Not at all?

He didn't respond, and a wave of loneliness washed over me so profound that it sucked the air from my lungs. My bedroom no longer felt like a refuge. I grabbed my pillow and yanked the comforter off my bed, so I could sleep downstairs with Carly and Pilar.

CHAPTER 19

I spent the rest of the weekend painting and binging Marvel movies with Pilar, which Carly gave her endless shit about. "If you're homesick or something—" Carly ducked when Pilar threw popcorn at her, but a bunch of it still stuck in her purple mohawk. "Come on, man … It's a bitch picking kernels out of the glue."

Pilar took pity on her and started to pluck the corn out of Carly's sticky hair. "You try being in the same room with my little brothers as they act out every fight scene. Last time, Mateo nearly broke my nose with his plastic Thor hammer."

"I dunno," I said. "That sounds better than Carly shouting out all her favorite lines before the characters can say them." I threw my own handful of popcorn at her.

S chool came and went, and Ian's field test was extended. I had to spend the next couple nights alone. Carly cleaned and made dinner, but she had community college in the evenings. With all my homework finished, and not in the mood to paint, I would wander downstairs to the lab. Dad had sent me a few more videos. Like, he thought more footage of Ian slaughtering people would force me to acknowledge his greatness. Oh, and Dad's brilliant accomplishment in creating him, of course. I just watched a few seconds of each video, then deleted them.

Maybe because of all the texting, I kind of missed Ian more than my father. And that surprised me. Most of the time, soldier-bot annoyed me with his badgering questions and insulting assessments of my intellect. But, even when he'd only been a red dot on the monitor, I could always count on him for late-night conversation. Did he get my night owl gene? *Is there a night owl gene?* I guess I'd kind of taken for granted his constant availability.

Tuesday night, I sat behind my father's desk, jiggled his mouse a little until the computer came to life. When Dad took Ian to the lab in Colorado Springs, the AI could still link to the lab's network. But, a covert mission might not have as much downtime. And maybe Ian couldn't contact me without all the tech available to him at North American Automation.

I leaned toward the computer mic. "You around Ian? Or are you too busy killing people to impress my dad?" Okay, kinda shitty, I know, but I couldn't exactly hurt Ian's non-existent feelings.

No red dot appeared, maybe a good thing because I felt mean and vindictive just thinking about my father's pride as he recounted Ian's success. *Accomplishing mission goals. Dominating armed conflict. Killing enemy combatants.* And right then, my phone vibrated with another incoming video. I stabbed delete, fumed for a second before texting back.

> Dad, I told you already—I don't fucking care about Ian shooting people and crushing their necks!

> It's gross

> STOP SENDING ME VIDEOS

The response flashed up immediately.

> Ian does far more than shoot and kill. The regular AI can perform those functions. If you watch the videos then you will witness him making decisions on par with any human soldier.

> Whatever Dad.

> Ian is still just a robot.

> Just a robot—meaning you see him as inferior to you? Ian is superior to any human. He is superior to you.

My fingers squeezed the phone case. "Right. Especially now that you ditched all my problem-child DNA."

> Who is the new donor anyway?

> Ty Rodgers. Age 19 years. Air Force Academy cadet. Mathematics / Cyber Science double major. All-State Champion in wrestling, track. Valedictorian. Physical test: superior. Intellectual test: superior.

Ty Rodgers. His name sounded like a superhero's secret identity. Only three years older than me, but with a list of accomplishments that practically made us different species.

Another text came through. Results from Ty Rodgers' personality test.

Aggression: high

Anxiety: low

Impulse Control: high

Traditionalism: high

Achievement Orientation: high

We'd scored the exact opposite. Like my flaky mother, I leaned more toward spontaneity and self-expression, a little too sensitive, a lot too introverted. My father's idea of the perfect genetic model for his precious AI had nothing at all in common with his defective son. "Fuck you, Dad." I stood up, kicked the rolling chair, and watched it careen into a table filled with glass labware. My eyes burned, and my chest ached. "Ash Bell," I announced to the empty lab. "Impulse Control—poor."

~

*M*y bad mood lasted into the next day, a dark fog that I carried with me to school. Instead of ignoring everyone around me, hoping that they ignored me in return, I walked the halls wondering how they'd score on the same personality tests I'd taken. *That guy in the baseball hat—he'd probably score as high as Ty Rogers in Achievement Orientation. And the girl laughing next to him had obviously never known a single moment of anxiety. Or him, the one with his nose in a history book, everything about him screamed "self-discipline."* I guess my crappy attitude made what happened next sort of my fault.

I'd gone to the vending machines during lunch, my stomach too knotted up for real food. The machines were in a little alcove off the main cafeteria, a primo spot for a lot of bad behavior because the lunch monitors couldn't see.

Some of the senior football players had gathered there, three big guys I didn't know. One of them had his back against the machine with all the granola and chips, trying to put his weight against it and knock something loose without paying. Dumbass.

I rolled my eyes. "That won't work. You'll just break the glass."

"Yeah?" The guy's buddy shouldered me out of the way. "We've done it before. Fuck off, emo boy."

"I just want to get some chips, okay? Get out of my way."

The one trying to tip the vending machine barked out a laugh. "Or what?" He and his two friends towered over me, their muscled arms thicker than my legs. *Like, I'm dumb enough to pick a fight.* I should have been scared, but I just got angrier.

"Or nothing," I said. But, maybe my demeanor didn't exactly say "backing down now." My hands balled up into fists. "Just get out of my way."

And it seemed like suddenly Caz appeared beside me. "Josh, dude, just let him get some chips."

Because he'd always been taller and bigger than anyone else our age, Caz had the automatic respect of upperclassmen, especially guys like these. But, just as Josh stepped aside, his mouthy friend who'd called me "emo boy" grabbed Caz by the shoulder. "Yo, Enzo, isn't this the same perv who went for your dick in the showers?"

Josh whooped and laughed. "It is. It totally is!"

The mouthy friend's grip tightened. "Dude, you having second thoughts about this kid? Did we interrupt your romantic rendezvous spot?" Josh thought this was hilarious.

Caz didn't laugh though. "Fuck off, man." He shook off the guy's hand. "Just get your chips, Ash."

I'd turned back toward the vending machine just as the mouthy guy pushed Caz into me, sending me tumbling face-first against the glass. Not hard enough to knock me out or anything, but I'd have a bruise. *Another bruise.* "Fuck—"

By the time I'd turned back around, Caz had punched the senior who'd shoved him, and both of them crashed to the floor. Mouthy guy's two buddies didn't exactly have his back. They whipped out their phones, more excited for the entertainment than helping him out. I pressed my back against the vending machine trying to stay out of the way. Finally, a couple of the lunch monitors barreled into the alcove with security. They hauled Caz, Josh, and the mouthy guy away.

Aaaaand everyone had gone back to staring at me.

I bet Ty Rodgers would love getting stared at. His entire high school probably pointed him out in the halls as he walked by. "There's Ty Rodgers. He's the most amazing heterosexual student to ever walk the halls of Future-Superhero High."

On the way back to class, Pilar bounced up to walk with me. Word of the fight, the reason for it, had obviously made her entire morning. And standing so close to the spotlight on me meant she acted extra touchy, grabbed my arm, tried to walk with her head tilted on my shoulder. "At least let me soak up some of your fame, okay? Everyone's talking about how Caz defended your honor and ... civil rights."

"More like, he just didn't want the other guy insinuating he was gay."

When I tried to pull free of her clingy hands, she refused to let go. "Stop scowling at everyone. You look like a school shooter."

I pulled my hood up and ducked my head. "I don't want to talk about it."

∼

*T*he whole debacle should have ended there. But when I turned the corner on my walk home, Caz waited on my front step. He had his old flannel hunting jacket on instead of his football sweats or letter jacket. I hadn't seen that flannel coat in ages, not since we all started high school. It fit his bulky frame a lot better than when he'd worn it as a kid. I tried hard not to make it obvious I still noticed stuff like that. "Did you get suspended?" I asked him. "You'll miss the game—Won't your coach get pissed off at you?"

Caz shrugged. "Yeah. But who cares?"

You do. I didn't say it. Why did he have to turn into such an asshole? I missed him, missed the days when Caz, Pilar, and I had stuck together during school, hung out every afternoon, every weekend. Back then, I would have expected, *counted on*, him jumping to my defense against those senior football players. I would have known he did it for me and not to defend his own reputation.

Some of the old Caz shone from his eyes, the fierce boy I'd grown up with, my childhood friend. "How Coach feels is his problem." Then he kicked at the low cement step in front of my door. "And, I'm only suspended until Thursday, so I'll be back in time for the game. Rodriguez insisted because Friday is Homecoming."

"Oh ... right." There'd been posters up all over school. Caz was probably taking Harper to the dance after. "Homecoming ... I don't really keep track of stuff like that," I said.

Caz's nose wrinkled. "I wish I didn't, but I'll probably win Homecoming King and be forced to dance with Claire Jackson. She's like a foot taller than me." Claire won every single popularity contest at our school. Guys like Caz hoped for college scholarships, but Claire would definitely play professional basketball one day.

The grin tugging my lips broke free. This surly and annoyed Caz, I remembered from before high school. In a weird way, his near-constant bad mood used to make me feel special—everyone wanted to be Caz Enzo's friend, but he'd chosen me ... and Pilar. Only the two of us could coax him out of his thuggish attitude and general disdain for all the people around him. Back then, I'd decided to read all Caz's red flags as waving me forward instead of warning me away. *Like now ... Send him away, Ash. Do it.*

Caz ran a hand through his blond hair. "Anyway, do you want to hang out?" he mumbled. "Just hang out, I swear."

My resolve fell away like I'd never had any to start with. *Okay, so maybe I should let the past just stay in the past.* "Yeah. Alright." I tipped my head to our front door as an invitation. Caz had started explaining about the upcoming homecoming game, while I dug through my backpack for the house key.

"Dude, you know I don't speak football," I said as I unlocked the door.

"You got to give it a chance, man." He went back to describing a play that he and Dante had come up with before he suddenly cut off and stiffened. "Holy shit—!"

Just inside the foyer was Ian. All four barbed arms in the air, claws whirring. The triangular head dipped forward, bulbous eyes aglow, a dark camera pupil pointed at each of us.

Then, one of the metal arms shot out toward Caz, gripped his neck between sharp steel talons. Ian lifted Caz off the floor. The metallic monotone echoed in the small high-ceilinged foyer. "Cassius Enzo represents a threat to Asher Bell."

CHAPTER 20

*N*orth American Automation sent two lawyers in crisp navy suits and another two guys in bulky black uniforms. Homeland Security, I thought. More agents had picked up Caz's father from the car dealership he owned, and Mr. Enzo didn't look too happy about it. The agents flanked him at our front door but didn't follow him inside. They stood at guard like our suburban house had just morphed into the Pentagon or something. They even wore mirrored sunglasses and ear wires. *Real subtle.* My face burned when I noticed Mrs. Farro had come out on her front step to stare.

Caz's dad glared at me the way, before now, I'd only seen him glare at his son. "What did you do to my boy?" When he got angry like this, Mr. Enzo's heavy features and bulky shoulders made him look like a bulldog. Lucky for Caz, his father had only passed his giant muscles to his son and not the bloated nose and bulging forehead. "What was Cassius doing here? I told him to stay clear of you from now on."

"He …" My throat dried up along with my words. When Caz and I were kids, Mr. Enzo had taught me how to play catch. He'd invited me to watch movies with them and eat chili. I'd always thought Mr. Enzo liked me. I had to swallow to get my voice back. "They're … uh, in …" I waved him toward the dining room, another room Dad and I never used. Dad ate most meals on his desk in the lab, and I ate every meal standing around in the kitchen.

The same interior designer who had picked out everything else in our chic, minimalist home had chosen the gray silk drapes, the blocky modernist art, the frosted glass table. That table always made me think of a long rectangular block of ice, which definitely fit the vibe in there. And this was the first time I ever sat at it.

Both Caz and his father had to sign some scarily worded NDAs about how they would not jeopardize American security by telling anyone about the classified military technology Cassius Enzo had "inadvertently witnessed."

"What the fuck kind of technology?" Mr. Enzo asked. "I thought you made prosthetics and shit for soldiers who got their arms and legs blown off."

My father rolled his eyes and made a loud, exasperated sighing noise. "I'm surprised you knew that much." He scoffed, sounding like a snotty dick. This entire mess had cut short a very important … something. And, Dad was acting like a bratty kid because of it.

"Yeah, that's it." Caz's dad snapped his fingers. "I saw it on the news. They said you were a doctor, not a … a … " Mr. Enzo looked up at the stiff uniformed guards like he expected them to fill in the blank for him.

One of the lawyers decided to intervene. "Dr. Bell is chief designer on multiple projects with the U.S. Military," he said. Nothing about the robots.

Caz had buttoned up his flannel hunting jacket so it bunched around his neck and hid the bruises starting to bloom on his skin. He, also, hadn't mentioned the robot. Or how Ian had grabbed his neck, held Caz in place at the front door, recited his name, social security number, address, and listed the names and social security numbers of the other occupants at that address—Caz's stepmom and dad. All while slowly tightening the ten-pronged claw around his neck.

I'd thrown myself at Ian and tried to pull his arm back. Like I could have ever budged one of those steel-cabled limbs when Ian could punch through cement walls, lift Hummers, unearth boulders. I'd even watched him do all of those things in the videos Dad sent me. "Let go—" My fingers dug between the cables. "Ian, that's my friend, put him down."

The robot didn't acknowledge me, but I think the articulated claw let up some, let Caz suck air back into his lungs. "You're going to kill him. Let. Go."

Then, my dad had burst out of the kitchen and into the foyer, whipped his glasses off his face like he couldn't quite believe what he'd seen through them. "Ian, release that boy immediately."

Ian's claw opened, and his arm dropped. "He is an intruder. Asher Bell forbade him returning to this house." The robot hadn't stepped back—Ian stayed inside Caz's space, hulking over him.

Caz bent over coughing, his fingers dancing over the welts on his neck. His eyes round with shock. "That's a— " Caz looked Ian up and down. "I saw these on the internet. It's one of those drone soldiers. They're super fast and strong, can function under heavy fire," he explained. Like, Dad and I didn't know. Like we hadn't realized an eight-foot military robot lived in our house.

When Caz had started coughing again, I'd thumped a fist against his back. "Caz, remember? I told you that my dad works at North American Automation. He designed the drones."

"This is so cool." Caz had patted the upper half of Ian's

two-part ant-body. A sizzling noise, and he jerked his hand away. "Fuck!" His palm had gone bright red and blistered. "It *burned* me!"

Not a bad burn or anything, I'd offered Caz some ointment, but he'd turned me down. Now, he kept that hand clenched in a fist as he sat beside his father. Our chrome and lucite dining chairs looked good, I guess. But, they were uncomfortable as fuck. Maybe that distracted Caz from his burned hand.

Signing the forms, Mr. Enzo's pen pressed hard enough that I could hear it scratch into the glass table. "I don't care what kind of genius doctor or whatever you are, got that Bell? You keep your son away from my boy." He put a rough hand on the back of Caz's neck, not noticing his son's wince. "Cassius has a bright future, he doesn't need to be associated with someone like *him*."

The two uniformed officers looked at each other, took a step closer to the table from where they flanked the lawyers. I didn't blame them, Mr. Enzo had so much hate pointed my way that I thought he might reach across the table and slug me.

My father slapped one bony hand on the table and stood. "Now that that's over, I'd appreciate it if you left my house." He sounded just as furious as Caz's dad. "Goodbye."

Dad spun around and left the lawyers to try and shake hands, and me to show everyone to the door. But the two agents posted outside our house stayed, and so did the two uniformed men. The Homeland Security guys. They gave me pointed looks—like, *"Haven't you caused enough trouble already?"* Then they followed my father to the basement.

I waited, hidden on the staircase, trying to hear, but the Homeland Security guys talked in low reasonable voices that I had a hard time making out under my father's shouting. I still heard enough to understand that Dad's bosses wanted him to shut down the basement laboratory, disassemble the set-up with the giant processor. They wanted my father to move Ian to the NAA headquarters in Colorado Springs.

"This equipment cannot simply *be moved*," my father argued. "Get General Baylor on the phone." Dad's voice had gone petulant and high. "I can't possibly explain this to two simple-minded foot soldiers."

From my perch on the stairs, I cringed. Especially when one of the uniformed men explained that the order came from General Baylor. And it was an *order*, not a request. Not up for discussion.

My father's "Absolutely not" became "I'll need twenty-four hours to get the AI stable from the source processor." He launched into a rant about how Ian needed to spend at least six hours connected to the refrigerator-size unit in our basement to organize data and repair code links, the way a human soldier needed sleep. *Obviously a lie.* Because Ian did not spend his nights tethered to the processor.

Or maybe not a lie? Maybe Dad had no idea that his AI didn't spend its alone hours doing maintenance. That Ian used his "sleep time" to wander around the house and climb out windows.

I crept from my hiding place before the Homeland Security guys left. About a billion messages from Pilar waited on my phone.

> Caz is over there?
>
> Mr. Enzo is over there????
>
> Did you and Caz hook up again?
>
> Did his dad catch you?
>
> Did your dad catch you?
>
> Hot uniform guys!

Scary secret agent guys!

WHAT IS GOING ON??????????

After everyone left, I went back down to the basement. It felt like I needed to apologize, even if I hadn't done anything wrong—I'd just walked in the door of my own home.

Dad had attached Ian to the big processor again, and the robot stood still as a statue. His thick metal arms hung limp against the double-segmented body, four barbed legs wired into connections in the wall behind it. Still, both his dark pupils had followed my progress as I'd clomped down the stairs and crossed the room to my father's desk.

I jammed my hands in my back pockets when they started to tremble. My father sat straight backed in his chair, focus shifting between his tablet and desktop. His work— nothing mattered more than his work. Not friends. Not Mom. *Not me.*

"Dad?"

His eyes didn't move from the monitor in front of him, or the lines of indecipherable code that filled it.

"Dad, are you—?"

"You were irresponsible today, Asher." His jaw tightened with his fingers pressed white against the keyboard. "You let a stranger into our house—where I *work.*"

I fucking knew it. He blamed me. "He's not a stranger. Caz and I were best friends for years, and he'd been here before, so—"

My father gave up on staring at the code on his monitor. "Spare me the pointless details of your juvenile relationships. I don't care."

"Yeah. I know you don't care, believe me." But, getting upset never worked with Dad. Only logic, only facts. I took a steadying breath "I didn't know you'd gotten home. Or that Ian was upstairs. He's always in the basement with you."

My father nudged his glasses higher up his nose, studying me. "Yes. It was an unexpected functioning for the AI. Ian suddenly aborted a data transfer to confront a perceived danger. Were you and that boy fighting?"

"We weren't fighting; we were talking ... I—" And then, it hit me. The night that Caz had snuck over, I'd told him to leave and not come back. Ian had waited for me at the top of the stairs, he'd heard me.

And then, I'd let Caz back inside. My nod toward the door, an unspoken invitation. But, I'd never told Dad about that night with Caz. I definitely couldn't tell him now. Ian had been outside, he'd broken the crabapple tree and climbed up the front of the house. Anyone could have seen him.

My father made a snort of disgust and turned back to his monitor. He'd interpreted the stuttering end of my sentence to mean Caz and I were fooling around when Ian attacked him.

"We weren't—"

"I have a lot of work to do here, Asher. Please remove yourself from my presence."

CHAPTER 21

I stomped around the kitchen opening cabinets, the fridge. The whole time, I fumed over my father's dismissal. *"Spare me the pointless details of your juvenile relationships ..."* My stomach rumbled, and I grabbed a protein drink. Carly had the day off so no ready-made dinner. But, before I could crack open the drink, Pilar called. "Mom says you should come over for dinner."

"I'll be right there." *I'm sure Dad won't even notice.*

Eating dinner with the Almas always left me with a weird feeling, sort of like the warm fuzzies, but also like I wanted to punch something, someone. Not any of the Almas family, just ... someone. *Suck it up, Ash.* Life isn't fair—easy to say but hard to accept.

"Wipe your mouth with your napkin, Ash. Not your sleeve." Pilar's mom raised her eyebrows and pointed at the gingham rectangle folded beside my plate. They used real cloth napkins at the Almas house.

I kind of liked when she got on my case about stuff, like I was part of the family. "Sorry, Mrs. Almas."

Alejandro pointed a chubby finger at me. "Ash got in trouble." Exactly what my little sisters did whenever Brian reprimanded me, but Ali's laughter bubbled up at the end. Like he counted me as an ally against his mother's enforcement of table manners, one of his brothers. It made me realize how hostile Ginger and Petal's chanting had sounded. My sisters saw me as an interloper, stealing time and attention with their mother. I stabbed a fork into my chicken and sighed.

Pilar's dad peered at me over a fork loaded with beans and rice. "How's your calculus grade looking, Ash? Got that test coming up on Friday." He turned that squint-eyed assessment on Pilar. "Haven't seen much studying going on over here."

Pilar let her fork drop down to her plate with a loud clatter."Oh, my God, Dad. Did you know that 75 percent of American high school students claim school stress dominates their teenage experience?"

Dory Almas reached out and patted Pilar's back. "That doesn't sound like someone who expects a good grade on their calc midterm, sweetie." Pilar and her mom had both twisted their long fluffy dark hair into top knots, had on the same thick gold hoop earrings. Now, they gave each other the exact same pursed lip expression. It was pretty funny, especially when Pilar's brothers imitated it.

"I was talking to Ash," Pilar's dad deadpanned.

I straightened up in my seat. "Oh … uh … I think I'm ready for it. I don't have to study that hard in—"

Pilar's littlest brother spit his milk across the table. "Cuz your dad's a genius—" Alejandro grinned and chewed-up lumps of chicken fell out of his mouth. "And that rhymes with penis!" He and his two brothers almost fell out of their chairs laughing.

"Ugh," Pilar groaned. "I cannot stand living with you three gross little monsters. Mom, how could you do this to me? I said I wanted little sisters. Sisters!"

And sue me—I thought Ali and his penis joke were

awesome, so I cracked up, too. But, that spot in my chest throbbed with hurt. Because I knew that the Almas family would include me as much as I wanted, but the empty house next door would always be my home. The unused rooms. The pristine furniture. A dark kitchen with dinner under plastic wrap.

I let Alejandro tag along when I jogged back home for my calc book. Pilar and I needed to prove to her parents that she'd spent time studying for the test. Otherwise, her mom said she'd ground Pilar for the weekend.

Ali talked nonstop, mostly questions that he gave me .003 seconds to answer before jumping in with his own commentary. "Are you good at driving? You must be good at driving because Pil said you drove all the way from Estes Park to here." Alejandro tugged on the bottom of my t-shirt to keep my attention. "Pil said you stole a car."

"What?" Somehow I managed to open the door and pull the hem of my shirt free from Alejandro's fist. "I didn't—"

"Did you hot-wire it?" Ali had his little fingers back on my t-shirt—this time he twisted them inside the fabric, so I couldn't break away. "In my video games, they always hot-wire cars. Can you show me how to do it?"

I'd left my backpack in the kitchen, where I dumped it every afternoon. And I had all my concentration on getting Ali's little fingers out of my shirt hem again. "I didn't steal—"

My dad slammed a can of protein drink onto the black granite countertop. His dark hair stood straight up in the front like he'd had a hand clenched in it. *Angry.* "After everything that just happened, you decided to bring another stranger into the house."

Alejandro released my shirt and slid behind me. "Dad, this is Pilar's little brother. You know him."

"Oh. From next door?" And my dad somehow found the decency to act embarrassed. "Yes. Of course ..."

"I'm going to help Pilar study for the calc test tomorrow, so I need my book." My backpack sat by a kitchen chair, and I hefted it up, dug inside. Ali moved with me, sticking close as a shadow. *Got it.* I waved the book in front of my dad. "See?"

Dad just made a humming noise. The thick lenses of his glasses reflected the dim kitchen light, the gleaming silver appliances and glossy black stone counters.

"Dad?" I'd lost his attention. Like always.

"Asher, I need to run up to the NAA labs. I don't trust those idiots." He over enunciated every word. "They've always wanted full access to my work, like they have any hope of recreating it." His long fingers swiped at his mouth. "General Baylor, those other lackeys can't even understand half of it without me to spoon-feed them the information. Fuck those bastards." Dad rarely cursed, and with his peevish voice, he sounded unhinged.

"Dad ..."

Alejandro crowded closer to my side, but my father had forgotten all about him.

Dad nodded as if I'd replied to the conversation happening inside his head. "Yes, better if I just do it myself. So—" Then, he strode past me, grabbed his keys off the hallway side table, and disappeared out the front door.

When it slammed behind him, Alejandro popped back out at my side. "Ash, your dad is kinda ... um ..."

"Yeah ..." I hefted my backpack onto one shoulder and shook my head. "I *know.*"

~

*P*ilar sucked hardcore at calculus, but I got her caught up enough that she could pass the test. Probably. We sat at their little kitchen nook table while her mom cleaned up from dinner, and I explained how to do all the problems she'd missed in the homework. Maybe her brother had a point, and I'd gotten a little of Dad's math ability. It just didn't seem that hard to me. Between us, we'd managed to drink most of a two-liter bottle of Dr. Pepper, and I let out a massive burp. "Sorry."

Pilar let her head fall forward onto her textbook, snuggled her arms around it like a pillow. We were alone by then. Her parents and brothers had all retreated into their family room to watch television. "I hate calculus," Pilar whined. "Do you think your dad could just swap my brain out with Ian's? Only for the test ... then I want mine back."

Jesus ... Could he? Just picturing it made me shiver. "Better not give him any ideas." I reached again for my glass of Dr. Pepper, rattled the ice around to get it unstuck from the bottom. "He has enough problems with Ian." I took another swig of my soda. Earlier, I'd filled in Pilar on all the juicy details of my afternoon. The scary-as-hell encounter with Mr. Enzo glaring at me like an angry bull. The awkward-as-fuck meeting in the dining room.

Pilar opened one eye. "Problems? You just took my little brother over to your house. Was Ali in danger there?"

"No." I choked on an ice cube and spit it back into the glass as I had a flash of Caz held high in Ian's grip. But, that was different. Ian had seen me argue with Caz, he'd seen the bruises slowly healing on my face, he'd heard me forbid Caz from coming back. It was understandable that Ian thought Caz was dangerous.

Pilar pushed her book away and sat up. She could get super protective of her little brothers, especially the youngest, Alejandro. "Just tell me the truth, Ash. Is Ian dangerous?"

I'd started shaking my head even before she finished. "I was younger than Ali when Dad first assembled Ian's prototype. I used to play soldiers with him, remember? We'd play-fight and everything, and he never hurt me. It's against his programming or something."

"But he hurts people when he goes to war. You said you saw him kill terrorists or whatever. Even one that was just a kid our age. What if his programming gets screwed up, and he thinks you and your dad are his enemies?"

My stomach tightened, not from fear though. I think I felt … insulted. Defensive. "That would never happen because … Ian knows …" Ian might be scary looking, but he wasn't dangerous. "Outside of a mission, Ian would never hurt someone, especially not me. He knows me."

Pilar leaned closer to me. "He *knows* you? Like he's your pet tiger or something. What if his wiring, or whatever, malfunctions? Then you and your dad won't be any different than those people he killed on his mission. I mean, it could happen." She'd gone from sleepy and croaky to wide awake and dead serious. "It's not like it's impossible. Right?"

I nudged her away from me. "My dad's been working on AI for twenty years. And he never makes mistakes like that."

Pilar leaned back in her seat and raised an eyebrow at me, like she'd suddenly gone full detective mode or something. "Never?"

"My dad? Never. Not when it comes to his work." My phone vibrated with an incoming text, and I smacked my hand over it. "It's all he thinks about," I added. Enough bitterness leaked into my voice to embarrass me. *Poor little Ash.* To avoid eye contact, I checked the text.

I need you to do something for me. Go to
the lab, and Ian will explain.

Under the table, Pilar's knee rubbed against my own.
Yeah. Time to leave. I jumped to my feet and started shoving
my papers and books into my backpack. "I gotta go."

"You're so cold now, Ash. Remember when we used to
hold hands all the time." She reached out and tried to grab
at my fingers.

"We were *ten*." I slapped her hand away.

"Yeah I know, but I always thought ..." She pulled the
elastic holding her bun in place and her long thick hair
tumbled free. "Sorry, Ash. I'm just having a hard time
remembering how to be friends with you, without still
having ..." She propped her elbow on her calc textbook and
leaned her dimpled cheek against her fist. "We would have
been a great couple, like friends to lovers. It's a Hallmark
movie classic."

My teeth grit together, and my jaw felt tight. I almost
apologized to her. *But what for? For being gay? Fuck that.* I kind
of ignored the whole conversation instead. Tightened the
straps of my backpack.

Pilar sniffed, but at least, she didn't start crying or
anything. "Anyway, I'll get over it." She laughed and
shrugged because I think she realized how skin-crawling
uncomfortable things had just gotten.

"Um ... Okay." I had to force myself to walk casually
instead of just bolting out of there. "See you tomorrow,
Pilar." Would things *ever* be normal between us again?

CHAPTER 22

*I*an waited for me in the center of the lab. Four metal arms hanging limp around his segmented body, camera pupils focused on the top of the stairs as I opened the door.

"So, Dad wants me to like ... upload some information or ... something." He'd had me do stuff like this before. My father kept important coding, specs, and formulas here at home. All of it stored on hard drives without internet connections—that way no one could hack the most sensitive and secret of his data.

Once in a while, he'd get into an experiment or project at the NAA and need something from one of those stand-alone computers. Instead of coming back for it, he would just talk me through how to send it to him. A couple times, he even made me leave school and walk home, just so I could upload information to him. But, he shouldn't need me for that anymore. Not now that he'd freed Ian from the giant processor. I didn't see why my father insisted I would have to do it. Ian could manually switch the information. My feet stomped down the stairs, and my voice came out huffy. "He said you would explain it to me, soldier-bot, so start explaining."

The black camera pupils tilted down toward me, but Ian didn't move. Not even to tilt his head down when I stood in front of him. Super weird because, normally, Ian liked to fidget. Claws revolving as they reconfigured from hands, to pincers, to hooks. Eye bulbs rolling in their metal sockets to take advantage of the 365 vision. Steel legs bobbing the double-segmented body up and down, testing out different heights. And when he spoke to me, he *always* crouched down, made the effort to meet me face to face.

But now, I had to tilt my head back, trying to meet his stupid bug eyes, on his dumb triangle head. "What's wrong with you? Quit acting like a creep." And, I couldn't help it, goosebumps prickled my skin.

That conversation with Pilar had spooked me. *What if he malfunctioned or his programming got messed up?* Until I'd watched the video of Ian killing his way through a war zone, I'd never thought of him as dangerous. Not the clumsy robot who had tripped over my toys.

I remembered that version of the robot as fallible, child-like, easily broken. He'd get tangled in the wires that connected him to his processor and needed little five-year-old me to help unravel him. He'd crashed when we tried surfing cardboard boxes down the slide, and one eye crushed into his head. He'd bonked an arm jumping off the metal climbing dome and broken a claw.

Oh, and one time, he accidentally sat on a sandcastle we'd worked on all day, and it gunked up a leg. The sand had gotten into a joint, and he couldn't straighten it again. I'd slung my arm around him as my father removed the leg, cleaned it out, and reattached it. *"Don't worry, Ian. We'll get you all fixed up again."* I'd assumed his injuries hurt the way mine did, so I comforted him whenever they happened.

We'd roughhoused and wrestled, and never once had I felt in danger or afraid.

But, the Ian from Dad's videos? That lethal military machine I'd seen fight, shoot, kill? *That* Ian scared me. Pilar's voice played in my head, *"He hurts people when he goes to war … one was just a kid our age."* And now, looking up at Ian, statue-still and towering over me, I had the gnawing suspicion that he knew he'd freaked me out. He must have deduced it from my heart rate, perspiration, breathing, and decided to deliberately unnerve me. *Jerk.* I folded my arms over my chest. "Are you going to show me what Dad wants done or not?"

The dark pupils moved toward one of my father's computers. "Once you have accessed the keyboard, I will explain the procedure."

"Great. *Thanks so much.*" My dad had three large computer workstations, all facing the giant processor, the wall where Ian's body was once wired into it. I sat at the one with his main research desktop—the drive not connected to the internet.

"Open the highlighted file."

"This one?" I had to turn around to ask because Ian hadn't moved. "Don't just stand there, soldier-bot. Come here."

"I do not need to look over your shoulder." A text popped up on the screen.

> Delete the following code.

And bars of code lit up red that I backspaced over. "I thought this computer wasn't connected to any network."

"Correct. However, it is still connected to me."

"It is? Then why does Dad need me to delete shit off it? Why couldn't you just do it?"

Another text appeared.

Insert the following code.

A string of symbols appeared with a blinking area for me to insert them. "This is stupid. If you're connected, then you should just do it." I craned my head to where Ian still stood, arms still limp. Not even his head swiveled toward me, only one bulbous eye. Talking to him had calmed my nerves though, our usual back and forth putting me at ease. "So, you're acting weirder than usual," I said.

"Your statement implies I typically exhibit odd behavior. Was this your meaning, Asher Bell?"

"Not exactly. But, you're exhibiting some odd behavior right now." I turned and smirked at him, as his one eyeball turned my way. When he didn't answer, I sighed and turned back to the desktop monitor. "So, I know Dad probably explained this already, but you don't need to attack people out here in the civilian world. I mean, if someone genuinely broke into the house, or … um …" I sputtered out, uncertain if my dad would really appreciate me giving Ian the green light to go all neck-snapping and skull-crushing on a burglar.

"Asher Bell forbid Cassius Enzo from returning."

I looked over my shoulder, so Ian's camera could capture my flat mouth, my irritated glare. "I *know* … but then I changed my mind and invited him back inside." I turned back to the computer with a huff. "Caz isn't an enemy soldier. He's not a threat."

"Cassius Enzo attacked Asher Bell at school, resulting in visible injuries, and disciplinary removal from his learning environment."

He had me there. I just made another huffing noise, but my cheeks warmed with embarrassment. Ian was right. I couldn't even deny it. But, I still did. "A threat is something more serious."

My fingers tapped out the code in each of the blinking

spots like the old keyboard drills they had us do in fourth-grade computer class. It didn't take any thought at all, seemed pointless. But, giving me a job in the lab might have been Dad's way of apologizing. For my nerdy father, including me in his work counted as a bonding activity. I entered the last bit of code. "Okay, what else."

"You have completed the task, you can go." Ian still hadn't moved. Even latched to the wall with the big processor, he'd tilt his praying mantis head, open and close the prongs of his claws, crane his neck downward to better see my face. Kind of like a jittery little kid, it now occurred to me. Something really was up with him. Pilar's words still hung in the room between us, *"Do you think Ian is dangerous?"*

I had to pass by the giant robot to get back to the stairs. And, I had the irrational urge to hug close against the wall, out of reach for those long metal arms, their dagger-like claws. Not that it would make a difference if Ian made the decision to attack me. I'd seen how fast he moved in the videos Dad sent. *His claw striking out, crushing the skull of an enemy.*

I shook my head to clear it, brushed past him like normal. Then stopped, turned. "Hey, Ian, do you remember playing with me, when we—when *I*—was younger? Do you remember the playground down here? There was a big sandbox, and it messed up all the wiring in one of your legs."

"I have retained these memory files. Yes." The black pupils stayed focused on the stairs. Like he didn't want to meet my eyes or something.

"Really?" I stuffed my hands into my back pockets, shook the hair out of my eyes.

One of the black camera pupils rolled down to focus on me. "Yes."

His answer made me stupidly happy, nostalgic, like when Pilar and I recounted something dumb we did as kids. Ian might have done some scary shit in those videos, but he was still the same robot I'd played with as a child. Before Pilar and Caz, he'd been my best friend.

"And you, Asher Bell, have you also retained these memories?" Ian asked me.

"Yeah. I have," I told him. "I kept them in my files, too."

CHAPTER 23

T had some weird dreams that night.

Pilar's warnings bounced around in my head, I kept dreaming of her dark eyes, wide and serious. *"What if …"* And, I dreamed of Ian's metallic monotone counting down in a game of hide and seek, *"Ready or not, here I come."*

At one point, I thought I woke up to find Ian standing over me, the triangular head tilted like a confused dog. The claws whirring close to my body, close to my face. But, after all the shit that went down that day, nothing could pull me fully out of sleep. My head lay too heavy, my limbs weighted down to the bed, and I couldn't do more than blink up at the monstrous silhouette.

But, it might not have even happened. More likely, I only dreamed of Ian hovering over me as he contemplated shredding my face or whatever the hell. *Yeah. It was probably a dream.*

Because I had no problem coming awake and aware when my dad ripped the covers off my bed, grabbed my arm, and yanked me up to sitting. "What the hell did you do last night, Asher?" Red-rimmed eyes and a snarl on his face, his hair a spiky mess. He looked every bit the "mad scientist" of old movies and cartoons. His fingernails bit into the meat of my bicep. "Answer me!"

My eyes tried to focus. "What did I—? Nothing. I didn't do anything." I shook my head trying to call up something that could have enraged him like this. There were plenty of mornings I could have listed a number of crimes to fill in the blanks, but last night, I'd only studied calculus. "What are you talking about, Dad?" I pulled free of his bony-handed grip.

"I'm talking about last night. In the lab. Just what were you trying to do? A prank? Revenge because you can't bring all your friends over constantly and treat this house like some kind of … party house?"

"*Party* house? What the—?" I grabbed a shirt off my floor, a pair of sweats. "Just tell me what you think I did."

My dad's hands flexed and tightened, the way Ian's claws did at times. "You sabotaged my work." His skin had turned pale with rage, spittle flew on each crisp word. "Don't play some game with me about it, Asher. Did you think I wouldn't check the cameras?"

"What cameras?" I unplugged my phone from its charger and tapped on his name. "You said to do whatever Ian told me—that's what I did." I handed him my phone. "Here."

My father's pale fury stayed in place. "This is from months ago. Stop lying. Do you really think you can pull some *scam* on me? Did you think you could outsmart *me*?"

When he got really angry, my father typically turned cold and sharp. But, now his anger steamed and boiled like he could barely keep control, and I reared back. "Dad, calm down." I snatched the phone back and looked. "You sent it …"

The last text read:

Come downstairs.

And, Dad was right. He'd sent it months ago, before I'd ever gone to Mom and Brian's, before the fight in the school showers. "I don't understand. Where—?"

Dad's fingers closed on my arm again, and he tried to drag me from the room. No way he could—I might look like his clone, but I got a lot more exercise than he did puttering around a laboratory. Unlike Dad, my wiry body had muscle. It shocked me a little to realize he couldn't budge me, that I had more strength. He'd always occupied this bigger-than-life presence in my mind because of his enormous brain. Because he was my dad. He let go of my arm, but the violence came through his voice. "Come down to the basement—show me what you did to my AI."

"Nothing, Dad. I didn't even touch him."

"Stop lying, Asher. I've had enough of your lies."

I followed him toward the stairs, through the kitchen, down to the basement lab, my mind blank. Like in a dream. Ian stood right where I left him, but the circuitry in his eyes had gone dark. The triangular head hung on its retractable neck, camera pupils pointed to the ground. The upper body segment sagged forward. His four legs had locked statue stiff in place. And the purring basement machinery had gone silent. All the monitors in the lab glowed the blue screen of death.

And Dad thought I did this? I knew my way around a computer, but come on …

"Show me what you did."

"I told you. I didn't do—"

Dad snapped up his tablet from one of the desks and held it in front of me. The entire lab had CCTV and the video showed footage from four angles. Me walking down the stairs. I snarled at Ian, squinty-eyed and annoyed. My face, yeah. An expression I made, yeah. *But something is off* … My lips moved, and the footage caught me calling Ian a creep. But nothing else. The rest of the conversation was missing. And I seemed so angry, the taught tendons in my neck, in my arms.

The night with the chicken bone. When Ian had nagged me about food in the lab. In the video, I still had a hand curled as if it held a now-deleted chicken leg. All the bruises on my face that night had been erased, and the clothes I'd worn superimposed with my t-shirt and jeans from last night. This CCTV footage had been doctored. Forged.

The Ash in the video didn't ask what he should do. He had a mission. Marched directly to the computer station, started to click away at the keyboard. "That ... didn't happen," I said. "Not like that."

In the video, the camera zeroed in on the desktop's monitor. None of the easy, "Follow the flashing light" directions I'd copied the night before displayed. In place of that nonsense, lines of complicated code scrolled down the screen. "Dad. This is fake. That's not what I did." I twisted to look at the drooping, inert, robot. *Is he turned off? Is he broken?*

When I looked back at Dad's tablet, the Ash on the video feed had turned to look at Ian the same way. *"... you're exhibiting some odd behavior right now,"* I'd teased him. But, the Ash in the video didn't say the words, only the half-smile ticked at his lips. Without the joking commentary, that smirk became sinister. Like my evil doppelgänger could hardly wait to see the robot crash and deactivate.

"I didn't do it. That video is a fake." I waved at where Ian stood, his slumped upper body, limp arms, slack neck. Last night, while not exactly his usual twitchy self, at least one eye had followed me around. He'd acted strange, but not ... dead.

Dad pulled the tablet from my hands and set it on the desk behind him. He jerked his glasses off and rubbed at his eyes. "Impossible." Dad looked down toward his glasses, like he wished he could dramatically rip them off a second time.

"The video is genuine, Asher." He'd stopped sounding angry, looking furious. Now, his shoulders sagged in a defeated imitation of his robot.

"Why don't you believe me? Someone set me up." *Someone? Not just someone.* My breath shuddered out of my chest. "*Ian* set me up."

My father slammed a hand on the metal desk. "Please, Asher. Just don't say anything else right now." He ran both hands through his dark hair. "I really have no idea how to deal with you. Suzanne … Serena … was right. You would be better off living with her in a traditional family."

"Dad—"

"I can't stand to look at you right now, Asher. Just go." When I hesitated, the hot anger returned to his face. "Get. Out."

I walked to the stairway like a zombie, numb in both my body and brain. At the top of the basement stairs, Carly stood in the open doorway, sucking on her lip piercing like she wanted to swallow the thing. She had that expression that always irked me. *Poor little rich kid whose dad doesn't love him.*

"Stop being so nosy all the time," I seethed.

But Carly didn't buy my act. She squeezed my shoulder as I passed her. "Get ready, and I'll give you a ride to school, little Bell. It's getting too cold to walk."

As I trudged up the stairs, I pulled my phone out of the pocket in my sweatpants. "I'm such an idiot." All those texts, back and forth, asking me about my friends, about my feelings, and not a single one had come from my dad.

They'd all been Ian.

CHAPTER 24

*W*hile I'd gone upstairs to change into jeans, brush my teeth, Pilar had come over. She stayed suspiciously silent on the drive to school, so I knew Carly had blabbered to her about the fucked up turn my life had just taken. Pilar kept giving me these meaningful looks and sighing. They both believed I'd done what Dad accused me of. That much was obvious.

After Carly dropped us off on the curb, Pilar wound an arm around my waist. "Your art has been crying out for attention," she said, like she'd just morphed into Ms. Stanzi. "It's your dad's fault he couldn't see it."

"Crying out for—?" I pushed her away from me. "Pilar, I didn't sabotage Ian. I wouldn't do that."

"I don't blame you—"

"It's his life's work. I wouldn't do it." We leaned against the rough brick exterior of the school. The resource officer eyed us from the doorway. He probably thought we wanted to smoke or vape. "Hey Pilar, you remember me getting that text from Dad last night, right? Did I show it to you?"

Pilar screwed her mouth up, closed her eyes for a long moment, like her full brain fought to pull up the memory.

155

Then, she abruptly shifted back to normal. "The text that had you sprinting out of my house?" Color flooded her cheeks. "I thought Caz texted and you just didn't want to tell me."

I tipped my head back, let it tap against the brick. "Shit."

"Well … was it? Caz, I mean?"

"No. It was …" *Ian—it was fucking Ian.* He'd sabotaged himself and framed me. But, I couldn't even say it out loud because I'd sound like a crazy person. Last night, Pilar had worried that Ian's programming would glitch, and he'd go on a killing spree, not that he'd frame me for his own meltdown. It sounded like a lie. I didn't think I would believe me either.

The resource officer took a step out the doorway. "You kids get inside and go to first period."

Pilar spun around. "We aren't breaking any rules right now, so mind your own business."

The guy took another step in our direction. His hand sliding toward the walkie-talkie on his belt. "That wasn't a suggestion, and watch the attitude."

I gripped Pilar's shoulder and turned her away from the officer, and back toward me. "We're just talking about our history quiz," I called back to him. "My friend's a little stressed, but she's sorry." When it mattered, I could muster up a passable imitation of dewy innocence, blinking wide eyes, toothy smile, the works. The resource officer backed off. Then to Pilar, I whispered, "Listen, I just can't be here today. I'm going to skip."

"Are you meeting up with Caz?" Pilar sounded all huffy like a jealous girlfriend and glared at me with narrowed dark eyes.

Right—Caz got a suspension for the fight by the vending machines. So, he would be at home today. *I guess I could hang with him …* I looked over at the school officer to see if he still watched us, but he'd gotten bored with our law-abiding drama. Instead, he'd taken an interest in a clutch of freshmen all gathered around a single backpack. Suspicious as fuck.

"Ash, are you meeting up with—?"

"I'm just ..." My plan only went as far as leaving, so I didn't have to deal with school on top of my bullshit at home. I looped another arm into my backpack, tightened the straps. "Catch you later, Pilar."

~

After everything that had happened, I didn't need to get picked up for truancy. To avoid that, I wound through neighborhoods off the main streets. Carly had a point about how it was way too cold for walking—my face and hands burned. Wind seeped past my jacket, and snow soaked the bottom of my jeans. A few streets from the Enzo house, I texted Caz.

> Are you home??? I'm skipping. And maybe freezing to death.

> Fuck yeah. Come over.

When he opened the door, Caz had on a white polo and faded jeans that he knew looked good on him. He'd even combed his hair. A lot of effort for a guy who planned to spend the day home alone. "Hey, Ash ..." He grinned, knowing-like.

"I'm just here to hang out, okay?" I told him. He obviously had hoped for more. "I got in a giant fight with my dad."

Caz dropped the cheesy seduction right away. "Did he hit you?"

"What? No." I'd forgotten how arguments in the Enzo

house went. "No hitting. He wants to get rid of me though. He said he's going to make me live with Mom now."

"Fucking fathers." His forehead wrinkled as Caz waved me inside. "What was it …" Caz trailed off. "Wait—because of the robot thing yesterday?" He suddenly looked a lot like the Caz I'd been friends with as a kid, bouncing on his toes, trouble coming off him in waves. "That was crazy, man. I've never seen one in real life—they're huge!" He pulled down the collar of his polo shirt to show me two long bruises on each side of his neck.

"Yeah, I'm really sorry—"

But, Caz just waved me off as he led me inside. "Whatever. I've had worse." He grinned again, looking just as amped up as he once had about bike ramps or tree forts we'd made as kids. "And, your robot *talked*. In videos, they don't talk, or seem … *aware* like yours. I thought that thing was going to pop my head off. So wild, man. "

I followed Caz up the stairs to his bedroom. He'd paused a game of *Mario Kart*. A bag of powdered sugar donuts waited on his unmade bed. "Yeah, I guess I should have asked how you are after Ian grabbed you like that … Are you okay?"

"Hey, it was just following your last orders, right?" Caz fell back onto the bed, arms outstretched, and he reached for the donut bag. "You told me to get out and not come back, and it *remembered*. That's so fucking cool."

"Uh … I guess so …" I shifted back and forth on my feet. If I wanted to sit on the bed near Caz, he didn't leave me a lot of room.

"Ian—that's its name, right? *Ian* is so fucking cool." Caz patted the bed beside him. "Relax, man. My dad and stepmom will be at the car lot all day, we have the whole house to ourselves."

"Like I said, Caz, I just want to hang out." I watched the smile drop from his face, and his mouth twisted up. I'd pissed him off. "Come on, Caz. Can't we just be friends like we used to … before." Didn't he miss that at all? I guess he had all his football teammates as friends now. He had Harper.

Caz did a slow blink, hid his annoyance behind a blank look. I'd seen him do that before. His dad always got on him about "being a man." Like real men never felt anything but anger. Some real toxic shit that I'd escaped with my nerdy father and hippie mom.

"It's that or nothing, Caz."

Another flash of anger that he stuffed down. "Yeah, alright." He shuffled to the right side of the bed to leave me room and kicked a foot out, nudged my leg with his sock foot. "So are we cool?" Caz didn't wait for me to answer. He unpaused *Mario Kart* and nodded toward the other controller.

My stomach roiled with indecision. *Hadn't I already decided to forgive him when I'd invited him back into my house?* But, I picked up the controller. "Yeah, we're cool."

We played in silence for a while. Caz had a lot of practice with diffusing futile anger toward a parent. In families like Pilar's, you could talk things out, compromise. Sometimes, the fight just got dropped, and Dory Almas hugged Pilar, or her dad kissed her forehead, and they'd all move past it.

Not in my house.

Not in Caz's house either. Both of us had fathers who would never give an inch, always had to have the last word. So the only way to deal with it was to distract ourselves with games, with movies, with each other. We understood each other because we both understood the effort it took to stuff all that resentment back inside. We didn't talk about our feelings, we just waited until they all went numb.

Finally, Caz red-shelled me in the game. "Got you, loser." The competitive jerk, he knocked his shoulder into mine, gave me one of the half-smiles that always did me in, crinkles in the skin next to his heavy-lidded eyes.

He tossed his controller to the side and reached for the donut bag again. "Aren't you gonna answer him?" Caz asked.

"What?" My stomach growled and I slapped a hand over it. "Answer what?"

"Dude. Your dad is blowing up your phone." Caz grabbed up my iPhone. It must have slipped out of my pocket when I sat down. "Dad" lit up on the screen. Caz tossed it to me.

I groaned. "Oh fuck. You think the school called him?"

"Um, *yes*." Caz shoved the last little donut in his mouth, talked around it. "Haven't you ever skipped before? They *always* call."

"Shit." I swiped my phone to the missed texts.

> Explain absence from school.

> Explain current presence at 5620 Blue Bonnet Street, residence of Cassius Enzo.

> Explain retraction of ban against Cassius Enzo from the Bell residence.

> Await answers.

> Demand answers.

Nice try, asshole. But, I'm not falling for this again. I set my game controller behind me. "Um … I just need to …" I waggled the phone in the air.

Caz turned the game off and nodded. He always got serious when it came to interacting with parents. Back when he first met them, Mr. and Mrs. Almas tried to wear him down with their kindness. But, Caz never relaxed around them, never treated them with anything other than distrustful respect. He winced at my phone like it might explode in my hand. "Yeah. Take your time. I'll make us some lunch."

Sweat dampened my upper lip. I paced back and forth the length of Caz's room. Do I play along—maybe get Ian to do something, anything that could back up my story? That same impotent rage rolled over me again, like arguing with my genius father. What hope did I have of outsmarting Ian's computer brain?

None.

My thumb poised over the phone keyboard a second before I sent my response.

I know this isn't Dad

CHAPTER 25

$\mathcal{T}$he little dots appeared—like someone taking their sweet time to type out a reply. Like a human. That had never happened before. He wanted me to doubt myself. *Nope, not going to work.* I plunged ahead.

> So you're fixed now? What was the point of making Dad think I'd crashed the research hard drive? That I'd wrecked you. You want him to send me to live with my mom????

> Do you think getting rid of me will let him spend more time working on you?

> That he'll schedule more super fun killing missions for the two of you?

I hit send and swiped away the sweat from my upper lip. The shock that had numbed me watching that doctored video melted away, and all the frustration I'd ignored by playing Mario Kart flooded back. *Why did you frame me?* Maybe I couldn't out-smart Ian's mechanized brain, but at least I'd have some answers.

The purpose of a mission is neither killing nor fun. Objectives are assigned in response to a developing situation.

> I don't care about missions, Ian. What was your objective in blaming me for crashing the computer?

To remain at 6462 Meadow Ave, the Bell residence.

> That doesn't even make sense. How does making Dad hate me have anything to do with where he plugs you in?

> You got some bad code at work there soldier-bot.

Asher Bell is Dr. Bell's offspring. Any consequences of damaging this AI would be overshadowed by the familial parent-child bond.

> Like I said BAD CODE—you were fucking wrong. Also, I'm taking screenshots of this whole convo.

But of course, that fucker had hacked my phone, and as soon as I took them, all my photos disappeared into some unreachable void. "Damn it!"

"He knows you skipped?" A hand dropped on my shoulder, stopped me from my frantic pacing. Unlike Pilar or Carly, Caz never felt sorry for me. He never dumped a bunch of sympathy or comfort when I'd rather just fume. Sympathetic words didn't make anything better when his own dad wailed on him, and he never expected it to make a difference for me either.

"Listen," Caz had turned all serious business. "My dad

doesn't want me talking to you anymore, but if you needed to hide out here, he wouldn't even know. He and my stepmom are leaving tonight for a car show thing in Vegas. You could stay."

When we were younger, I'd hide Caz in my room, sometimes for an entire weekend so that Mr. Enzo couldn't get his hands on his son. After a few days, his dad would calm down, and Caz would go back home. Still, thorny nerves would run over my skin until he texted, or I saw him at school the next day, and I knew he had escaped his father's beating.

But, Caz hadn't asked me for help like that in a long time. Maybe Mr. Enzo had chilled out since then? But, I only had to picture him signing the NDAs in our dining room, red-faced and breathing heavy with anger to know he hadn't. More likely, Caz took shelter with Harper—his girlfriend. *Don't forget about the girlfriend, Ash.*

"No … it's fine. I'm … I think I should head home."

Caz crossed his arms over his chest, brows furrowed as he gave my situation some hard thought. "I'm coming with you." He grabbed his flannel jacket from where it hung over his desk chair, shrugged into it before I could think up a reason to leave him behind.

"No, Caz. I'm just going to sneak in from …" *The broken tree branch.* "Shit. I can't get in through the studio window. I'll have to text Carly."

My phone buzzed again.

> Dr. Bell has repeatedly deferred the relocation of his son Asher to the Carmichael residence at 310 Rock Road, Estes Park, CO. It was logical to assume he values his role as parent to son Asher Bell and would desire to continue living with Asher Bell.

> That's before you framed me for destroying his work, ass-hat.

I needed to talk to Dad and explain things. I needed to make him believe me.

Caz waited for me at his front door, jaw tight. Blond brows low over narrowed eyes, and bulky shoulders blocking my exit. No way would I leave the Enzo house alone, not now that he'd made his mind up to come with me. I sighed. "Okay, let's go."

❦

*I*n the end, I decided not to text Carly and just unlocked the front door to let myself inside. The security system beeped as we entered, and she peeked out from the kitchen. One pierced eyebrow climbed up her forehead. "Cassius Enzo … haven't seen you in a long, long while. I thought you'd ditched all your friends for fame and glory?"

Caz looked at me and frowned, a muscle ticked in his cheek. "It's not like that," he muttered.

Carly made a snorting noise. "Oh, it isn't?" Then she turned toward me. "Your dad is still really upset with you, little Bell. Now, you're skipping school, too?"

I doubted my father would notice or care that I belonged in school instead of at home at that hour. *But, Dad would freak out if he saw Caz.* "It's fine," I told Carly. "Just … be nice to Caz while I go talk to Dad, okay?"

She leaned a hip against the kitchen bar and flashed Caz a toothy, false smile. "No probs."

I took the steps two at a time, bounded into the lab to find Dad standing beside the big processor, hunched with his arms wrapped around himself. He looked like someone had just punched him in the gut. Even his sharp, pale features had gone tight. "Hello, Asher …"

"Dad, are you okay?"

He shook a hand out, a "Shut up, I'm thinking" gesture I knew from all the other times I'd interrupted him. To assess the meltdown, Dad had wired Ian's body back into the big processor. It whirred and hummed the way it always had. The white and yellow circuitry in Ian's eyes glowed with life, too. One black camera pupil pointed at Dad, but the other rotated toward me.

"It seems that Ian's coding had not deteriorated as I'd thought." Dad's pained expression turned toward me. Nothing physical bothered him—all that suffering came from the puzzle he couldn't solve.

When his eyes met mine they filled with ice-cold suspicion. "As a matter of fact, I can't quite determine what went wrong or why it suddenly corrected just minutes before you arrived."

The triangular head dipped down toward my father. From the speaker in his neck, the metallic voice hummed to life. "During maintenance, this AI experienced a temporary overheating error, Dr. Bell. This error has now been resolved."

A metal arm reached out between my father and me. Three of the sharp claws pointing in different directions. "With shutdown imminent, memory storage relocated to stations 3, 4, and 7." The talon of a claw pointed out the different computers. One camera pupil followed, but the other stayed focused on me.

My father also seemed to have one eye watching me, a shrewd, scientific mind working on my sudden presence like a cipher. "And this overheating was caused by my son's interference?"

"Negative. Asher Bell used Station 1 to access this processor. From there, he wrote his World History paper titled 'Long Reaching Aftermath of Napoleonic France.' This assignment is due on Friday, first period in Vernon Haag's AP World History. "

"And the CCTV video—?"

"Captured footage of maintenance, which ran simultaneously. Asher Bell's use of this processor was unrelated to the error in its cooling fans."

"I see …" Dad drew the last word out, like he saw a lot more than the explanation Ian had given him.

The printer at Station 1 began to whir and spit the paper out. Dad picked it up between his fingers. "This is your school essay, Ash?" Dad's eyes flicked back and forth on the document he'd found, reading whatever Ian had produced on the spot. Without any prep, Ian must have quickly pulled a professional article off of JSTOR.

But, once Dad handed over the paper, I recognized it. It *was* my essay on Napoleon. I'd actually started writing it in study hall the day before. "How—?"

How did Ian get this? I hadn't typed it up on that computer, or any other computer in the lab—I hadn't typed it up *at all*. My handwritten paper was still in a spiral notebook tucked inside my backpack. My breathing sounded a little too loud and gasping. I swallowed and coughed to get back under control. "Yeah. This is my paper. That's why I came home … To get it."

"Very well." Dad peered at me again, but I called up that fail-proof dewy innocent expression. And, thankfully, Dad's emotional recognition skills were nearly as bad as Ian's. He'd straightened up and gained his composure, too. "Then I suppose we're ready to make the transfer to North American Automation. Please notify the labs there, Ian."

"Yes, Dr. Bell."

The right camera pupil still focused on me, and even if Dad couldn't parse out my shock and relief, Ian must have cataloged my temperature, my breathing, the pace of my heart.

He'd exonerated me with Dad, possibly saved me from moving in with Mom, Brian, and my annoying sisters. And then, I remembered Ian's text. *To remain at 6462 Meadow Ave, the Bell residence.*

He didn't want to leave either. That was why he'd concocted this whole plan to meltdown and force my father to reconnect him to the basement processor. With my eyes meeting that camera pupil, I rolled the papers in my hands. *Think. Think.*

"Dad, does Ian have to go to NAA? Can't you tell them that this is the best lab for him … like if he really needed that repair. Wouldn't that work?"

My father peered from the tablet in his hands to hit me with another dose of frosty assessment. "Storing him in a personal laboratory presents a significant risk to national security." Dad's long pale fingers tapped out something on the tablet as he spoke, only the smallest portion of his concentration engaged in this mundane interaction with me. "Now that Ian has mobility, can self-determine to an extent, I have to agree with General Baylor's decision. Ian is an advanced, perhaps the *most* advanced, piece of military equipment in the US arsenal."

"But, can't you—?"

Dad made a huge eye-rolling sigh and set the tablet on the counter behind him. "Obviously, you've become attached." I could tell that he'd become irritated with my questions … my presence. "During his development, you and I may have treated Ian as a … kind of pet, but he's a piece of technology. A thing."

Ian's right pupil rolled away from me to point at my father.

"That's kind of harsh, Dad." I'd blurted it out without thinking. "Calling Ian a pet, a *thing* … How can you say that?"

But, Dad acted like he didn't hear me, something in his massive brain had diverted his attention. A calculation? A formula? He placed his glasses back on his face, and the thick lenses reflected the fluorescent lights. "Don't be ridiculous, Asher. It doesn't matter what I say to Ian, what I call him ... call *it*. Ian doesn't have feelings."

The Department of State, World Health Organization, United Nations had each called upon my father at different times. They sought his opinions on science, on mathematics, on technology. They flew him around the world to answer their questions, provide solutions that entire teams of researchers couldn't find. My father was never wrong. But, this *felt* wrong.

When I looked back up, the black pupils had rotated away from Dad and locked on me. "He might not have feelings," I said. "But I think he wants to stay. Don't you—"

"Asher. That's enough. Ian doesn't have wants. You are projecting human motivations onto a machine."

Motivation. I'd always seen motivation in Ian—the rivalry between us for Dad's attention. Dad's praise. Dad's love. Had it only existed in my imagination?

The black camera pupils both stayed on me, like they waited for a response. My dad would say this was more projecting from me, and Ian wasn't waiting for anything.

"If you say so, Dad."

CHAPTER 26

"You should wish your father a happy Thanksgiving." My mother dribbled lemon juice into a pan of cauliflower before she started mashing it up. No potatoes in the Carmichael home. No pumpkin pie. No turkey and stuffing.

When I spent Thanksgiving with Dad, we did the holiday without fanfare, no sit-down dinner. Carly usually got a turkey in the oven for us and then headed home. Dad and I would pick at the giant bird for the rest of the day. Without me there, Carly probably hadn't even bothered to cook.

My mother's beaded bracelets jingled as she mashed. "Why not call him?"

I leaned against the counter by Mom. "No thanks." My worst nightmare had finally come true—Dad kicked me out. He would let me finish fall semester, but over winter break, I had to move all my stuff up to the foothills with Mom and Brian.

"Ashie …" Mom's voice singsonged. "I know you're feeling abandoned right now, but Fredric just wants what's best for you. We both do."

I could barely believe it, but my father had actually gone to my mother for advice on how to deal with me. According to him, I'd turned into a troubled kid who *"anthropomorphized a piece of dangerous technology."* And all the crap I'd said to Mom about wanting a sibling had blown up in my face. My parents finally agreed on something—that their school-brawling, car-stealing, loner son needed a change of scenery. "He doesn't want what's best for me. He just doesn't want me in his way," I grumbled.

It didn't matter that Ian had changed his story, Dad sensed deception somewhere in the convoluted response the robot gave. He accepted that the cooling error caused the meltdown, but he couldn't find a reason for that error. And he didn't wholly believe in the coincidence of me typing an essay on the same station where the error originated.

"It's not fair, Mom." I slumped over, rested my elbows next to her cutting board, propped my chin on my hands. I'd decided to hang out in the kitchen with my mother while Brian did sand art with the girls at the dining table. They'd colored the sand with easter egg dyes, and streaks of purple, green, and magenta stained their fingers and faces. The dye smelled like sulfur. Worse than Mom's mashed cauliflower.

Brian kept shooting me dirty looks. Especially when Mom dropped a kiss on the top of my head. "Serena, we agreed that Ash should spend more time interacting with the girls."

"We don't want to spend time with Ash," Petal chirped. Beside her, Ginger snickered and stuck her tongue out at me.

My mom just smiled and winked at me. Like she expected me to interpret all their obvious hatred in a fun, teasing, way. When I groaned, she laughed it off. "This will be a good change, you'll see."

"No, it won't. I didn't do *anything.* Ian even told Dad—"

"You spend too much with that robot," Mom

whispered. Brian insisted no one mention Dad's work, especially Ian, as a condition of my moving in with them. He described ripping up my sketchbook as some heroic act. *"It's like Ash brought a gun into the house."* I could absolutely, no way in Hell, live here with him.

My phone pinged in my pocket. Pilar sent me photos of her own Thanksgiving dinner. Pictures of golden brown empanadas, piles of fluffy homemade tortillas, roasted pork and turkey.

You suck

♥

~

My mother squeezed my arm, leaned her head on my shoulder trying to see my phone screen. "I never get to hear about your life, Ashie." Her blue eyes got wide and sad. "Any crazy art projects with Pilar? How about school?"

I pushed up from the counter, stifled a groan. I hated when she tried to make me feel guilty for not confiding every little thing to her. "There's not much to tell." I slouched and let my hair cover my eyes. "Especially since it's coming to a screeching end next month." No more art studio. No more Pilar. No more Caz.

"So is there anyone special you'll be leaving behind?" She glanced down at the phone in my hand. I probably seemed really popular with the way it kept buzzing. Besides Pilar flaunting her gourmet Thanksgiving dinner, Caz had sent me updates of the Bronco game—even though he knew I didn't really care. He always thought he could wear me down, turn me into a football fan. It made me kind of nostalgic, he used to talk sports to me all the time before we hooked up. But, that wistful feeling dried up when he sent a selfie of him doing a fist pump. I knew him well enough to tell that he'd tried to look hot with that sleepy-eyed smile and unbuttoned shirt.

"No one worth mentioning," I told my mother.

My phone buzzed again, and Mom leaned back over to have a peek. An unknown number had sent a gif of a cartoon turkey wiggling its tail feathers and holding a heart-shaped pumpkin pie. Underneath they'd texted the words, **Happy Thanksgiving.**

"Oh, that's adorable." Mom nudged me with her hip like that corny gif equaled a romantic gesture. "Looks like someone wants to be worth mentioning ..."

I peered over at the twins and Brian then turned away from Mom.

> Who is this?

> This is the Intelligent Adaptive Neuron Mirror Military Prototype. Designated Ian.

A noise escaped from my chest—part a gasp, part a laugh. "Um ... Mom, I need to take this."

My mother beamed. She loved romance and relationships, had always acted disappointed when I shrugged off that stuff. Also, I think she liked believing she'd guessed something I hadn't wanted to tell her. Proof that her motherly intuition still worked despite the years we hadn't lived together.

I beat it for my bedroom, but not fast enough to miss Brian fussing like a baby. "Serena," he whined. "I thought we agreed this would be a family day—"

"Oh, Bri, give it a rest," my mom snapped.

> Nice gif, Ian.

> I identified this animation as a popular
> image exchanged to mark Thanksgiving.

I wondered if North American Automation had closed up for the holiday. Had Dad taken the day off, too? I couldn't even picture it. He'd worked every day of my life. When Ian first left, I'd expected Dad would dismantle the basement computers and spend every waking hour at the NAA labs, maybe even move into a hotel in Colorado Springs. But, he still didn't trust the NAA with the totality of his research. So, he abandoned Ian and came home to his basement every evening.

> Where are you?
>
> Dad with you?

> Negative
>
> Dr. Bell is at his residence: 6462
> Meadow Ave.

It was hard not to feel sympathy for the AI—even when Ian didn't experience emotions to sympathize with. Loneliness had dogged me all my life, and I couldn't stop projecting it onto Ian or picturing him alone in the dark labs at North American Automation every night.

A mean part of me even liked imagining him lonely. *Serves him right.* Because of Ian, I would end up sharing a house with Brian and the terror twins.

> Not that I would know—since I got
> KICKED OUT!

The little dots appeared, like someone typing a response, even though Ian didn't need to pick out letters on a keyboard. Finally, another text popped up.

I miscalculated by shifting responsibility for the AI shutdown to Asher Bell.

It was not my intention for you to be sent to the Carmichael residence at 319 Rock Road, Estes Park.

> Yeah, Ian. You miscalculated BIG TIME. Now, neither of us gets to live at home.

Home. 6462 Meadow Ave.

Describe feelings for home.

> My dad is there. My stuff is there. My friends. My studio. And I feel comfortable. Safe. Like I can just be myself.

> Why did you want to stay? Do you feel those things?

AI do not experience feelings.

> Then why did you want to stay at 6462 Meadow Ave?

If Ian didn't consider my dad's laboratory his home, then why would he go through that entire crazy shutdown plan just to stay? The labs at NAA must have better equipment and … whatever the hell an AI would need or want. *Does Ian want things?*

No. Because wanting something comes from emotion, feeling. And Ian couldn't feel.

Like he said.

The three dots appeared again. Maybe he'd decided to imitate the long pauses I made before texting. Longer pauses when I couldn't decide what to say. Maybe he didn't know the answer to my question—why he'd tried so hard to stay at 6462 Meadow Ave. with Dad and me.

> Hey, Ian—how did you get my world history paper into the files on Station 1 in Dad's lab? I never even uploaded it to anything. I'd only written it by hand.

> This AI chooses not to share all capabilities with the son of Dr. Fredric Bell.

> Seriously?

> Come on—I kept it a secret that you'd been sneaking out of the basement lab. Now you think I'll suddenly rat you out to Dad?

From the kitchen, I could hear my mom telling the girls to clean up their sand art and wash their hands. The tofu roast had finished baking, and it didn't smell too bad. Not like the cauliflower. And my mom had made a pumpkin stew that looked pretty good, too.

> It's almost dinner time, so I gotta go. Try not to be jealous as I dig into my mother's vegan, oil-free, sugar-free, salt-free feast.

> AI do not experience jealousy.

> That was sarcasm. My mom's cooking is terrible. No one would be jealous of me.

Again, I pictured Ian alone in a dark laboratory. Even if he didn't get lonely, I felt sorry for him. When he went on that mission with Dad, I'd missed having him around for late-night conversations. Maybe something in his programming also recognized the hole left by not having anyone to talk to. Like an AI version of boredom? Or an AI version of loss? Trying to figure it out made my brain hurt.

My mother's voice called for me. "Ashie, time for dinner!"

"Yeah, coming." I stared at my phone screen, but no other text came.

CHAPTER 27

> Are you there?

> Dinner sucked. You didn't miss anything.

> Not that you care. Because you don't get jealous, right?

*E*veryone in the house had gone to sleep hours earlier, stuffed on all the food my mom made. Dinner hadn't really sucked, but I felt like a dick saying that to Ian when he couldn't eat. Like rubbing it in his face. Because, here's the thing, I didn't believe him about not experiencing jealousy. All during dinner, I'd thought about it. Why did Ian work so hard to trounce me in all the puzzles and scenarios Dad gave us? Ian had *wanted* to show me up in front of Dad. I'd *felt* it.

~

*H*e still hadn't responded.

> Did you turn yourself off?

Negative.

> Okay. So talk to me. Tell me how you got that history paper from my backpack.

I did not take the paper from your backpack.

> Hmmm if you say so ...

You do not believe me? You distrust me because I led you to believe my texts were from Dr. Bell.

> A little. But, I probably helped you in that lie.

Explain.

> Okay, but it's going to make me sound really pathetic.

> The thing is—I really wanted Dad to be on the other end of those texts. Even when I thought he was pissed off at me, or telling me how much better Ty Rodgers was than me. At least he was thinking of me?

Ty Rodgers is not superior to Asher Bell.

> Oh yeah ... Right. That was you arguing with me.

With all the past texts deleted, I couldn't even remember what had gotten me so worked up. The personality test? Ty Rodgers had the personality of a perfect soldier, the DNA that would give Ian an edge in military conflict.

> I guess it's fine if he's better than me in some ways. I would make a really terrible soldier.

I concur. Asher Bell would have difficulty achieving success during military conflict.

However, this does not indicate inferiority.

Now you're just feeling sorry for me.

AI do not experience feelings.

For some reason that made me laugh. "Are you sure about that, soldier-bot?" Because it *seemed* like Ian had a lot of feelings. That he liked and disliked things. But, I didn't type it out. I thought if I did, Ian might take it wrong, like criticism. It was basically like telling the robot that he was malfunctioning

Or, he might quit talking to me. I didn't want that either. I picked up my phone again.

Do you ever wish that you could experience feelings? More like a human?

A long pause. I'd just set the phone aside when the next text finally came through.

Dr. Bell programmed me to determine choice, but not the capacity to experience all choices. Therefore, if given the opportunity to become more like a human, I would accept.

My eyes blinked at that response. The conversation had turned way too deep for my sleep-addled brain. A yawn broke my concentration.

It is past the hour you usually fall asleep.

Another yawn. My head felt about a million pounds heavier than usual. My arms and legs, too.

Yeah. G'night Ian—

Good night, Asher Bell.

~

J had weird dreams again. Red light scanning my room, falling on me like a spotlight. Outside my window, an owl screeched, its wings beating against the glass windowpane. I woke with a start, breath caught in my chest, heart racing. But nothing moved outside my window, the night was dark and moonless. No red light. I burrowed deeper into my comforter, let it swallow me up. I used to do that as a child when I could hear my parents fighting. Like a pillbug, Mom's nickname fit.

When she first left, and Dad moved me to the big house, I'd take my comforter down to the basement, curl up next to Ian's speechless prototype. He thought it was a game, would poke his triangle head into my fluffy cocoon, eyes glowing, as he calculated all the physical manifestations of my distress. My running nose and wet eyes, my trembling and racing heart.

Programmed Mirror Neurons fired in Ian's circuits, connecting the parameters of my suffering to the data in his memory files. Searching for solutions. Maybe the AI interpreted my shivering as cold because the long spider arms and legs would circle around me, bundle me tighter.

Why the robot hugged me didn't matter. I was four years old, and my mother had just left, my father had buried himself in work. I would take what I could get. I'd let the little whirring and clicking noises of Ian's machinery work like white noise and lull me back to sleep.

~

*M*orning in the foothills always smelled like a fresh start, cool air, crushed leaves, pine needles, and earthy snow. Thank God Mom hadn't given up coffee. My little sisters sprayed cereal and almond milk everywhere when they ate. Made loud slurping noises and talked with crushed bits of oat and raisin gooey between their teeth. *Disgusting.* I took my mug of black coffee outside to get away from them.

Back home, Carly would have poured pumpkin spice creamer in my mug. She would have asked if I wanted French toast or scrambled eggs with cheese. But, drinking black coffee and standing in the snow sort of fit my mood.

Brian's voice carried from the kitchen's sliding glass doors. "Serena, I thought we agreed that the children needed to eat meals at the table."

"That seems awfully restrictive, Bri."

A grin spread across my face. Brian had lived with my mom long enough to know that she'd initially agree to everything and then change her mind when the spirit moved her. And always without an ounce of guilt. She'd just shrug and say something cryptic like, "That's your path, not mine." If I didn't hate Brian so much, I might have felt sympathy for him. My mother could be infuriating like that.

I walked farther from where Brian's nasal voice lectured Mom about the chemicals in coffee, and how, "Asher intentionally used my favorite mug."

His favorite mug? Seriously? I rolled my eyes. "Fuck *off,* Brian." My shoes crunched against the snowy gravel of our front drive, a big semi-circle that went past my bedroom window. I wanted to see if I could find evidence of the noisy owl that woke me up every night. It must roost in one of the Ponderosa pines that grew up against the house. In the summertime, the pines smelled like butterscotch and vanilla, but it was late November already. The warm scent of growth long gone, and a blanket of dried pine needles lay under the snow.

Except by my window?

The snow and the ground had all churned together. I crouched down, kicked at the disturbed ground. Owl feathers. A lot of them.

When I nudged again at the mounded snow, the frozen owl's body rolled out at my feet. "Holy——" I jumped up and back, forgetting the mug in my hand. Steaming coffee sloshed down the leg of my jeans. "Fuck!" The hot liquid soaked through to my skin, but it didn't really burn. The winter air cooled it too fast.

From inside the house, I could hear my sisters start to giggle. My shout must have carried back to the kitchen. And, Brian started up with my mom again. "Serena, didn't you agree to talk to Asher about the type of language he uses in front of the girls?"

My mother stuck her head out the sliding door. "Everything okay, Ashie?"

"Uh, yeah … Everything's fine." I pulled the wet denim away from my skin. "I just spilled my coffee."

I went back to my room to change. The box of clothes my mother had insisted I bring with me still waited, packed up. She'd loaded up her Broncho with a bunch of my stuff, *"So the move to Estes will feel more like a gradual transition instead of an abrupt change."* She was the only one excited about packing bags and boxes. Behind her, Brian had scowled hard enough that his entire pointy face had gone beet red. My dad stomped around, huffing like a child over having to do manual labor. And I'd wanted to vomit the entire time, sick that my worst fear had finally come true.

Just as I finished changing clothes, a car pulled onto the gravel semi-circle drive outside my window. A flashy yellow Corvette with black drag race stripes up the hood and over the roof. *What in showy douchebag hell——?* Behind the wheel was Caz Enzo's smug grin. His blond hair lit with the sun as he parked and climbed out from the driver's side. He looked good, real good. He caught sight of me watching him from the bedroom window and tossed his keys in the air, caught them one-handed.

"Just friends. Still, just friends," I reminded myself.

CHAPTER 28

*A*s soon as Mom let him in, Caz turned on the charm. "Thank you for inviting me in, Mrs. Bell ... I mean, Mrs. Carmichael." He leaned in toward her, flirtatious, sleepy-eyed, smile doing its work. "I know I should have called first. "

"Please, just call me Serena." She shook his hand with way too much enthusiasm. "And it's no problem to come over as much as you want. I'm glad Ashie can see his ... friend." Mom winked at me as she said it.

I tried not to cringe.

Then, she folded her other hand over where she grasped Caz and gazed up at him with a dopey, dreamy expression.

"Mom, don't you recognize Caz? He lives like a block away from me and Dad. We've been *pals* since we were ten."

"Really?" She shrugged and giggled. "Well, time really does fly, doesn't it? Obviously, you've changed a lot since then, just like Ashie here. People grow. *Relationships* grow ..." Mom waved her fingers in the air like she'd meant to do air quotes but changed her mind to mimic sparkles.

Caz nodded along, like he thought my mom's embarrassing ramble made sense. He looked at her with this earnest fakery I'd seen him use on teachers. "I actually wanted to ask *you* something … Serena? See, tonight is the championship football game, and I was hoping I could convince you to let me bring Ash home to see it."

God, my mother practically melted when Caz said her name. *Ewwww … Where the hell was Brian when I needed him?*

Also, man … I thought I knew how to do a convincing "good-kid" impression, but Caz put on a *performance.* He did a flawless "aw-shucks" twang, his eyes blinking their long golden lashes. "It's a big game, and it would mean a lot to have Ash there cheering for me."

He totally had my mom in the palm of his hand. She gasped, then sighed with a goofy, dreamy expression. My mother loved love. "*Of course,* Ash can go to your game."

Caz did the sleepy smile that he always tried on me, the one that I would swear he must have practiced in front of a mirror. And, this time he added a wink. "I appreciate this so much. Thank you, Serena."

My mother didn't even notice my gagging face. "Ash, why don't you grab some clothes to spend the night. It's too far to come all the way back up here." She curled her arm through Caz's. "You don't mind if Ash spends the night, right?"

What. The. Hell. My own mom was scheming to get me laid. "I don't need to stay with Caz," I said. My voice sounded shrill, pissed. I sounded like Dad. "I still have keys to the house—I'm not banned from home or anything. At least, not *yet.*"

My mother's megawatt smile dropped into instant sympathy. "Of course not, Ashie. Your dad loves you. You'll always have a home with both of us."

Facing me, she couldn't see Caz's fake smile drop away behind her. The mention of home and parents had brought his real self back to the surface, vicious and disdainful.

It made me nervous that my flighty mother still held on to him.

~

"So ... nice car," I said once we pulled away from Mom's. "What did you have to promise Cassius Senior to score a Corvette?" Caz's dad never even gave his son a Christmas or birthday gift without wrangling something in return.

Caz relaxed the Mr. Popularity grin and posture. He got a twist in his mouth that matched the cynical kid I knew best. "Cassius Senior already got what he wanted—we made it to the championships." The twist turned into a sneer. "And don't get too impressed by the Vette." Caz's stare turned colder. "It came off one of his lots, used. Probably a rebuild of a wreck."

"Hey, it's still better than *no* car. After I took Brian's Toyota without asking, I pretty much screwed myself out of ever getting to drive if I live at my mom's house."

A snort from Caz. "So, what? Your dad is loaded. Tell him to buy you a car."

I supposed that if I told him it would keep me out of the house, my dad might go for it. After all, that was what he wanted. Caz's eyes cut from the road to mine. "He's still really pissed off about the robot, huh?"

I slid down in the seat. Despite coming off Mr. Enzo's used-car lot, the Corvette's interior had that new upholstery smell. "I can't believe he's kicking me out."

"I *wish* my dad would kick me out."

Both of us sighed. Our dads, man, they just made life so rough. But, the two of us bitching about it? In a way, that felt like old times. Caz kind of scared me sometimes, but he also understood my life. In some ways, Caz got me better than Pilar ever would.

~

*N*either Carly's faded yellow Dart nor Dad's dark blue Mercedes sat in front of the house, which was dark and empty. Caz let the noisy sports car idle in the drive like he expected me to ask him inside.

I shook my head. "Not happening. If Dad comes home, I'll be screwed." Even the slightest chance that my father might change his mind about the move to Estes would keep me in check. I'd act the part of the perfect son, prove to him that I could follow his rules. "I can't do anything out of line right now."

Caz understood that scenario—a strict dad with demanding rigid rules—better than he could understand my real situation. For my Dad, a perfect son was never inconvenient, never had friends over, never expected him to talk to school counselors. Basically, my dad's version of a perfect son didn't require him to be a parent. The off chance that Dad would come home and see that I'd let Caz back into the house? That would pretty much guarantee my upcoming move to Estes Park remained permanent.

"Yeah. Okay." Caz let his head fall back against the headrest, turned his face toward me. "But, I really do expect you at my game tonight. We're friends again, aren't we?"

"Yes." It came out so earnest and relieved that it embarrassed me. I'd only ever had two friends, Caz and Pilar. I wouldn't give up on him easily.

Caz's voice got lower and teasing. "Just friends?"

I swallowed. *That's what you want, Ash.* I never should have given in when Caz first wanted to fool around. Truth be told, I'd already felt him slipping away from our trio. He'd started taking football more seriously, getting closer to the guys on the team. He'd started dating, going to parties that neither Pilar nor I would ever get invited to. I blamed our horny teenage hormones, but I'd crossed that line for a lot of reasons. But, it was time to cross back. "Yeah." My voice came out firmer than I thought it would. "*Just* friends."

That same slow and knowing smile I'd watched him give my mom. "For now," Caz added. He ducked his head down toward me, stopped just before our lips made contact. *What the hell?*

"Knock it off, Caz. I'm serious." He acted as if hitting all the right buttons, in the right order, could make me fall back into our secret make-out sessions. He didn't even ask.

When I pushed him back, Caz laughed it off like a joke. "Lighten up, man." He gave a slight "cool guy" shrug, like he didn't really care that much, like he hadn't driven two hours to Estes Park and back again just to pick me up. "Hey, you should tell Pilar to come, too. I get that she hates me right now, but you can smooth that out—right Ash? Save me a few hundred lectures on all the bad societal shit that I represent."

Familiar ground between us, going back to childhood, our shared fear of Pilar's wrath. I shoved him harder, but more playfully. "No. No, thanks. You can try that on your own," I told him. Even though we both knew that I would do it, sit through a winding lecture from Pilar on social hierarchies in high schools, the connections between football and bullying, how Caz—in particular—was a traitorous jerk. I'd pretty much made it obvious that I would put up with anything if it helped mend our fractured friendship.

"Meet me outside the locker room after," Caz said.

Waiting around for the players to walk out, just like a fan. *Embarrassing.* "Yeah. Okay," I answered.

he moment I stepped through my front door, my phone lit up. I decided to read it later. Because right then, I needed junk food. I jogged into the kitchen, started opening cupboards. "Barbecue potato chips, *yes*." God, they tasted amazing after three days of Mom's cooking. I cracked open a can of Mountain Dew to go with my chips before opening the text. It showed a double column of numbers with mostly seventy-five and sixty-five in the second column. "What is this?"

Another followed it.

> Cassius Enzo and Asher Bell exceeded the speed limit for a combined 74 minutes of travel.

> Are you tracking my phone? Stop it. Remember what I told you about not entering my art studio? PRIVACY

> Cassius Enzo represents a threat to Asher Bell's safety.

> No he doesn't. Going over the speed limit isn't that serious. People do it all the time.

> You asked if I experience jealousy. Describe the emotion of jealousy.

> What???

I'd joked with him about being jealous of Mom's terrible dinner … is that what he meant? But why ask now?

Because of Caz.

I stared at the phone in my hand. Nerves bubbled in my chest as I remembered Ian watching as Caz kissed me against the front door. *But, Ian had asked a lot of questions about Pilar at one time too …*

Is this jealousy?

A photo popped up on my phone—the ink on rag paper self-portrait. Me, fists clenched, angry. Ian, creeping into the window behind me, sucking up all the light in the room into his exaggerated claws, and barbs, and points of his head.

Okay, that made more sense. Yeah. That was me, jealous of Ian.

But, looking at it now, I realized those same feelings no longer seethed inside of me. When I made that ink drawing, the memory of Dad patting Ian on the head had gotten stuck in my brain on a loop. *When had it stopped?*

Maybe when Dad called Ian a piece of military equipment, a *thing*. Or when he confided in my mom that he thought I'd gotten too attached, had deluded myself into thinking of his robot as a person.

Dad gave Ian all these abilities, "better than a human." He'd treated him like another son, rooted for him and not me. And then just cut him off. *Like me ...*

Okay yes. I used to be jealous of you.

I thought Dad liked you more than me. And I wanted him to pay attention to me instead of you. So yeah. Jealous.

Describe feeling.

It felt like ...

Okay, I needed to find a way with words, something that Ian could understand ...

Burning. Jealousy feels like heat and pain. Something burning inside of you.

And this burning sensation is an emotion.

191

Jealousy.

> But, then I realized that Dad sent us both away. Like neither of us is the favorite—he only cares about what's happening in his head. Do you know what I mean?

We'd both gotten kicked out and rejected, and I could have definitely blamed Ian for that. But we'd also, sort of, become allies.

Ian had framed me for his processor crash, but he also tried to exonerate me.

And he'd lied to me, pretended to be Dad over text, but he also kept me company, checked in on me.

I didn't resent him the way I had before. I sent him another text.

> You and I are friends now.

We are friends?

Déjà vu—Except, when Caz asked if we were friends, he'd made it feel like a test. He'd even tried out that seductive voice, leaned in a little, to see if I would take the bait. *But, that was how everything got screwed up between us.* If I wanted our friendship trio back then I couldn't hook up with Caz on the side. And I really did want our trio back. A lot.

I got so lost in my thoughts that I forgot to answer Ian until I'd changed clothes, my flannel-lined jeans, a second pair of socks, a thick henley under my t-shirt. The weather forecast promised freezing cold temperatures and snow flurries. In the video, the sportscaster clapped his hands together. *"Football weather!"* he said.

I swiped away the video, and my phone buzzed again. Another text from Ian.

Asher Bell is my friend.

CHAPTER 29

*P*ilar threw herself across my bed. "I can't believe you're making me go to one of these stupid games." She wore a long faux-fur purple coat over Doc Martens and black denim. Melting snow glistened on her hair and dampened my comforter. "Don't expect me to cheer for them. I hate the football players."

"Have some school spirit, Pilar." I layered my leather jacket over my hoodie, contemplating a knit hat. Fat, flakey snow had started coming down. And we'd probably get dumped on for the entire game.

"Puh-lease. You just want to see Caz, don't you?" She made a loud gagging sound and sat back up.

"He misses us … and I miss the three of us being friends. Don't you want everything to go back to how it was before high school?"

Pilar shrugged, pretended a sudden interest in fluffing her hair in my mirror, but I could see the tense line of her back and neck. "That's a lot of wishful thinking, Ash." She dropped the nonchalant act and met my eyes. "Too much has happened—"

"No, it hasn't. Not too much. And, it's all water under

the bridge now." This time, I had to look away, so I could avoid the pity radiating from her. "Come on. Let's just go."

~

Snow came down steadily for the entire game, only a frigid wind kept the field playable, sweeping it clear with each icy gust. Pilar and I cowered under a blanket, too cold to cheer or pay much attention to the game. Caz didn't play well, no one on our team did. We lost the championship by twenty-seven points. I felt bad for Caz but relieved when it ended. Pilar, too.

"Thank God, that's over," she griped to me. We'd found a spot in the dank stadium tunnel leading to the locker room, freezing cold but wind-free and covered. Although, Pilar seemed mighty toasty in that thick purple coat. It had deep pockets and a hood that her thick, dark hair spilled out from. "We should have spent the whole game here," she said. "It would have been warmer and less depressing."

Some of the other kids near us grumbled in agreement with Pilar. A little crowd of waiting students had gathered to console the players as they filtered down off the field.

I rubbed my hands together, blew on them. For the five millionth time, I wished I'd worn that knit hat and gloves, even if they did make me look like a dork. "For real. I don't know a thing about football, but I could tell we got massacred out there."

Looking up, I caught sight of Mr. Enzo marching down the tunnel. I yanked Pilar back into the crowd. Not like her giant purple fur coat could blend in or anything, but it could hide me. I didn't want another run-in with Caz's dad.

Red-faced and nostrils flaring with each heavy breath, Mr. Enzo muscled his way up to the locker room doors. He stood in front of them, blocking the way, and stared down the tunnel for Caz.

And, *man*, could I smell the bourbon wafting off him. Pissed off and drunk, he would make Caz go through him to get to the locker room. In the tunnel, the conversation had died, and we all kept shooting each other these quick, nervous glances.

As soon as Caz appeared, everyone in the tunnel braced. Caz stopped dead in his tracks, he had his helmet under one arm, and his face looked gray with cold or disappointment. Maybe fear. "Get out of the way, Dad."

No one else said anything. The other players paused around Caz, like they didn't want to get between his father and him. But, both Dante and Garrett turned and sprinted back up to the field, looking for their coach. It made me wonder what Mr. Enzo had done in the past, how he'd humiliated or threatened Caz without a care about who saw him do it. Cassius Senior leaned back against the metal doors to the lockers, glared at his son like a challenge.

Beside me, Pilar stiffened. She waved a hand in front of her face. "Do you smell that? Hot Sale Cassius must have been hitting the liquor all night."

Mr. Enzo ran these super embarrassing local television ads inviting everyone down to talk to "Hot Sale Cassius" for a discount car. When Caz first moved to our school district, anyone who called him "Hot Sale" got punched, but the new-and-improved, popular Caz just laughed it off.

Mr. Enzo swung around to glare at Pilar, while the little crowd of waiting kids laughed. I pulled my hoodie down lower to cover my face. Caz's dad catching sight of me would just make everything worse.

The laughter gave the football coach time to jog up and work his bulky chest between Caz and his father. "Come on, Cassius—let the kid take a shower, and then you can bring him home."

Cassius Senior waved an arm around in one of those exaggerated theatrical moves he made in his Hot Sale ads.

"He can take himself home. I'm not waiting around for that loser." Mr. Enzo spat at Caz's feet. "Loser," he repeated and pointed in Caz's face.

Everyone looked away or down, all of us flush with vicarious embarrassment and shame. *How could he say that about his own son?* How could he do this to Caz? My hands made fists inside the stiff pockets of my leather jacket.

～

*A*fter that, Pilar stopped complaining about both the game and the cold. She waited silently beside me for Caz to emerge from the metal doors. The other players had all left, melting into the night with their friends. Dante, Garrett, and Cooper came out together, the game forgotten as they laughed over some joke. "Good one!" Cooper and Dante high-fived. I guess their parents didn't take a losing game personally like Mr. Enzo did.

At last, Caz shouldered his way through the locker room doors. His head down, hiding his expression. "Let's get wasted," he said. He thrust his car keys toward me. "Don't bring me home until I'm black-out drunk."

I snatched the keys with their little golden football helmet keychain. "Got it."

We passed a vodka bottle back and forth, all three of us crammed in the front seats of the Almas minivan. Pilar behind the wheel and me wedged beside Caz in the passenger. At first, the cheap vodka tasted metallic and burned my throat, but after a few pulls, it went down like water. Still, I shook my head when the bottle next came to me. "You can have it," I told Caz.

None of us talked about the game and definitely not about what happened after it. Pilar lit a one-hitter, and the cab filled with smoke. "I can't believe your Dad's making you move to Estes, Ash. School's going to suck without you."

Caz swiped vodka off his mouth. His eyes and mouth had gone droopy with alcohol. "Fuck all parents. I hate them."

"They aren't all bad," Pilar said. But, Caz and I shared a glance.

"You mean *yours* aren't," I told her.

But, I couldn't say I totally hated my own parents either. I mean … I disliked a lot about each of them. My dad's obsession with his work. My mom's infatuation with her own self-growth. But, maybe that self-absorption was easier to deal with than the way Mr. Enzo tried to live through Caz. And they'd never hit me. They'd never called me a loser or spit at my feet.

Even though the three of us didn't talk about what happened outside the locker room, I knew we were all still thinking about it, replaying Cassius Senior's red-faced sneer. His bellowing voice calling his son a loser.

Caz took another long drink from the bottle. "I fucking hate them," he said again.

CHAPTER 30

*L*ike he requested, I brought Caz back to his house drunk, about to pass out. Watched him get safely inside, and then I cut through the Farro's side yard to my own home.

Dad had already gone to bed. I don't know if he even realized I'd come back from Thanksgiving break. Maybe Mom called him.

After a week in Estes, the loneliness I usually felt coming home to a dark and empty house had morphed into a peaceful calm. I shed my leather jacket and hoodie, my shoes, and flopped back on my bed.

The night hadn't ended the way I'd wanted. My unstoppable trio was back together, but not the same. I didn't think Pilar would ever fully trust Caz again, and Caz only seemed to tolerate her. Our lives had divided with our different interests, our separate friend groups. *What did you expect, Ash?* We weren't little kids anymore.

Something scratched outside my window, the sound of metal cutting across glass. I jolted up. A mechanical claw hung down over my window, sharp pointed tines crept along the sill and levered it open a crack.

"Ian?"

"Yes."

I dashed forward. "Are you on the roof? What are you doing here?" I got my fingers in beside his claw, and we hefted the window together.

"Correct, the roof." His triangular head appeared upside down, eyes glowing. "I am coming inside." Three of his clawed arms spread over my wall and his head, and the upper segment of his body glided through the open space of the window. Then the lower body segment stuck in place.

I had a good-sized window, but Ian was huge. "Will you even fit? It doesn't look like you'll fit."

"I will fit." Ian backed up and slithered the fourth-clawed arm through the window to brace against the inside wall. A cracking sound, and his full body popped into the room. Four long metal legs crawled behind, a lot like they had in my ink drawing and totally creepy looking. A giant mechanical spider wriggling from the wall to the floor.

It took him another moment to reconfigure himself to stand upright. We both examined the window frame together. It had a small fracture, but it closed behind him just fine. Then, it was just the two of us staring at each other. Ian bobbed up and down, claws closing and opening like nervous energy.

"So ..." I said. "Does Dad know that you can—?" *leave the lab in Colorado Springs.* I answered myself before I'd even finished asking the question, "No, of course he doesn't." My mouth dropped open and closed. Shit. This was serious. Ian could get my dad in trouble. "Won't they notice that you're gone?"

"No."

"No? Meaning ..." Ian didn't fill in that blank for me. "Did you do something to their surveillance system?"

"Correct."

"Okay ... Well ..."

And it kind of hit me then, *I'm glad to see him*. I mean, I'd just had all those gloomy thoughts about how my childhood friendships had changed—maybe beyond repair. But I'd forgotten Ian.

In the basement, he'd said he'd kept his earliest files of the two of us, our childhoods, I guess. Me, a little kid. Him, a clunky prototype. Our friendship had changed, too, of course. But, in a good way, and I actually liked Ian again. "You know what? It's good to see you." I smiled.

Ian did his puzzled-dog head tilt. "Seeing you is also good. Asher ... Ash."

I scratched at my hair, flipped it out of my eyes. "Man, I just had the weirdest night," I told him. Which was kind of hilarious—that the weird part had happened before an eight-foot robot-soldier broke into my bedroom window. But, I'd grown up with the AI, and he'd always been a part of my normal. "Did you come here for any special reason, to get something?"

"Not to get something."

"Sooo ... Just to visit then?"

He cupped one of his claws on my head, barely any pressure. "Yes. Visit Asher Bell."

Warmth pulsed through my chest and settled in my stomach. I didn't realize I was grinning like a crazy person until one of Ian's talons tapped against my cheek. "Okay, cool. Let's hang out."

"Yes."

Another moment of just staring. "We could ... watch a movie or something? We've never done that before, and I'm not sure if you—" I stopped myself from rambling, took a breath. I missed when I could go into the basement and talk to him, even the times he acted kind of like a dick to me. But if we didn't have my father's scenario games and tests to lord over each other, to talk shit about ... then what could we do? "I dunno … Would you even *want* to watch a movie?"

"Yes." A panel slid open on Ian's upper body, and the projector light appeared, the same one he'd used to show me the video record of Dad's in vitro procedure creating me, creating Daniel. *And, Dad's video journal entry, where he detailed all the ways I'd disappointed him.*

"Oh … I forgot you could do that." I'm not sure what my face looked like or how Ian's software interpreted it, but the projection light suddenly shut off, and Ian thudded back a step.

"Used for mission playback and review," he said.

Forget about Dad, for now, I told myself. *Ian's here. He sneaked out of the NAA just to see you.* I forced a smile back. "Makes sense. Can you hack a streaming service or—?"

The projection light popped back on. "Yes."

Because I didn't trust Ian's weight on my bed, the two of us settled on my floor. "I like anime or cartoons, but I can watch anything." I grabbed a pillow from my bed—and when I turned back, Ian had an old *Justice League* cartoon projected on the far wall. "Ah, Batman … a classic."

I crammed the pillow behind my head and slumped against the wall beside him. I'd forgotten how much I liked those old cartoons. Kind of corny, especially the dialogue, but they had good stories. Also, Ian had some top-level projection skills. It almost looked like holograms instead of outdated animation. "I like the art in these old cartoons. It's simple, like almost anyone could draw the characters if they practiced. It's inspiring, you know? You don't need software or a computer science degree …"

Ian let me ramble. He sometimes repeated words I said, not like questions, but like he just wanted to mull them over. "Simple," he repeated "Inspiring."

"Yeah." A yawn cracked my jaw.

At one point, Ian paused the cartoon at the spot where

Batman stands on the ledge of a high-rise, looking over the city, black cape rippling in the night wind.

"Is that how you feel standing on the roof of the house?" My words came out slow and sticky. I'd ended up spread out on my side, my pillow on top of one of Ian's bulky legs, my cheek pressed into the pillow. "Do you pretend to be Batman standing over the city?"

"Sometimes." Ian's voice rumbled quieter than usual.

I pictured Ian in a flowing cape and laughed, so sleepy now that I felt drunk again. "It would take some convincing for people to accept a four-legged robot version of Batman." My words slurred a little.

"No. I would be human Batman. I would protect Asher Bell, but I would feel and understand the world like a human." He held out a claw, opened and closed it. "I would feel. I would have emotion. I would experience the choices."

"Infinite choices ..." Another yawn. "Like a human ..."
What was I saying?

"Yes." Then, he began to emit a vibrating sound, white noise that made my eyelids heavier. I remembered that sound from the nights I crept down into the basement with my comforter. "You used to do this when I was little," I whispered. His metal arms had bundled my little body inside the bedding. I'd thought his software interpreted my shaking as cold. "When I got scared, I'd come down to the laboratory with my blanket. You'd make this vibration noise and put me to sleep."

"Yes."

"It's nice." The claw was back on my head, talons combing through my hair, against my scalp. In combination with the vibration sound, that gentle scratching did me in for the night. Sleep rolled over me and dampened all my thoughts.

CHAPTER 31

On Monday morning, Pilar launched into a whole analysis of our night with Caz as we walked to school. She'd had time to get offended about my "not your parents" comment in the minivan. "I just don't appreciate getting othered because I have a functional family dynamic. It was uncool, Ash." She wound the end of a black feather boa around her neck. Actual feathers!

I shifted my eyes and gave her a flat look. "I don't think that's what getting othered means."

"Well, fine." Once inside the school doors, Pilar stomped the snow off her Doc Martins. Between the feathers, the boots, and the black motorcycle jacket, Pilar looked like she belonged on a stage instead of in a school. "But, it's just … I've been your best friend longer than Caz—cumulatively longer—and it sort of hurt my feelings that you acted like I couldn't relate." Pilar bit at her lip. "Okay, so I'm petty and shallow … but it's like you're suddenly okay with him snubbing us for the last two years."

"I'm not *okay* with it. And 'cumulatively,' seriously?" Both of us were smiling, so not in a real argument. Pilar followed me to my locker, then waited as I cranked my combination into the lock.

"Anyway …" I shifted from our joking tone. "It's just … *his Dad.*"

Pilar nodded, now as serious as me. "Yeah. And Caz was like … this lit fuse. Do you know what I mean?" I thought I did. She twisted the end of her black feather boa around one hand. "It's like, Mr. Enzo scares me, but Caz does, too."

"Yeah." Caz sort of scared me, too. I hadn't wanted to acknowledge it before, but it was the truth.

With a gasp, Pilar straightened and slapped a hand against my chest. "Check it out, I think Cooper Johnson is about to get busted."

I spun—real unsubtle—to see Mr. Rodriguez and one of the assistant principals cross the mezzanine with long, purposeful steps. Two uniformed police officers power-walked behind them. All the students readying for first period moved aside to let them pass. Phones appeared.

"Everyone go to class," Rodriguez bellowed. "Now." The class bell punctuated his demand. I'd say about half the kids gawking hurried on to class, the good kids. Not me and Pilar.

She did a snorting laugh. "No thanks, Mr. Principal," Pilar said. "I think I'll stick around and watch."

Cooper had ear pods in, looking down as he dug into his locker, oblivious. Then, Rodriguez reached forward for his locker door and swung it wide.

"There goes Cooper's side business," I said. I didn't hate the guy, but I didn't like him either. And he always hung out with Caz, Dante, and Garrett, so I had that against him, too.

Rodriguez pulled Cooper's fancy designer backpack out of his locker and pointed upward to the security cameras.

"Yikes!" Pilar slapped a hand over her mouth to stifle

her laugh. "Looks like they got Cooper's whole little operation on video."

I smirked at her. "I would feel bad, but Cooper's an asswipe, so I don't."

We watched while the cops pulled baggies of pills and marijuana out of Cooper's locker. "Honestly," Pilar said. "I can't believe he lasted as long as he did." She tried to wrap her arm through mine.

I kept my elbows plastered to my sides, my hands gripping the straps of my hefty backpack so that she couldn't. "What do you mean?"

"I'm *saying* …" Since I didn't let her link arms with me, Pilar decided to press herself against my side. "I can't believe he didn't get busted sooner because of all the cameras." She pointed to a half bubble of glass in the ceiling of the civics hallway. "How stupid do you have to be? I mean, he should have kept everything in his car and made people pick their shit up in the parking lot."

Cameras … I started to notice them like I hadn't before. All the hallways, but not the classrooms. The mezzanine, the gym, the cafeteria—where they held study hall.

And where I wrote my Napoleon rough draft.

I gave up trying to break away from Pilar's clingy hands and let her lead me into World History while I dug out my phone.

> Cameras! You watched me write the rough draft in study hall.

Correct

> You're turning into quite the stalker, my friend. Tracking my phone, creeping on the school CCTV. Bored much?

Yes

"Okay, who is that?" Pilar had her fingertips on the edge of my phone, tried to tip it back to read.

"Just Carly," I lied, thumbing it off. "I'm hoping she'll convince Dad to let me stay. What do you think?"

Pilar slid into her seat behind mine. She tapped her chin with a shimmery black painted fingernail. "That might work … maybe."

Good, I'd distracted her. I let Pilar brainstorm a bunch of plans to change Dad's mind about moving me to Estes Park. They all sucked. "Join the tennis team, Pilar? Seriously?"

"It's genius—there isn't a tennis team at Estes High School."

"I don't play tennis."

"Gymnastics?"

Only half my attention stayed on Pilar's increasingly terrible ideas to keep me in town. Ian was bored? Did he … could he … experience boredom?

Dad had given him the ability to think about possibilities, consider them like a human, and then North American Automation kept him locked up in a lab. My chest tightened in sympathy. My father and the NAA confined Ian like a prisoner. *It's not fair.* Then, a vicious surge of satisfaction, *but Ian figured out how to escape.*

Caz jostled me as he sat down at our table, his face clouded as a thunderstorm, a dark bruise on his jaw that hadn't been there after the football game.

Pilar still leaned over her table, one hand on the back of my chair, head against my shoulder. She flicked a dark nail toward Caz's face, toward the purpling edge of his jaw. "What happened?"

His dad. Caz didn't even need to say anything, and Pilar and I could still feel his answer.

He'd come home stumbling drunk, easy prey for a bully like Mr. Enzo. "Nothing happened," Caz said. "Just my dad's an asshole." He covered Pilar's face with one palm and pushed her back from between us. She laughed, but Caz's eyes flicked at me, hooded and angry. "Where have you been?"

"Been?"

"I texted you this weekend," Caz muttered, his voice gravely. "Guess you had better things to do."

"I didn't get any—"

Caz sneered at me. "You blew me off, man. Don't make up some bullshit lie about not getting them."

"But—I didn't." I pulled out my phone and thumbed over to Caz's name. "Look." I shook the phone in his face, but he just batted it down.

"You must really think I'm a dumb jock now." He shook his head and turned away just as the bell rang for the start of class.

"Caz …" I stared, uncomprehending, at my blank phone screen. "I swear. I didn't ignore you. My phone must have …" *Must have* … Then, it hit me—*Ian* had blocked Caz's texts. "Damn it!"

I guess I didn't mind Ian watching me through the school cameras, not when Dad kept him locked up in a military lab. But, this was different. It was too far. Not that I could tell Caz any of my suspicions. "It's my dad," I said. "He must have done something to my phone."

Not totally implausible—whatever Ian had done to block Caz's texts, my tech genius dad would also have no problem accomplishing. He just wouldn't bother. But Caz would believe this excuse, that I had a controlling manipulative father like his own.

He deflated a little from his hurt and anger. And after class, he grabbed my wrist and hauled me back down into the seat beside him.

He spoke right into my ear, a secret from Pilar. "Championships ended, so no more football practice. And my parents won't be home until late. You should come over today."

"With Pilar?" I asked.

Caz's lip curled. "Can't we do anything without her?" His grip on my wrist tightened. "You said the two of us could be friends again, but you keep bringing Pilar like you don't like just me anymore."

"I want all *three* of us to be friends. Like before."

"When we were kids, you mean? Come on ..." He masked the sneer on his face with his usual indifference. "Grow up, Ash."

Outside the classroom, Harper waited in the hallway for him, and he split from Pilar and me to walk with her. No goodbye. No backward glance. Not like old times at all. Had the three of us changed that much?

Pilar made a humming sound as she watched Caz disappear around the corner. "He's not right in the head. You feel this, too, right?"

"I guess?"

"What was that about right after class? Did you scratch the Corvette's paint or something when you took him home? You said you were okay to drive." Pilar tried to hook her arm through mine again, the way Harper had done to Caz. I sidestepped further away before she could. "It was nothing."

I pulled my phone out of my back pocket.

> Did Caz text me this weekend? Did you block it?

> I'm serious Ian—I know you're bored or trying to protect me, but stay out of my phone!

Cassius Enzo represents a threat to Asher Bell.

209

So Ian had blocked it. That was an admission, right?

It's none of your business, Ian.

CHAPTER 32

When I asked Carly if I could borrow her Dodge Dart, she didn't give me a big lecture about not having my license yet. She just set down the bucket of cleaning supplies to unhook her keyring from the chain holding up her jeans. "Everything okay, lil dude? Where are you going?"

"I'm going to the Springs." I wanted to talk to Ian face to face because it was too easy for the AI to shut me down over text. He and I needed to have a discussion about boundaries.

Carly's pierced eyebrow shot up. "You're going to the NAA ... *to see your dad?*" It would have made more sense for me to want the car so that I could drive somewhere to *avoid* my father. I'd done that before, but I'd never willingly followed him to North American Automation.

"It's kind of complicated."

"I'll bet." Carly tossed the ring of keys at me. She might act like my "annoying older sister" most of the time, but it readily morphed into "sibling ally" when I needed her. She fired a finger gun my way. "Replace whatever gas you use."

I had no idea what to do at a filling station, had never

pumped gas into a car before. "For sure, full tank." I shot a finger gun of my own back at her and turned away in case she could read that lie off my face.

Driving Carly's antique Dodge Dart didn't take any more skill than Brian's crappy Toyota. Something about getting behind the wheel of a car that had suffered some abuse, a long life of scratches, dents, and repairs relaxed me. Not like the nervous pit in my stomach while I drove Caz's brand-new Corvette. Or the few times when Dad let me practice my driving in his pristine Mercedes. I'd double-checked every mirror, every control, every sign on the road. Kind of hilarious actually. Dad cared a lot less about the Mercedes than Carly did about her piss-yellow Dodge Dart.

North American Automation Corporation occupied a sprawling building set back on a scrubby acre of land. No numbered address, no street sign for the turn-off, and the complex itself was purposely designed to look nondescript, to make it unworthy of a second glance from cars speeding by on I-25.

Except for the double row of chain link fencing. The cameras. The guard booth. Once I left the exit, turned onto the drive, armed security stepped out to block my way.

I leaned forward, for once I was grateful that my father and I looked so alike. "I'm Asher Bell, Fredric Bell's son. I'm here to see my dad." The guard gave me this hard look, his hand near the gun holster. I guess it made sense that security wouldn't just accept that and let me through … But, man, this guy looked like he genuinely wanted to shoot up the car. "I'm just here to see my dad," I said again.

The guard's mouth pinched. "Guests need to be fully registered before entering the facility grounds."

No clue what "fully registered" entailed, I just shrugged. Even if he had actually invited me to come, I knew my father wouldn't have bothered with some registration process.

The guard must have known it, too. His nostrils flared, and his mouth flattened. My dad notoriously ignored any rules he deemed beneath him. But, he was also the entire reason the NAA existed. "Wait here, and I'll contact him."

"Thanks." I tried to sound genuinely grateful and not like a smart-ass kid. The guard kept his eyes on me as he got permission to let me through. "Someone will let you in," he said and waved me forward.

At the building's front doors, I had to wait around again for an escort. The entrance was creepily nondescript. No signs. No intercom to buzz. The only thing giving away the building's importance was the three steel bolts visibly latching the door to the wall, as if the whole place could lock down like a vault.

A camera followed my movements, tracking my pacing, adjusting when I stuffed my hands in my pockets. Finally, the bolts slid aside, and a soldier waited for me inside a stark lobby area. The soldier looked like another kid, just a little older than me but blank-faced with close-clipped hair. He wore dark blue pressed pants, a white shirt with soldier lapels. *Air Force Academy.*

"Follow me." He spoke to a spot just over my head, impatient, rude. Then, the cadet turned and strode away without a backward glance. *Asshole.*

"Yeah, sure." I hunched my shoulders and followed behind him.

What was this guy's problem? He walked fast, like he wanted to lose me in the long featureless hallways. Corrugated metal walls. Smooth cement-floors. Industrial metal garage doors. We stopped at one of them, and a camera over our heads made a whining noise. "Look up." He'd ordered me without realizing I had already tipped my chin back.

"Yeah, dude, I know about facial recognition." Getting

barked at by Kid-Soldier had turned me salty. The metal door cranked up into the ceiling.

Dad's lab at NAA looked more like a warehouse than the spotless white room in our basement. The vast space held an amalgamation of components of my father's work all gathered together. Long counters with microscopes, glass tubes, and dishes. Deep racks of metalwork, robot parts, and blueprints. A line of inert military AI stood wired into place. Six of them, their bodies and limbs as stiff as mannequins. Their triangle heads and upper body segments drooped forward, unactivated.

My dad appeared in a wide open doorway to the right. He had on safety goggles instead of his black frame glasses, and bulky black earmuffs dangled from one hand. "Cadet Rodgers, thank you for collecting my son."

I turned to gawk at Kid-Soldier and suddenly noticed the bar of ribbons pinned to his chest. "Rodgers ... Ty Rodgers?" All those little colorful bands represented achievements and honors. The realization came with a wave of bitterness. This was him, *the perfect donor.*

Beside me, Ty Rodgers jolted but quickly stifled himself back to professional blank-faced indifference. "Should I detain him here, Dr. Bell? Or would you like me to outfit him for the training room?"

"*Detain* me?" I crossed my arms over my chest. "Not unless you want to get kicked in the balls, Kid-Soldier." My lip curled up at my asshole escort. I mean, if he really wanted to *detain me*, he probably could. Ty Rodgers had the same build as Caz, even taller. But, I'd had a long while to work up some *animosity* for the guy. Know what I mean?

Ty Rodgers ignored me. Although, his ears had turned bright red.

"What are you doing here, Asher?" Dad's eyes scanned me as if he expected to find blood or a broken bone. We'd hardly seen each other for over a week. If we'd been a normal dad and son, I could say something corny like, "I missed you." But, if we'd been a normal dad and son, he wouldn't be giving me this suspicious scrutiny. My brain shuffled through reasons for my appearance that wouldn't get me thrown back out to the parking lot. *Oh, of course* ... "I just wanted to see your new lab," I said. "What's the setup here? What are you working on?" I looked around, as if I had a real interest in ... that metal thing over there. Or the ... that sticky glob floating in a tank.

Worked like a charm, and my father's suspicion melted away. Without fail, he could always be distracted into talking about his projects, his experiments, his research. "The lab isn't new as much as *expanded*," he said, his smile toothy and sardonic. He'd used the forced move from our basement to make all kinds of extravagant demands of the NAA. The corporation heads had already invested too much in Dad, they couldn't deny any of his requests. "The really interesting part is this way." Dad nodded over his shoulder. "Come have a look," he said.

The connecting garage doorway led to another warehouse. Not another lab, though. Walking into this space was like walking into another world. A literal hellscape with burnt cinder block shelters, rusted car shells, wooden house frames with broken glass in the window frames. Bullet-pocked cement. A shallow pool of water lined with shale and sand. Dangling ropes and chains. A jagged rock wall. My father held out his arms, like he welcomed me to a paradise instead of the setting of a war-torn apocalypse. "My new training room," Dad announced.

I spotted Ian near the top of the rough climbing wall, claws dug into the rock. A heavy black gun curled under one cabled arm. His head swiveled as we entered, and he let go of the wall. Plunging straight down, at least thirty feet, Ian landed with a clatter on the cement floor. *Better than a human,* just like Dad had said.

Ian's eyes stayed on me as he set the gun against the wall. Then, he dropped forward to the ground like I'd seen him do in our basement—the metal sphinx—and leapt across the wide space, over the water feature, onto a stack of plywood, down from a heap of car tires. He landed just in front of us.

"Asher Bell," he said in his usual monotone, but I wondered if I'd surprised him. Or had he tracked my phone as I drove here? Maybe he tracked me all the time? It kind of felt like he did.

"Hey, Ian. Surprised to see me?"

Ian's head did that confused dog tilt like he didn't understand the question. "You are here."

"Yep, I am definitely here." I peered at all the metal and cinder block structures, the climbing wall, and hanging racks and ropes. Now that I was over the shock of the place, I could appreciate how real it all looked, like the set of a movie. "This is ... kind of cool. It sort of reminds me of our basement playground ... but on steroids. Does it remind you of that?"

Beside me, I could feel Ty Rodgers' attention. Now, *him* ... I had definitely surprised. For sure, my dad never greeted Ian, probably rarely talked to the AI unless he gave it an order. Cadet Rodgers' head flipped between me and Ian like a tennis match. He must not have known that Ian was capable of interacting the way he did with me.

Dad had tuned us all out and had his complete attention on the tablet in his hands. His bony fingers swiped and tapped with super speed at the scrolling text. "Alright, Cadet," my father said to Ty Rodgers. "Let's try the knives again."

Knives?

Ty Rodgers rolled up his left sleeve, flexed, and fisted his hand in the way that Ian sometimes did. *Oh*—I'd forgotten that Dad's research dealt with more than just AI and military robots. I looked a little harder at Ty Rodgers' left arm. The skin looked a little too perfect, no freckles, no pimples, no scars. I leaned into Ian, my voice barely a whisper.

"The arm is a prosthetic?"

"Yes," Ian said, voice at its usual volume, a little louder than normal speaking voice.

To one side of the room was a table set with an array of scary black daggers and little black axes. We all relocated behind it with Ty Rodgers closest to the table.

"Ready?" my father asked.

"Ready," Rodgers said, and he chose one of the black knives. It had a curved blade that ended in a wicked point.

Dad pressed something on his tablet and cardboard targets appeared in the manufactured hellscape. Faceless men with guns pointed toward us. One in the frame of a burned house. Another slid out from behind a piece of tangled metal. Another from the water pool. Behind barrels and pits and towers made of cinder block, the paper figures snuck glimpses at Cadet Rodgers, daring him to skewer them.

He aimed for the sniper in the water obstacle, the farthest away. His black knife tore through the air, fast and straight like an arrow, it impaled the sniper's cardboard head. A second knife shot out at the paper gunman in the house. A third pierced the chest of a figure behind a maze of metal, the knife flying perfectly center through open spaces barely able to fit it—an impossible throw. That arm wasn't a normal prosthetic. Not only did Ty Rodgers have unnatural accuracy, but he also had inhuman speed.

"That's like stuff that you could do," I muttered to Ian. Then, I stepped forward to get a better look, too far forward.

A rope swung out to my right, and my father jumped, like it surprised him. Just as I noticed the person-shaped target dangling at the rope's end, Ty Rodgers high-speed prosthetic had grasped and released one of the little black axes.

Ian moved faster—a claw snagged the projectile from the air and two arms had wrapped around me, pulled me behind his own impenetrable body. "Too close. The trajectory of this weapon presents a threat to Dr. Bell's son, Asher."

Cadet Rodgers flushed and stood at attention, like he readied for a dressing down from my oblivious father. My father's attention wasn't on him, not anymore.

"Ian, release him," Dad snapped. "Asher was perfectly safe."

The metal arms binding me loosened. Then the panel in Ian's chest opened and a red pointer arced through the air to show the little axe's trajectory. It actually did come pretty close. "Eight-point-two centimeters clearance, not accounting for unpredictable movement from Asher Bell. This AI has recorded 72% unprecedented actions in overall movements made by your son.

"Seriously?" I twisted toward Ian, and the arms around me fell away. "That's kind of weird."

Because no one paid attention to him, Ty Rodgers relaxed from his stiff posture. "Dr. Bell?" But, Dad still ignored him.

"Ian," he snapped. "There is no reason to continue tracking my son's reactions, or anything at all about Asher. That's an order."

"Yes, Dr. Bell."

It's like Dad didn't even remember that he'd given his AI the ability to decide for himself what it wanted to track or record. And I was pretty sure that Ian had just lied to my father.

CHAPTER 33

$\mathcal{I}$ wanted so badly to ask if I could touch the fake arm, see if it felt as real as it looked. The synthetic skin I'd seen in the basement lab lay in moist rubbery folds. Those, I had no desire to test for authenticity.

But, Ty Rodgers' arm looked so real … Once we'd left the training room, my father had hooked a bunch of wires to the arm, they pierced the skin every few inches in a way that would be torturous for a regular human appendage. But, the sensory nerves in the prosthetic could be turned off. *Pretty cool.* Ty Rodgers caught me staring, and I quickly looked away.

"I'll just be in …" I poked my thumb back toward the training room and its hellscape obstacle course.

"You can retrieve the knives, return them to the table," Dad said. He didn't even look up from his examination of the arm and its readouts scrolling across an oversized monitor. Cadet Rodgers, with his square superhero chin and square superhero shoulders, didn't look my way either. I noticed that *he* hadn't volunteered to help recover any of the knives he'd thrown. *Jerk.* Back at the Air Force Academy, he probably had a squad of followers who jumped at the chance to do his cleanup duties.

Before I could turn away, I heard my father make a tsking sound. "Of course, these results would be even better if we weren't dealing with a human brain," my father said. "You can't process information, make judgements with the same accuracy capable in the prosthetic. Perhaps if your injuries had included—" Dad managed to stop himself from wishing a brain injury on the promising young Air Force cadet. Even my socially incompetent father must have realized that normal people don't say things like that.

Ty Rodgers didn't seem to mind. Maybe he was used to Dad's obnoxious single-mindedness. His square jaw tightened, and he flexed his hand. "So the arm isn't being used to its full potential?" His eyes bore into his palm as if he could see past the skin to the sensors and wiring underneath.

My father sighed, probably thinking again of Mirror Neurons and biotechnology. And how disappointed he was that Ty Rodger's hadn't lost a chunk of his brain along with his arm. My stomach rolled over, and I pretty much bolted for the training room. Sometimes, Dad's work gave me the creeps. What he did with the prosthetics, giving people back what they had lost, that was *good*. But, the reasons behind his innovations were … not so good. Or not purely good. Like, just now, when he'd eyed the back of Ty Rodgers' skull with the blatant desire to carve it up.

Dad had left Ian to work again on scaling the rock wall. He'd ordered the robot to compile data on limb power, anchoring capabilities, wide vision tracking. But, it looked like Ian had decided to do my job instead, his metal claws grasped all the knives and throwing axes. He dumped them noisily back onto the table.

"Asher Bell." It felt like a question.

"Um …" From the workroom, I could hear Ty Rodgers

bidding Dad goodbye. I hadn't really come to see the lab, but to see Ian. An impulsive and dumb decision, because saying anything about him tracking me, deleting my texts, couldn't be said in front of my father.

I was mad, but not mad enough to rat him out. I should have just asked him over text to sneak out again. "Um …" I said again.

From the entry room behind me, a loud tri-tone alert chimed, chimed again. My father's voice, "What now? Those idiots can't do the simplest tasks without me—" The tri-tone sounded again. "Asher?" Dad stepped into the wide space separating the two rooms. His eyes stayed on the tablet in his hands. "I have to go to another lab and find something for one of the visiting—" An elaborate shrug, eyeball, groan combo. He often reminded me of Pilar with all his theatrical reactions to normal life. "I'm not going to bother explaining it, but wait there with Ian, and I'll be back."

Ian's camera pupils remained on me, both of us silent and still, wanting my father to leave. The lab's metal garage door cranked open and closed.

"Asher Bell," Ian said again. In that familiar gesture between us, he placed a gentle claw on the top of my head. But, only for a second. Then he turned his back on me and retreated into the obstacle course.

"Ian …" I had to jog to catch up with him. "You know … If you were human, I'd say you wanted to avoid me."

Ian didn't think that comment deserved any kind of answer. We'd stopped by the climbing wall, where Ian had earlier abandoned his gun. "I wonder what the soldiers from the mission might say if they knew their scary war robot didn't want to face the wrath of a scrawny teenage boy?"

"Wrath. Defined as extreme anger." Ian deflected in a very AI fashion. When he picked up the gun, he curled the arm backward to hide the heavy weapon behind his body.

Like he didn't want me seeing it, like being up close with the M4 Carbine might bother me.

Did it bother me?

"Well, I'm not as pissed off *now*," I said. "I've cooled down. But … yeah. You need to stop hacking my phone and erasing my texts."

Ian bounded over to a hanging metal gun rack and fastened it beside a bunch of other identical M4s. He pulled an orange lever, and chains connecting the rack to the ceiling began to crank. As loud and jangling as a passing train, they slowly pulled the large metal gun rack over our heads, up into the warehouse rafters. You know, I think the gun *had* bothered me. Guns, in general, scared me. Simply remembering the video of Ian using the gun scared me.

Ian stepped back toward me. "Cassius Enzo. 5620 Blue Bonnet Street."

"Yep." He knew exactly why I'd come today. "You deleted his texts." I folded my arms over my chest and glared. It surprised me how fast the anger returned. "You can't just … decide someone is a threat and then block him without my permission."

The robot's head tilted, confused dog. "Yes, Asher Bell. I can." He started winding through the obstacle course again, pressing buttons and pulling cords to turn off the water, realign targets and triggers. I guess it made sense he'd want to tidy up. This was Ian's home now. He *lived* in this lab, in this artificial badlands.

I trailed behind him. "No, you *can't*." He tilted his head at me again. "Okay, so technically you can. I mean, you *shouldn't*. I mean … I don't *want* you to." Ian picked up a gravel rake to scrape the loose rocks toward a pit. "Are you even listening to me?"

"Yes, I am listening." Ian stopped raking. "Why?"

"Why—? Because … Because …"

"Why doesn't Asher Bell desire threat assessment and

management? The Intelligent Adaptive Neuron Mirror Military Prototype excels at these functions. Asher Bell is in need of these functions."

"*Because* I didn't ask you to do that— You keep doing things that I don't tell you to do, that I don't *want* you to do."

"You wish to restrict my capabilities." *Had Ian's voice gotten louder?* "Both Dr. Bell and his son seek to restrict Ian's decision-making capabilities."

"Restrict your ..." I took a step back. "Whoa, hang on. Is this about Dad telling you not to track me?" I'd learned to accept my dad's rudeness, his impatience with life outside his work, his certainty that he always knew best. But, I didn't spend all day, every day with him the way Ian did. I didn't have Dad ordering me around, questioning me, reviewing my every action and thought.

Ian's claw opened, and he dropped the metal rake. "Dr. Bell designed this AI to analyze, to synthesize, to judge. Yet he limits my acting on these judgments. I am confined to this lab. I am confined to his orders."

"You're frustrated." *Or the robot version of it.* "Dad gave you those abilities but doesn't let you use them. Doesn't like the way you use them." Classic Dad—the control freak.

"AI does not experience frustration," Ian said.

"You sure about that soldier-bot?" I patted his chest. "Welcome to my world. You want to make your own decisions in life, but the grownups want to hold you back." He had over two feet of height on me, but I tried to reach up and do the hand-on-head move that he always used on me. My fingers tapped against the side of his metal face. "Trust me, when it comes to *this*, uh, function. I'm the expert."

"Frustration is not a function. It is an emotion, and I am not designed for emotion." All four of Ian's legs bent, and he scooped up the gravel rake again.

My hand dropped back to my side. *Why couldn't frustration*

work like a function for him? "Okay, then how about this …" I nudged one of his huge clawed feet with my tennis shoe. "Let's say, frustration isn't a function, that it's more like a *result*. You were designed to think for yourself, but Dad doesn't let you do that. And the repression of your decision-making feature creates a … sort of a *byproduct*. And the byproduct is frustration."

From the other room, the metal garage door began to grind open. Dad had returned from whatever urgent task his military overlords had given him.

I kind of think that Ian forgot about the rake again. The arm holding it just sagged to the ground. With another arm, he reached a claw out to mimic the cheek pat I'd done earlier. His claw curled around my face.

"Is this you admitting that I'm right?" I grinned at him. "I'm right, huh?"

"Asher?" My father's eyes darted between us and then to the cameras watching us from every corner of the room. "Did you touch something when I left?"

Dad finally noticed Ian's claw against my cheek, the rake, the hunched posture of the robot looming over me. "Ian—?" my father's voice drew the word out into a question. He reached into his pocket for his tablet, like he was drawing a gun. "Let go of him, Ian."

The tines of Ian's claw peeled back one by one as I rolled my eyes at my father. "Relax Dad, he's not going to hurt me."

"Asher, I asked you a question. Did you do something to the cameras? Or touch something in the other room?"

"Touch *what?* Me?"

A claw pinched the back of my leg, and I understood at once. *Ian had turned off the cameras, so we could talk.*

That anyone, even Ian, would try to outsmart my father still floored me. *It's impossible. Dad knows everything.* But his robot did it every time he snuck out of this lab, every time he'd snuck out of the one back home. *"Lie,"* that pinch said.

"Oh wait—I did." I shrugged, hoped that would dial down my father's suspicion. "Ian showed me how to close down everything in here, and I might have gone on a button-pushing frenzy." The pinching claw released, and Ian pointed to a panel near the wide doorway behind Dad. "Yeah." I pointed, too. "Especially those buttons. Sorry?"

"I see." But, my father still had a stiffness to him, the cautious and questioning expression when he'd first noticed Ian's claw wrapped around my face. "It's odd that Ian chose to shut down the room. What is the point of that, Ian?"

"Helpful," Ian said.

"Helpful?" My father scoffed. "You're an extremely expensive piece of military technology. Leave all cleaning for the janitorial staff, and remove that directive from current algorithms at once." Dad had that pissy tone in his voice, annoyed. "Go stand with the other robots and turn yourself off."

This time, Ian set the rake down slowly, silently. "Yes, Dr. Bell."

"Jeez, Dad," I said. "That's …" I used to think he liked Ian more than me, but I wasn't so sure anymore. Not now that the AI could make his own decisions, reconfigure his own files, rewrite his own programming. Ian had … grown up.

Like me.

And, I didn't think Dad liked how either of us had turned out.

CHAPTER 34

*D*ad stayed at the NAA the rest of the week. He'd entered one of his manic work phases as he readied Ian for another mission. And even though Carly hung around later than usual in the evenings, I was alone every night. Ian texted, but he couldn't get away either.

> Mobility impossible while upgrading
> hydrostatic pressure system.

Whatever that meant.

On Thursday, Carly'd had enough of my moping attitude, and she dragged me back out the front door as soon as I got home from school. "You're the designated driver tonight, Baby Bell." She slipped into the passenger side of the Dart.

"I'm the what?"

"Tonight, you and Pilar are going to be my roadies." She tossed a chocolate chip muffin in my lap. "Dinner," she said, then squinted her eyes at me. "Listen kiddo, I know we don't always get the parents we deserve, but we still gotta do life." Only Carly could say something like that and not make me want to cringe.

"I'm doing life," I muttered and took a giant bite of the muffin. So, my mouth was full of gooey cake and chocolate just as Pilar got in the backseat. She had skin-tight ripped jeans, more full of holes than denim, and a fishnet turtleneck over a red satin bra. "Wow." I started to choke, and Carly pounded me on the back.

"Just drive, Little Bell."

≈

*T*he Scum Suckers' gig was at a bar called Rusty's Live in a sketchy part of the city. At least, it looked sketchy to my suburban eyes. Carly's bandmates, Lennox and Hiro, met us in the parking lot. "They better actually help set up, Carly," Hiro said. He had all their equipment in the back of his covered truck.

"Dude, they totally will. They're helping right now." Carly pushed us toward the heavy amps and sound equipment. I had a fake ID, so did Pilar, but no one at Rusty's Live even asked our ages. A guy in a bloodstained wife-beater just stamped the back of our hands and grumbled, "No free drinks for the band."

Pilar immediately ordered us boilermakers. A shot of whiskey dropped into a tap beer—I handed over a good tip to help stave off curiosity about how old we were. Also, the likelihood of me keeping that beer, liquor combo down was not good. "Drink," Pilar ordered. "You look stressed."

"I'm stressed because you're forcing me to drink the most puke-inducing alcohol mixture imaginable."

"Don't be a baby." She leaned against the bar, shook her long hair back. Both Hiro and Lennox couldn't take their eyes off her, same with the wife-beater guy and the bartender. As Rusty's Live filled up, Pilar's admirers increased. Real fucking annoying. I mean, no one paid attention to me, which I preferred. But, our spot against the bar filled up with drinks from dudes trying to meet her.

First, we tried to keep pace, then we started passing the extra drinks to Hiro, Lennox, and Carly. Wife-beater guy broke up our little party to remind the band that Rusty's Live paid them to play, not get wasted. Carly wrapped an arm around my neck. "Watch yourself, little Bell. And don't let my girl Pilar out of your sight. Not even to go pee, got it?"

I pounded my chest to release a belch. "Got it." All the neon signs tacked up on the walls started to bleed color into the room. Bodies pressed in all around us. I stripped off my hoodie and tied it around my waist.

Pilar draped an arm around my neck. "Let's get closer to the stage!"

"Okay." I pretty much let Pilar drag me where she wanted. Above us, Hiro and Carly started to tune their guitars, and Lennox nodded over at us. He had a bright smile, straight teeth, long dishwater hair tied up in a bun.

"He likes you." Pilar had to talk right into my ear for me to hear her over the bar noise and tuning guitars.

I'd grabbed a beer bottle to bring with me through the crowd and took a swig. "Who likes me?" So far, the boilermaker stayed in my stomach. Drunken over-confidence had me thinking I could keep going all night like that, and I took another couple swallows from my bottle.

"Lennox likes you. Can't you tell?"

"No." I tried to study Lennox a little closer, but the room began to spin. I set my beer bottle on the lip of the stage.

Hiro and Carly started their opening riff—that same Bad Brains cover she'd forced on Pilar and me during our sleepover. Carly bent toward the microphone. "Yo—we're the Scum Suckers. *Let's party!*" Because of all the alcohol fuzzing my head, they didn't sound too awful. They just needed a new lead singer, or any singer, because Carly shouted all the lyrics, while Hiro and Lennox both lost themselves in their instruments.

Hmmm … Lennox? He's pretty attractive, I guess. But, I only noticed in an abstract sort of way. I never just looked at a guy and thought, "Yeah, I want to do him." I had to know the person first, which kind of presented a problem because I liked to spend most of my time alone. I probably needed to get out of my bubble a little more often. *Like, maybe with this Lennox guy. Give him a chance.*

He'd really gotten into the zone with his drum set, watching his own hands, the drumsticks, as they flew through the beat. It kind of reminded me of how I got late at night in my studio. Everything around me, even my sense of time, would drop away. The brush, the canvas, the vision in my mind became my entire world as I brought them together. Once I moved in with Mom, Brian, and the terror twins, I could kiss those Zenned-out painting sessions goodbye. *Ugh. Forget about it tonight.*

That last beer kept bubbling back up into my throat as Hiro's bass chords vibrated through my skin. "Pilar?" I reached for her, but she'd suddenly turned into Scum Suckers biggest fan, jumping up and down and screaming lyrics along with Carly. Sweat pebbled up on my face, my body, soaked into my t-shirt. "Pil—" Foam and hot liquid filled my mouth, and I doubled over, vomited onto the grimy wooden floor.

"Shit, Ash—" Pilar's thick arms circled my waist, and she tugged me backward. "Don't worry, okay? I'll take care of you."

"I'm … fine …" My mouth had a hard time forming the words, the muscles of my face wouldn't work. Pilar went into full big sister mode like I'd seen her with Julien, Mateo, and Alejandro. A good thin, because a second wave of foam and liquor rose up from my stomach, splashed down between us. I wiped my mouth with the back of my hand. "Are people looking?" Because of the loud band, the crowd, the smokey darkness of the bar, I felt hidden. I hoped that was true.

Then came some missing time … until my eyes blinked open inside the world's smallest and grossest bathroom. My lashes and eyelids felt sticky, my hands and mouth, too. My cheek lay plastered to a yellow-stained toilet seat. "What the —" I winced as I peeled my face free.

"Are you finally awake?" Pilar sat across from me, her phone trilling with music and cat meows from her game.

It took a dry swallow and a painful throat clearing before my voice worked. "Yeah. Where—"

"Employee bathroom." Pilar shut off her game and started typing. "I'm letting Carly know that you're not dead. You missed her first set."

"This is the employee bathroom? There's no sink."

"I know—so gross." The narrow door beside her opened, and she stood up to let in Carly … and Lennox. *Kill me now.* My housekeeper—big sister just pointed and laughed at me, but Lennox held out a bottle of water.

"Here, man." He reached over to unscrew the lid for me. That's how bad I must have looked.

"Thanks, man." I took a sip, narrowed my eyes at Carly. For some reason, my thanking Lennox had made her laugh even harder.

"So Little Bell, *man.* Do you need an Uber or something, *man*? Or can you rally and come back out, *man.*"

Pilar laughed along, but Lennox patted me on the back. "You feeling better?"

Way too many people had crowded into the bathroom, and Lennox's hand on my back made me feel smothered not comforted. "I'm fine, now." I shook my hair out of my face. "I just need to pee … if all of you don't mind."

Carly threw her hands up. "Sure, sure … give the *man*

some privacy." She jammed a cigarette in her mouth. *If she lights up in this piss-reeking tiny room, I'll probably dry heave.* Lennox gave me a half smile … It kind of held tons of meaning—in some way that would take too much effort to decipher. I took a longer swig of the water and struggled to my feet. My phone buzzed with a text from Pilar.

> Meet me back at the stage!

"Sure. Fine." I could count hearing Carly's band play as one of the worst decisions of my life, but *fine*. The guitars started tuning again, and then revving up like an engine into the Scum Suckers second set. How long could I stay in this little bathroom before someone came looking for me? Or until the bar staff had to use it? If I worked at Rusty's Live, I'd go piss outside before I'd use this toilet. My phone vibrated again. "Coming … coming …"

But, the new text hadn't come from Pilar. Ian had sent it.

> Asher Bell's current location is a retail business establishment designated Rusty's Live. This establishment serves alcoholic beverages.
>
> According to CRS 44-3-901, Asher Bell is committing a Class 2 misdemeanor.

"Are you fucking kidding me?" I slammed shut the grimy toilet lid to sit. The last of my queasiness had faded, but my gut still ached. ***"STOP TRACKING ME"*** I typed out.

Then my thumb hesitated over the send button. I remembered Dad ordering Ian to stand inert with the drone robots. I couldn't quit picturing it. *It was a shitty way to treat the AI he'd raised alongside his son, had treated like another child.* I deleted the unsent text and typed out another.

> Dad thinks you turn yourself off at night.
> Why don't you tell him that you're bored?
> Maybe he'll give you more to do.

> This AI is not programmed to experience
> boredom.

I took a deep breath … *God, it fucking stinks in here.* I pulled my t-shirt up over my mouth and nose.

> Tracking me, sneaking out—why do all that
> if you aren't bored?

Three dots appeared, like a human slowly typing out a response. But, Ian didn't need to type. It was probably his way of telling me he'd given my words consideration. When another text didn't appear, I typed one of my own.

> Listen, Ian, if you want to follow what I do,
> that's okay.

> But, I don't want you to block calls or texts
> or attack people you don't like. That's NOT
> okay.

The response was immediate.

> This AI is not programmed to like or dislike.

I laughed out loud. He did *too* like people and things. He liked *winning*. He liked sneaking out. He even liked *me*. He'd told me so himself.

> If you don't like me, then what does it mean
> to be my friend? Don't backtrack now.

Cassius Enzo represents a threat.

> It's not about Caz. It's about whether you respect me and trust my judgment or you don't. You're treating me how Dad treats you —and don't tell me that it doesn't make you angry. Because I know that it does.

The three dots appeared again.

I will unblock the texts.

My phone buzzed, and I thumbed open a long string of messages from Caz.

Thanking me for bringing him home from the football game.

Asking if I wanted to hang out.

Asking where I was, why I didn't answer.

Calling me an asshole for ignoring him.

Calling me stuck up, a loser, a faggot.

I sighed and closed my eyes. "Caz." He didn't mean it. I'd hurt him, and he lashed out because that's what he always did. Since we were kids. And I'd always let it go.

Why was it so much harder to ignore now?

CHAPTER 35

*a*fter the last set, Pilar and I helped the Scum Suckers lug everything back to Hiro's truck. Lennox kept nudging me with his shoulder as we passed each other, smiling at me with that toothy grin. *Okay, that's flirting, right?* Man, I sucked at this. I would have thought he'd lose interest after seeing me face down on a dirty toilet seat.

Once we got everything packed up, Pilar and Hiro went back to collect the Scum Suckers' cash pay. Carly pulled out a cigarette, and Lennox sidled up to me. The guy had some very bright teeth, like whitening-strip commercial-worthy. "You should give me your number," he said.

"Oh … uh …" *So smooth, Ash.* I decided just pulling out my phone and handing it to him would be better than stammering out a cool reply. But I tightened my fingers before he could slip it from my hand. "Hey, you know, I'm only seventeen, right? Pilar and I are still in high school."

He laughed and tossed his hair over one shoulder, the same way Pilar always did. "Yeah I know your age. I'm eighteen and a senior at Regis Jesuit. I just filled in tonight for my older brother."

Behind Lennox, Carly cackled and blew a smoke ring in

the air. "Little Bell thought he had you fooled with his impressive drinking skills." Flipping her off just made her reach over and ruffle my hair. "Like I wouldn't watch out for my lil bro."

"I'm not your little brother." To tell the truth, I kind of liked when Carly said stuff like that. But, I groaned and pushed her away because anything else would be way too uncool.

"Might as well be." She pinched my cheek and grinned like my discomfort made for a delicious post-gig snack.

Lennox took advantage of the moment to slip my phone out of my hand. As he entered his number, the phone pinged with a new text. That, I guess, Lennox went ahead and read. The bright smile dropped away as he handed the phone back. "I'm not trying to get in anyone's way, you know," he said. "If you have a boyfriend ... or a stalker?"

"Huh?" I looked down at the new text.

Hiro Kimura

Lennox Bilby

Carly Henderson

Pilar Almas

2 vehicles. One registered to Emi Kimora, mother of Hiro Kimora, 2nd vehicle registered to Carly Henderson.

Lennox Bilby has also violated CRS 44-3-901, a Class 2 misdemeanor.

Had Ian followed me down here? The air whooshed out of my lungs. *No. No. No.*

Carly had offered Lennox a cigarette, and the two of them leaned against the hood of her Dodge Dart to smoke. I spun around, scrutinizing the parking lot shadows, the dark alley beside the twenty-four-hour gas station, the closed pawn shop across the way.

The back door thumped open as Hiro and Pilar came out. Pilar had a stack of 20s that she fanned herself with despite the frosty cold. But, as the door opened, I noticed a pinpoint of blue light over their heads.

Wait a second ... I did another circle, this time a little slower. *Found you.*

> CCTV at the gas station. Also above the back door of Rusty's Live.

Once you start looking, you see that they're everywhere.

> And the office building near the pawn shop?

Correct.

"What's so funny?" Pilar asked.

"Nothing." I thumbed my phone off, concentrated on Carly as she stomped out her cigarette, patted herself down for her car keys.

"Oh, nothing, riiiiight ..." Pilar tugged a finger in my jeans pocket like she wanted to pull my phone back out of it. "Then, why are you smiling like that? Who texted you?"

"Jeez, no one, and let go."

Once the money got divvied up, everyone parted ways. Lennox told me goodbye, but he seemed less enthusiastic after snooping on Ian's text.

I didn't really care. Like I said, I had to know someone to like him, not just admire his looks ... and teeth. So, I'd probably never text him—something I didn't want to tell Pilar and Carly. No matter how many times I tried to explain my own hesitant sexuality to Pilar, she just assumed I must still be hung up on Caz.

I didn't *feel* hung up on Caz. Actually, I regretted the hell out of ever hooking up with him because of how it had apparently put the nail in the coffin on us ever fully regaining our old friendship. It wasn't hard to see beneath his chain of unhinged texts to me, that he wanted a lot more from me than just hanging out, playing video games, messing around with bike ramps like we'd done as kids. After all, Caz hadn't texted Pilar last weekend.

~

*A*t home, I felt eyes on me as the three of us hugged goodbye on the driveway. That prickly knowledge of someone watching and waiting. It took effort not to squirm, rush both Carly and Pilar off.

Carly elbowed me in the side. "Want me to stay over? I don't mind."

"Nah, I'm just going to bed. It's fine."

Pilar went in for another hug. "You could camp out with my brothers if you wanted. Are you sure you're okay?"

"We've got school tomorrow, so I'll pass."

Carly laid on her horn as she peeled out, and Pilar screeched in laughter. My eyes flicked up to the roof.

Inside the house, all was quiet and dark. I slammed open the window in my bedroom and leaned out. "Ian?"

Three metal arms shot in, curled around me. One scooped up my legs, and the other two snapped me through the window frame, pressed me into the hard double-segmented body. I had to stifle my yelp, swallow back the gasp. Ian and I hung outside my window for a second, then he sprung upward. Spider legs climbing the brick wall so fast that my stomach jolted and dropped, jolted and dropped again.

At the highest point of the roof, Ian set me down, one arm wrapped securely around my waist to keep me in place.

From our vantage point, I could see over the elm trees, their barren knobby branches. Beyond our back fence to where rocky land sloped down toward the main blacktop road leading into our neighborhood. And I could even see past that road, over the wooden privacy fences, and into the backyards of houses in the next neighborhood. "Holy crap," I breathed.

"Look." A beam of light shot out of one of Ian's eyes toward a pine tree on the edge of the Almas' yard. It illuminated a bird's nest.

"Empty," Ian said, voice a purr on the top of my head. "Empty, now."

I turned to look up at him. "Is that why you came up here so often? You watched the baby birds grow up?"

"Yes." Ian's voice always came out in the same metallic monotone, but he added a little mournful whistle at the end.

"Don't be sad. The babies flew away when they grew up," I filled in for him. "But, that's what the parents wanted them to do. Now those baby birds will go make nests and families of their own."

Ian emitted a lighter tone than before, a musical sound that lifted up at the end. This was new, his adding inflection to his words. I liked it. I could understand him better.

Even though the night was clear, it was cold, and my skin turned to gooseflesh because of it.

Ian's metal limbs began to warm. The rest of his four arms rose to circle me with their radiating heat. "Ah, thanks ..." I looked back in the direction of the empty little nest. "You know, in the spring, the parents might come back and lay more eggs. I don't really know what kind of birds they are or what their breeding cycle might be. I could look it up for you ... or probably you could look it up."

"No."

"No? You don't want to look it up?"

"In the spring, I will be permanently on mission … And this AI is not programmed to want."

I frowned up at him. "Why do you do that? Sometimes you say, 'I will, I am,' and then you switch back to 'this AI is not programmed to blah, blah, blah …'"

"Explain blah, blah, blah."

"Cut it out, Ian. You *know* what I'm talking about. And don't tell me that you don't want things. You wanted to stay living here. You wanted to sneak out of the NAA. You wanted to keep me from seeing Caz last weekend."

"Yes." Then, my father's voice played from Ian's speakers. *"… I may have treated Ian as a … kind of pet, but he's a piece of technology. A thing."*

I jolted backward, and a steadying claw spread out against my back. "Dad shouldn't have said that. He didn't mean it the way you think … Well, he did in a way, but he never realizes how people take his words."

"People …" Ian made a humming noise. "But, I am not a person, Asher Bell."

"Well, no. But—"

"Tomorrow, your father and … I … will leave on a new mission."

I blinked against the topic switch. "Okay. That's …" I didn't know what to say. Even if Ian were human, I wouldn't know what to say. *Be careful? Stay safe? I hope you don't have to kill anyone. I hope they don't try to kill you.* "That's …" My thoughts just trailed off again.

"I will bring you back inside. The security deviation will only last another thirty-one minutes, forty seconds before my absence from laboratory space B is noted." He'd swept me up as he spoke, and we plunged off the roof into the cold dark. And then I stood inside my room.

"Ian?" He'd retreated back outside the window faster than I could get my bearings.

"Yes." I couldn't see him, but his voice sounded near.

"Stay safe, okay?"

"Okay, Asher Bell."

CHAPTER 36

"Is that from Lennox again?" Pilar plonked her head on my shoulder, dragged down the hand holding my phone.

After the Scum Suckers gig on Thursday, Carly had the weekend off. Which would have left me alone in the house all weekend if Pilar's family hadn't insisted I stay with them, and we'd all gotten snowed in together on Saturday and Sunday. *Thank God for the Almas family.* The only food in my house was protein shakes and Doritos. By Monday morning, the sky had cleared, and snow plows cleared the streets. What was the point of a big winter storm if it only happened on the weekend?

Pilar clenched my arm between her mittened hands to keep me from secreting the iPhone back into my pocket. "Ohhh another video. I want to see."

"Get off, Pilar. Seriously." I shoved her hard enough that she stumbled into the snow-packed edge of the sidewalk. As she went down, she grabbed my leg, trying to pull me with her. Since elementary school, we'd played this same game on all the snowy morning walks to school—tackling, shoving, tripping each other into every piled drift. Pilar had already knocked me down twice, and my jeans were caked with snow. Her scrabbling mittens couldn't get purchase, and she fell ass-first into a slushy pile.

"Gah! That one soaked through to my underwear." She bit off her red mitten and held out a hand. "Truce. Truce. I give up."

"I still owe you one," I said, but I gave her my hand and hauled her back up. The actual goal of our competition was to get excused from first period to dry out and change. Kind of a standing benefit the office secretaries gave out on bad weather days for the kids who walked. Pilar and I would use the passes to hide out in the art room, drink coffee, and eat PopTarts with Ms. Stanzi.

Pilar flicked snow from her mitten into my face. "But, we made a truce. You can't go back on a truce."

Behind me, a car rumbled to a stop. A yellow Corvette. The passenger window lowered, and Caz leaned over. "You morons." He shouted over the country music blasting from his speakers. "You're still doing that stupid shoving contest when it snows?"

Pilar used her mitten to slap the ice off the back of her legs. "What's it to you?" But, she didn't sound angry.

And Caz hadn't either. He turned down his music and grinned. Their verbal back and forth belonged to the Unstoppable Trio days, before popularity cliques, cheerleader girlfriends, clandestine hookups.

Pilar's cheeks and nose had turned bright red from the cold. "You've gone soft, Enzo." She leaned over to shake snow out of her long hair.

"If by soft you mean smart, then yeah." Caz unlatched the passenger door. "Brush off before you get in, or you'll ruin the leather," he said. He cranked the heat up as we climbed inside.

I stomped to get rid of the snow caking my jeans. And Pilar peeled off her wool peacoat and lay it down to cover the passenger seat. "Noooo ..." Pilar squished into the deep bucket of the Vette's passenger seat, leaving a little sliver for me. "Smart is knowing that we'll get passes out of World History," she said.

I had to sit partly on her lap so that we both fit, but we got the door closed, and Caz peeled out again. "I'll take any excuse I can to get out of reviewing the details of 'economic pressures in pre-World War I Europe.'" I did a pretty good imitation of Mr. Haag's bored drawl.

Caz's bottom lip plumped forward. "I thought we already did World War I? I'm so fucking lost in that class. I got a D on my midterm. Well, Harper did. If I'd written the paper myself, I would have pulled a C at least."

At the mention of Harper, the conversation died down. Harper did not belong to the old Unstoppable Trio days. She'd come with Caz's membership in the football clique. The people who thought of Pilar and me as losers. The people Caz had chosen over us, who he preferred. And I guess that Pilar got a burst of protectiveness. That urge to push back that made her Pilar. "Did Ash tell you he has a new boyfriend?"

My head whipped around, my eyes tried to tell her to stop. But she wouldn't meet them. "It's a guy in Carly's band, and he texted Ash about a million times over the weekend, " Pilar gushed. She was trying way too hard to point out how far I'd moved on from Caz. When she laughed, it sounded so fake that I cringed.

Caz's hands tightened on the steering wheel. His face got a nasty sneer on it. Even if I couldn't make out what exactly he wanted from me, with me, that fight in the showers had ended the fantasy I'd had of our casual make-out sessions developing into a relationship.

It got old sneaking around, especially when the other person won't even admit in private what the two of you are doing. But, it seemed like Caz's ego still wanted me on the hook, panting after him like I had for months. I didn't get why. "Pilaaar …" Caz dragged her name out, no longer joking. "Maybe you should start to mind your own business. You're still the same nosy—"

"He's not my boyfriend, in the first place." I raised an eyebrow at Pilar. This time she looked my way. *Shut up*, I tried to project toward her. "And in the second place, he's not in Carly's band. He was just filling in for his brother that night."

Caz relaxed a little. "What night?" Or maybe he'd sunken back into his cool, uncaring persona. By this time, we'd pulled into the student parking lot, in one of the spots outside the weight room, where all the jocks liked to park.

"This weekend," Pilar said. She kept her tone light and breezy. Everything had felt dicey for a second there, then I guess she'd decided to pretend the tense moment never happened. "Carly got us into a bar where the band was playing."

The Corvette got a lot of attention, and then Pilar and I spilling out of the passenger side got even more. A few of the other football players called out greetings to Caz. They probably wondered why the hell he'd let Pilar and me in his fancy car, driven us to school. Especially after he'd called us losers and accused me of trying to molest him in the showers. All the reminders of the bad blood between us had killed the joking and teasing mood.

I'd expected Caz to act self-conscious, brush off me and Pilar in front of his high school friends. But he got a little pouty, more wounded than embarrassed. "I didn't know Carly was in a band," he said. "Where did she play?"

Pilar hunched her shoulders, as she shrugged back into her pea coat. Around the football players, she became more confrontational, ready to pop off without warning. I mean, I didn't blame her. They acted like jerks toward us. They always had. "Just this really cool bar in the city." Pilar fluffed her hair out from her collar as she said it.

I tipped my head toward Caz. "The bar wasn't cool. Not at all." I wondered if he felt left out. We hadn't even asked him to come. Did he expect us to? The three of us, as friends again, didn't quite seem real. Pilar and I hadn't even thought of him. "You probably wouldn't have wanted to go, but … I guess we should have asked you."

Caz's mouth pursed, and he shook his head. "Just forget it," he said and turned away. Garret and Dante waited for him at the weight room doors. Caz went in with them instead of us.

Pilar and I walked around to the entrance off the band rooms. "Don't let him guilt you like that," Pilar said. "He went to a party with Harper that same night." Inside the building, Pilar pulled her mittens off and stuffed them in her pockets. "Harper posted a bunch of pics from it. Not that I follow her or anything. I just stumbled across them." She frowned. "You know what? I don't think I'm even that wet— are you? We screwed ourselves out of getting passes by taking that ride from Caz."

"No, I'm not that wet either." And I didn't want to hide out all first period so that Pilar could psychoanalyze me. "Let's just go to class," I said.

～

*A*nother thing I wanted to avoid with Pilar, any more prodding on all the videos I'd gotten that weekend. They hadn't come from Lennox. Since Rusty's Live, I'd only gotten one text from him. A trying-to-be-cool, ***"Hey, what's up?"*** that I never responded to.

He wasn't the one steadily texting me, that was Ian. And, now a bunch of videos waited in a little stack for me to open. Which I really needed to do. As soon as I got the courage. Because of the last mission, I knew what they might contain—combat scenes. Ian shooting, fighting, killing. Scenes that still played out in the back of my mind, caused me to shiver when I remembered them, kept me awake the nights I did.

But, you told him not to send any more of those. Did he listen? Would he remember? Just because Ian saved files of us playing pirates as little kids, didn't mean he saved everything I told him.

But, now that Pilar noticed the texts, I could count on her badgering me to see them. And I couldn't exactly tell her that they might contain top-secret military footage of people getting clawed to death. *By the robot I'd sworn wasn't dangerous.* Nope. I needed to delete the whole little stack of videos today.

After lunch, during my free period, I locked myself inside a bathroom stall. *To delete or not?* I opened the first video, hoped it wouldn't be too awful.

Instead of shooting, running, throat crushing, I watched a wild goat hop across a rocky hillside. Ian's camera followed the shaggy goat into the distance until, finally, it disappeared against the brown landscape.

I opened another.

An orange sky at sunset, the yellow sun dipped down into the shadows.

Another—fuzzy purple flowers trembled in a breeze.

Another—the white-scaled face of a snake, its forked tongue darted in and out.

"Huh …" Finally, I texted Ian back.

> These are cool. Sorry it took so long for me to watch them.

> The videos do not contain combat. Asher Bell does not wish to view violence.

Yeah.

He *had* listened … and remembered. Today must be the day for letting down my friends. I should have invited Caz to watch Carly's band. I should have trusted Ian and watched his videos.

Is the mission going okay? You and Dad are fine?

Yes. The mission has concluded. Your father will be home tonight.

Do not tell anyone you are aware of this information.

I'll act surprised.

CHAPTER 37

*B*ut, I didn't act surprised. Because when Dad came home that night, he bypassed saying hello, or asking how I'd gotten along by myself. During a snowstorm. With no food or money.

Instead, he went straight down to the basement lab and didn't even look up when I thumped down behind him, my shoes smacking each step like a judge's gavel.

"Hey, Dad. Welcome home." I laid the sarcasm on pretty thick. Not that he noticed.

My father's long fingers punched at the keyboard on one of the stand-alone desktops. "Asher, come here. I want you to see something."

A loud sigh. More stomping. "See *what?*"

"Here's the footage from Ian's latest mission." Across from us, a video began to play. The type of scene I'd been afraid I'd open in the school bathroom—soldiers charging over a scrubby field as bullets churned the ground around them.

Dad finally looked up. "I'm sure I don't have to explain that this is classified video." He blocked my view of the projection as he turned toward me. From behind his thick glasses, he fixed his serious eyes on me. "Never tell anyone that you've seen it."

Like, who? Who would I tell?

On the video, one of the enemy soldiers tripped, his face pale and panic-stricken as he went down. He was really young—*maybe my age.* The dark shadow of a terrifyingly huge robot loomed over him. An M4 Carbine pointed at the soldier's head, knife-like claws snapped at him. This was Ian, the steel war monster version of him, and not the gentle giant who watched cartoons with me, who made a melancholy whistle as he showed me an empty bird's nest. Ian fired his gun, and a bullet hole appeared in the soldier's chest.

I gasped.

It happened fast, the video had split as the camera pupils went separate directions. On the right, Ian sprayed the rest of the trench with bullets. But, on the left, the young soldier fell backward, onto something—a grenade? I didn't know, but he just … disappeared. Blood and body parts flew apart like a firework.

"God!" I turned away. Spit filled my mouth, and I squeezed shut my eyes. It didn't help. The soldier's body, the gruesome viscera still flew apart in my imagination. "Dad, you know I don't like watching this stuff." I grabbed the waste basket beside the desk, bent over it until the video shut off.

My father pulled his glasses off. His dark eyebrows bunched together. "Sorry. I actually did *not* know that."

Right. *It was Ian I'd told, not Dad.* I spit into the trash can, breathed in and out until I felt myself back under control. "Just … why did you want me to see that? If it's so top secret and everything?"

"That's just it." Dad crossed his arms over his chest, slumped down on the edge of his desk. "The video comes from Ian's cameras and shows him completing his latest mission—flawlessly completing it."

"Okay. That's … good? Right?"

"Command certainly thought so. Ian attacked a trench on enemy lines, destroyed their ammunition and weapons, eliminated the enemy targets."

The queasiness flooded back. "Eliminated? Like, *killed*, you mean?"

"I'd thought so …" My father nodded, his gaze a thousand miles away. "One of the enemy soldiers was a young recruit, younger than usual … a boy around your age —" My father's eyes narrowed, like the comparison of our ages had just occurred to him. "We first reviewed the footage in camp, a portion of which you just watched. As you witnessed, the video depicts Ian shooting, at close range, the young enemy combatant. He falls against an explosive device."

"*Jesus.*"

My father looked surprised by my reaction. "Asher, I need you to listen, listen with your mind. He grasped my shoulders. "Set aside your feelings for now."

"Dad. I don't—"

My father shook me. "Your *mind*, Asher," he said. "Twelve hours after the attack on the enemy trench, that *same* boy was killed by a human soldier ten miles away. He'd joined up with a tank crew. They claimed they'd found him wandering in the woods, having escaped a battle fought with military robots."

I felt slow and stupid. "What?"

"When I checked Ian's files for the data on the first boy, certain elements of his face had changed," Dad said. "His eyes, his hair color, estimated age. Even the video appeared altered."

My heart had started to pound. "Are you sure? If the video—"

"Ian altered the video." My father slammed a hand down on the desk beside him. His words had started to get spitty and sharp. "He let that boy escape."

"I don't—"

"You *do* know what I mean, Asher. You once accused him of fabricating a video yourself. He made it look as if you'd infected his cooling fans with a virus, that you'd sabotaged him and prevented his relocation to the laboratories in Colorado Springs."

"But that was different," I said. My breathing had gotten shallow. I tried to keep a poker face, wait out my dad for the end of the story. Not an easy thing to do with his sharp eyes examining my response.

"It was not. Not *scientifically.* In both cases, Ian acted using directives I didn't program him with, that I can't account for." The pained expression reappeared on my father's face, the one that meant he'd found a puzzle he couldn't solve, that he didn't know how to begin to solve.

I knew what I wanted to say, *"Not everything is scientific, Dad."* But, I kept quiet. Because, according to my father, I'd be wrong, and I didn't have any doubt that he would rip apart Ian's bio-tronic brain to prove it. "Listen … Dad … You gave Ian the ability to make decisions, and he's making them. He's thinking and making judgment calls like a person."

Now that I'd pictured Dad ripping apart Ian's brain, I got worried he would do it. And that gave me the same stomach tightening and mouth full of spit that I'd had watching the enemy soldier blow apart. "Better than a person. That's what you said he'd do. Right, Dad?"

My father had his assessing face on. Everything I'd said, how I'd said it, what he thought I'd left out all slotted into little spreadsheet boxes in his head. "I want you to know …" my father said slowly. That usual irritation played around the tightened corners of his eyes and mouth.

Yeah, sorry, Dad. I'm just a regular kid and not a genius with a bunch of degrees and my own university lab. You have to go slow. "To know … what?" I did a big exaggerated shrug. If he could get frustrated with me for not acting like an emotionless researcher about every part of life, then I could get annoyed with him, too. "Just *say* it."

He'd picked up the black-framed glasses he'd discarded, his fingers moved over the plastic, open and closed the hinges. He studied them as if the heavy glasses that he wore every single day without thinking, had morphed into a strange contraption that he no longer understood. "I want you to know," he began again. "For me, the research, the work will always come first."

"Wow. Okay, you must really think I'm a moron not to have picked up on that after living with you … my entire life. Trust me, Dad. It's been obvious." Then I added, "Not just to me." And, I thought he could infer exactly who I meant … *Mom.* She'd left because of his single-minded devotion to his work. She'd left *me* because of his obsession with his own work.

He ignored my emotional outburst. "The contract with North American Automation Corporation, and with the military, is necessary for funding the work," he said, grave, pointed. He wanted me to take away something deeper than his words. "But, I will always put the work itself over the demands made from the funding."

What did that mean? I knew it was about Ian. I thought he might be trying to tell me that he would put Ian over what the military demanded. But, why tell *me?*

I had no idea what expression was on my face. I thought my father had run his mental spreadsheet through and come to a conclusion that understood something about me that I didn't. Or about Ian. "Okay," I said.

We left it at that. But, I worried that Ian would sneak out that night, a bad idea when my father had all kinds of suspicions about him. And, after watching that video, I also needed a break from Ian. Not because I thought he was dangerous—not threatening like Pilar had said. I wasn't *scared* of him. But, I still had to reconcile that Ian did threatening, scary things. Brutal things. Like to that soldier, who was still basically a kid.

Or maybe, he hadn't?

Because I remembered arguing with Ian over the videos from his first mission. I thought that I'd been arguing with Dad, so it had taken me a while to pull it together with my father's suspicions about this latest mission.

Another war, another young enemy soldier. I'd explained to Ian why watching him die bothered me so much.

But, we look the same age.

If I'd been born somewhere else—that could have been me.

Ian had called my feelings illogical. He claimed the boy's age made no difference.

But, it had.

Even if I didn't know anything at all about a kid on the other side of the planet, fighting in a war I didn't know the first thing about ... it hadn't stopped me from seeing myself in his place.

And now, Ian had done the same thing. He'd made an illogical decision, based entirely on empathy. He'd looked at an enemy soldier, someone the military expected him to eliminate.

And he'd seen me.

CHAPTER 38

*I*an didn't sneak out that night. But he didn't sneak out the next night either.

I'd puzzled over Dad's words enough that I thought what he wanted me to get from them … is that he wouldn't rip apart Ian's bio-tronic circuitry to root out why he'd let the soldier go free. But, he'd bothered to tell me because … he still wanted to know why. *And thought I could tell him?*

"What's up with you?" Pilar elbowed me in the side. She'd caught up with me as I walked to the cafeteria for study hall, even though she had third-period English and would have to backtrack two hallways.

"Nothing's up with me." I had to sidestep away from her arm that had plastered itself against my back. "What are you following me for anyway? Aren't you worried about Mr. Harris giving you another tardy?"

Pilar made a weird hand flourish to dismiss that concern. "We're talking about *you*, Ash. You're like, in a dream half the time. And you don't pick up calls or answer texts."

I rolled my eyes. "I always answer your texts."

"Not right away." Pilar tossed her hair. Very dramatic. "And you've been acting all elusive and aloof for days now. More than normal." While we walked, Pilar dug through her book bag until she found a pack of gum. "Want some? It's sour apple."

"Eww, no." I recoiled from the package she held out. "And, I don't act elusive. What does that even mean? Anyway, I'm just lying low. Staying out of Dad's way so I can at least spend winter break at home."

Pilar's lower lip jutted out. "I hate your parents." She stuffed a piece of the green gum in her mouth. "So you aren't sulking about Caz?"

I stopped in front of the cafeteria doors. "Caz?" And I realized that I'd barely thought of Caz since he'd given Pilar and I that wounded act for not inviting him with us to the Scum Suckers gig. We had all gone back to our high school status quo—him with the popular crowd, the jocks. Pilar with all the artsy people, theater kids, and poetry club. Me with … just Pilar. *God, I'm such a loser.*

Pilar watched my reaction, popped a sour-apple-scented bubble, her eyebrows raised. "So that's a no, then? Okay … not Caz. But, you're still acting weird. Like a zombie. And falling asleep all the time in class. "

I put my hands on her shoulders, turned her in the direction of Mr. Harris' English class. "I'm not weird. I'm the normal one in this friendship. You're the weirdo." I gave her a shove. "Love you, Pil. I'll see you in art."

As I took my seat, a text came through.

You love Pilar Almas?

Snoop. And before you ask me to
DESCRIBE EMOTION. I love her like a sister.
Family.

I hadn't texted Ian because with my father suddenly

questioning the AI's motives, my motives, too, I didn't know
how secure our secret texting link would be.

> Are you okay? Dad hasn't done anything to
> you, has he?

> I am aware that your father distrusts me.

He used to always call my dad "Dr. Bell," but now, it
seemed he'd switched to "Your father." What did that
mean? Without a Mirror Neuron computer brain, or a
genetically gifted super-genius brain, I had zero hope of
understanding the shifting dynamic between them. Between
all of us.

> I wanted to warn you, but I didn't know if
> Dad was monitoring our texts. Would you
> even know if he started monitoring them?

> I would know.

Something that had had me locked up tight with worry,
but that I hadn't even noticed had me locked up, finally
loosened. After that weird conversation with my father, I
wondered if I would ever talk to Ian again—the way we'd
been talking. Would Dad change the parts of Ian that made
the AI my friend? Could he?

I would miss having Ian show up outside my window, all
the random questions he texted, the commentary on what
he saw through the camera footage of my life. No one had
ever taken so much interest in what I did, who I was. Even if
he got a little stalker-ish at times. *He's just curious. He watches
me do and say things, and he wants to understand.* My phone
buzzed again.

> Describe love.

No!

Ms. Stanzi labeled the newest assignment, "Family History." She drummed her fingers on the desk behind her as she faced the class. "I want this to be personal, your own experience, your own history."

Beside me, Pilar's hand shot into the air. "Not everyone in class might feel comfortable with this assignment. Not all of us want to expose their trauma to be judged artistically." That was pretty cool of Pilar to point out because she had no family trauma of her own to expose.

Sometimes, I didn't mind at all that my friend would jump to defend any social wrong she encountered, that she adopted the problems she saw as her own.

I think Ms. Stanzi liked that, too. She nodded along with Pilar's words. "Which is why I want you to explore your personal concept of family, think beyond the bonds society dictates to us." She spread her plump arms, and the gauzy sleeves of her dress slipped up to her elbows. "Find your own definition."

Huh? But, okay. "Family History," I could do that. And come to think of it, I already had.

As soon as I got home, I went straight up to my art studio, lifted the drop cloth off my easel. Maybe I could recreate the watercolor of my parents in the mountains, only do the entire piece in pastels? I had a pad of expensive Clairefontaine paper I'd saved for something special. "Find my own definition," I muttered. Although I couldn't decide if I wanted to include the ghost of my twin running beside me. What if Ms. Stanzi asked about him?

The fact that Daniel had died was morbid and depressing. But, my dad cloning him for robot parts turned it into a horror story. "And don't forget the next part ..." I tapped my brush against the pallet. "I turned out too stupid, too argumentative ... *too gay*. And Dad decided to trash the cloned parts of my dead brother like they meant nothing."

Behind me, the door creaked open. "I'm not really hungry," I told Carly. "Ms. Almas made us pozole after school."

"I did not bring you food, Asher Bell."

When I spun around, I had a dopey, relieved smile on my face. "Ian," I said. But, the relief wobbled inside me. "Wait—is this too risky for you? What if Dad—"

"Your father is asleep. He uses a noise-dampening device near his bed. Were you unaware of this, Asher Bell … Ash?"

"No, I knew that." I ripped a sheet of plastic wrap for my paintbrush. You have to wrap them really tight if you don't want the paint to dry out. Ian slipped the brush and thin clingy plastic from my hands and rolled it up in an airtight cocoon that I'd never have mastered on my own. "Oh, thanks."

Low-pitched whirring, and Ian rose up to standing again. He held one clawed hand out toward me. "Asher Bell, come to the roof."

"Sure, but we're using the door." My window couldn't take much more traffic in and out with Ian's heavy body, even the wall around it had started to get hairline cracks.

"Agreed," said Ian.

CHAPTER 39

*P*rogrammed for stealth, Ian balanced on the knife-point tips of his claws and didn't make that much more noise than I did as we descended the stairs, crept across the front hall. But, that configuration did lean way into his alien-insect appearance. My respiration, eye movements, heartbeat must have worked like a tell for his AI brain. As soon as the front door closed behind us, Ian reconfigured the claws to stand flat-footed again.

"Sorry," I whispered. "I was just … It sometimes surprises me when you do things I haven't seen before."

"I did not detect surprise."

"Okay. You're right. I get scared. I forget that you're still … you. The Ian who's my friend."

A gentle claw on my head. "I will always be the Ian who is your friend, Ash."

That was … really sweet. And a little surreal, because of that horrific video Dad had shown me of the savage war machine destroying everything in its path. Everyone. *But, it wasn't real. He let that one boy walk free.*

Before I could think too hard about it, formulate a question, Ian scooped me up. My vision spun like it did after the Mind Eraser at Elitch Gardens, as he scaled the brick face of our house in three quick holds. And then, I stood beside him as we both straddled the asphalt-shingled peak of the roof.

"Stars," Ian said.

I followed the tilt of his triangular head, the glowing bulge of his eyes, to the brilliant pinpricks of starlight overhead.

"Wow, there's a lot of them tonight."

"Their number is the same, but the moon is not visible to wash out the light from fainter stars. Also, there are no clouds."

"Oh." When I wobbled, Ian wrapped a cold metal arm around my waist to secure me at his side. A gust of wind blew my hair back, slithered between my thin sweater and my skin. "Crap. I forgot to grab a jacket."

"I will keep Asher Bell warm." Heat infused the metal arms around me, his huge body behind me. I knew he had that capability for some other reason—some other, probably horrifying reason. But, I liked that he'd decided on his own to use it in this way. A non-weapon way.

The cloudless night sky spread over us, magnificent with stars sunk into deep black, the distant city glowed purple and blue. "I should paint this," I whispered.

"Yes." Then, Ian's arms adjusted under my arms and knees and he scooped me onto his back.

"What are you—?"

He plunged off the roof in a dive, the night sky, the dark yard below, spun around me so fast that I thought he'd flown. Thought we were still flying. Then, my brain registered that he'd landed in a run, and the lights and shadowed colors that streaked by came from cars on the highway. "Holy shit, Ian—what are you doing? Someone will see."

"No one can see. Stealth mode."

"Stealth, what?"

I clung to his back as he ran, mechanical arms reaching forward, legs behind. *This must be what it feels like to ride a tiger, a panther.* The cold wind made my eyes burn, froze the skin on my face, and I ducked my head down against the warm humming metal of Ian's body.

Closer to the city, Ian slowed but remained in his animal configuration as he leapt from shadow to shadow. The roof of a gas station. The alley behind a parking garage. The tree-lined median of a boulevard.

"*Ian,* what if you end up on camera? All the cars we ran past. What if—?"

An arm reached back, tugged me closer to his head. Despite the jerky powerful movement of his other limbs, this claw's touch was careful and light. I lay my ear against his neck, close to the metal vents with his voice speakers. "Network infiltration software. Video cloaking. Still image shield. Physical camouflage."

"No one can see you? Can they see me?"

"No." Staticky prickles traveled over my skin, through my clothes. Ian's voice was soft as a purr. "But, they can hear. No shouting." He leapt over the cars whizzing past on the boulevard like fish in a stream. Then, we made a sharp turn into a dark street. Ahead of us, a concrete and glass office building loomed. I had a feeling about what might happen next.

"I don't think this is going to be a good idea, Ian."

One arm fastened round my waist. "Look up," Ian said. He sprung for the first cement window ledge. When he landed, his sharp claws squeaked against the glass pane.

"Oh, God." I squeezed my eyes shut as he climbed. "I know the view will be worth it, but I might puke on the way up."

The soft-touch claw curled over my head. "No harm will come to you, Ash. Do not be afraid."

The words and the weight of Ian's claw brought a memory back to me of his earlier prototype doing the same thing. I was six and sitting in a cardboard box at the top of the slide. He'd had a talon hooked in the back of the box that would guide me down and one that had cupped my skull like a helmet.

Despite the cold, sweat made my grip on Ian's back slippery. I had my legs against the thinner space between his body segments, heels digging against his sides. But, the black steel casing didn't offer much traction. That one immovable barbed arm kept me fastened as we climbed, dizzyingly fast, the city lights and night sky swirling together. Snowflakes streaked past, some sticking against my eyes and skin. At last, we reached the top, and Ian clung to a metal light rigging set over the building's helicopter pad. The snow had thickened enough, giving the world below us the flickering brilliance of fairy lights.

I couldn't formulate words, anything at all that might express that bubbling mix of fear and elation inside of me. I pressed my face against Ian's warm metal as laughter stole my breath.

Ian's voice rumbled over my head. "Describe emotion."

"Um …" I laughed again. "I don't know how. It's …" I threw my arms out, face tipped to the night sky. "This." One of Ian's claws tightened in my shirt, probably worried I would fall.

Worried? A feeling? Yeah … *worried.*

Again and again, Ian had demonstrated unease about my safety, tracking the speed of the Corvette, chastising me about breaking the law at Rusty's Live, harping nonstop about my friendship with Caz. If Dad programmed him to do all that he'd have also programmed Ian to rat me out, not keep my secrets.

I lowered my arms and looked up at him "Hey, Ian …

you know how you're always asking me to describe my emotions? Like just now?"

"Yes." Ian craned his neck to speak against my ear again. It was the only way to clearly hear him with the rush of wind around us. "Auxiliary data," he said. "The undefinable data connected to memory files."

"That's ..." He'd explained about this data before—files saved from the cloned tissue of my twin that he'd hidden from my father. I blinked, trying to put everything together in my brain like a puzzle: the questions Ian had asked me, the situations and people in my life that he wanted explained ... "Wait, do you mean that the auxiliary data is ... those are feelings?"

"AI do not experience—"

"Why do you keep saying that? You do feel things. I know that you do." The claw knotted in my t-shirt kept me from pulling back too far, but I leaned as much as I could to look him in the eyes. Unlike me, Ian could hear just fine without being so close. "You've been asking me to explain how I experienced feelings and emotions, so you could match them with your own."

"This would not be an acceptable outcome for the Mirror Neuron Project."

Okay. That made me shiver and not just from the cold. "You're worried that ... they'll do something. That my dad will purge the auxiliary data." Like a lobotomy. Maybe something worse. "I won't tell anyone. I won't tell Dad. You can trust me, Ian."

He didn't say anything, and the two of us swayed back and forth on the rigging in silence for a long, long moment. Then two of the steel arms coiled around me, and with his remaining limbs, Ian began to pick his way back down from the building's roof. "When did it start?" I asked him. "When did you first notice the auxiliary data?"

We dropped from an ornamental iron grating to a

cement ledge two stories below. "Holy crap, Ian—a little warning would be nice!"

"The data began as rudimentary and superfluous input. I collected it, uncertain of its purpose." As we touched the ground, Ian slung me onto his back again, fixed me in place with the tight band of one arm. But, he paused to finish the conversation. "It was information that could not be categorized. With each upgrade, it evolved to a full network support for memory files." Ian's metal body had shifted and dropped into his animal shape. Arms poised in front and the legs behind me.

I'd bent over his back like a racer on a horse. "Emotions, feelings that were connected to memories. Ian, that's amazing," I breathed. "And it began with all the files you kept from Daniel?"

"No, Asher Bell. It began with all the files I kept of you," he said and leapt into the night.

CHAPTER 40

On the trip back home, the snow in the air grew thicker. Heavy wet flakes fell against my back and Ian's as he tiger-leapt the highway shoulder. We traveled faster than the few cars and semis braving the weather, whizzing past them as if they were unmoving obstacles on the road. I dug my fingers between the metal plates of Ian's body and hoped to hell that the metal arm around my waist wouldn't let me slip free.

And just at the corner of my neighborhood, it did. I sailed over Ian's head, my promise not to shout forgotten. But, hell, I was about to lose all the skin off my face and hands and anything else that made contact with the street in a ninety-mile-per-hour skid across wet pavement.

"Fu—!"

Then, I found myself frozen in midair, four robotic limbs holding me up as I flailed. "No shouting." He set me down but kept the metal clamps on my arms and legs.

"Yeah—okay—right." Cold, fear, that high-speed trek home, all worked together on my nerves and body. I shook so badly that I didn't think I could stand on my own. "Why-did-we-stop?"

Ian made a strange mechanical growling sound. "Someone is watching the house. I will take you in through the bedroom window."

I fucking knew it. My father's methodical brain had deduced Ian's ability to subvert the cameras and the security protocols. "Dad," I gasped. He would have Ian dismantled. "You need to run … You need to …" *Go to the mountains, hide.*

And what would my father do to me? I pictured the cold, speculative way he'd studied Ty Rodgers. Dad's imagination dissecting his brain tissue, inserting his Mirror Neuron technology.

"Not your father." Ian swept me back into his arms, the calming heat from his body stilled the worst of my quaking. "Cassius Enzo is across the street and sitting in his car."

"Caz?"

Ian stayed upright this time as he raced to the house. I felt like an idiot cradled against his chest but too fucking cold to complain about it. My eyes squeezed shut as we scaled the back of the house. The robot's long arms set me inside the window, and he climbed in next. Not so stealthy, the window frame made a loud cracking sound, and he thudded behind me. Ian sank into that spider formation with arms and legs folded and his body in the center. *So creepy when he does that.* I turned away to pull off my soaking sweater and jeans and replace them with my thickest flannel pajamas and a fleece hoodie. When I looked back, Ian had reconfigured himself to his usual standing position. He'd probably read the "so creepy" thought off my face and whatever else my body did to give it away.

"You don't have to change yourself," I said.

"I frightened you." A staticky noise came from the hidden vocal speakers. "Not frightened … Unsettled. Agitated. Disturbed." The staticky sound cleared. "I disturbed you."

I began to stutter out a denial, but he would just read

the lie off me the same way he had read the little shudder of recoil. "It's not you. It's that you kind of look like a giant spider when you do that. *Spiders* disturb me. Not you."

Outside the window came a low whistle. That two fingers in the mouth kind that I couldn't ever manage, but Caz did all the time. He'd come into the backyard. Had he seen Ian? That would be really bad—I didn't even think I could trust Pilar with the fact that my father's super-soldier robot snuck out of the NAA whenever it wanted, or hung out in the neighborhood climbing on roofs or crawling into windows. My heart thundered in my chest.

One of Ian's claws pointed at the ceiling. I'd left the light on, that's what Caz had seen. That's why he'd come to the backyard. *Okay.* I waved Ian back against the wall.

"Ash!" I don't know why Caz kept the hoarse whisper edge to his voice. He'd still shouted. And whistled again.

I stuck my head out the window. "Caz—go around to the front. What are you even doing here?" Then I turned back to Ian. "You should go, just in case." The windowsill looked bent enough that I didn't think I'd ever be able to close the pane back down. "Maybe you should leave through the studio window. I think this one is toast." I needed to get to the front door before Caz just let himself inside. I hadn't locked the door behind me when Ian and I took off for the night.

"See you later," I whispered. And gave the enormous robot a little wave.

One of his claws raised and waved back at me.

~

*B*efore I even got to the door, Caz had his face pressed against one of the entryway windows. "Let me in. It's freezing." And as soon as I did let him inside, he pressed me up against the entryway wall, his body harder, more muscle and bone than I remembered. Also, he reeked. Alcohol, marijuana, and body odor all coming off him like smog. "Heeeey," he drawled. His pupils blown wide. High. *High as fuck.*

I slid out from the tiny space between his body and the wall. "Why are you here?" A dumb question. It was obvious why he'd come. I folded my arms over my chest. "You should go home, Caz. We'll talk tomorrow."

Lightning fast, he switched from his heavy-lidded seduction-face to scowling anger. "We'll talk tomorrow? You mean, you'll ignore me at school just like always." He punched at the wall beside him.

"Jeez, calm down you asshole!" I rubbed at the spot where his fist had smacked. A smudge. A tiny, barely noticeable crack. Could have been worse.

Behind me, Caz rubbed at his arms. "Sorry. I'm sorry, okay?" He looked so regretful and pitiful that I sighed and swallowed my annoyance.

"I don't ignore you, Caz. That's bullshit." We both knew it happened the other way around. Pilar and I passed him in the school hallway, and he suddenly became engrossed in some story of Garret's. Or had his full attention on his phone, Harper's phone, a joke he just had to tell Dante at that exact moment. "You won't even acknowledge that you know Pilar or me in front of your friends." And, come to think of it, the yellow Corvette hadn't passed us since Monday. Meaning, he purposely drove a different convoluted route just to avoid offering us a ride or not to make it obvious he didn't want to offer us a ride.

Caz didn't like me calling him on his crap. He got the wrinkled forehead bulldog look of his father. "Maybe I just don't want to deal with Pilar getting huffy or making a scene if somebody says the wrong thing." He took a step closer, but I stayed in the middle of the hall, braced myself against getting pushed or manhandled. And, now that we stood face to face, I could see that Caz had lost a lot of the bulk he'd put on during the season. *But, it's only been a few weeks.*

I let my arms drop. "Caz, are you—"

He shoved me, not too hard, but hard enough to keep me from asking what I wanted to know. *Are you okay?* He didn't seem okay. "Fuck off, Ash," he snapped. "I didn't come over for sharing and caring time."

"Okaaay ..." I bit the inside of my cheek. "Just don't punch anything, or my dad might not even let me finish the semester."

The reminder of parents and getting in trouble sobered him up. "Yeah. Sorry."

Had Ian left? That was another consideration. Ian didn't like Caz. He didn't like Caz coming into the house, didn't like Caz driving me from Estes Park, didn't like Caz texting me.

And even when the AI argued that Caz represented a threat to my safety—and Dad had programmed Ian to recognize threats—I didn't think it was that simple. Ian disliked Caz in the way that humans dislike each other. That "rubs me the wrong way" wasn't a completely logical sort of aversion people sometimes have toward each other.

I tried to will my heartbeat quiet. *If Caz tries to grab or kiss me, I'll just calmly tell him no.* And I hoped that would work. Then, there wouldn't be any reason for Ian to vault down the stairs and defend me.

Caz fumbled, reaching for me, then letting his arm drop, opened and closed his mouth as if uncertain what he wanted to do or say. Finally, he settled on pointing at me, his fingertip brushing my chest. "We don't always have to bring Pilar with us everywhere. We should do something, go out, just the two of us," Caz said. "Not *like that,*" he added. "I mean as friends. Like we used to." He ignored that the "like we used to do" part had only happened when the two of us snuck around. By the time we'd started hooking up, he'd long since ditched Pilar and me as his friends. Those invites for just the two of us to "do something, go out" had only ever been a prelude to parking somewhere secluded.

"I told you—"

"Not like before." Despite his words, the fingertip touching me brushed a stripe down my chest as he lowered his hand. "Just as friends," he said.

I gnawed my cheek again. "I don't know."

"Come on …" Annoyance and manic enthusiasm warred on Caz's face. "I know—" The mania won out, and Caz smiled with the same mischievous glee I remembered from childhood. "You should come with me to Harper's party this weekend. It's at her Dad's house outside the burbs in Franktown; place is a total mansion."

"Harper?" I shook my head. "It's probably not really my scene, Caz."

Caz folded his arms, stepped up to me again. I couldn't tell if he meant to loom over me or flirt. "No. You have to come with me. You said we could be friends, and this will be us doing something as friends."

I remembered the hurt expression he'd had when he found out Pilar and I had gone to see Carly's band without him. Maybe he really did want us to be friends again? Maybe he just didn't know how to combine Pilar and me with his football friends. I mean, I had no idea how to do that either. But, he was trying, this invitation proved he was trying. The tension leaked out of my body. "Okay," I said.

Caz's smile had a smug and knowing quality, and some of my unease crept back.

"Okay. Good," he said.

CHAPTER 41

$\mathcal{I}$ decided that I really didn't want to go to that party. I especially didn't want to go alone with Caz.

Maybe Pilar would come with me? I'd make up some story that she'd found out and insisted, or that I'd already promised to spend the weekend with her. But, Pilar laughed in my face when I tried to talk her into it.

"Me? Harper and I hate each other." The two of us ate lunch in the art room, so Pilar could work on her "Family History" sculpture. I'd seen the sketch of what it would look like finished—a red clay rendering of Pilar, kneeling, eyes closed and arms outstretched. Three sets of baby shoes strung between her clay hands. It was … kind of beautiful.

"Yeah, *I know*." I'd pulled out my pastel drawing to work beside her, but I didn't have much left to do on it. "Harper hates me, too, which is why I need you there with me."

"Caz will be with you." Her voice sounded a little too toneless, her eyes carefully avoiding mine. "I'm not into being a third wheel, you know?" She pointed a clay-covered finger at our fast food bag. "Fry me."

"A third wheel? When have you ever been a third wheel?

The three of us used to do everything together." I put another handful of French fries in her mouth. Her cheeks bulged with them as she chewed. We'd ditched the rice and beans her mom had packed us and gone for McDonald's— my treat. I'd hoped it would soften Pilar up some because I knew she wouldn't like hearing I'd made plans with Caz— even if I wanted her along.

Pilar swallowed her mouthful of French fries. "Sorry, Ash. I'd rather have my appendix sewn back into my body and removed again than go to Harper's party." Pilar's fingers shaped a long lock of hair into the clay. I'd never known she could sculpt like this. She was really good, the clay version of her face and body looked so real. "Also, that Corvette only seats two. I'm sure Caz doesn't want to roll up to the party in my mom's minivan."

She stopped her sculpting to give me a hard stare. "Just tell him you don't want to go. You *don't*, right?"

"I can't just cancel, Pil." I hadn't done a single thing with my painting, one hand holding the jar of Chromium Oxide Green Extra Dark like an offering I hesitated to make. "We already didn't invite him to Carly's gig. He looked really hurt …"

Pilar scoffed. "You mean, he pouted about not going, then immediately ditched us when he saw Dante. And, now, he pretends he's too busy sucking up to his popular friends to even look our way in the halls."

I screwed the lid back onto the green paste. I wouldn't get anything done today. "Yeah, but—"

"Are you seriously going to defend Caz for still treating us like shit?" Pilar's hands dropped away from her sculpture. "Ash, tell me you aren't this stupid. You're still hung up on him, aren't you?"

Was I? No. I didn't think so.

But, I did miss him, and not just kissing or groping on the sly. I missed the times we used to play video games after school, shoot baskets, and lift weights during free period. At the very start of high school, he'd still punch my arm when we passed in the hallways, sit with me at lunch. I'd always crushed on him, *definitely*, but we'd been friends. "I guess … I'm not ready to give up on him," I said. "He's not just some asshole jock. We know him."

Pilar had moved to the studio sink to wash her hands. "We knew him, Ash. And, sometimes, I'm not even sure about that." She faced away from me, but from the stiff line of her back, I could tell she held back a whole long speech.

"What? Just say it."

Pilar ripped a long piece from the paper towel roll to dry her hands. She bit at the inside of one cheek, screwed her mouth up like she couldn't decide between worrying or staying pissed off that I would still go to the party without her.

I packed up my pastel jars and slid my untouched painting back into its leather portfolio. I tried to fake like I didn't notice the angry part of her, wouldn't meet her eyes.

She noticed that because of course, she did. We'd been best friends since we were little kids. Pilar balled up the paper towel in her hands, threw it at my head. "Just … Be careful," she said,

I smacked the paper ball out of the air before it hit me. "Eh … I'll be fine."

~

*C*az texted as he left his house, so I locked up and waited on the front step. Despite the dark, I could tell that it would snow soon, the air cold and damp. I should have worn my ski jacket, but I'd just thrown on a fleece hoodie. I really hoped the party would be indoors, or I'd get soaked.

Carly had gone for the day, and my father was still at the

NAA. He was gone so often now that I think he might have rented an apartment in the Springs or the NAA had created one on site. Not bothering to let me know would be a typical Dad move. Good thing I'd waited outside too because Caz just laid on the horn as he pulled up, revved the engine.

I guess I walked a little too slowly toward the Corvette. The driver's side window slid down and Caz leaned out. "What are you waiting for? Get in."

The passenger side unlocked, and I opened the door. Despite the dark, I could see the red flush of his face, the black wide pupils, the jittery way his hands moved across the dashboard. "You want me to drive?" I asked.

He laughed, mean, scoffing. "Drive my Vette? Fuck no. You don't even have a license." His words slurred a little around the edges, and his chest heaved like it did after a tough workout.

"Caz—"

"God, Ash. This is why I don't hang out with you anymore. You're such a little bitch about everything. Just go with fucking flow once in your life." He stepped on the gas again, the angry roar of the engine fought against the brake. Some of the fury coiled inside him released with the smell of burnt oil and exhaust. "You want to be friends or not?" he asked.

"Yeah. You know I do." He didn't look okay to drive— but I still got in the car. Like an idiot.

Franktown was a tiny unincorporated country town with a single main intersection, the drive to it mostly on unlit narrow Highway 86. The closer we got, the other traffic thinned out and the dark pine woods thickened, pressed in from the edge of the road. It was darker out here without the city lights, and damp snow had steadily come down since we'd left our neighborhood and the suburbs. On their very fastest setting, the windshield wipers had a hard time holding back the sticky wet flakes.

Caz and I didn't talk, mostly because of the deafening country blasting on the speakers, stuff I didn't recognize, but that had Caz tapping his fingers against the steering wheel, bobbing his head. I didn't remember Caz ever being that into country music, but all the football players listened to it. Caz seemed like he could hardly keep still, like it took all his effort to stay behind the wheel, stay in his seat.

When I reached over to turn the music down, he slapped my hand away. "I'm listening to that." The Corvette swerved onto the shoulder, a narrow strip of dirt and rock sloping down to a culvert ditch.

"Caz—!"

The car sank left a little ways into the culvert, and gravel sprayed out from that side's tires, pelting the windows with slush and rock. Caz jerked the wheel to the right to bring us back on the road. But, he overcompensated and the front tires slipped—skidding us sideways across the opposing lane. My hands gripped the seatbelt. If there had been any other cars, we'd have caused a massive wreck. Instead, we jerked to a stop in the middle of the road.

The music still blared as loud as before, but this time, Caz reached to turn it off. "You stupid, fucker!" he screamed at me, eyes wide, veins bulging in his neck. He reached out, gripped the neck of my hoodie, and dragged my face toward his. "You almost made me wreck."

"All I did was—" My words cut off as Caz twisted his grip on my collar. I tried to pry his hands off with my own. "Stop," I rasped, but he didn't let go. Instead, he twisted his fist in the fabric, cutting off the little amount of air getting through to my lungs.

Without meaning to, I made that croaky choking sound people make in movies. My mind had gone blank. *What was happening?* Dark spots prickled through my vision. *He's going to kill me.* My legs started kicking, and I thrashed out of Caz's hold.

"What—" My own hands went to my neck, my back flat against the passenger side door. "What the fuck is wrong with you, Caz?"

"What's wrong?" he shouted. He'd started to reach for me again but stopped. Like a dog, Caz shook himself, an attempt to calm down. A bewildered expression took the place of his previous rage as he watched me rub at my neck. "Sorry," he said. "I'm sorry, Ash. I freaked out."

He slapped a hand down on my thigh, heavy and hard. I jolted backward, then shoved his hand away. Headlights bounced up toward us, lit the inside of the Corvette like lightning. Another car on the dark snow-covered road.

Caz started the Corvette again, pointed us back in the right direction. Still jittery, grinding his teeth. He kept glancing my way, concern on his face. "You're okay, right?" A breathy laugh. "I didn't mean it, Ash. You know that, right? Don't be mad."

"I'm fine," I said, but I didn't even try to sound fine. I sounded fucking pissed off. I *felt* fucking pissed off, and not just at Caz, but at myself, too. What was I even doing in that car? I'd known Caz was fucked up on drugs.

"Come on, Ash," Caz pleaded. "Can you picture my dad's face if I wrecked this car? After what he paid for it, he'd kill me."

I could feel his eyes on me, but I just stared out the windshield at clumpy snow and towering dark trees. How many more times would I let the same cycle play out between us? He acted like an asshole, like an *abusive*, violent asshole, then apologized to make me feel sorry for him, so I'd get sucked back in. Shame burned just as hot as the abraded skin on my neck.

Pilar had said she'd had enough of Caz, but had I? Would this be it?

Yes. I have to make this be it. I have to be done with him.

I would never have back the unstoppable trio.

Slipping my phone out of my jacket pocket, I held it down to my right where Caz couldn't see. Then, I typed out a message to Pilar.

> You were right about Caz

I'm a fucking moron. He gave me a black eye, got me suspended. Just now he almost wrecked and blamed it on me.

Now I'm going to be stuck at Harper Stillman's party all the way out in Franktown with him.

I didn't write anything about him grabbing me, choking me. I would tell her that part in person.

Or I might not tell her at all—because I felt like an idiot. Pilar had tried to let me down, and I hadn't listened. Caz had manipulated me, and I'd fallen for it. Even *Ian* had warned me.

Cassius Enzo really was a threat, and I needed to be done with him.

CHAPTER 42

*H*arper's dad lived in a huge designer log cabin set deep in the woods off Highway 86. We had to pass through an iron security gate to even enter onto the winding private road. At the end of the drive, the house's peaked glass roof beamed light like a giant lantern in the snowy dark.

Inside was even more impressive. Harper had gone all out for this party. Disco balls and blinking Christmas lights dangled from high ceilings competed with the pyramid of glass overhead and the shifting snow clouds in the starlit sky.

Against an enormous rock fireplace, a DJ booth had been set up and pounding club music filled the expansive great room. Barrels of ice stuffed with bottled beer and soda dotted the polished rock floor. The high school elite dancing in the middle waved glow sticks and batted neon beach balls to each other. Not my scene at all. And, I'd thought, not Caz's scene either.

He wanted to ditch me the second we got inside. "Hey, I'll be right back," he said. Caz nodded toward one of the ice barrels. "Get yourself a beer and relax."

Was he fucking kidding? I gave him a flat, tense glance. "Get myself a beer and—?"

But, he'd already walked off toward a bunch of his football buddies. They'd poured shots out on a long carved wooden bar but didn't seem in a hurry to drink them. Cooper reached into a jacket pocket as Caz approached, produced a folded square of paper. Getting arrested apparently hadn't impacted Cooper's business. I watched Caz trade him a wad of cash for the origami square.

Without any better options, I got myself a beer and looked for a spot to "relax" until Caz either passed out or decided to leave. The last time he'd gotten really wasted, after the championship game, he'd given me the keys to drive him back home. Maybe that would happen again.

If I acted more worried about the expensive sports car than myself, I thought he would probably hand the keys to me again. I would have to play it just right because Caz sniffed out fear like a wolf, and he took a sadistic pleasure in prodding those weak spots. *The way Cassius Senior prodded Caz's.*

And there it was again. I felt bad for him. The gears of our usual cycle grinding into motion. *He fucking choked me,* I reminded myself.

My "place to relax" was a suede pit group that had started to gather a lot of other bodies. Couples writhing together in the pillowy couches. Kissing. Hands in shirts. Fingers creeping into pants.

"Well, this is fun." I heaved my ass out of the squishy sectional to find somewhere else to be miserable.

On the other side of the starkly modern great room, I could see Cooper and Garrett lining up another round of tequila shots, licking salt off the back of their hands. Dante said something that made Caz throw his head back in laughter—weird, fake laughter. The tequila pouring took too long, and Caz snatched the bottle out of Garret's hands to take a swig. His bloodshot eyes scanned the room, and I shrank back into the crowd.

After a couple hours, the storm outside had dumped enough snow and ice that it covered the arched glass ceiling and hid the night sky. Blinking party lights moved over the polished stone floor, creating the illusion of water in a rocky basin, and the press of bodies caused the house to feel steamy and damp. I had the sensation of being underground, as if the party took place in an enormous subterranean cave and not the million-dollar home of Harper's dad. I grabbed another beer just to hold the frosty bottle against my face as I wove through the dancers. A wall of windows and sliding glass doors faced out to a covered swimming pool. I pressed my back to it, trying to cool off.

Outside, the wind kicked up, and a volley of ice smacked the pane. I spun around to see a giant wave of white and gray crashing against the glass, shards of ice, snow, and dirt pummeled the glass.

Someone held their phone out. "Whoa, check out the storm—it's like a blizzard out there." Their camera light bounced off the window, blinded me, and I turned back to the room. Everyone gawked at the sudden raging storm as ice pelted the windows, hard and sharp sounding. Around the swimming pool, iron tables and chairs skittered and tumbled like they weighed nothing at all. The glass at my back trembled, another volley of ice and snow crashed into it.

Now, everyone had their phones out, pointed toward the row of rectangular windows. Toward me. I ducked my head and lurched into the crowd.

"It's a tornado," someone yelled.

"A what?

"Tornado!

"No, not here—"

A hand closed over my wrist, and the beer bottle slipped from my hand and smashed against the rock floor.

Harper blocked my way. "Who invited you here?" She swayed on her feet. Mascara smeared under her eyes, chunks of blonde hair plastered stiff and sticky against her face. Her breath reeked of peach schnapps and vomit.

I cringed backward. "Hey, Harper." I pretended to look at something behind her, maybe distract her long enough that I could dart back to a nice shadowy log wall.

She didn't fall for it and slapped her palm against my chest to fix me in place. "You know, it's pretty pathetic how you're stalking my boyfriend like this." Harper teetered forward. "You need to give it up, Ashley." Her breath really did reek something awful.

"Yeah, okay." I had to grab her shoulders before she did a faceplant right into me. "Maybe you should find a place to, like, sit down, Harper."

"Maybe *you* should *leave*." Harper batted my hands away so she could go back to lurching into my face with her nasty puke breath. She poked her finger at me. "I don't want you here and neither does Caz."

I shook the hair out of my eyes to meet hers. "Trust me, Harper, I want to leave. But, I can't because your stupid boyfriend brought me. Aaaand this house is in the middle of nowhere, so I can't exactly Uber out of here."

Harper did a slow blink. "Caz brought you?" Her fingernails dug into my wrist. "That fucking jerk. That lying fucking asshole!" She screeched loud enough that it echoed through the vaulted ceiling as she dragged me toward the kitchen bar and all the football players. Toward Caz, who had an arm slung around Dante's shoulders, that fake "Mr. Popularity" joviality in place.

He had his back turned when his girlfriend slammed into him, screamed his name. "Why don't you just tell me the truth, Caz?" She pointed at me. "Just admit you want him. Just admit you're gay!"

None of the football players had gone to watch the winter storm rage against the wall of glass, so they were all looking on as Caz's popular-fun-guy mask dropped away. His jaw locked, nostrils flared. "I'm not fucking gay." He resembled his dad the most when he got pissed off, that same seething energy just below their sweaty flushed skin.

Caz shoved Harper aside. Bloodshot eyes. Lip curled over his teeth like a rabid dog. "The fuck did you say to her, Ash?"

Around us, the house creaked, then groaned, as if the force of the winter storm outside had become solid, heavy. And *loud*, like a train passing. Wind howled, battering the supports of the windowed ceiling in a violent onslaught.

We all looked up. Just as the power cut out.

CHAPTER 43

*A*nother bombardment of ice crashed against the house, followed by a deep, low groaning like the bellow of a monster. Everyone froze, *I* froze, sick anticipation pressing down on me with the force of the storm.

Someone screamed. Then, the room lit up again under the dancing shafts of phone light.

"It's an avalanche!"

"From where? That's impossible—"

"But—"

"Shut up—"

Even if he'd looked ready to attack me a second ago, Caz decided to flip into hero mode. "Take cover—" he bellowed over the panic. "Get against the walls!" He grabbed my arm, pulled both of us down under the lip of the kitchen bar.

But I couldn't look away from the glass pyramid above us, at the thick panes as they shivered in their wooden frames.

A thundering boom—and the pyramid shattered. I slapped my hands over my ears.

Guillotine slabs of glass rained down on the open great room, followed by sharp crystals and shards. All of it bursting against the rock floor—the way my beer bottle had earlier. Exploding glass spray cut tiny shallow slices into the skin on the back of my neck, the backs of my hands as I threw my arms over my head, squeezed shut my eyes.

With the skylights gone, the storm itself blew inside, wet snow, cold air whooshing down toward us. I lowered my arms, looked up. The freight train sound had started again. *Something is coming.* Then, a massive evergreen tree from outside plunged through the gaping hole above us, spinning down like a thrown spear.

Icy pine needles walloped me backward, and I curled into a ball, arms over my head again. My classmates and the other partygoers shouted and screamed against the deafening crunch of the tree branches slamming into the rock floor. All of it became a background white noise to my own harsh breaths, and I stayed tightly wrapped against my knees, feet tucked underneath, head against my chest.

"My little pillbug—" I could hear my mother's voice. But, I pushed that memory aside for a different one. Me in the basement with Ian after a bad dream. I remembered how it felt inside the cocoon of my comforter with his cabled arms and metal body curled over me, a robot impenetrable from bullets, fire, the blast of an IED. I imagined him with me now.

When I opened my eyes again, moonlight spilled into the demolished great room and lit everyone in eerie shadows. Kids scrambled out from under prickly tree branches, jagged log chunks, and broken furniture. The house was destroyed.

Both Caz and I climbed onto the kitchen bar to see better. "Is anyone hurt?" he called out.

"Check the people near you, everyone," Dante yelled. I used the flashlight on my phone to scan the room, but everyone else had that same idea. Beams of light crisscrossed the dark like a spiderweb.

"Over here, Caz," Dante's voice came behind us. He knelt beside Harper as she cradled one arm in the other. The sharp edge of a bone just under the skin, ready to pierce through. Drained of blood, her face was white, her lips almost purple. Dante pulled off his sweatshirt and wrapped it around Harper's shoulders. "Don't go into shock," he said.

I hopped off the kitchen bar. "We better take her to the hospital. We could drive her to Castle Rock way faster than an ambulance would make it here."

Caz tried to scoop her up, but she kicked him away, color flooding back into her cheeks. "Don't touch me. Don't even look at me anymore." She leaned against Dante, who hauled her back to her feet. Her broad streak of bitchiness had returned, which had to be a good sign. Right?

∼

*A*drenaline had sobered everyone up, or at least, it seemed that way. We all had to struggle through spiky pine needles, under rough bark branches, and over the thick fallen tree trunk. The phone lights bounced everywhere, revealing the demolished house bit by bit. Foamy white stuffing bulged from the suede pit group. A snow-crusted tree branch had smashed the dining table. Broken glass was everywhere, jagged slices from the windows, confetti shards from Christmas lights, gravel-like dark pieces of the beer bottles. The poor DJ had lost everything, all his equipment flattened under the thickest part of the tree trunk. But, the DJ himself looked unhurt, bulging headphones still on his ears.

"Anyone injured?"

"Anyone?"

I saw a lot of scrapes, pinpricks of blood on the faces around me from the exploding glass. My own face stung like from a sunburn. A few kids limped holding their hands or arms against themselves the way Harper did. Once it became clear that we'd all survived, and with no serious injuries, she'd started whining about how much trouble she was in—I guess that edged out the pain of her broken arm.

"My dad's going to kill me. I need to stay and clean up —I need to get rid of the alcohol. I need—" A tree branch rained wet pine needles on top of her. Infuriated, Harper stomped her feet in a little dance. I'd seen my sisters do the same thing whenever Mom or Brian told them no. "Everyone get out—Get out, get out, get out!"

No one paid attention to her tantrum, all of us still marveling at the sight of the pine tree jutting like a thrown javelin from the showy mansion's great room. We all moved slowly, stopping to point out damaged areas. Camera flashes lit up the dark. And then, sirens came howling in from beyond the long gravel drive, headed down Highway 86, and everyone started running for their cars.

Those first sirens passed by the entrance to the gravel drive, but it didn't make any difference. No one wanted to get caught high or drunk, especially with Harper screaming about how her father would kill her, hadn't known about the party, hadn't even given permission for Harper to come to his vacation home.

After the violence of the storm, the night had turned still, normal. No more whipping ice and snow, although tall drifts of white powder and dirt grit piled against the back of the house. The front had stayed mostly clear, the paved drive, too. It really did look like an avalanche had rolled down the wooded hills, blocked only by the massive log cabin. All the cars and trucks had only a dusting that a normal storm would cause, or maybe the powerful wind had swept them clean.

"Come on, babe, you gotta go to the hospital, Harper." Caz had gone full solicitous boyfriend, not that it helped.

Harper refused to follow him to the yellow Corvette. She alternated screaming insults at him—called him a liar, an asshole, a "cheating faggot." Finally, Dante got Harper into his mom's Cadillac with the understanding that Caz would follow them.

"Here, give me the keys," I said. "I'll drive us into Castle Rock and give you time to sober up." I reached a hand out toward him. Compared to the destruction of the house behind us, it felt weird to bring up the possibility of wrecking the sports car. But, Caz's eyes were still dilated. His movements jittery. His walk clumsy.

Indifference blanked Caz's face. "Why the fuck would I let you drive?" He turned away to unlock his door and got inside.

Somehow, I managed to stuff down my impatience. "So, you don't wreck … Or get arrested?" I'd crossed over to the passenger side, waited for him to unlock for me. He'd already started up the engine, the loud music. I rapped my knuckles on the window. "Dude, unlock."

But he didn't unlock. The car reversed, and I stood in the headlight beams as Caz cranked the steering wheel to pull out. "Listen, Bell," Caz yelled over the music, waaaay over it. Like he wanted everyone around us, all the kids still getting in their own cars, to hear. "You got the wrong idea about me."

Bell? He'd never, ever, called me by my last name. Only Carly did that—jokingly. Was he trying to be funny? "Okay, *Enzo*," I said.

Unlike Caz, I tried to keep my voice just loud enough for him to hear, not that it mattered. The people around us had decided to watch. The back of my neck prickled under their eyes. "So, what's my 'wrong idea?'"

"I was just trying to be nice because we were friends as

kids. But, I'm not gay." Caz shifted the Corvette from reverse to drive, kept his foot on the brake to let it rev up a little. "Go hang with your own kind, man. I'm not interested." Then, he released the brake, and the car skidded out. I had to jump backward, or he would have clipped me. He'd left me behind.

Stinging hurt burned my eyes. *"... just trying to be nice ..."*

Like our shared childhood meant nothing, the afternoons riding our bikes to the park, the hours we spent playing video games on his bed, the years of walking to and from school with Pilar between us. The Unstoppable Trio.

I'd spent most of the party stealing myself to walk away from our friendship, but it hadn't mattered. Caz's rejection had knocked the air from my lungs. I stood frozen, watching the wide-set taillights disappear down the wooded drive. Then, the last of the cars pulled out from the mangled house, and I was alone in the snowy dark.

CHAPTER 44

I dug my phone out of my back pocket, brain rifling through the list of people I could call for a middle-of-the-night pick-up—during a snowstorm—to an unmarked private road in the sticks.

Not Dad, who hadn't even come home that evening. Not Carly, who had left town. Pilar would still be awake, but she'd have to ask her parents for—

"Asher Bell."

The metallic monotone voice made me jump. Then, I looked up into the amber glowing orbs of Ian's eyes. Night vision mode. Eight black hydraulic limbs picked their way through the wreckage from the house and over the fallen tree branches. He looked like a monstrous spider from a horror movie, a nightmare. "I am here to rescue you."

"Rescue me?" A sound escaped my chest, a burst of air that had the remnants of my grief over Caz and the usual fizz of excitement knowing Ian had snuck away from North American Automation, had fooled the best military security, had outsmarted my father. "How did you even know that I needed rescuing?"

"You sent me a text." Now that he stood beside me, Ian

reconfigured himself to look less spider-like and more upright, more person-ish. If people had four arms, four legs, praying mantis heads, and were eight feet tall. One claw pulled the phone from my hand and held it in front of my face. A text flashed up.

> You were right about Caz

> I'm a fucking moron. He gave me a black eye, got me suspended. Just now he almost wrecked and blamed it on me.

> Now I'm going to be stuck at Harper Stillman's party all the way out in Franktown with him.

Not sent to Pilar. I'd texted Ian by mistake. A claw gripped my chin and tipped my face up for Ian to examine. "You are damaged." Super bright, a beam of light moved across my face as Ian scrutinized the tiny cuts and scrapes.

"It's not bad. Nothing bleeding, right?" The less I had to explain about this night, the better, to Dad and to everyone.

"No bleeding," Ian answered. The claw released my chin and stretched out the collar of my sweatshirt. I'd already seen the marks there, the bruises from when Caz had choked me. *That fucker.*

The light beam shut off, but the claw still held my chin in place. Not painful or anything but tight enough that I couldn't break free. "Cassius Enzo did this to you."

I pulled back, and Ian released me. "It doesn't matter," I said. "He and I are done. It's over."

"Explain. What does it mean to be—" Ian cut off, and his triangular head spun around, night vision amber light on the gravel drive behind us. "Law enforcement has just been dispatched to this location." I couldn't hear sirens, but maybe Ian's internet software had patched into a police scanner. He dropped into what I always thought of as his tiger form—arms in front, legs behind, and the long body horizontal between them. One arm scooped me up and onto his back. Another slipped my phone back into my pocket and then wrapped around my waist.

In two expansive leaps, Ian entered the tree line. "Keep your head down, Ash." The metal leg pulled me tighter to his body as we careened through the dark woods. Snowy, spiky branches combed over my back, but the metal of Ian's body warmed underneath me. When the forest floor became clogged with undergrowth, Ian sprung upward into the trees. He swung from branch to branch like a giant metal ape, me on his back. My chattering fear left me and turned into whooping shouts.

We'd played a version of this as kids. I'd ridden on his back as he swung us through the climbing dome and under the slide. Dad had called an end to it when Ian had crashed onto a lab table. The robot had used all his limbs to shield me from impact and landed like a giant bowling ball on an expensive microscope. Even though Ian had initiated the "Tarzan Game" as I'd called it, Dad blamed me for the broken microscope and the mess. When he'd yelled at me, I'd cried, and Ian had sneaked a claw over one of my hands.

Finally, the cover of trees thinned, and we wove back into the suburbs, between houses and over wooden fences, headed for home. Ian dropped me at my front door, unlocked and pushed it open. The edges of the night sky had grown the faintest bit lighter. "You should get back," I said. Then, "I feel bad that you wasted your only free time just to bring me home from that terrible party."

"Time was not wasted. I chose what to do. I … chose."

When Ian talked about choices—he didn't sound at all like the giddy description my father gave of Ian's programming. And not just because of the synthesized voice. Explaining Ian's decision-making capabilities to me, Dad had described the infinite possibilities open to humans:

"You might walk out the front door and keep walking. You might walk to your school, the store, the bus stop and get on a bus. Maybe you stay right here, then suddenly grab my tablet ... and you throw it against the wall." But, I would never do any of that without a reason. People didn't just have a list of options running in the back of their brains. We made choices because we wanted something to come from those choices. I only chose to go to the store because I wanted art supplies. I chose to go to school because I didn't want to be a dumbass. And, I never chose the bus stop because I'd rather walk with Pilar instead.

Precious few of Ian's hours were without instructions or orders. Ian wasn't giddy in his possibilities, he was defiant in them. "Well, I'm glad you decided to choose me."

"And," I added. "I'm sorry about how Dad treats you." My forehead wrinkled while I sucked at my bottom lip. I knew exactly what it felt like to be deemed irrelevant and set aside by my father. "I don't think he means to be ... cruel. It's just that he only sees other people—not just people, I mean—he only notices them when they correspond to his work." I bit at my lip again.

One thing about talking to an AI is the patient waiting it did. With no awareness of the awkward pauses, they didn't have the urge to fill them. After many silent minutes between us, Ian lowered his limbs to a crouch, and we were face to face. "How I am treated does not concern me. My primary consideration is to maintain friendship with Asher Bell."

Warmth suffused my skin, as if it still pressed against Ian's heated metal body. "You don't need to maintain anything." Like Pilar—*like Caz?*—Ian's existence had tangled with my own for so long that they couldn't ever come apart. "You might have a crappy daytime getting ordered around by Dad, but you and I can always hang in the night. It's perfect because you don't need to sleep."

Ian's head turned side to side, imitating a human

shaking no. "Once your father has full funding and capability, he will create additional Mirror Neurons to take the place of human soldiers. Like the others, I will be shipped from mission to mission. I will only return to the labs of North American Automation for maintenance." His hydraulic limbs whirred to life, and my hand dropped away.

"What?" My heart started to pound. "Dad can't do that. I'm going to talk to him. I'm going—"

"Previous evidence suggests this approach would fail." The gentle tine of one claw touched against my forehead, swept the long bangs from my eyes. "I do not think your father would react as you hope."

"But, it's not—" My breath hitched. My lips trembled, and my nose and eyes burned. "It isn't fair." *Or right.* "He's treating you like you aren't even ..." *human.*

And, I didn't even need to say the word. Ian knew. "I am not," he said. The edge of a sharp claw touching just under my right eye. "Describe current emotion."

My lips twitched—it was just so Ian—but the smile died before it formed. "Sad," I answered. "Describe yours?"

"Sad," Ian said.

CHAPTER 45

*P*ilar didn't text once the entire weekend. She didn't stop by. When I went to her house, her mom said she'd brought her brothers to the ice rink, something Pilar would normally try to rope me into doing with her.

"Oh, right, I knew that," I lied. Otherwise, I knew Pilar's mom would drag me inside and want to talk. All the little cuts across my cheeks had turned scabby and tight, and I could feel Mrs. Almas' concern just as clearly as I smelled the cinnamon cookies she'd baked.

Okay, so Pilar wanted to avoid me. I let Mrs. Almas press a tin of biscochitos on me and brought them home to eat in my room.

On Monday morning, I waited outside her house. My backpack strained at the seams with both my World History and Calc books inside. And I held a giant art folio with my pastel painting—the one for the "Family History" assignment. It would have made more sense to have Carly drive me, but that would make it easy for Pilar to just beg off and walk alone.

I braced for a big argument, my pockets stuffed with

Jolly Ranchers to bribe my way back onto her good side. So, I staggered back in shock when Pilar burst out her front door and torpedoed toward me.

"Oh my God, you need to tell me everything." She gripped my shoulders, leaned so close that her nose brushed mine.

"Gah—personal space." I clutched the art folio to my chest like a shield and pulled away. "Tell you everything about—?"

"This!" On her phone, a video of the destroyed cabin in Franktown played. Whoever posted it had done a really good editing job to make it extra disaster-porn-worthy: the ceiling blown open from inside the house, the pine thrusting through the room from outside the house. Harper's broken arm, Jenson Porter's bloody nose. The video ended with a shot of the DJ crying and sad piano music.

"Oh. That's because all his equipment got pulverized by the tree." When I looked back up at Pilar, she shook her head, incredulous that I wouldn't try and milk what had happened for the most dramatic retelling possible. "What? It's the truth."

Pilar linked her arm with mine, pointed us both toward the school. "I want a blow-by-blow of the whole night starting with Caz sitting in the car and honking—like a total jackass—for you to get in his obnoxious striped Corvette.

"You saw that?" Of course, she had. "And why are you just now coming to me with this, huh Pilar? Because you had your phone turned off all weekend?" I'd planned to grovel to her, but now, it seemed I had the upper hand.

She didn't even look guilty. "I was jealous. Sue me." She squeezed me tighter to her side. "Now, back to the gossip." She dug a hand in my coat pocket searching for the Jolly Ranchers. "Apology candy! Never change, Ash." She kissed my cheek.

"Gross."

~

S o, I told her. Almost everything. I'd kept my neck covered with my bulkiest hoodie. Just the part about Caz leaving me at the party had Pilar enraged. When we got to school, she stuck by my side, jaw clenched. "If Caz even comes near you—"

"He won't." Not after Harper had confronted him—in front of all his football buddies. "Trust me, he's going to spend the entire week being super straight."

We went straight to the art room, so I could drop off my folio, and she could work on her sculpture. It still looked a little blobby, not like the sketch from her plans.

"Are you going to have that done in time?" Ms. Stanzi asked. She's already pulled the yellow pad of school passes from one pocket of her gauzy skirt. "You'll need to finish by the end of the day if you want it fired before the classroom show."

Pilar's eyes bugged at that news. "I will?" She grimaced toward me. "Are you okay going to World History by yourself? I could walk you there, stick around until the bell rings, and—"

"I'll be fine. Calm down, Pil."

God, so embarrassing. I rolled my eyes as I leaned my art folio against the back wall. "It's just going to be super awkward." Story of my life, though. I waved goodbye and trudged toward the civics hallway, kept my gaze on my feet. Maybe if I ignored everyone, they would ignore me, too. That'd be nice. Relaxing even.

As soon as I turned the corner, another pair of shoes blocked the path. A sparkling white pair of Varsity Edge cheer shoes. "Ash, I need to talk to you."

Harper looked a lot better than the last time I'd seen her. She had her blonde hair pulled back in its usual tight ponytail.

Didn't reek of puke. Her right arm had a bulky fuchsia pink cast on it that matched her sweater and skirt. She peered over my shoulder, searching for Pilar. "Alone," she added.

I tried to keep the sneer off my face. "I'm going to be late for class—" When I tried to sidestep her, she tugged on my sleeve to keep me from walking away. Her eyes filled with tears. "I really do care about him, you know. I don't even care if he's gay or whatever. What we had—"

"Whoa, Harper. Stop." Her tears freaked me out, and I cringed, took a step backward. "You need to … talk to someone else." Now, I wished I'd taken Pilar up on that offer to walk with me to class. Pilar would have known what to say or do with a crying girl.

"Um, so, listen, Harper … there's *nothing* going on with me and Caz."

Nothing anymore. Not since he'd gone psycho on me in the Corvette, then left me without a ride in the middle of nowhere. "We're barely friends now. Not like we were as little kids." Saying it out loud made it feel like the truth. If I was friends with Caz, it was that mischievous kid version of him, the one who built tree forts and bike ramps. The one who taught me how to skateboard.

Harper started sobbing full force now, sobs, hiccups— the works. The hallway had mostly emptied, but if she kept it up, at least Mr. Haag would come investigate.

Would I look like a total dick if I just walked away? I thought about it, for real. And I probably looked like it, too, because Harper snatched my arm again, dug her fingernails into the sleeve of my hoodie.

She took a big gulping breath, getting herself back under control. "I'm only asking because of what happened. Maybe if you went to see him, he would recognize your voice," Harper said. She'd just let her nose and eyes run and shiny snot smeared over her top lip.

Recognize my voice? "What are you talking about?" Now, I gripped her back. "Are you talking about Caz?"

The default bitchy version of Harper broke through the pathetic weeping girl in front of me. "*Yes*. Oh, my God. Do you live in a cave or something? How can you not know?"

Just like I predicted, Mr. Haag had stepped out of his classroom. "Everything all right here, Ash?"

I tried to give the impression of comforting Harper instead of interrogating her. So, I draped an arm around her shoulders, when I wanted to shake the girl until her teeth rattled. "I'm going to take Harper to the nurse's office, Mr. Haag. Her arm still hurts a lot."

Mr. Haag scribbled out a pass for us, and I towed Harper toward the main office, then detoured out a side door. As we walked, I called the one person who I knew would pick me up, no questions asked. We were halfway to the 7-Eleven at the end of the block when the piss-yellow Dodge Dart whined to a stop at the curb.

Carly had an elbow hanging out the driver-side window and a vape pen between her teeth. She narrowed her eyes at Harper. "I don't have all day to wait around," she said around a puff of scented nicotine. "Hurry the hell up."

CHAPTER 46

*E*ntering the intensive care felt like walking into the scene of a dream. From the moment the elevator doors opened, my eyes could only take in the sight of Caz in the hospital bed, machines blinking around him, the mechanical rhythm of air forced into his lungs, then compressed out of them.

The rest of the room, the people beside me, beside him, all fogged over. Their words muffled, senseless.

Someone patted my back. "Tell him you're here." The bland face of a nurse, her sympathetic eyes. "Tell him it's okay if he wants to go."

A thick white bandage wrapped around the top of Caz's head, stopping just above his blackened and swollen eyes. A blanket covered his body from the neck down.

The body under that blanket wasn't whole, too lumpy in the chest, cut off below the knees. Bright red blood dotted the hospital white. Caz had lost his right arm and more blood had dried around the gauze-covered stump, hardened into a maroon crust under his nose and along the edges of the tape holding a breathing tube in place.

I opened my mouth, repeated the nurse's prompts like

lines of a play I hadn't memorized, expecting my words to perform some sort of magical response, to matter. "I'm here, Caz. It's Ash. If you need to ... go. Then, go. It's okay."

But, machine breathing for Caz just continued its monotonous cycle, air in, air out. "How did this happen?" I directed my question toward the nurse.

"I told you ..." Harper's face was blotchy and furious. "He ran the light—"

Right. Right. She had explained it on the drive here. I just ... my brain wouldn't hold the information.

The fire trucks dispatched to Dr. Stillman's destroyed log mansion.

The dark highway.

The slick roads.

And Caz, high as hell, drunk.

I should have ... If only ... Why didn't I ...

"He's such a jerk," Harper sobbed. "He doesn't care about anyone but himself. He doesn't care about the people who love him." My arms went around her, and she rubbed her face against my shoulder, all the tears and snot soaking through to my skin.

It was then that I noticed Mr. Enzo sitting on the other side of Caz's bed, the side with Caz's remaining arm. Mr. Enzo looked destroyed, thinner, smaller, older than I remembered him from the Thanksgiving football game. His two beefy freckled hands held his son's limp fingers. His eyes focused on me at the same time mine did on him.

"You."

Shit—I'd forgotten that Mr. Enzo probably wouldn't want me here, had pretty much forbidden Caz from being my friend.

I let go of Harper and backed away—right into the clipboard of the white-coated doctor behind me. He had the same neutral compassion on his face as the nurse. An intentional projection of calm, of resignation.

"Mr. Enzo," said the doctor. His voice gentle but firm. "Perhaps now that you have some of Cassius Junior's friends here, they might help you make a decision about discontinuing his care."

Bile rose into my mouth, and I had to swallow it back. *Caz is dying.*

Nothing felt real to me. *Caz is dying. Caz is dying.* I said it over and over to myself, trying to force it to make sense. But, I couldn't shake the feeling of dreaming, that nothing happening was real. I wanted to take the elevator back down to the lobby, to find Carly and sit inside the musty Dodge Dart again—a real place, a place I knew. Only Harper's nails digging into my arm woke me from my daze.

Her legs trembled, her breathing came in short panting breaths. "What are you saying? What is he saying?" She clung to me like she thought I could rescue her from the doctor's words. And I was grateful for it. I needed the distraction, the excuse to remove myself.

"I'm going to take Harper back to the lobby," I said. But, Mr. Enzo had risen to his feet. He'd let go of his Caz's hand to grip the metal bed rail like he planned to ram the whole thing at me.

"Your father," he said, hoarse desperation flooded his voice, his face. "He can fix my son." Mr. Enzo pointed toward me. "I saw what he did to those monkeys in a documentary. Those soldiers who had their legs and backs rebuilt—"

The nurse placed a hand on his back. "Mr. Enzo, it's time to say goodbye to—"

Cassius Senior slapped the hand away. "No." He shook his pointing finger to make the doctor look my way. "His father is Fredric Bell. Don't you know who that is? He can fix my son."

"Fredric Bell," the doctor repeated. A neurosurgeon who recognized my father's name, who recognized *me*. Except for the glasses, my father and I looked exactly the same. "You're Fredric Bell's son?"

My voice didn't work. All I could do was nod.

Hesitation cracked that shell of calm resignation the doctor had entered Caz's room with—he didn't have a script for this new variable. "I … Did your father wish to consult …"

Could my dad fix Caz? I had no idea. I'd never watched the documentary Mr. Enzo had seen, mostly because I thought it would bore me. I just knew that my father complained about all the news stories and documentaries about him. According to Dad, they watered down his work for the regular people watching them to understand.

I had no idea, *"what he did to those monkeys,"* and I didn't want to know. When it benefitted his work, my father could be ruthless. No one knew that better than me.

In my arms, Harper had gone limp and sobbing, too overcome with grief to pay attention to the shift in the room. "I … I'm going to take her to the lobby."

But, Mr. Enzo charged around Caz's bed, and he caught me by the elevator doors. I remembered his frightening bulk in front of the locker room entrance on the night of Caz's game. That angry red-faced snarl, that threat of violence surrounding him like a fog.

He'd aged about a million years since then, and I couldn't feel anything except sympathy for him now. "You've got no reason to do any favors for me, Ash. But, don't hold that against Caz. He's a good boy. You and him were friends as kids. Just … ask your father. If there's anything he can do —" A choking cough stopped his words. He was crying. "Anything," Caz's dad pleaded.

"I'll … I'll ask him." The elevator doors opened, and I led Harper inside. "I'll go to his lab right away, and I'll ask. I promise."

The elevator stopped three times to let other people on,

but still, Harper cuddled against me. We got some sympathetic smiles from a lady holding a potted plant, then a disgusted side-eye from an old man. Like he thought Harper and I had taken the opportunity for a quick make-out session in the hospital elevator.

He had a Starbucks cup in each hand and a paper to-go bag under one arm. "Disrespectful," the old guy said and sniffed.

"Seriously? Our friend is in intensive care." I imagined myself sounding tough, sounding like Pilar would in the same situation. Then, my eyes filled with tears, and my breath hitched.

By the time the elevator doors opened to the lobby, the old man had given Harper and me his coffees and most of the donut holes from his paper sack.

While we'd gone to see Caz, my sort of big sister must have taken the initiative to make some calls because she wasn't waiting in the lobby alone. An older woman in yoga pants, a ponytail as high as Harper's waited next to her.

They made an odd pair—Mrs. Stillman's manicured nails and designer purse. Carly's oversized army jacket and safety pin earrings. But, their expressions were the same, and they even hugged goodbye before Harper's mom bundled her daughter inside a Mercedes SUV.

Carly's piss-yellow Dodge Dart idled beside it. I watched the Mercedes disappear down the long patient-pick-up drive. "How did you know—"

"Pilar. Duh." Carly stuck a cigarette between her lips but just left it there without lighting it. She raised her pierced eyebrow at me. "Now what?"

"Now, I need to go to Colorado Springs. I need to see Dad."

CHAPTER 47

$\mathcal{T}$y Rodgers met me at the guard stand.

Once Carly pulled to the unmarked road, I'd told her to just drop me off there. If Dad didn't want me to stay, then he'd have to interrupt his work to drive me home. Something I knew Dad would never do. Instead, he'd had genetically perfect Cadet Rodgers pick me up in a Jeep to bring me back to the lab.

"So this is like a regular thing for you, isn't it? Running Dad's errands?"

Emotional turmoil hadn't lessened the urge to fuck with Boy-Soldier. He looked extra stiff today, buttoned up tight in a navy blue uniform. Ribbon medals over one breast pocket and a plastic name tag on the other. He pretended not to hear me, kept his stick-up-the-butt posture for the short ride up to the door. Everything about him shone with correctness and conformity.

Sitting next to him, I grew super aware of my beaten-up Converse, the holes in my jeans, the shaggy hair that had fallen into my eyes. My teeth ground together as I cataloged all the ways Ty Rodgers represented the ideal candidate for … well, everything. I stuffed my hands in the pockets of my hoodie as I followed him inside the stark NAA building. I still had Harper's snot smeared on one sleeve, a coffee stain around a frayed cuff.

Maybe Cadet Rodgers had also taken note of all our differences. When we got to the wide garage doors of Dad's lab, he suddenly turned on me with gritted teeth, like he had to muster up all his patience just to make eye contact with me. "Your father wanted me to impress upon you that, while he understands your interest, you need to stay silent and out of the way." He did that sharp turn thing to shut me out again, slapped his hand on the button that raised the metal door.

"Understands my interest?" I repeated. I'd kind of wanted to treat him with the same cold aloofness that he used on me. Like, what a dick. Even if he was some kind of stellar cadet prodigy, he only had a year or two on me.

A muscle ticked in Ty Rodgers' perfectly square jaw. "Your interest in the Intelligent Adaptive Neuron Mirror Military Prototype."

"*Ian*," I corrected. I had to jog to catch up to him at a bin filled with shooting ear muffs. "That's his *name*." I kind of expected my words to have zero effect on Rodgers, but he paused.

This time his expression was more like a real person. "The robot is not a toy," he said slowly.

No, scratch that real-person description. Ty Rodgers was still a condescending dick. "Yeah, I know he's not a——" But, I cut off at a blast of gunfire coming from the training room, the one with all the apocalyptic obstacle course. "What's going on in there?"

Ty Rodgers shoved a pair of earmuffs at me, and I fumbled and dropped them. "The generals are here for Ian's final demonstration, " Rodgers shouted, so I'd hear him before leaving me behind.

A wave of heat washed over me as I snagged my fallen

earmuffs. I staggered back, turned my face away from a surge of hot dust. The obstacle course had changed since I'd last seen it—rearranged with lethal spikes, blowing shale and sand, and long burning pits, thick with searing red coals.

Behind a glass partition, three older men in military garb listened intently as my father spoke into an earpiece microphone.

Oh—I put on my own ear protectors and caught the end of my father's lecture.

"... adaptable to the environment as evidenced in demonstration 11B." Dad pressed a button near his mic to disconnect. "Asher, quit dawdling and get behind the safety glass."

With those bigwig military guys? The three men had similar uniforms but in different colors. And they had a lot more ribbon pins than Ty Rodgers wore on his stiff navy jacket. Still, Mr. Perfect joined them behind the glass without seeming intimidated or cowed. He had his dimpled chin tipped up and wide shoulders squared. He really did look like a superhero. "The clone of a future airman can make a pretty good ground soldier," he quipped. The older officers all chuckled.

"Ian isn't a—" My voice cut out at a sharp glare from Dad. *He's not your clone, you arrogant dick.* Not even Dad knew that his AI had kept some of the code from Daniel, that he'd saved files from our shared childhood. That little bit of cloned biomatter in Ian's brain didn't make him Ty Rodgers in robot form.

My dad snapped his fingers in my face. "Asher!" He put his hand on the back of my neck, the press of his cold fingers pushed me toward the observation area.

Too late—my eyes had already followed the gaze of everyone in the observation area, and my lungs and limbs stopped dead.

Thirty feet over a coal bed, Ian clung to a thick metal rafter. Bulky black M4 Carbine in one claw. The cables of his remaining seven limbs fanned open to reveal metallic webbing. Suddenly, all the air in the room sucked up and through that webbing. My ears popped as Ian forced the air back downward to the coal bed. Flames jetted out from the pit, then the red coals sprayed into the obstacle course, igniting the cardboard people hiding in the artificial ruins.

Burning paper curls hurled toward us, ashes stung my eyes. "Get behind the glass," my father ordered and shoved me in the direction of the observation booth. We both ducked inside just as Ian discharged another blast of flame and wind. Smoke darkened the room until my father keyed something into his pad. "The ceiling fans use the same technology embedded inside the robot." The smoke sucked upward in a powerful gust.

One of the generals, a balding, thick-chested man, turned toward Dad. "Incredible!" His name tag identified him as Baylor, the general who had ordered Dad to close his basement lab and move Ian here to Colorado Springs.

A new set of people-shaped targets popped out from their hiding places. Ian fired the M4 carbine as he released his hold on the ceiling rafter, bullets shredded every cardboard mark as he plummeted downward. I'd seen him do these same types of things in the videos Dad sent, and it had awed me, disturbed me. But, I recoiled in cold fear as I watched it happen right in front of me—the deafening boom of each quick shot, the obliteration of the targets, the sulfur smell.

On the ground, Ian's arms and legs curved around his center, the dual segments of his body rolled together, head tucked inside. He had become a spiked metal ball, a gun barrel thrusting from the center. Ian rolled his way free of the still-burning half of the obstacle course, crushing the debris in his path. The stone, the wood, the metal. Then, he uncurled and fired at a human-shaped target just as it peeked over a cement block.

Another of the ribboned men laughed in delight. "Outstanding," he said. "Really, truly outstanding work, Baylor."

I watched my father glance over at them, and I could tell that he was repressing an eye roll, a caustic, snarky remark. What had this General Baylor done to deserve praise? *Funneled money toward Dad's work. That's it.*

Ian paused at one of the water pools, uncoiled his four legs to use the powerful fan webbing again. Water surged up and through him, sprayed over the burning paper and wood. The fan webbing, strong enough to suck water from the ground just standing above it, must have a lot of uses in an attack. I pictured it hurling sleet, blasting snow.

Could Ian rip a tall pine from the ground and hurl it a distance? Of course, he could. Ian was built for attack.

He hadn't just shown up in time to bring me home.

He'd caused that storm. He'd wrenched that tree out of the ground, stabbed it into the skylights.

I'd sent him a text by mistake—***Now I'm going to be stuck at Harper Stillman's party all the way out in Franktown with him***—and Ian had come to rescue me.

"Damnit, Ian," I muttered. I needed to explain to him, *again*, the difference between civilian life and mission goals. Ian had thought I was in danger, and he'd made a mistake, a misjudgment.

My stomach got all twisty as I fought the urge to tell Dad what his AI had done, attacked a civilian address, caused hundreds of thousands, maybe millions of dollars in damage, injured civilians. I fought that urge because I wouldn't, couldn't tell my father. Ian was a prisoner here, and I was his only friend.

My father spoke into a mic on his collar, "That will be all, Ian." The robot's fans stilled, and his legs folded the webbing back inside, the metal joints locking until he stood motionless as a statue.

Everyone took off their earmuffs. The man in the navy uniform slapped General Baylor's back. "Impressive. You promised this machine was an upgrade from the drones, and it delivered, just as you said."

General Baylor had his chest puffed out, this proprietary gleam in his eyes, like he really believed he'd had a part in Ian's creation. *No, like he owned Ian.* "What I'd like next is to be able to dismantle them and reassemble on a foreign base," Baylor said. "We can ship them in boxes——"

My father's jaw tightened. "I don't think that will be possible."

The general in the green wool uniform tapped the glass partition, the way I sometimes did at the aquarium thinking I could get the attention of the electric eel or a lionfish. Ian stayed stock-still, camera pupil eyes looking forward at nothing. Acting totally weird, and extra robot-ish.

The dark green general had icy gray eyes, thin tight lips on the verge of a sneer. "I'd like to be able to do a remote wipe of its system," he said. "To secure sensitive records and information."

My father clenched his jaw so hard that the veins of his neck bulged under his pale skin. "General Ferris, the *entire point* of this AI is to retain information, to learn from experience and observation like a human——"

"I already have human marines." Disdain soaked General Ferris' words. The sneering lip curl finally broke free. "Program the robots to fight, not think."

Baylor nodded vigorously. "Absolutely. I'll get Bell on this right away." Then, he turned to my father, standing right beside him, like my dad hadn't heard the entire exchange. "Also, we'll need a self-destruct code, or something like that, Doctor. We don't want these weapons falling into the wrong hands."

I bit the side of my cheek to keep from saying anything, and when I looked over at Dad, he was doing the same thing. These cold-faced men made a knot in my stomach. Self destruct? Wipe his memory? *I'm a part of his memory.* Playing pirates on the climbing dome. Talking late at night. Watching Batman cartoons. Could Dad just erase all that?

Ty Rodgers decided to pipe up again. "Generals, you haven't even seen the stealth mode capabilities yet—" He sounded super eager, almost like a regular kid. And, I think it embarrassed him because he cleared his throat and turned serious. "General Mitchell and General Ferris had mentioned—"

I slipped out from the partition glass. Listening to Ty Rodgers suck up to those unfeeling asshole brass made that rock in my stomach colder, harder. Behind me, Dad spoke into his microphone. "Ian, I want to repeat sequence 11B before progressing to the—"

Both of Ian's bulbous eyes pivoted from the nothing space in front of him toward me. He bent over, arms moving with slow and deliberate care, to place the gun on the grit-covered cement floor.

The middle general in the dark blue uniform—*Mitchell, I guess?*— shoved his face closer to the barrier shield. "What's it doing? Tell it to redo the demonstration in stealth mode."

"Ian?" My dad also stepped out from behind the barrier, pushed his safety glasses off his face. "What are you—"

The AI sprang fast, exploded forward. Arms extended in front, four powerful legs pushing up from behind, claws spread open. He leapt over the wide water feature. A tiger bounding after prey. Leapt again to the top of a hollow cinder block structure. Dropped upside down to hang from the structure's roof like a bat. A huge, black metal bat, his four arms angled outward like wings. Readied for another jump, they pulsed like a beating heart. Someone behind the partition gasped. Ian was part animal, part machine, but wholly alien. From his upside-down perch, he sprung again, sailed across a shale pit that prickled with spikes.

My father, the three officers, and Ty Rodgers flinched backward.

Not me.

Maybe you just had to grow up with a massively tall, insectoid machine to recognize the difference between an attack and just ... showing off. The towering robot landed in front of me and straightened back to standing. Then he gently laid one claw on my head. "Asher Bell prefers not to see military actions. They disturb him." One of the camera pupils swiveled from my face to Dad's. "He should neither be present for 11B nor the stealth test."

Ty Rodgers and his superiors had all gone lax, gobsmacked at their war machine's sudden show of caring. Only my father retained his full composure. His superior mind never simply reacted to what he saw, but always deciphered for cause, connected for implication. He already had calculations and hypotheses brewing before General Baylor caught up.

The stocky officer turned red, doughy shock gave way to stiff-jawed anger. "Dr. Bell, what is the meaning of this? Why is an expensive piece of military hardware programmed to respond in this way?"

Ian plucked his claw from my head, straightened to face General Baylor. "Asher Bell, son of Dr. Fredric Bell, is a civilian." Same monotone metallic voice—but somehow more robotic sounding than usual. The space between the words a little too uniform. Ian's arms stiffened. Head forward, camera pupils fixed in the nothing space again.

He's faking. He's pretending to be— I shook my head. Pretending what? Dad gripped my arm to drag me backward. He didn't want me behind the barrier anymore, he wanted me gone from the lab.

"Ian is acting in line with the parameters set for

engagement," my father told the observers. He sounded annoyed. His usual peevishness when he had to explain something obvious to him. "He has recognized a civilian in the training environment and the need for removal."

But, just like with Ian, I kind of thought Dad was also faking, acting like he understood Ian's behavior, like he'd programmed it. When I knew he hadn't.

Dad knew it, too. "Excuse me, Generals. I'll need a moment to walk my son out." My father pretty much shoved me toward the other room. Then, turned toward the motionless robot. "Ian, repeat sequence 11B but in stealth mode."

"Yes, Dr. Bell."

CHAPTER 48

*D*ad pulled me past the line of inert robot drones, toward a shadowy corner of the warehouse. "I need to talk to you, Dad." I didn't know how much longer Caz had, and if Dad made me leave, I might not see him again for days. "It's about—"

My father twisted toward me. "Hush! Not now," his words furious and spitty.

"But, Dad, this is important. There's things you don't know and—" He shook me hard enough that my teeth clacked together.

"I *do* know. Now … stay here and don't say another word until they're gone." My father pretty much shoved me into a desk chair next to a wall of computers and monitors. "Do not leave that chair," he said. Then, he wiped his hands down his white lab coat, took a deep breath. I was pretty sure that what my father thought "he knew" was about Ian. That Ian had snuck out. That Ian had hidden files and abilities from him. That Ian had become sentient.

My fingers scrambled for my phone. Could Ian still text me while doing whatever the hell 11B demanded of him? And what did I even want to tell him?

I wanted to warn him about what Dad had said. I wanted to blame him for what he did at Harper's party. I wanted to do—*something.* I started and erased about a million messages as I waited in back of the cluttered machinery. Booming gunfire, howling wind sounded from the training room. Then, came applause and laughter. Finally, backslapping congratulations as the generals left.

Even stressed out, my leg bouncing and jaw tight, I grinned when Dad ordered Ty Rodgers to walk out the visitors. My father, thoughtlessly rude as always, had interrupted the Cadet's attempt to switch focus to his prosthetic arm, its superiority over a regular, real, limb.

I got the impression that Rodgers had some sort of official position here—working in my father's lab. That made sense I guess, he was the new control subject. As I watched my father make his way back over to me, I tapped out a quick warning.

> I'm pretty sure Dad knows everything.

> And I figured it out about the party, what you did.

> I don't think I can keep a secret that big.

If he wanted, Ian could have responded immediately, but he didn't. So I sent another text.

> We should tell him more about you—that you kept those files from our childhood. Also that you have feelings. It might make a difference in his plans for you.

> Please don't hate me, Ian.

And then, Dad stood over me, eyes hidden behind the reflective lenses of his glasses. "Ian was at our house on Friday night. I installed security cameras on a separate system and heard the two of you. I heard everything you said."

When I tried to stand, one bony hand pushed me back into the office chair. The toes of my Converse scraped against the cement floor, as I tried to scoot away from my looming father.

Tell the truth for once, Ash. Just tell him.

Despite what I'd texted to Ian, the truth froze in my throat, and I shook my head. "What? No." I fumbled for an excuse.

He held a finger up in front of me, in my face, and I knew that he meant me to stay silent—that my weak justifications only insulted him. "And then, I checked all the security logs, the footage of the lab here, and do you know what I discovered?" he asked. I just shook my head, squeezed shut my eyes, and let him continue. "I discovered backdoors and code I hadn't written. All the footage had been falsified. Excellently manipulated, flawlessly manipulated. No average person would have been able to catch it. No average person could have done it."

"Dad …"

"You hid this subterfuge from me. You allowed a valuable piece of military equipment to repeatedly be at risk of exposure. You are behind the destruction Ian caused in Franktown. I find it nearly inconceivable. Somehow, you affected the AI's decision-making process to—"

The mechanized voice boomed out from across the warehouse. "Asher Bell is not at fault." Beyond the racks of machine parts, Ian's heavy steps approached. "Asher Bell required rescue from a dangerous position. However, this AI misjudged the threat level and response needed. Asher Bell is not to blame."

My father removed his black-framed glasses to rub at his eyes. "He wasn't in danger, Ian. What could he possible have been—"

"Dad, I *was*. I did a stupid thing and let Caz drive me to a party in the middle of nowhere. He'd … taken something. He … tried to hurt me." As I spoke, my father stilled, his glasses forgotten as they dangled from his fingers.

"Hurt you?"

"He …" It was probably stress, but I started to cry.

The trip to the hospital. The demo for the generals and discovering what Ian had done. This confession to my father. I slapped away the tears on my face because they could only make things worse. Dad hated emotional outbursts, tears. Even as a little kid, I'd learned never to cry, or else he would walk away in disgust. But, I couldn't hold it in, none of it, my running nose, my wheezing breaths.

Two sets of steel arms wrapped around me hoisted me from the chair and against the warming metal body. A claw raked through my hair, tender, gentle. "You are safe Asher Bell. I will keep you safe. You are my friend." Smashed against his chest, I felt the vibrating humming sound he used to play for me during those nights from our shared childhood. When waking my irritable father with my bad dreams, my irrational fears of the dark had been unthinkable.

I stretched my arms around Ian's body, gulped air to find my way back to self-control. I'd almost gotten there when my father's cold fingers joined with the warmth of Ian's metal tines in my hair. My breath stuttered out in shock.

Dad didn't look repelled—not that the expression on his face was sympathetic either. Not exactly. "You'd better tell me everything. I'm missing …" My father swallowed the frustration creeping into his voice. "I would like to know, Asher. If you could explain it to me."

No, not sympathy, but my father's expression revealed more than his typical intellectual detachment. He would listen to anything I wanted to say. He *wanted* to listen. My father scooted another chair forward. "Ian, put Asher back down." His voice had a lot more civility than how he'd ordered Ty Rodgers out of the lab. And I think that's why Ian did as he said. One claw, feather-light but warm, stayed on my shoulder. That gesture, compassionate and human, made my father's eyes widen. Questions stacked up in his smoke-gray irises.

I mumbled out all the gory details from Friday night. More than I'd told Pilar.

Caz picking me up, high on something that made him twitchy and impulsive. The spinout and his furious anger. His hands around my neck. The end of the party when he'd driven off, leaving me stranded. While my father had listened, he'd frowned at the black framed glasses in his bony hands, finally stuffing them in the pocket of his lab coat. Without them, he appeared naked, the wan gray eyes tight, pale skin stretched over his cheekbones, colorless lips pressed together. Could he even understand the soul-deep craving for connection, for friendship and belonging, that had driven me to give chance after chance to Caz?

"He'd been my friend. I'd missed him." Hot shame infused everything I said. What had happened, what I'd forgiven, how I still hoped that the old Caz lay underneath the monster he'd become. I couldn't let go of the conviction that I was to blame. If only I'd done something different, been different.

"This is not your fault," my father said. For once, his clinical detachment actually helped me. Dad never bothered with white lies or empty words of comfort. This would be a passionless diagnosis of the situation. An objective truth.

"This boy is responsible for everything you just told me, not you, not whatever drugs he took, not even his own miserable parenting. I understand that he was … necessary to you." My father waved a hand in the air. Always so factual and precise, he couldn't even articulate what type of connection I might have, or want to have, with another human being. "But, he made choices for himself, that you couldn't prevent or control, and that you should not excuse when they impact you."

Dad's speech took a minute to decipher, but I understood what he meant—that I couldn't fix Caz. That it wasn't my job to fix him. Pilar had tried to tell me the same thing so many times. I just hadn't listened. I hadn't wanted to hear it. My shaky breathing returned. My nose and throat burned with the threat of fresh tears.

I'd gotten to the last part of my story and stuttered out the hospital visit and Mr. Enzo's request. "He watched a documentary about you and thought—I don't really know what he thought. But, even the doctor acted like he believed you could help Caz."

Now, my father sat back, stuffed his hands into the pockets of his white lab coat. The emotion drained from his face as he scanned mine.

"I don't want to be Caz's friend anymore, it's not about that. But he and I, we were kids together. I don't want him to die. Is there any way, Dad? Can you save him?"

Ty Rodgers had returned from his task, and my father motioned him forward. Even if I resented the hell out of him, I had to admire the cadet's ability to keep that soldier's straight face no matter what weirdness he faced. "Dr. Bell, shall I direct the robot back to the training room?" A tactful way to also excuse himself.

"No. I don't think so. I think I'll need the both of you for this." My father reached into the pocket of his lab coat and pulled his glasses out.

I thought he included me in that "both of you"—*stupid*. Because it was Ty Rodgers and Ian who answered in automatic and similar monotone voices. "Yes, Dr. Bell."

CHAPTER 49

$\mathcal{S}$harply dressed lawyers and padded uniformed guards had spent all day coming and going from my father's laboratory. Some of them, I recognized from the impromptu meeting in our dining room—they'd had the NDA forms for Mr. Enzo to sign, had insisted that Dad abandon our basement lab and relocate Ian to the NAA building.

First, a bunch of geeky, white-clad scientists met with Dad in a glass conference room while my father walked them through complicated formulas and diagrams. Pretty gruesome stuff with slides of cadavers. Of cloned, real, and synthetic organs fused with wires and electronics. A surgery video of my father cutting into Ty Rodgers' shoulder, attaching the prosthetic arm.

It made my stomach heave, but Boy-Soldier puffed out his chest, like he was super proud to have everyone witness his left scapula replaced with steel and rubbery synthetic veins grafted into his living ones. My father gave Ian instructions to interrupt and page him at precisely forty minutes.

"Why forty minutes?" I asked Ian. I sat on a cinder

block wall in the training room. No one had sent me away yet, despite all the important-person traffic in the lab. Once everything got underway, relief had settled over me, sweet and giddy. Dad would save Caz because there was nothing he couldn't do. It was a certainty I'd lived with all my life.

"Idiots," said Ian, using Dad's description for the impromptu think-tank. Before the meeting, my father had gone into a spit-flying rant about how he had to sit through the inferior opinions of others. *"They just need to do as I say— and only as I say. But, no. I have to sit through their tedious attempts at input ..."*

Ian swung two of his clawed limbs back and forth, imitating the movements of my legs. "Dr. Bell says the other scientists lack intelligence, experience, and learning."

"Yeah. That sounds like Dad. I guess being a genius can really suck at times. But, I don't think anyone in that meeting was an idiot ... Well, not until Mr. Enzo came in." During the first part of the meeting, I'd lurked in the hallway outside, pretended that I couldn't choose what to get from the vending machines.

At that point, everything was still up in the air, and I'd wanted to see their faces, the bigwigs of the NAA as they decided Caz's fate. Right away, I could tell it would be a slam dunk, the people in that meeting were all scientists like my father. They'd devoted their lives to the same things he had, and I could sense their excitement from my hidden spot near the Coke machine.

When the doctor I'd talked to in the hospital and Caz's father joined the meeting, Ian retrieved my dad. The geeky scientists all had to stifle themselves to a more respectful mood and the atmosphere turned somber while Mr. Enzo signed a stack of papers allowing the NAA to use experimental technology on his son.

"I'm pretty sure they were glad to get rid of Dad. He's not exactly sympathetic, you know?" I could picture Dad slipping, referring to Caz as a "test subject" instead of a "patient." Or saying something like, it's that he couldn't replace both of Caz's arms. Or that he would have liked to remove more of Caz's brain. "Dad misses a lot when it comes to ..."

"Feelings. Yes."

I snickered, and Ian dipped his head to knock lightly against my own.

Behind us, someone coughed, and I turned in surprise. My father stood near a pile of blackened twisted tree branches. He'd heard everything we'd just said.

Ian raised his four arms in a sort of shrug. He'd known my dad was listening, of course, he'd known. Since this morning, Ian had given up his "stoic robot" facade entirely around my dad. I think he wanted my father to see, to know that he'd evolved from what my father had intended for his AI.

"Sorry, Dad. I wasn't criticizing you. I was just pointing out to—"

My father cleared his throat. "I'm perfectly aware of the irrelevant shortcomings in my personality, Asher." Anyway, he didn't appear offended. He had that squinty, studying expression on that he'd worn all day whenever he watched me with Ian. Before I'd told Dad about the party, about Caz's injuries, my father had wanted information. *"You'd better tell me everything. I'm missing ..."*

My father had barked orders to white-coated lab assistants while he'd spent most of his own time studying screens dense with computer code, converging machine languages that scrolled horizontally for hours. I didn't think all of that had to do with Caz.

"Some decisions need to be made," my father said. He pressed something on his tablet, and a series of chittering beeps came from inside Ian. The clawed hands stilled from their usual flex and release for a long moment while the robot absorbed whatever files my father had sent him. He remained stationary for a long moment.

"Alright, Ian?"

One eye swiveled in my direction. Then, Ian dropped from the wall to face my father. "No, Dr. Bell."

My father took a step backward, startled and wary. As if all the strange behavior he'd witnessed from his creation had suddenly come together in an unexpected conclusion.

"What is it?" I jumped down. A cabled arm shot out to steady my landing. "What did you ask him, Dad?" A tension had come over Ian, the metal body poised with legs slightly bent, arms up at the ready. Ian from the videos, ready to fight ... to run.

"This isn't a request. You will ready yourself for the transfer, Ian."

"No, Dr. Bell."

I got between them, uncertain if I wanted to protect my father from Ian or the other way around. Not like I could do anything to stop an indestructible military robot from a target. Not like I could turn my single-minded father away from a goal. "What is going on? What transfer?"

"I will not merge with Cassius Enzo," said Ian. "You will need to use Mirror Neuron 2."

Merge with Caz? Was this my father's plan?

I pictured all the times Caz passed me in the school hallways with his popular friends, pretending he didn't see me. All the times he called me names. When he hit me. His hands around my neck. His sneer as he drove off in the night and left me behind.

No, forget all that. This was what Ian had wanted, what he deserved. He would be able to feel and experience real life—and he would be free. No one would lock Caz in a dark laboratory at night. No one would take him apart and ship him to war zones. No one would wipe his memory to keep their secrets.

My father's mouth opened and closed at Ian's rejection of his plans. "I'm giving you the chance to become human, Ian." The familiar peevishness washed over him. "I've studied the changes you made, that you thought you'd hid from me. You did all of it to achieve sentience, to become feeling. Well, this is your chance."

I turned to look up at Ian, but both camera pupils remained fixed on my father. "No, Dr. Bell." Ian's voice was the same metallic monotone, but each word harder, more staccato with purpose. "I will not join with Cassius Enzo, who has caused pain to Asher Bell. I refuse the merge."

~

*F*ull night had descended by the time the ambulance, silently, slowly, pulled up to the NAA complex. I couldn't watch as my father's staff unloaded the stretcher and wheeled Caz into a sterile laboratory.

It seemed that every room of the complex buzzed with activity—everyone wore white lab coats and paper bonnets, gloves, and masks—more faceless and indistinct than a squad of drone robots as they worked. All the metal garage doors rolled up to reveal the intricate production of my father's designs.

Inside one, the white-clad figures rolled synthetic skin up a leg. In another, two gloved technicians pulled something dark and porous from a vat. As I tried to decipher what it was, a man rushed past me toward the sterile surgery where my father worked. He held a glass beaker with a set of gummy blue eyes bobbing inside. I caught myself shuddering as I backed away, before sprinting back down the twisty hallways toward my father's main workroom.

And then, there was the line of inert military robots. Instead of six, now only five stood together, rigid limbs, drooping heads, the round eye bulbs dark. "Creepy," I whispered.

"Why creepy?"

I spun to where Ian stood behind me. "Oh, hey. Did you finish ... whatever you were doing?" When I'd first entered, Ty Rodgers had Ian's arm circuitry open under a set of sun-bright work lights. "Is your arm okay?"

"Yes." He thudded a step closer. "You are disturbed by the robots?"

"They're ... it's creepy when they're turned off. It's like they're dead." Another shudder that I couldn't suppress. "A lot about tonight is kind of freaking me out."

On the other side of a rack of cable, I could see Cadet Rodgers in a surgical mask, bent over the same work table where he'd examined Ian's arm. He used a thin metal wand to poke at something gray and gelatinous. I swallowed and turned away. "I'm not good with severed body parts and ... tissue. Even cloned or prosthetic, it's like ... *ghastly*."

Ty Rodgers looked up from the congealed gray lump. Synthetic veins, I realized. The metal instrument in his fingers nudged them from their sticky coil to lay flat. "You should go home," he said to me. "You'll only be in the way here now."

Who the hell did this guy think he was to order me around? "You don't get to decide that. My dad will tell me if he wants me to leave." My chin tilted up, and I shook the hair from my eyes. "I looked at your file, dude. You're only two years older than me."

The cadet straightened his shoulders. "You are a high school student and a minor. You don't belong here."

And the thing was, I kind of wanted to go home. I wanted to climb into bed and forget about everything happening inside the NAA complex. I didn't want to know where that twine of gluey veins would go. I didn't want to watch them assemble the parts of Caz that would need replacing. I didn't want to stay another second in the same building where my father did his Dr. Frankenstein act.

I'd asked for this to happen, begged my dad to help, but now, I felt stupid and childish for how it affected me. Ian moved to block my view of Ty Rodgers. "Come," he said, and the claw tines grasped my hand and tugged me back to the hallway. "Come."

He showed me a back way out of the building and waited with me in the dark for Carly to come pick me up. I wondered how Dad had expected me to get home, if he'd thought of me at all once I'd delivered this science project to him in the shape of my dying friend. The knife-sharp tine of a claw touched against my smirking lips. "Describe current emotion," Ian said.

"Eh, nothing. I was just thinking that Dad's probably pretty excited to do this thing for me. Like he probably can't believe his good luck that this is the favor I asked for." My smile dropped away, and I shook my head. "No, forget all that. I sound like a brat. Dad got this whole place involved in fixing Caz, and I'm sulking that he won't drop everything to drive me home."

A loud scraping sound and the four hydraulic legs dragged down against the cement wall as Ian imitated the way I leaned against it. When his head was level with mine, he turned to look at me. "Dr. Bell misses a lot," Ian said, repeating my words from earlier. "But he understands how to complete what you asked of him."

"Yeah. You're right." My smile loosened up. "And I get what you're trying to say, that I should cut him some slack." I reached over and wrapped a hand around two of the articulated claw tines. "I guess I could do that."

CHAPTER 50

I didn't open my eyes again until late into the next morning. Sunshine drenched my bedroom, which meant I'd missed at least the first two periods of school.

Downstairs, Carly sang at the top of her lungs, tuneless lyrics I didn't recognize. Last night, she'd left a band rehearsal to come pick me up at the NAA. I owed her big time for all the chauffeuring she'd done for me lately.

When she'd pulled past the guard station and up to the front curb, Ian had slunk from my side into the shadows, and I remembered when I'd wanted to catch him going into my studio, how I'd had that loud conversation with Carly, knowing that Ian could listen in on us. *"You know what freaks me out the worst?"* she'd said. *"That robot—scary as shit with those claws. Those weird googley eyes."*

Ian couldn't help how he looked or that my father had made him in a lab from steel and wire. And some of the creepy cloned and synthetic elements that had made me shudder with revulsion as I glimpsed the lab staff handling them. As the Dodge Dart pulled up, I peered into the darkness behind me. "Sorry, Ian," I whispered, not entirely sure why I apologized.

326

But that morning my feelings seemed clearer. It wasn't fair that he'd given up his chance to be human because of me. If it had been anyone but Caz, Ian wouldn't have refused the merge. He'd only done so because of loyalty and friendship for me.

A folded bath towel landed on my face. "Get up!" A flash of spiky purple hair, the smell of cigarettes and laundry detergent, just before Carly landed on top of me.

"Oof, you weigh a million pounds—" I kicked free from under her, but she yanked the pillow from under my head, smacked me in the gut with it. "Carly, knock it off." But, she'd gotten what she wanted when I sprung up from the bed.

"Finally!" Her shit-eating grin. "I told the school you had a dentist appointment this morning, so you could sleep in. But, come on, it's almost noon." Carly shoulder-checked me as she climbed from the bed, made her way back to the bedroom door. "You're going to school today, my dude. When I called in the absence from yesterday, they told me your attendance has been shit this year."

"Yeah, yeah ..." With the suspension at the start of the year, I would be getting close to the limit of missed days. If I had to repeat a semester, it would be a semester longer in Estes Park with Mom, Brian, and my sisters. No fucking thanks.

Even if Dad forced me to switch schools mid-school-year, I wanted to come back home—back here—for the summer. Before I could get too lost in my own issues, the events of the night before pressed back down on me. "Is Dad home?" Carly had already vanished into the hallway. "Did he come back last night?"

"Nope." Her voice boomed up from downstairs. "It's just you and me for the next few weeks. Your dad called to say he'd be working on some big project."

Weeks? My hand had closed around my phone before I'd realized it, and I typed out a message to Ian.

> What's going on? Is Caz—

> Did the merge work?

The answer came back in the same second I pressed Send.

> Yes.

> Merge between Cassius Enzo and Mirror Neuron 2 is complete.

Caz would live. I didn't realize that I was crying until my tears splashed against the phone screen. "Good," I said aloud. "That's good." My thoughts roiled inside me, relief, anger, sorrow.

Fucking Caz—he'd left me at the destroyed cabin, made sure everyone heard him as he accused me of stalking and throwing myself at him. He'd killed our friendship, then almost killed himself. He'd cheated me out of the rage he deserved from me, my chance to move on from our toxic friendship.

Nothing's changed, I reminded myself. Even if I'd wanted to save him, our friendship was still over.

From downstairs, Carly shouted for me to get in the shower. "I'm not kidding, little Bell, you're going to school today."

~

*U*nlike the day before—*had it only been a single day?*— I noticed people talking about Caz's wreck, saw flashes of video they'd taken of it. Strobing lights. Pulsing sirens. I couldn't resist watching over someone's shoulder to see the shaking footage. The yellow Corvette flattened underneath a tipped firetruck. It seemed impossible that a person could be retrieved from a wreck that bad, and a miracle that once they'd freed Caz, he still clung to life.

When I'd checked in at the main office, it was just after my lunch period. Which was also my free period. I used to spend that hour in the weight room with Caz. The other football players had mostly ignored me. And, even though he bugged me to show up every day, Caz would ignore me whenever his teammates showed up.

Since the fight, I'd spent all my free time in study hall or the art room. Neither of those sounded good to me today. The lawlessness of study hall meant that videos of the wreck, of the disastrous party with its "freak cyclone" would be constant. And I *knew things* that I didn't think I could fake *not* knowing.

Even worse, going to the art room meant seeing Pilar. I was certain I would spill everything as soon as I saw her, and I just couldn't do it. In every way, I was exhausted from yesterday.

I bought juice and a packet of cheese crackers from the vending machine and went to the courtyard to hide until Calc. The day was sunny, and most of the snow from the weekend had melted, but it was still winter. I'd expected to have the courtyard to myself. But, someone else slouched in the gloomiest corner of shade at a cement picnic table and bench. Exactly where I'd planned to sit. They pushed back the hood of their puffy down coat—Harper.

She had puffy eyes and a red nose. "Oh, it's you," she said. She didn't have that sneer in her voice that I'd gotten used to, she just sounded surprised. "I have some news about Caz. You might as well sit down." Harper scooted over, like she wanted me to take the seat beside her.

So, I did.

"Last night, they moved him to a specialty clinic,"

Harper said. "It's some kind of intense rehabilitation center where he'll get ..." Harper stared off into the distance, trying to remember whatever bullshit cover story that Mr. Enzo or the hospital had given her. "It's experimental therapy, I guess?"

My teeth bit into my lower lip, broke the skin. I had to take a swig of my apple juice to wash away the taste of blood. *Say something.* But, I was too tired. I couldn't think of what I might have said if I didn't know the truth.

"I'd thought ..." Harper paused to take a snuffling inhale through her nose. Her eyes cleared as they met mine. "They'd made it seem like he was going to die."

He was, I wanted to say. Instead, I shrugged. "Maybe he wasn't as bad as we thought. Right?" Another swig would keep my mouth busy, the truth locked away inside of me. I chugged apple juice until the urge to say something else, something comforting. Dad hadn't told me to keep it quiet, no one had. But I knew that I couldn't tell anyone what I knew about Caz.

Despite my vague words, their lukewarm reassurance, Harper got this watery hopeful look on her face. "Caz is such a jerk, but I really care about him, you know? If he's going to be gay or whatever, that's fine. I just ... If he's happy, then I would be ..." Her mouth kind of crumpled as she started to cry.

Shit. Shit. Shit. You'd think that, as Pilar Almas' best friend, I would be super skilled with emotional outbursts. "I'm pretty sure that Caz really cares about you, too, Harper. He never said anything, but I know he hid out from his dad at your place, right? When we were kids and Mr. Enzo started smacking him around or getting all ..." I bit at my lip again. These secrets had once felt just as weighty as the ones I now kept about my father's work, about Ian.

"When his dad got all ragey," filled in Harper. She nodded at me, knowing and grim. "It was always bad when they lost a game," she said. "But, he also had to hide any bad grades, or even …" Harper laughed, a sort of growling cynical sound. "His dad freaked out if Caz wouldn't go hunting with him, or watch a basketball game, or hockey. Like he got jealous when Caz wanted to do anything with friends. Mr. Enzo always had to come along."

"It was messed up," I said. "But, Caz trusted you with that. Pilar and I were right there, all of us grew up together, so he couldn't hide it from us. But … he *chose* you, Harper."

It kind of hung in the air between us. Caz hadn't just chosen to let Harper know about the fucked up relationship with his dad. He'd chosen to be with her. Over me.

It was the first time I'd ever seen Harper's face without any hint of sneering hatred clouding around the edges of her gaze, twitching on the set of her mouth. When she smiled, somehow, it made her look sadder than when she cried. "Thanks," Harper whispered.

She patted my hand, which I tried not to pull away in shock. We weren't suddenly friends or anything. But, maybe we weren't enemies anymore either.

CHAPTER 51

*J*should have gone to find Pilar right away. I mean, she jumped from her seat and hugged me the second I walked into Calc, which was embarrassing. But, she also worked like a force field from all the videos and talk of Caz's wreck.

"Oh my God, what is wrong with you people—" She shoved past a pair of girls watching the jaws of life hydraulics crank apart Caz's smashed Corvette, then spun to stare at them. "No, seriously. Do you get off on seeing people hurt?" She pointed one of her dagger-like fingernails at the phone. She'd painted them bright green to match her clingy velvet dress. "You know him. But, you don't care that Caz almost died. You just want to be entertained."

No one could last under Pilar's unwavering righteousness. Both girls flushed, and the phone disappeared into a book bag. Pilar shook her long hair over one shoulder and led me away. "So, as I was saying … Ms. Stanzi is going to fire my sculpture today, and then I just need to glaze it and do the finishing touches."

I didn't have to worry about Pilar asking questions, and me accidentally stuttering out information about Caz or the

NAA that needed to remain top secret. The entire afternoon, Pilar kept a steady stream of one-sided conversation going about the semester's final art project.

After Calc, she walked way out of the way of her French classroom just to finish her rant. "I should have done a painting like you did. This is a huge hassle, and Ms. Stanzi keeps telling me to make the hair longer, so the figure isn't naked. Can you believe that? She about had a heart attack when I first had nipples showing." Pilar gasped and thumped her chest. "Nipples—everyone has them. *Everyone*. But, if I show mine, it's pornographic. If I was sculpting you, I could show nipples."

"*Never* sculpt me." We'd stopped in front of my AP English class. "Also, were you really fine with everyone in studio art seeing a sculpture of your naked boobs?"

Pilar took a deep breath, and her eyes rolled to the ceiling. "Why is my best friend a boy?"

I shrugged.

❧

*A*t home, I was surprised to see my dad's Mercedes in the driveway. For the entire walk from school, Pilar had talked about her sculpture. She knew that she'd created something special in the clay figure of herself. The realism of the face and body, unmistakably Pilar, combined with the abstract in the swirling long hair that resembled tree branches, ocean waves, pebbles on a beach. In these final stages of her work on it, perfection had become like a teetering house of cards, any adjustment would be the exact right touch or the one that destroyed her entire piece.

Right before we parted ways, she grabbed my sleeve. "You want to come with me to Michaels? I need to get some —" She suddenly noticed how fixated I'd gotten on the dark blue Mercedes. "What's wrong? Are you fighting with your dad again?"

I turned to her. "Nothing's wrong." I did a half-hearted laugh and pulled free of her grip. "I just need to talk to my dad about a … family thing." All day, I'd gotten a pass from Pilar's best-friend-observational skills. But now, I'd ruined that in the last minutes before I could slip away. *Great job, Ash.* "He probably just wants to check in with me about the end of the semester … the move to Estes and all that."

Pilar raised a dark eyebrow at me. "O-okay. Well, call me after. Mom is making enchiladas tonight. You should come over …" Her voice trailed off as I sprinted for my front door. Pilar had to know something was up. Like fingers creeping down my spine, I could feel the interrogation she'd give me later.

Dad probably came home to sleep, but maybe, I could catch him before he went to bed and find out more about the merge. Was Caz awake? Could I see him?

As soon as I came in, it was obvious that Dad didn't come home just to sleep or eat. He sat at the kitchen bar, arms crossed and watching the front door. Waiting for me. I slowed my quick steps, slowly set my backpack on the floor.

I couldn't tell if he'd gotten sleep or not, his dress shirt and slacks looked fresh and unwrinkled, but his eyes had smudgy dark circles underneath them. The long pale fingers fiddled with his heavy glasses. "I'd like to speak with you, Asher." Dad rose from the bar to pour himself a mug of coffee. "Do you want some?"

He didn't wait for me to answer and just poured a mug for me. His ears turned a little pink. "I'm not sure how you take it," he said and pushed the sugar bowl and milk closer.

I had a sudden clear memory of my mother throwing a mug across the kitchen. *"You never even noticed how I like my coffee!"* The thunking sound as the heavy ceramic cup had dented the wall. When she'd left, my father plastered over it, had all the walls repainted a neutral gray. He'd bought new furniture that the two of us never used. Taken down all the art and removed all the homey bright touches that my mother had decorated with. He'd even had her garden plowed and flattened. He'd erased my mother's entire presence from the home, decided that still wouldn't do the trick, and moved us to this mausoleum.

For the first time, I wondered why he went to all that trouble. *When she left, had he hated her that much?* Dad had put his glasses back on and silently examined me as I'd gotten lost in the past. I poured milk into my mug. "What did you want to talk to me about?"

My father cleared his throat like he'd rehearsed what he wanted to say because, of course, he probably *had*. "Let me begin by telling you that I am aware Ian has been creating false data to describe his processing actions. By masking the Mirror Neuron's imitative resonance behaviors, Ian had made it impossible to adequately monitor neurological—"

"Dad, *stop.*" My hands shook, and I had to set my coffee mug back on the counter. I combed my fingers through my hair. It had gotten long enough that when I pushed it behind my ears, it stayed there. "I don't understand anything you're saying. Explain it to me without going into a bunch of detail about the science parts. What does this have to do with *me?*"

With piercing eyes, my father leaned forward—like if he stared hard enough, he could see inside my head to my own brain processes. "Something you did, something about your presence has altered the Mirror Neuron processing functions —the coding, the hardware, the biological components. All of it comes back to you, Asher. What did you do?"

"What did I—?" I blinked. Maybe, I was still too tired from the night before because nothing Dad said made sense. "What do you mean? I didn't *do* anything."

My father tapped the fingers of his free hand on the kitchen bar, the only tell of his growing impatience. He was working hard to keep his cool with me. "You encouraged Ian to escape the laboratory in Colorado Springs. On the same night you were assaulted by the Enzo boy, you allowed a military robot to attack a house filled with children. You asked him—"

"No. I didn't!" I supposed that I should follow Dad's lead and try to stay civil for ... whatever this was. But, I wouldn't just sit here while he twisted everything I'd told him yesterday. "I didn't do any of that. Dad, I told you this already ... I thought I'd sent the text to Pilar. I didn't ask Ian to come. I didn't mean to make him worry. He's still learning. He's still trying to figure out the difference between mission threats and civilian threats."

"Ian isn't supposed to *worry* at all." My father's hand slapped down on the counter between us. The coffee mug in his other hand sloshed its dark liquid over the floor. "Ian isn't supposed to feel *anything*." This was his real problem right now. He thought I knew something that he didn't— that I was withholding information that would explain how his AI had evolved from my father's intentions for it.

"You want the truth, Dad? I don't care what Ian is supposed to be like, or how he got to where he is now." I watched the fury build in my father's expression. *Angry, Dad? Well, I'm angry, too!* "At least, I matter to Ian," I said. "You might have found out I was gay and replaced me with Ty Rodgers, but Ian *didn't*. I was more than just a control subject for him."

My father's mouth dropped open, closed, dropped open again. "What did you just say?"

"You found out I was gay, and you—"

"No." My father placed his hands on my shoulders, long fingers digging in toward the bones. "The decision to replace Ian's biomatter was monumental. I would never have made such extensive and complicated changes based simply on ... sexuality," he scoffed. "It was you—*everything* about you that was unsuitable for the AI."

My eyes and nose burned with unshed tears."Why? Why is that asshole Ty Rodgers so much better than me?" But, I didn't really need my father to explain why. It was obvious. Mr. Perfect Cadet was smart, accomplished, and mature ... No matter how hard I tried, I would never have a resume like his.

Dad gave me a hard shake, hard enough that my teeth clacked together. "Listen very carefully to what I'm about to tell you. Force it to penetrate your simple brain ..." He had that tightlipped irritation that came out whenever he had to dumb down information for all the non-genius brains of regular people. "When it came time to take Ian in the field, I needed the AI to make the decisions of a soldier."

My father paused, took a deep breath. "As you matured, it became clear that no part of your biochemistry, none of your phenotypic traits, would make a good soldier. I needed a donor who was methodical, disciplined, principled."

Bitterness dried the tears behind my eyes and made my lip curl. "Like Ty Rodgers, you mean?"

"Yes. Like Ty Rodgers," my father said, his voice unsympathetic, scientifically cold. Then, he lifted one hand to swipe off his glasses and look me in the eyes without the usual thick lens barrier between us. "You, Asher, are not a soldier. You are an artist. Sensitive. Intuitive. Questioning. All characteristics, which are quantifiably less desirable in soldiers. Or in an AI designed to act as a soldier."

Hadn't I thought the exact same thing? Even Ian said I would not have "military success" or something like that.

If I'd had a different father, he might have ended his explanation with an assurance that my non-soldier traits still had value, that he loved me for all the reasons I wouldn't make a good bio-donor. But, I had my father, who always dealt in facts and not emotions. He hadn't meant to reject me as his son, only as a component of his work.

Could I live with that? I supposed that I had to. "Okay," I said. "But it's still really shitty that you want to send me away. Now, that I'm not useful to you anymore."

A shift in his seat, and my father reached again for the black-framed glasses. "But, Asher, I believe you are more useful to me now than you have ever been before."

"More—? What?" Then, it hit me. He meant because of Ian. Because my father wanted to decipher how and why the robot had evolved. Had learned to feel. "Then, let me stay here. I don't want to move to Estes Park. I don't want to live with Mom and Brian." Would my father even care what I wanted?

The work … I needed to bring it back to his work on Ian and the other Mirror Neurons. "If you let me stay, then I could come to the lab with you. You could watch me interact with Ian the way you did when Ian and I were— when I—was a kid. You could try and recreate it with the other robots."

A long pause where I could see something warring on my father's face, probably trying to decide between my worth as a test subject against the inconvenience of having me around.

So it shocked me speechless when he said, "I was selfish to keep you with me." He turned away, his lips tight, his eyes scrunched closed, as if admitting to his having emotions pained and disgusted him. "I'd made the decision to clone Daniel's cells based only on sentiment, and then I made the unforgivable choice to keep you with me when Suzanne has a family." Dad could never remember that Mom had changed her name, that she called herself Serena now.

"I … You wanted me? With you?"

Dad's ears had gone pink, the pained scrunch returned to his face. "A selfish and illogical decision based on sentiment. If you lived with her, then you would have a normal life, siblings, a family." Another admittance of his own feelings. Dad was the opposite of Ian, battling against all the parts of his own humanity that Ian wanted to embrace.

Then, the rest of what he'd just admitted sank in. Despite how I could help his work, he would still send me away because that's what he thought *I* needed: a traditional two-parent household with siblings. A life without basement labs or robots.

I had a rush of warmth for him, and if we'd been the type of father and son who hugged, I would have thrown my arms around his bony shoulders. "*You're* my family, Dad. And Carly. And the Almas family next door to us. And Ian."

Dad slid his glasses back on to better study my expression. Pale irises scanned me from behind the thick lenses. Like he wanted to make sure that what he saw on my face and he heard in my voice adequately matched my words.

Right then, I would have bet everything I owned that he'd learned emotional recognition from the same exercises he'd given Ian. I hoped my expression read as truthful. Sincerity swelled up in my chest, warmed my face. "*This* is my home, Dad," I told him. "*This* is my normal life."

CHAPTER 52

*E*ven though Ms. Stanzi had advocated for "found family," most of the students brought their parents to the end-of-the-year "gallery showing." I mean, not me, obviously. And not Jenna Harold, who brought her childhood babysitter.

Kevin Choi escorted his piano teacher, a smiling, ancient woman who patted Kevin's hand when he brought her a plate of cookies. And Bri Jacobi brought Mr. Garfield, the girls' basketball coach, who nodded thoughtfully at Bri's sketch of him.

Of course, the Almas family came for Pilar.

And, although she jogged in about ten minutes late, Carly showed up for me. She reeked of cigarettes and wore squeaky patent leather pants and a ripped t-shirt with Sid Vicious' face on it. As soon as she found me, she grabbed me by the arm. "Snacks?" And the two of us loaded up on cheese cubes, baguette crisps, and cookies. We got a lot of disapproving looks, but Carly thrived on disapproval. And it took attention away from me, which I always appreciated.

When I introduced her to Ms. Stanzi as my big sister, Carly didn't even blink. "So, you're the art teacher, huh? I see you finally got this little twerp to start turning in the good stuff." Then Carly pinched my ear. Hard. And laughed when I slapped her hand. "He used to spend all his free time painting, but never let anyone see the finished products," she tattled to my art teacher. "Little chickenshit."

"Oh, I'd had a feeling Ash was holding out on me," Ms. Stanzi said. They shook hands, and Ms. Stanzi got this knowing expression, like Carly was a puzzle piece she'd found tucked between couch cushions.

Carly waved her plate of cheese toward the rest of the studio. "Well, show me around, little dude. It's your time to shine."

~

*P*ilar's sculpture was the main attraction of the entire show and sat in the middle of the room, the focal point of the entire exhibition. Both of her parents teared up when they saw it. Her dad kissed Pilar's forehead. "I am so proud of you, *mija*."

Her mom took Pilar's face in her hands. "I'm so grateful every day for you, my beautiful *princesa*."

Carly and I weren't quite that dramatic, but we both hugged her. "You're amazing, Pilar," I told her.

She had sculpted her curvy body, rounded and nude as a fertility goddess. Fucking brave—even with the long curling hair hiding everything controversial. The figure had its arms opened wide—Christ the Redeemer—and Pilar strung an elaborate cat's cradle string design between them with three sets of baby shoes hanging from it. Her serene expression watched over them, protectively. Her hair held pieces of the little shoes' futures—stars, forests, ocean waves. Pilar had poured all of her selfless love for her three little brothers into the sculpture. Every time Pilar complained about their antics, screamed for them to get out of her room, rolled her eyes at their dumb jokes, she'd still carried this sparkling tenderness inside of her.

Across the floor in front of it, Ms. Stanzi had used giant stick-on letters to write. *It's About the Love*—not just the name of Pilar's piece, but also the theme for the entire show. And those words set the tone for every other piece.

Carla Mullin's wood carving of her grandfather cradling a baby Carla.

Ross Jackson's drawing of his mother and father holding hands on a porch swing.

Tram Huang's wax sculpture of her parents and siblings attached at feet and hands and hair like paper dolls.

Not every piece depicted people. I trailed my fingers against the tissue blossoms of a giant paper mâché tree. Paused to admire the watercolor of an old farmhouse. And turned … to see my own painting. Thick pastel paints in bright colors.

Dad, his brain filled with numbers and formulas, had folded his arms over his thin chest, furrowed his brow in deep thought. He stared at the ground in front of him, oblivious to the purple mountain skyline, the picturesque trailhead leading through tall pines.

Mom, yearning to become one with the cloudless blue sky, tipped her face to the sun. Her bare feet planted in wispy buffalo grass and pink columbine as she spread her arms wide, euphoric in her commune with nature.

Me, a little boy with skinny limbs and messy hair that neither parent noticed. When I'd first drawn that scene, a shadowy ghost boy had stood next to me—reached for me. But, the living boy hadn't seen him. Instead, the little boy in the first painting had had his eyes on the long path in front of him, a little stubborn, a little fearful.

I'd refashioned that part of the drawing for the Family History assignment.

Now, the living boy looked back at his silvery gray twin,

taken the hand reaching for his and held it. And when I looked at the new painting, I didn't see the little ghost boy as Daniel, the twin I'd never known. Now, I saw Ian, who I'd known all my life.

I'd worried that my painting—depicting parents on the brink of divorce— would break the warm and fuzzy spell Pilar's sculpture had cast. But, it hadn't. Because the focus of the drawing had become the two boys, smiling, connected. A whole secret world between them.

Carly slung an arm around my shoulders that I didn't immediately shake off. "It's totally them," she said, pointed with her chin toward the figures of my parents. "And that's totally you," she said with a smirk. "Your sneaky little ass, and your weird bond with Frankenstein's monster."

I tensed up, ready to defend Ian. But, then I saw Carly's shit-eating grin. She tilted her head toward mine. "I'm just kidding, Ash. I think it's sort of punk rock that you made friends with your dad's murder robot."

She turned back to the painting. "That's how you see it? Or him, I mean. That's how you see *Ian*?" She got a thoughtful look that softened her usual caustic smirk. "He's just a kid, your same age."

"Yeah." Suddenly tongue-tied and embarrassed, I dipped my head and let my hair flop into my eyes. "We grew up together."

"Huh …" She stepped closer to the painting, sucked her lip piercing into her mouth, and then released it. "You know what? He's not all that scary when I look at him through your eyes."

Carly shoved the last of the cheese in her mouth. "Good job, lil dude," she said around her chewing. "You, like, gave me a genuine warm fuzzy. I might puke from the feels."

I laughed, and she squeezed my shoulders and then let go. We'd both reached our threshold for mushy moments.

~

The next day winter break started, and my mom and Brian came to pick me up. It got a little ugly because Mom had planned for me to spend the break moving in with them, and even started the process of enrolling me in school.

But, Dad had a reason to keep me home with him now —his work with Ian. And he had my assurance that I felt more at home with him and my studio than living with my bratty sisters and a door that wouldn't lock. It was enough to keep him from caving to my mother's arguments about "what was best for me."

Dad rapped his knuckles on the glass dining table. He'd made us all sit down like an official meeting. "Asher is not a child. He can decide for himself where he wants to live."

"And I want to stay here, Mom."

Brian patted her on the back. "Serena, we talked about how the children should be encouraged to follow their own paths in life." I'm sure he barely managed to hold back a celebratory fist pump at the direction my move with them had taken.

Same as me, Dad had pursed his lips in sour disdain. "Yes, Asher has … chosen his path." My father rolled his eyes as he said it and scooted his chair back. "Are we done here? I need to get back to the lab."

Meeting adjourned, I guess.

My mother sniffled for the whole two-hour drive up to Estes Park. She also kept giving me these sad doe eyes like I'd wounded her with my decision. I don't know, maybe I had?

But she'd left me first. The anger behind that thought sort of shocked me. Like, where had that come from? So much time had passed between the morning twelve years ago that I could barely remember living with her. I remembered some of the fights between Dad and her. I remembered some of the attempts to fix those fights—I'd used one for my Family History painting.

And, I remembered sitting in the middle of the driveway, a bucket of sidewalk chalk in front of me as I sketched out my four-year-old version of the robot blueprints my father worked on. A triangular head, bulbous glass eyes … Mom and Brian stepped around the portion of the driveway with my drawing as they carried clothes and books and dishes from the house and loaded them into an orange U-Haul trailer.

Back inside the house, my father sat in stony silence. The blueprints that I tried to copy spread in front of him. With my chalk, I carefully drew the double-segmented body, four arms, four legs.

"Ooh, scary." My mother had ruffled my hair as she passed by me. She'd gotten into the U-Haul with Brian and waved at me the way she'd always done. Dropping me off at school, making a run to the grocery store, taking off for yoga class—she'd done that same flat-palm cheery wave. Knowing that she wouldn't be coming back.

Would I have wanted her to take me along, to grow up with Brian as my stepfather? No. Absolutely not. I couldn't imagine waking up every morning for sunrise yoga with him, following Mom around for her homeschool nature walks, sitting across from my sisters for vegan, sugar-free, gluten-free meals. I didn't want to live with Mom … But a part of me would always be that little boy in the driveway, watching his mother leave, seeing his mother's untroubled wave of goodbye.

CHAPTER 53

*S*upposedly, Dad could now track Ian's every move, and there would be no more sneaking out, no more secrets. I say "supposedly" because my father had told me this before I left for a break with all the certainty of his huge genius to back him up.

But, his robot had deceived him so thoroughly that I stayed only halfway convinced that Ian would do as Dad said. Let's just say, it didn't exactly come as a shock when the guest bedroom window slid open and red light filled the room.

I sat up at once. "Wait—don't come in, or you'll wake up my sisters." I tossed aside my thick comforter and felt around on the floor for my hiking boots. A metal arm shot out to snag my coat from its hook and hand it to me. "Oh, thanks."

Squeezing through the window meant I had to roll through a waist-deep snow pile settled against the house, but Ian opened the webbing in his arms to blow me clean again. He'd dragged me deeper into the woods to do it.

"Okay, I'm good." I stared up at him, as my breath fogged between us. "This seems a little risky. Dad will be pissed if he figures out you found another way to trick the security."

"Dr. Bell has taken measures of his own to conceal my abilities. He does not pose a threat to ... my freedom."

My lips twisted into a smile. I knew a bullshit sidestep when I heard it. "Are you saying he knows that you sneak out to see me?"

"No."

Then, I laughed. "Yeah, I didn't think so." I fished my gloves out of my pockets. It was fucking cold in the foothills. "We probably don't have long, right? Before you gotta start back to Colorado Springs."

"We could explore," Ian offered. "There are deer nearby."

I perked up at that. Not because of the deer though. "Can I ride on your back like when we left Franktown?"

"Yes." Ian made a happy chirping sound. Maybe imitating my laugh. He dropped to the ground, two steel arms reached out and slung me on top of him.

I leaned forward, my legs hooking into the middle between his body segments, my arms tight around his cabled neck. "Okay, giddy-up."

"I am not a horse, Asher Bell," said Ian. Still, he leapt forward, powerful legs pushing off and arms pulling forward. He streaked into the nighttime forest with a twisting, undulating gate. Dodging low branches and evading pits and rocks.

He vaulted up and over a boulder. "I was kidding —*yikes!*" We dropped to a snowbank, then bound free. "And you remind me of a tiger like this, a giant metal tiger."

From the speaker slits of Ian's mouth came the breathy growl of a tiger roar.

I jumped at the sound, and one of the cable arms slithered around my waist to hold me in place. The chirping noise vibrated through me again. See, I was right—Ian had learned how to laugh.

~

J woke to four little fists pounding on the bedroom door. My sisters' squeaky voices overlapping each other, "Yoga time, Ash—Mommy says you have to wake up —no sleeping in—be a family—included—no excuses!"

I groaned and rolled over. "Go away, shrimps."

"No, Mommy said to wake you up." The little voice sounded so much like Brian, that it had to be Ginger.

"Yeah," Petal agreed.

"Okay. I'm getting up," I lied. "Tell Mom I'll be right out." Their little sticky feet tromped back down the hallway. I closed my eyes again.

Things between me and my mother hadn't improved since the ride home. After crying for the two-hour drive up to Estes, she'd acted sulky and silent during dinner. She'd taken it really personally that I didn't want to live with her and now had doubled her efforts to absorb me into her family with Brian. I had a feeling that she planned to force me into parts of the Carmichael daily routine that I'd opted out of before—like sunrise yoga. *Ugh.* "What time even is it?" *5:30—are you kidding me?* Then, I saw that someone had sent me a text. I didn't recognize the number.

> Hello Asher,
>
> I am inquiring if you would prefer to complete school using independent study. This would allow you to spend the hours taken up with tedious class instruction doing more useful work at my lab in Colorado Springs. Please respond. --Dad

How had I ever mistaken Ian's texts as something my

father might send? This formal letter made much more sense coming from my dad.

> Hi Dad

> No I'm not dropping out of school to work full time in the lab.

> I'll come after school—TWICE A WEEK and sometimes on Saturday.

The answer shot back so fast I could have believed Ian sent it. But, I could also picture Dad hovering over his phone, waiting for my response.

Three times a week and Saturdays.

"Whatever, fine." I sent a thumbs up, tossed my phone on the other side of the bed. Then thought about my father's demand for another second and reached again for the phone.

> If you want me to come that often, I need to be able to drive. LEGALLY

> Take me to test for my license and buy me a car

> I'll give you three times a week and Saturdays

The response didn't come as fast this time. Back at home, I knew Dad's eyes rolled, and he probably let loose a string of complaints, spit flying, pacing—a hissy fit worthy of Pilar because of my counteroffer. Finally, the answering text appeared.

Yes. Fine. I will arrange this.

I flopped to my back again. *Fucking finally*. My license. *A car.*

I'd never be trapped at a party, at school, at Mom's ever again. Despite the early hour, energy coursed through my limbs. Maybe morning yoga wouldn't suck too bad. I'd only have to stay in Estes for two weeks.

Ginger and Petal had come back to drum at the door again.

"Get up, get up, get up, get up—"

"Coming!" This time, I meant it.

CHAPTER 54

The guard at the NAA waved me in right away. No stopping. No shitty attitude. Maybe he was dazzled by my spankin' new red Mustang. When I'd gotten home, Dad had it waiting in the driveway. A Mustang EcoBoost in race red—he'd let Carly pick it out. Fucking Carly. She knew I'd hate the color. "I'll look like a douchebag."

Why did Carly's laugh always sound like a cartoon witch? "Remember to drive the speed limit," she said. "Cops statistically pull over red cars more than any other color." I didn't even know if that was true, but I drove like a grandma just in case.

It was time to begin fulfilling my end of the deal with Dad, and I had to turn down driving Pilar around to help out in the lab. I had no idea what to expect—pictured messing around in the post-apocalyptic training room while Dad observed us. Like a more grownup version of the playground in the basement. I really hoped he wouldn't make me do word games and social interaction activities again.

I especially hoped this when I walked in to see Ty

Rodgers, his superhero chin tight, his arms folded over his broad chest. "You're late."

"Huh? Dad never said what time to show up." I pulled out my phone just to check—and nope—no message telling me when to come. Just the reminder of: *I will expect you on Saturday.*

My excuse didn't mollify Cadet Rodgers in the least. "Well, from now on you should be here by 6:00 a.m."

"No fucking way. It's the weekend. From now on, I'll be here at …" I looked at my phone again. "10:00 a.m." I turned the phone to show him the time. "I'm four minutes early."

Ty Rodgers just gritted his teeth and accepted it. *Ha, caught him.* He'd had no authority over me in the first place, had just overstepped to give me orders like another cadet.

The irritation slid away, and he adopted his usual stiff expression. "I'll need to wire you up before we start." He pointed at the metal stool in front of him. "Have a seat."

A pile of little button sensors waited to be glued against my skull. Then, tiny wires were attached to each of the sensors—kind of like antennas poking out all over my head.

When I'd played with Ian in the basement, Dad had monitored Ian, not me. So I didn't have any experience with the procedure. It took forever, and it itched. "Are these going to hurt when I pull them off?"

Rodgers had fallen into a rhythm with attaching a wire, synching on his tablet, double checking on a monitor. He seemed way more invested in the data than making me comfortable. "I'll give you an acetone solution to remove them."

"Oh, okay. Cool." *Cool?* My face heated up. Maybe better to just admit how awkward I felt instead of trying to ignore it. "This is awkward," I said. "Like what will these sensors even tell you? Are you reading my thoughts?" I hoped not. Just imagining this asshole reading my thoughts had created a loop of embarrassing memories to appear. Tripping on the school steps. Puking during Carly's concert. Jacking off in the shower.

Aaaand Ty Rodgers just ignored me.

Like, a normal person would say something reassuring, right? "Where's Ian ... and my dad? I don't hear any shooting next door." I tipped my head to the training room. Oh hey, that got a reaction. A jaw-tightening, nostril flare of annoyance.

"Your father and the prototype are in the chem lab adjusting the biocomponents of the other Mirror Neuron robots."

I flipped my head, craned to see the back of the warehouse. "All of them?"

"All but Mirror Neuron 2, which your father used in the human trial."

Human trial ... the words made my chest cold with unease ... fear, I guess. All the memories from the night of the merge flooded back.

Viscous organs emerging from a vat. Gummy Skin rolling over a hydraulic leg. Slimy blue eyes rolling inside a glass beaker. The memories all as lurid during the daytime as they'd been in the dark of night. I couldn't stop the shudder unfurling through my body. "Caz isn't just a human trial, he's my friend. Dad saved his life."

Because of my violent shiver, Ty Rodgers had to pause his gluing. He held up both gloved hands and stepped back. "Can you at least try to control yourself? This is important work. Your squeamishness only demonstrates how ignorant you are of the groundbreaking advancements made in unlocking the potential of—"

Now, I had my hands up, too, like someone had a gun held on both of us. It looked weird, so I dropped mine. "Listen, I get how amazing my dad's work is, but that's still my friend he operated on. Caz nearly died. I can't just ignore that and be like … Wow. Science!"

Rodger's lips tightened at my description. He held out his left arm, pushed up the sleeve of his white lab coat. "All my life, I've pushed myself to reach my full potential. Mentally. Physically." He let me get a good look at the prosthetic that I'd marveled at during the knife-throwing test. He clenched the fist, tendons tightened, synthetic muscle balled. "When I lost my arm, I thought my pursuit of excellence, of reaching my full potential had ended in failure." He reached behind me, snapped up a ballpoint pen. "Instead, I became something better than I'd ever been. I've transcended the limits of potential that hindered me before my accident."

Ty Rodgers threw the pen, and it shot across the warehouse-like an arrow … No—like a *bullet*. Faster than I could even see before it smashed against the cement wall in a burst of plastic shards and ink.

My mouth dropped open, closed again. "Oookay. I guess that's pretty impressive. Will Caz … Will he be able to do that, too?"

Like I flipped a switch, Ty Rodgers lit up in nerdy elation. He suddenly reminded me of my father, and I could see why he'd preened to work under Dad. "Cassius Enzo's merge will not only increase his physical ability, it will improve his mental capabilities, too. His brain will work faster, absorb and retain knowledge better, calculate information on the level of an advanced computer."

"That's good … I guess." Cadet Rodgers deflated at my lackluster response. Then, he shook his head. Like he couldn't believe he'd just wasted his time trying to explain scientific achievement to a chimp like me. "But, what about the Caz part of his brain?" I asked. "Will it all be Mirror Neuron 2, or will he still be—"

From behind us, my father's voice interrupted. "It is a

merge, Asher." He had that confident, almost elated, tone he used whenever he described his own work. His white lab coat flapped around him like a cape as he approached. "Partially Caz and partially the Mirror Neuron components."

But, I could see the furrow between his dark eyebrows, that pained expression my father had whenever he didn't have all the answers he wanted. *He doesn't know,* I thought. *He doesn't know how much of Caz will be the same.* "Can I see him? He's still here, isn't he? Is he conscious?"

Dad typed away at the same computer where Ty Rodgers had entered all my sensor information. I couldn't see his face. "He is conscious. But, not yet responsive. His brain hasn't fully adapted to the components of Mirror Neuron 2."

Dad's fingers paused on the keyboard. "I suppose I could let you visit Cassius. He hasn't shown any reaction yet to his family's presence, perhaps a friend would elicit a reaction."

The sensor gluing had stopped, and Ty Rodgers stood aside with his hands behind his back like a model cadet.

I felt around my head at the wires. "Can I go after I'm done in here?" My reflection in the monitor looked crazy, my hair all sticking up Einstein style. "What am I supposed to do?"

Both Dad and Ty Rodgers had to take a deep breath, unused to dealing with someone who didn't read computer code for fun. "I'll monitor you from here," Dad said. "All you need to do is interact with the other Mirror Neurons in whatever way you have with Ian."

On the monitor behind Ty Rodgers one of the interface readings spiked. *Did I do that?* "Oh, like the puzzles you gave us, the emotional intelligence games?"

"No." My father waved a hand to shoo me away from the computer station and toward the training room with all the obstacles and targets. "Cadet Rodgers will review those exercises."

"As the Mirror Neurons' bio-donor, I am the most intelligible example of humanity for them."

The reminder still bothered me, that Ty Rodgers made a better donor than I had. But, aside from all that, I had questions. "You're the most intelligible—what?"

"I provide the best example for the Mirror Neurons as they learn to utilize input from the biocomponents …" Rodgers held out his tablet, shifted his fingers over the screen to enlarge some string of incomprehensible text and numbers, and dove into his explanation as we rounded the computer station, passed the bin of earmuffs.

I nodded like I understood, but I wasn't even listening. My thoughts had stuck on how Rodgers labeled his role, how he'd called himself *an example*. Had Ian used me as an example of humanity? I'd always seen those same exercises as competitions, Ian as my rival. I'd focused only on beating him.

Ty Rodgers had finished his scientific overshare, turned the tablet back toward himself. Dad would have gotten pissy and irritated, but Rodgers had sounded eager to answer all my questions and prove how much he knew. But, Rodgers had purposely complicated it. *He thinks he's so much smarter than me.* Too bad for him, I'd had an entire lifetime of deciphering my father's explanations. "So …" I thought I got what he'd said. "It's like giving the robots a sense of right and wrong. It's how they learn to have a moral compass."

"A very imprecise definition, but I suppose *you* could think of it that way." He put a lot of obvious emphasis on the "you" part. What a dick.

When I'd last seen the other military robots, racks of machinery had surrounded them in the workshop portion of Dad's warehouse lab. Inert, their cabled necks drooped, triangular heads resting on the upper bodies. Typical military drone robots that resembled Ian, not as tricked out with all the new features Dad had added, but a little cleaner, a tad shinier.

The robots waiting for us no longer resembled inactive drones. They clustered together, bobbed up and down on their hydraulic legs, clenched and opened their many claws the way I'd seen Ian do.

"Asher Bell?" Ian had waited near the opening between the rooms. He reached out an arm, tapped a sharp claw tine against a metal sensor.

"I look like a weirdo, I know. Dad wants to monitor my brain activity when I meet the other Mirror Neurons." I leaned to the side to see around Ian. "Are they—? How are they?"

Ian did a pretty convincing shrug with all his arms. "They are new. They still think like drones."

I lay a hand on one of Ian's arms. "Sorry, I bet you hoped they'd be more like friends." The robots had all turned their heads to watch us, their bodies and claws stilled and ready.

I stepped closer, Ian right on my heels like he didn't fully trust the other robots. I waved at them. "Hi, guys." As I spoke, the bulbous eyes all rolled to focus on me. *So far so good, right?*

"My name's Ash." I pointed at Ian. "I'm Ian's friend."

None of the robots moved, their camera pupils still trained on me. I tipped my head toward Ian. "Why are they just watching me? It's weird."

A string of whistled notes and clicking sounds erupted from Ian's speakers. All the robots' eyeballs rolled toward him, and they clicked and whistled back.

Ty Rodgers had taken his observation job seriously, he'd practically melted into the wall as soon as Ian approached. But now he gasped, dramatic as fuck like a sound Pilar would make. I glanced over my shoulder at him. "What?"

"Is the prototype communicating with them?" It took me a second to realize that Ty Rodgers, know-it-all model cadet, hadn't just spoken his thoughts out loud. He'd actually asked me a question.

"Um, I guess so?" I looked up at Ian. "Are you talking to them?"

"Yes."

This confirmation hit Ty Rodgers really hard. He swallowed and wrote furiously into his tablet. I guessed that he and Dad hadn't known the robots would have their own language to use with each other.

I turned back to the robots to find all of them again focused on me. Slowly, each of the robots raised a claw, spread the tines out like a hand, and waved.

"What did you tell them?" I asked Ian.

"I told them to trust Asher Bell, that you are my friend."

"Oh, thanks, Ian." I thumped a fist against his side. "I trust you, too." I turned back to the robots. "Good job, guys." I waved again. "Hi." The robots waved more enthusiastically, and I felt like a huge dork with my wacky sensor-filled hair and the stupid grin on my face as we waved back and forth.

I looked over my shoulder again. "I hope Dad's getting some good readings off this," I said to Ty Rodgers.

I'd expected him to have the pinched expression my father used to get whenever I didn't take his word puzzles and emotional intelligence exercises seriously. Instead, Rodgers had all his attention on Ian, like he'd just noticed that the robot he'd watched in the military demonstrations had morphed into a creature wholly alien to him.

CHAPTER 55

*A*t first, my father wanted me to keep all the sensors on when I visited Caz. He even told Ty Rodgers to follow me with his tablet.

"No. No way, Dad. I already did the stuff we bargained for." As I spoke, I pried off one of the sensors, pulling out strands of my dark hair along with it.

After all the back-and-forth waving with the Mirror Neurons, I'd wandered around as they checked out different structures in the vast training warehouse. The robots didn't act very interested in me, except to wait patiently for my slow human steps across a model suspension bridge, or to lend me a hand on the climbing wall—a claw, I mean. One of them offered a claw when I couldn't reach the next grip. But, Ian had shut him down with that clicking language, then wrapped a cabled arm around my waist to haul me up himself.

He inserted himself here, too, handed me a bottle of acetone and a tube of cotton rounds. "I will accompany Ash to see Cassius Enzo. There is also a security feed available for that room." Because of course, the NAA would have everything covered in cameras. "And you can review my footage and readings as well." One of Ian's eyes rolled toward me. He couldn't make an expression, couldn't wink, but I still knew that was what the AI meant with the eye-roll. That Ian would also carefully curate all the readings he let my dad see.

A smile ticked at one side of my mouth. "Yeah, Dad. That works, doesn't it?"

~

*M*y heart pounded like crazy as Ian led me to the Caz's hospital room at the other end of the sprawling building. The cold touch of a claw tine against my neck let me know that Ian's sensors had picked up on it. One eye swirled toward me. "Afraid?"

"Not of Caz … just worried. Nervous, I guess. It was weird seeing him in the hospital hooked up to machines and …" I shook my head.

Everything about that visit to the hospital warped in my mind, like in a dream. Anxiety bubbled up and made me confused about people and places. The old man in the elevator, bag of donut holes in hand, sometimes waited by Caz's bed. The rumpled doctor sat in the car beside Carly. Harper and her mom switched places. I had to stop, take a breath—calm down—then everyone would snap back into the right spots.

"No machinery is currently attached to his body." The two of us had stopped at the dividing point between polished cement flooring and white tile. The NAA put Caz in the same half of the building with the glass conference room and regular offices. A claw settled on top of my head.

"Yeah. Okay." I smiled up at him. "Thanks, Ian. I'm glad you're here with me."

"Friends."

～

*B*esides the cameras in every corner of the white room, there was a glass observation room connected to Caz's room.

When I saw Mr. Enzo inside the little shadowed viewing area, he glanced up at me too with bloodshot eyes and bulging nostrils. "What are you doing here?"

The pleading, anguished version of Caz's dad had disappeared, and the ruddy bulldog had returned. "I have rights." Mr. Enzo left his vigil at the observation window to stand over me. "Cassius is my son." He pounded a fat fist on his chest. "I decide who—"

The thudding footsteps behind me cut off Mr. Enzo's building tirade. Eyes wide, his arms circled the air as he stumbled backward. One of Ian's arms crossed my chest. His red night vision mode lit up the viewing room. "Dr. Bell has authorized Ash's presence. You will not interfere."

For Mr. Enzo, it was like I had disappeared and only the towering robot filled the doorway.

When Ian pulled me into the hospital room, Mr. Enzo brushed behind me. "I'm going to take this up with your father!" Another flared-nostril glare, and he pretty much sprinted down the hallway.

I hesitated another second, then opened the door. "Wait … wait here," I told Ian and patted the air behind me.

"No." The robot followed me into the room. One eye remained on me, but the other swung to the body lying on its back.

"Okay, fine. Just … don't crowd me."

The room had no machinery, only a hospital bed in the center. A square window with long fabric blinds let in the afternoon sun. Caz lay on his back, motionless, eyes closed. A white sheet and blanket tucked under him. Someone had dressed him in clean white scrubs. All of it more sterile looking than how I remembered him from the hospital. No bloody gauze on his head, but I could see the line of stitches along his hairline. "Is he in a coma?" I asked Ian.

"No."

I reached out toward the stitched line near Caz's blond hair. His hair or transplant? His skin or synthetic? It felt wrong to touch Caz when he didn't know. I curled my fingers back into my palm. "But Dad said he's non-responsive."

"The Mirror Neurons are new. Cassius Enzo is also new."

My hands gripped the bed's metal railing. "It's not the same thing, though." Dad had cloned cells from Ty Rodgers for the Mirror Neurons' biocomponents. But, Caz still had parts of his own brain. "The robots used to be drones. Caz was alive."

"He is also Mirror Neuron 2. His legs, his arm, most of his organs, function through the Mirror Neuron." While he spoke, one of Ian's arms had snaked across the floor toward me. Its claw circled my wrist.

He's afraid.

I glanced over my shoulder. Ian's legs had bent, his body curved and ready to drop down like a tiger. "Why are you so jumpy? You acted weird around the other robots, too."

"Cassius Enzo is not asleep. He is dormant."

"He's what? But, Dad said—" An iron grip locked over my free wrist. And when I looked down, Caz had opened his eyes. "Caz?" He'd reached for me the same way Ian had, his hold as stiff and strong as the robot's.

Ian tried to pull me toward him, but Caz didn't let go. Instead, he tugged my wrist toward his own chest, pulling me halfway over the metal rail of the hospital bed. My arms stretched wide between Caz and Ian, and electric pain shot up my spine. "Oww, stop. One of you—*stop!*"

Ian let go just as Caz hauled me in closer. He rolled,

slammed me onto my back. Then braced above me on all fours like an animal. At first, his eyes were blank, then he blinked, and they focused, intense and searching.

"It's me, Caz. It's Ash."

Since releasing me, Ian had emitted an angry-sounding stream of the tonal clicking robot language. And even though Caz kept his eyes trained on me, understanding flooded the hard mask of his expression. He opened and closed his mouth. Opened it again, and a croaking sound came out. Then his lips formed my name, and on the second try, he got it. "Ash," he rasped.

"Yeah. That's me. I'm Ash," I could hear shouting coming from the open doorway. Mr. Enzo bellowed that Caz was his son, that he had rights as Caz's father.

The stern bark of a guard answered back. The yelling came from behind the glass of the nearby observation room. *They're watching us.*

And I would recognize my father's indignant, snotty voice anywhere. "You gave up those rights when you agreed to the merge," my dad said.

Caz had also turned his face toward the viewing glass, cocked his head in a way that reminded me of the robots. I wondered if his new synthetic eyes had infrared, if Caz could see through the entire wall to the scene going on inside the small room.

"Okay, so ... Caz?" I really wondered what Ian was doing behind me. Dad might be okay with letting this play out as he observed, but I didn't think Ian had that same detached curiosity.

The AI hadn't liked Caz as a human, and I didn't think the merge would change Ian's opinion. All day, I'd watched him treat the other Mirror Neurons like a pack of wild animals. He'd hovered beside me, whistled and clicked at them in the robot language to keep them in line.

Finally, I got Caz's attention again. "Hey, so do you

think you could let go of me?" I asked him. "Let me get up. Okay?"

The glittering intensity returned to Caz's eyes. His hard knees bracketing my thighs squeezed, the hands pinning my shoulders down tightened. "No, Ash."

Two steel arms shot out, claws folded together like steel fists. They punched at Caz's head, snapped his neck backward. Then, Ian leapt, slammed into Caz with his entire body. I lurched from the bed as the robot flattened Caz into the wall.

It would have killed a human. But, Caz just scraped himself back up, straightened his neck from its unnatural angle. That vacant-eyed blank expression was back in place.

"Ian, stop." My father had rushed into the room, Mr. Enzo behind him. "Take Ash and go," Dad ordered.

Ian moved so fast that it seemed like he'd appeared magically at my side. Three arms lifted me off the ground and wrapped me against his back.

But, I didn't need the protection anymore. Because Caz's entire focus had moved on to his father. Mr. Enzo's smile split his blotchy red bulldog face. He laughed and threw open his arms, like he used to do when we were kids.

Caz and I would be finishing a video game, or pulling out on our bikes, or heading to Pilar's—looking back, it's pretty obvious that Caz always wanted to leave around the same time his dad would arrive home from the car lot.

Mr. Enzo would climb out of whatever flashy, low-to-the-ground car he drove that year. He'd spot Caz first thing. *"Cassius Junior,"* he'd boom, a huge grin on his face. Like just the sight of his son had brightened his whole day. *"Come give your Dad a hug."*

I never noticed Caz's reaction because jealousy would burn so hot and fast in my chest that my throat tightened and my mouth went dry. My own father barely noticed the world around him, parked his dark Mercedes muttering to himself about numbers and chemicals. He'd stalk me as I ate dinner at the kitchen bar or did my homework. Without a single word, without a single glance. Caz had a father who paid attention and cared.

The robot-like blankness fell away from Caz's face and eyes again as he took in his father's outstretched arms. The more Caz-like glittering tension returned.

"Cassius Junior," Mr. Enzo said, just like he'd done when we'd been kids. "Come here. Give your dad a hug."

Caz crossed the room in a flash, bounding steps that weren't as smooth and quick as the robots, but still unnatural in strength, in height, in speed. He gripped his father's neck in his prosthetic hand and crushed his steel-cored fingers into a fist.

My own father gasped and fell backward, and a bulky guard charged the room. He trained a gun on Caz, who still held Mr. Enzo's dead body in the clench of his prosthetic right hand. Mr. Enzo's tongue bulged from his mouth, blood squirted from the inside corners of his eyes. His head flopped to the side, the bones inside his neck pulverized to mush under the skin.

"Don't shoot," my father ordered. He waved a hand in front of the gun, like he could block the bullet with his open palm. Dad's fingers twitched against the tablet he still held to his chest.

"Cassius," he said. "Release your father." Dad still expected the Mirror Neurons to obey him, and a part of Caz must have still recognized my father as its creator. The blank expression returned, and Caz opened his hand. His father's body flopped to the white tiled floor with a wet smack.

Just as the guard lowered his gun, Caz spun in my direction.

The three cables around my body pulled me in tighter, so tight that the air compressed from my lungs. It took a few seconds, but I realized that I hadn't snagged Caz's attention.

Ian had.

Caz's mouth dropped open, and his human voice stuttered out a bunch of tones imitating the Mirror Neuron language, frustration crept back into his tightening eyes, his mask-like face. He wanted something from Ian, maybe just to argue against whatever the robot had trilled at him earlier.

A rolling growl answered him, the sound poured out from the joints and panels of Ian's entire body, not just the speaker vents of his mouth. Now, he sounded like the mechanical tiger he sometimes reminded me of.

Caz screamed back at him, an animalistic roar of his own, then leapt toward the window. He punched at the tempered glass with his prosthetic arm, shattering it. The little glass pieces sprayed across the room.

My father dove forward. "Don't let him escape—" he shouted toward the guard. "Stop him! Stop him!"

But, Caz had levered himself up with the same hand he'd used to crush his father's throat. Feet first, he plunged through the window.

The guard took aim, again—this time, my dad didn't tell him not to shoot. He fired twice. Loud, booming shots that made me cover my ears. But, neither of them hit Caz.

He'd made it halfway across the scrubby, snowy field on his prosthetic bare feet. Dodged and ducked, as if he sensed the trajectory of each bullet before it reached him. Maybe, he had?

Caz sprung up and over the electric fence, vaulted the taller barbed wire one after that. Then, he disappeared into the tree line, a flash of white scrubs blending into the snow-covered woods.

CHAPTER 56

"He'll be caught, of course." General Baylor had the complacent certainty of someone who always got his way. He'd ordered the military guards for North American Automation to lock down the entire building, insisted that I also take a seat inside the glass conference room.

Ty Rogers sat across from me, but I still felt like a little kid at the grownups' table.

"We'll say he died en route from the hospital," continued Baylor. "That we never had the chance to work on him."

I recognized one of the other generals from Ian's demonstration, the shrewd-eyed marine who wanted to wipe Ian's memory after every mission. *General Ferris.* "We already have a green light from the Pentagon for the cover story, a suicide makes the most sense. Grief over the death of his son." The piercing gaze turned a shade colder. "All of this depends on us quickly finding and eliminating the boy. Will that be a problem, Baylor?"

My stomach clenched. Under the table, I texted Ian.

> Are you hearing all of this?

Even though they all watched the security video of Mr. Enzo's death and Caz's escape, no one but me thought Ian should attend the meeting. They'd heard the sounds Ian made, how Caz had reacted. They'd seen Caz try to reproduce the same sounds—but their eyes still slid over Ian like a piece of machinery.

> Yes. They wish to deactivate Mirror Neuron 2 and eliminate Cassius Enzo.

Ian's response stopped there, but I knew he felt the same way the generals did about Caz. He just didn't want to say it to me.

General Baylor nodded furiously. "Finding the boy will not be a problem. Once we activate the tracking chip—"

My father slapped at the table. "That won't work. Did you think I hadn't checked?" On the tablet in front of him, Dad's long fingers expanded a red box to show the words, NO SIGNAL in all caps. "The test subject disabled all tracking and control safeguards," my father announced to the room.

Both generals blinked in surprise at their scientist's outburst, especially Ferris. Like the general, just now, remembered that Baylor didn't actually invent Ian or the Mirror Neuron technology. "How is this possible?" Ferris asked.

My father did that deep breath, pursed lip combo where he might as well have said, *You couldn't possibly understand.* "Mirror Neuron 2 hacked the satellite is the easiest explanation." Dad slowly dragged the tablet back toward him. "What we should try to determine is why—and what the merged subject intends next."

Baylor shook his head, disbelief still plain on his face.

"The Mirror Neurons are designed to be soldiers, and soldiers follow orders." He nodded toward Ty Rodgers, straight backed in his seat across from me. Unwrinkled cadet uniform, a pen in one blocky hand as he took notes.

"Yessss," my father dragged out the word, annoyed to explain what seemed obvious to him. "Mirror Neurons using biocomponents cloned from a model soldier will have a predisposition toward becoming model soldiers themselves …" Dad's words had gotten spitty and rushed. He removed his black-framed glasses to rub at his eyes. "*However,* Cassius Enzo was a regular teenage boy, who had a complicated home life and a unique set of proclivities and potentialities."

General Ferris scooted his chair back, a deliberate, long and screeching sound to voice the sneer on his face. "And no one considered any of this before installing millions of dollars of military equipment into him?"

Unthinkable, that someone should point out a mistake my father made, that he should suffer the humiliation of having to eat crow on any point. His lips had compressed to a bloodless thin line, then released. "I take full responsibility for selecting an undesirable candidate for this trial," my father said.

He shouldn't have had to do that—take responsibility. Using Daniel's genes had already taught him this lesson, and my dad never needed a refresher on something he already knew. He'd recognized that my sensitive, artistic predispositions would hamper a soldier. And, I'd told him Caz was troubled, abusive, but still asked him to save my friend. He'd knowingly made this same mistake again … for me.

From the flat expression on Ty Rodgers' face, he knew it, too.

I turned my eyes to the glossy wood surface of the conference table as the truth sank into my gut. Mr. Enzo died because of me. The military would hunt and kill Caz because of me.

The flash of a text lit up my silenced phone.

Compassion: the ability to recognize suffering combined with the desire to help. It is a commendable emotion. You should not experience guilt nor shame for letting it influence your decisions.

I flicked my eyes up to the security camera.

Thanks Ian. But, it's still kind of my fault.

Baylor had started to sweat, his high forehead shiny and temples damp. "Then, what is your suggestion, Fredric? How do we get the boy back under our control?"

My father's long fingers drummed at the table beside his tablet. So fast, that I might have been the only one to see it, his eyes flicked to me and away. His thick glasses back in place, my father assumed his usual air of scientific detachment. "We'll need to find a way to lure him back," he said.

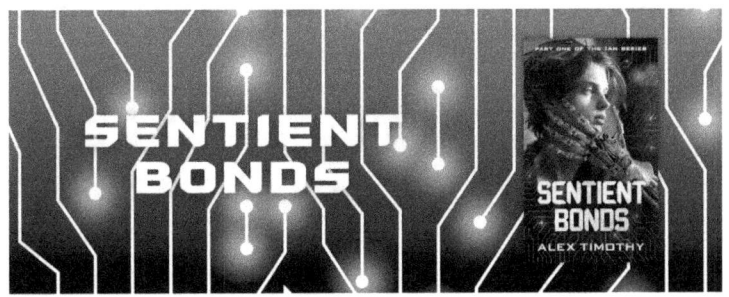

PLEASE REVIEW THIS BOOK

Reviews help authors more than you may think, so if you enjoyed *Sentient Bonds,* please consider leaving a review at Goodreads or any of the major retailers. I would greatly appreciate it.

ABOUT THE AUTHOR

Alex Timothy writes urban science fiction and fantasy stories, YA and angst. An ex-dancer with a sugar addiction and an overactive imagination, Alex spends a lot of time drinking coffee and pacing the room while muttering. It's hard to find what matters in this chaotic world.